THE WICKED
AND
THE DEAD

LOOK FOR THESE EXCITING WESTERN SERIES
FROM BESTSELLING AUTHORS
WILLIAM W. JOHNSTONE AND J. A. JOHNSTONE

The Mountain Man

Luke Jensen: Bounty Hunter

Brannigan's Land

The Jensen Brand

Smoke Jensen: The Early Years

Preacher and MacCallister

Fort Misery

The Fighting O'Neils

Perley Gates

Guns of the Vigilantes

Shotgun Johnny

The Chuckwagon Trail

The Jackals

The Slash and Pecos Westerns

The Texas Moonshiners

Stoneface Finnegan Westerns

Ben Savage: Saloon Ranger

The Buck Trammel Westerns

The Death and Texas Westerns

The Hunter Buchanon Westerns

Will Tanner, Deputy US Marshal

Old Cowboys Never Die

Go West, Young Man

Published by Kensington Publishing Corp.

THE WICKED AND THE DEAD

The Hair-Raising Tale of Hack Long
and His Outlaw Gang

WILLIAM W. JOHNSTONE
AND J.A. JOHNSTONE

PINNACLE BOOKS
Kensington Publishing Corporation
www.kensingtonbooks.com

First Printing: April 2024

ISBN-13: 978-0-7860-5121-2
ISBN-13: 978-0-7860-5122-9 (eBook)

10 9 8 7 6 5 4 3 2 1

Printed in the United States of America

CHAPTER 1

The bare prison courtyard deep in Coahuila, Mexico, was hot as Hell's foyer, and Hack Long would have given anything to be somewhere cooler. Dirt and rocks packed by decades of hooves and human feet reflected the desert sun's rays back against the brick, rock, and adobe buildings, making the enclosure feel like a massive oven.

He sat on the ground in a sliver of shade with his back to the rough exterior wall, chewing at a tough piece of meat that could have come from a cow, bear, horse, donkey, or wolf. Dog, for all he and the others knew. He'd eaten plenty of dog in Two-Horses' village over the past few years, when they were in the Indian Nations.

It didn't matter. The plain, familiar stew was nourishment, and they all needed to keep up their strength for the next struggle to survive that was sure to come. Bland food was strange down in Mexico, because the smell of onions, peppers, and spices that wafted from the *comandante*'s office and the adjoining guards' barracks made their stomachs rumble several times a day.

He and the boys figured the grub they brought to them was boiled up well before anything else was added, other than the salt needed for the prisoners to survive, providing another form of punishment for all those locked up in that hellhole. Only on Sundays were their tortillas and beans flavored with *nopales* and chilis so hot they seemed to be an added punishment instead of a treat.

Hack and the hard-eye boys with him ate every bite of whatever the Mexicans dished out and were proud to get it. They had to stay strong, because only the fit could survive in a world of bandits, murderers, and thieves.

There were two kinds of men in Purgatorio. Predators and prey. Sometimes, Hack was of the mind that only the wicked survived, while the dead were finally released from the tribulations that delivered them to dry graves outside the penitentiary with startling regularity.

The Long Gang, as they were known both inside and outside of the prison, had long ago proved capable of protecting themselves, but it was essential they continued to project a sense of menace worse than what they'd been dragged into.

That made them harder men than when they had stumbled through the gates of the Mexican prison in chains. None of them were without scars, and over half of those they shared were earned in attacks and fights that usually resulted in the deaths of the instigators.

Every day, they had only fifteen minutes to eat before going back to the copper mines, though it always seemed much shorter. On that day, Luke Fischer lowered himself to the hard ground beside the gang leader and adjusted his position to keep an eye on the other prisoners. "You feel it?"

"I do." Jaws aching, Hack shifted the tough piece of meat to the other cheek and chewed some more.

One of the newer inmates, a man with a wispy mustache, passed the American prisoners, looking with dead eyes for a safe place to eat from those wolves who stole food. Swift attacks to take the weaker men's twice-a-day allotment usually spilled more than they gained. The slender young man named Escobedo had only been there for a week, and in those few days, he'd lost half of his portions as well as his shoes.

Eyes glassy with hunger, work, and fear, he sat only a dozen feet from the Norte Americanos and wolfed down his meal. Two fresh cuts from an altercation the night before marred the smooth skin over one eyebrow and on the opposite cheekbone.

Andelacio Morales rose from where he squatted with a clot of other prisoners near the long row of cells and swaggered across the bare yard. Hack couldn't *stand* that man because he stunk so bad. That's part of why he and the boys steered clear of him whenever possible.

He was also the worst, most blackhearted human being Hack had ever seen. Morales's worn-out shoes crunched on the hard-packed gravel. Even the hot air stilled as the man towered over Escobedo, who kept his eyes lowered to the tin plate between his knees. Escobedo seemed to collapse inward as his spirit vanished. Hack sensed that he wished to sink into the ground.

Morales towered over Escobedo and spoke to him in Mexican. "Your portion."

The younger man quickly tilted the bowl to his mouth and swallowed without chewing. His Adam's apple bobbed as he swallowed, and Hack wondered how he got any of that gristle down without chewing.

Morales's face twisted. "The rest of that's mine."

Like a child, Escobedo twisted sideways to protect the bowl until he could get the last mouthful.

For the past several months, the Long Gang had stayed out of the trouble that swirled around them like a *chiindii*, the Navajo word for a dust devil. That's what those little fights in the yard reminded him of, the skinny twisters of sand that walked across the desert floor. Those kinds of fights were as common in Purgatorio as breathing.

Knowing what was coming next, Hack put down his

empty bowl and rose, using only the muscles in his stout legs. The corners of his eyes tightened, and he wondered why he was getting involved in someone else's business.

It didn't matter. That familiar tingle in his head rose with a hum. There are some things in this world the wanted outlaw wouldn't tolerate, and one of them was people who preyed on other, weaker men. The red tinge at the edges of his vision would soon narrow down to a tunnel with only Morales at the end. It had happened more times than Hack or his best friend, Luke, cared to admit.

He shifted over to make Morales see a fresh target rather than his young victim. "Go away and leave him alone."

The hulk of a man didn't take his eyes off Escobedo and the tiny bit of food left in the wooden bowl. "I'm not talking to you, *gringo*."

Across the yard, Juan Perez perked up. From the corner of his eye, Hack saw the head guard grin at the incident boiling to life in the hot sun. That evil man liked nothing better than watching a good beating, and he didn't give a whit about who was on the wrong end.

When Hack was a young man, his old daddy had always said to get the first lick in on a fight and to use anything that came to hand. The only things Hack had nearby now were his fists, and Morales was hard as the packed ground under their worn-out old boots.

"But I'm talking to you, *estupido*." Hack's right fist shot out in a blur and landed squarely against Morales's jaw, spinning him to the side. A hard left landed on the point of his nose, which exploded in a gout of blood that gushed from both nostrils. The cartilage crunched under Hack's large knuckles, and the man's expression went dull.

Morales staggered backward before regaining his balance. Pursuing his advantage, Hack followed up with two more swings that immediately split the skin over Morales's eyebrow and split his cheek. The stunned man blinked several times to clear his watering eyes. Half a dozen of his *compadres* gathered behind him like regimental troops, as if preparing for a charge, shouting and urging him on.

Still behind Hack, Luke Fischer barked a laugh and rose to square off with the others. Using his fingers to comb back a tuft of brown hair from his forehead, he set his feet in case somebody charged. "Darn, son. I think I just saw water shoot out of six holes in his head."

The other members of the incarcerated Long Gang heard Luke chuckle. Two-Horses, Gabriel Santana, and Billy Lightning put their bowls on the ground and stood as one. The boys drifted behind Hack and scattered out. Had the members of the Long Gang been armed, that action would have had the makings of a shootout, with deadly results. They were all experienced gunmen and had done their share of killing both good and bad men.

Instead, they faced Morales's lackeys and prepared to fight.

Morales was an experienced prison brawler, and a couple of hard licks and a little blood didn't faze him all that much. A large man, he'd survived innumerable fights by using his weight and power. He shouted and rushed in to get his hands on Hack, where he could use his considerable prison experience gained from years of preying on weaker men.

Hack was far from weak and had no intention of letting that happen. Planting his right boot, he cocked his arm as if ready to swing. The instant Morales ducked his head to plow a shoulder into his chest, Hack settled back to use his own motion against him.

As a former town marshal, train and bank robber, and range rider who'd fought his way across most of Texas, bustin' knuckles with someone else was nothing new to the gang leader. He'd learned long ago to let a man use his own leverage against himself and almost felt comfortable with what was about to happen.

When Morales charged, Hack swiveled and dodged, at the same time grabbing the inmate's arm, and he used the man's momentum to swing him headfirst into the prison wall. The convict's skull and shoulder hit the solid rock and brick with a crack. The impact stopped the man's charge, and his knees buckled.

Morales went down for a second, but using the wall to steady himself, he regained his feet and pushed off with both hands, addled for a second time in fifteen seconds. He shook his head to clear it and blood flew. Gritting his teeth, he growled like a furious coyote and rushed at Hack.

Those friends of his were moving in, and Hack had to finish up fast. Only men who lost their tempers wanted to continue a fight just to maim and hurt. He wanted that mad dog down for good in the eyes of those who saw him as their leader, so he wouldn't have to look over his shoulder every day for the rest of the time they were there.

Morales shook his head a second time to clear the cobwebs, and droplets of blood flew like rain once again, splashing on those nearby. His face was a mask of blood that poured from his nose and a gaping split in his forehead wide enough to look like a second mouth. The edges separated enough to show his white skull, which was soon covered in red.

Hack reluctantly gave him one thing, the Mexican prisoner was tough as a horseshoe nail and had no intention of stopping. He came in again, and Hack swung a soft left that the inmate easily blocked, but it left him open, and an uppercut that started at Hack's rope belt and aimed at the top of Morales's head finished the fight. His teeth clacked from the impact that shattered his jaw, and he dropped in his tracks like a puppet with the strings cut. He hit the ground blowing bloody bubbles mixed with broken teeth.

Breathing hard, Hack faced Morales's friends and squared off with them. "This'll be the rest of you if y'all take one more step. This is over." He pointed at Escobedo. "And you leave this man alone."

Still making eye contact to maintain their machismo, Morales's men drifted off like leaves in the wind, leaving Morales unconscious in the dust. Hack's boys stayed planted where they were in case someone whirled to charge. When all the inmates were back to their places in the shade, they relaxed and went back to their own small pieces of ground.

Escobedo nodded his thanks and pushed his back closer to the rock and mortar wall, as if ensuring no one could get in behind him. He tipped the bowl into his mouth and finished the food Hack had fought for.

Hack licked his thumb and rubbed at the now raw knuckles on his left hand. With all the roosterin' between them over with for the time being, he picked up his own wooden bowl and returned to his previous spot in the shade to suck in another mouthful of the now-cold stew.

The shirt hanging on his thick shoulders wasn't much more than a thin rag, but a new rip in the back that ran from shoulder to waist parted when he sat. "It's a good thing this storm is coming." He picked up the conversation with Luke as if they'd never been interrupted. "They won't make us work for a day or two while it passes through, and Escobedo there can rest up."

Luke scratched at his brown whiskers. "I'm surprised you stood up for that feller."

Hack chewed for a moment longer and nodded at Escobedo, who watched his tormentor's lackeys haul the unconscious man off. "He'll make it now, maybe. Did you hear what happened in his cell last night?"

Luke swallowed the last of his meal. "Escobedo's tougher'n you think. He whipped Torres one-on-one."

Two-Horses stood in the sun, picking at a callus on his thumb. His face was wide, jaw solid, with prominent, protruding cheekbones. It was his White man's blue eyes that set him apart from his Comanche roots. Round in shape and always narrowed against the light, they spoke of mixed blood that almost no one, white or red, could abide.

He seldom spoke, but he seemed surprised Hack had waded into a fight that didn't have anything to do with any of them. "So why'd you help him?"

"Because what they did wasn't right. Torres paid one of the guards, and I figure it was Perez, to open Escobedo's cell after lockup. Torres slipped in, and about five minutes later they had to carry what was left of him out. They locked the cell again, and nobody said a word. That's why I think Escobedo can handle himself, but two fights so close together can drain a man down to nothing.

"The truth is, I don't like it that Perez is playing games with everyone in here. Next time it could be me or you or any one of us who's not up to snuff at the moment and can't defend themselves."

"Why did he let Torres into Escobedo's cell in the first place?" Gabe Santana wanted to know. Besides Luke, Gabe had been with Hack longer than the others. A lithe, slender man with black hair, olive complexion, and somber eyes, he'd been a man to ride the river with from the first time Hack laid eyes on him up in Llano County.

"Because I heard there was a bet over who would win."

The youngest of their group, Billy Lightning, scratched at a red spot on his forearm where a scorpion had stung him a week earlier. Looking more like a schoolboy, Billy had only a few light whiskers along his jawline and a dusting of blond strands on his upper lip. "Torres woke up in the hotbox this morning. He's still in there as far as I know."

"I knew a guy who spent three days in the Yuma hotbox," Luke interjected. "Killed him deader'n Dick's hatband. Fell out about five minutes after they let open the door. It was a crying shame for a tough man like that."

"I bet Torres wishes he'd never tangled with Escobedo."

Santana stretched his legs in the dry sunshine, studying what was left of his worn-out boots.

Billy used his thumb to rub at the knot left by what he'd grown up calling a stinging lizard, which was a local description of scorpions. "You could have let Escobedo handle himself. Now you'll have Perez thinking about you and what he can do to us."

"Don't matter. I dislike Morales, and now that's settled," Hack answered. "Sometimes you have to refresh folks' memories, too."

Taking advantage of the time out of their cells and the mine, Hack adjusted himself in the narrow shade thrown by the twelve-foot wall to keep the sun off his head. The guards allowed each man a cap, of sorts, but it fit so snug, the hot material made Hack's skull feel like it was baking all day. He'd often thought he'd give anything for one of the tall sombreros worn by the locals that provided a cushion of air on top and a wide brim to shade a man's face and shoulders.

Shoot, he'd even settle for one of the military-style caps with the leather bills the guards wore. They were a by-product of the French influence there in Mexico, but Hack really wanted a good, soft felt Stetson like he'd worn across the river. All Texans love their hats, horses, and depending on the man, their dogs or women.

Only one prisoner had a hat of any sort, and that was Torres, but it would go into the grave with him if the hotbox took his life. The guards took what they wanted when a man died, and the rest was either distributed to the peasants in the nearby community, or buried.

As the boys finished their thin stew, the Long Gang sat quietly for the last few minutes allotted for dinner until an old man with sunken cheeks stopped beside them and spoke in Spanish.

"Ah, *los terribles cinco*. Do you feel it, the air?"

"The five of us aren't so terrible, unless these boys get

riled, but it seems a little hotter out here than usual," Hack said. "Of course, this place is only a couple of notches below the boiling point in Hell, anyway."

The man smiled, revealing only two bottom teeth left in his head. "The wind, it comes from the south. There is a storm on the way. *Muy malo.* This time of the year, they blow off the *baja* and bring rain and life to the desert."

The last to finish his stew was Billy Lightning. He paused with the bowl still against his mouth and swallowed. "I *thought* I felt something in my bones."

"I am an old man and have seen it once for each decade of my miserable life. If I was much younger, I would ready myself to escape from this hellhole when the storm hits."

As was his habit in the Mexican prison, Hack glanced across to the guards huddled around a water bucket in the shade of a stick-and-timber portico leading into the *comandante*'s office. They were laughing and paying more attention to a dice game than their prisoners, knowing the noonday heat would dampen any ideas of trouble.

"Have you ever seen it done, an escape from this place?"

"No, but I've heard about it. No one has broken out of here in nearly twenty years. The last time was the dark of the moon, but the one before my time was when fifteen men climbed the wall. Only five got away. The others were killed by the Apaches they used to track them. For every man killed, the one who did it received two pieces of gold."

"Apaches working with Mexicans?"

"Civilized Apaches who live that way, in the Chisos Mountains."

A tingle ran up Hack's spine and an idea formed, making him feel more alive than he had for months. "How long does it take them to get a tracker from out there?"

"It would be at least a day, unless a couple were in the village for supplies or mescal."

"There's no way to get out of the cells, though, once it starts storming."

"You can be like Torres. Bribe Perez there to let you out for a midnight fight. If it was me, I would tell him you knew Escobedo outside and needed to settle with him. Perez loves to gamble like he's doing over there right now, shooting dice, and would welcome to see a match with you and Escobedo, and he'd bet on you to win."

"Well, I've already stood up for him."

"So you could kill him yourself."

Hack forced a grin off the corners of his mouth. He'd been there for so long his mind didn't seem to work, and that idea had never occurred to him. And here it was, an old man giving them all a way out, served on a platter. "Then I could take Perez, get his keys, and let the others out."

"That is a good plan."

"Why're you telling me this? This is your plan, not mine."

"Because I am too used up to fight and run. I will die here, but the other reason is that I don't like Perez and would like to see his dead eyes open and collecting dust."

Luke drew in the dust with a forefinger. "Mighty hard talk, just because you don't like the man."

"He cheated me in a dice game when I first came here and took my shoes." The old man looked down at the worn-out *huaraches* on his feet. The pitiful sandals had been repaired so many times with strips of leather they almost looked like small mops. "My good shoes would not fit him, but he sold them in the village and used the money to entertain one of his ladies of the night."

Close enough to hear, the rest of the guys remained silent, but they were working things out in their own minds. They'd learned not long after arriving at the prison that groups involved in too much discussion brought suspicious guards. They were Hack's men but had their own minds and did what they wanted. They came and went when the Long Gang was working north of the river. Though these were his core group, there were others from time to time.

Instead of gathering to hear, Two-Horses and Gabriel Santana were stretched out along the wall, pretending to sleep. Billy Lightning sat four feet away, sanding a callus off his hand with a rock. They were all listening, and if one were close enough to feel the rising tension and elation, it was easy to tell that the men who'd resigned themselves to incarceration were once again ready to ride.

CHAPTER 2

The chief guard, Juan Perez, rose from an arbor shade reserved only for him and his men and sniffed the air like a dog, filtering much of the scorching air through a mustache that sprouted thick and heavy against his nostrils. In addition to the dust and manure coming from a corral outside the walls, there was a hint of dampness.

He kicked a resting guard's foot and poked another's shoulder, prodding them from the raw wooden benches against their quarters' wall. "Get up. These men need to work and a storm is coming. The *comandante* will want one last shift back to the mine before the rain falls."

Though he and the *comandante*, Raul Mendoza, would have preferred for their prisoners to work from morning to night, they long ago discovered that a full day in the mine would kill them and that a dead prisoner couldn't make money for the *jefe*'s pockets. Instead, they dug for half a day, then returned to the prison as the second shift took up shovels and picks to worry copper from the mine, then they'd switch again.

Although he acted as if irritated, Perez was pleased with the changing weather. He heard the day before that his favorite cantina server was back at work. Juana had been taken to Mexico City by a soldier loyal to Porfirio Diaz, the country's president, but for some unknown reason, he'd sent her packing, and that was fortunate for Perez. A rainy day meant he could leave the prisoners in their cells and visit with her to spend his money.

It wasn't that they couldn't work in the mines while it rained, but Comandante Mendoza was afraid the inmates would use the weather in an attempt to escape as they were moved back and forth between the mines and the prison. Better to let them remain behind bars, and besides, everyone wanted some time off, and that went for him and his men, too.

He paused to stare in the direction of the little mining village that lay between the ancient structure that was once a mission run by friars and the entrance into the low, barren mountain that looked like an animal's burrow.

Against a backdrop of gathering storm clouds and lit by the sun, which was not yet covered, two spirals of buzzards turned lazy circles over areas of interest. Perez studied the scavengers, wondering if they were human or animal bodies that lured them to those particular portions of the sky. He loved the scavengers, and he once even had the opportunity to share a *trabajador*'s pleasures while letting her do all the work as he laid on his back and stared out of an open window to watch the carrion birds float overhead.

Maybe it would happen again sometime soon. With that pleasant thought in mind, Perez remained where he was in the shade as the guards kicked the afternoon shift upright and those who'd been in the mines that morning went to their hot cells. Spending time in those hot, airless cubicles was a different kind of punishment and wasn't considered as a pleasant gift.

Finally bestirring himself, Perez used a fingernail to pick at the dirt crusted in the corners of his eyes and followed the men past the hotbox. He paused beside the sunbaked door in the windowless structure made from hand-packed adobe. "Torres, are you still alive in there?"

The man who'd been beaten within an inch of his life by the newest inmate groaned an answer, and Perez chuckled. "It seems that you are. Feel better, my friend. We need another match between you and the boy who put you in there." He gave the hotbox a slight kick, doing nothing but dislodging crumbling sand and rocks. "You cost me a lot of money, amigo. That's why you're in there. You need to earn it back and, possibly, your life."

It was a blistering afternoon. He watched the prisoners march out the front gate and went inside *la oficina del alcaide* to cool off a little and visit with the *comandante*. Raul Mendoza always had interesting stories to tell.

CHAPTER 3

Lockup came at the end of the day as the filtered sun settled over the distant mountains, where a dark, odd color crept into the sky. Having grown up in Texas, neither Hack nor the boys were strangers to violent weather. Blue northers appeared in the fall, the coming line on the horizon always blue-black as it rushed southward, bringing icy cold winds, rain, and oftentimes sleet or hail under the right conditions.

Springtime north of the Rio Grande often brought ugly green skies that blotted the sun and birthed fierce hailstorms with stones as big as a man's fist and, more often than not, cyclones that stripped the land of leaves, trees, houses, and barns, sometimes even taking the grass itself.

This rising storm approaching from the west looked different as the winds rose and blew perpendicular to the advancing clouds, throwing dust and sand into the air that settled on the oily exposed skin of everyone in Purgatorio. The inmates were already used to being dirty and gritty, but the winds added one more layer of filth that covered everyone within the rock walls, guards and inmates alike.

Perez shouted for everyone to return to their cells in his dry, raspy voice. It was a welcome order, and the prisoners figured it was because of the rising storm. The guards didn't want anyone to be outside when it arrived to use the weather as a possible means of escape.

Eyes squinted against the flying debris, Hack took his place in front of the four-person cell he shared with Luke, Billy, and Santana. Two-Horses had a cell of his own for reasons no one could explain, though they often pondered it when they had the chance.

Billy was of the opinion that because Two-Horses was half Comanche and half White, one of the other prisoners would kill him for being a half-breed. It wasn't that the *comandante* cared about the death of a convict, but losing a good worker might put him behind.

While armed guards stood with rifles ready at their backs and fully prepared to shoot anyone who stepped out of line, Perez started on Hack's left, opening the flat-barred iron doors and shoving the prisoners inside. Another *guardia* at the opposite end of the long cellblock snapped the locks closed once they were inside.

When Perez reached his cell and motioned for the four of them to enter, Hack hung back as the others filed inside and whispered so only the sadistic man could hear. "I want to offer you a deal to make money."

Perez's eyes narrowed and he paused, already interested. The last bit of light at the end of the day came from a direction that should have lit the color deep in his irises, but there was only blackness, as if looking into a foreboding cavern. "You have no money, *estupido prisonero*."

"But the other guards do. I want to fight Escobedo tonight. He thinks he's tough since he nearly killed Torres, who is likely dead in the hotbox."

"Is that why you fought Morales? To show Escobedo how tough you are?"

"You got that right. You know as well as I do that he's tougher than he looks. With Morales and Torres out of the way, I'll be top dog in this place. Any time a new prisoner comes in, you set us up and I'll whip 'em."

"What do you get out of that?"

"Extra food, and maybe a woman every now and then."

The other prisoners waited, curious at the delay but looking at the ground lest they draw Perez's ire, which usually resulted in a fist or a whack with the hard, slender mesquite cudgel hanging from a leather strap around his wrist.

Hack knew they didn't have much time, though. "We fight in his cell, and you can bet on me. The other guards will probably think he's tougher, but no matter, you bet everything you have, and I'll win it." He needed to hammer the first point home. "All I ask this time is for a couple of *pesos* to buy some extra food. I'm tired of eating this pig slop every day."

Greed lit the guard's eyes, and Hack knew even if the fictional fight happened, he'd never see a single coin. The guard didn't have much more time for discussion. Fraternization was against the *comandante*'s rules, and Perez could lose the privileges he'd earned since they'd been there.

Perez was one of the oldest and most experienced guards, and they all knew he left the prison twice a week to go into the village for tequila and a couple of hours with the prostitutes who made a living by entertaining men with a few *pesos* in their pockets. No matter what Hack offered, Perez needed to maintain that perk.

"Are you sure you will win?" The man who smelled worse than a pigsty rubbed at the three-day growth on his cheeks and smoothed the black mustache that grew so thick it hid most of his mouth.

"I will if you lend me that pair of brass knuckles I've seen on your hand when you get mad at those stupid *criminales* who aren't smart enough to stay out of your way. When I beat the newcomer, I'll drop them on the floor, and you can pick them up when you're first in the cell. It's a guaranteed win."

"Get inside, *gringo*!" Perez made up his mind and pushed the big prisoner into the cell. Snapping the padlock and giving the hasp a yank to make sure it was secure, he nodded as if satisfied they were sealed in for the night. "*Bien*. It is a deal."

Hack built a frightened face to make him think he was worried. "Don't let them all crowd around to watch. Those dimwits'll start hollering and bring the *comandante* down on us. Keep them away. When I walk back here to the cell, they'll know I'm the winner."

Perez processed the play slowly. "I will be back once the *comandante*'s lights go out."

He stared to turn away and then stopped. "You better not lose, or it will cost you your life."

"I never lose."

"You're in here, aren't you?" Perez gave a phlegmy laugh and moved down to the next group of inmates waiting for what little cool respite the night would bring.

Feeling as calm as if he were sitting in church, Hack watched the second-floor windows until the *comandante* blew out his lamp and went to bed. Instead of jangling nerves, he felt nothing other than resignation and the urge to get out of that prison and back to Texas, where they all belonged.

The wind blew for another hour until it lay and not a breath stirred. It wouldn't be long before the weather arrived. It was so quiet they heard the horses in the corral a hundred yards away. Feeling the coming storm, one snorted and another stomped its hooves.

The guardhouse lights were on, and Hack kept watch on the constantly shifting shapes that were backlit by soft lantern light. One of the guards came out and made water against the side of the building, the sound as loud as a cow peeing on a flat rock.

Luke sat with his legs crossed on the floor, with its stones laid tightly in place so as to prevent digging. There was little opportunity of that, though they considered the idea when they first came to the prison. The entire front of the cell was steel bars, and anyone standing in the courtyard could see the four quilt pallets and anyone on them, so they gave up on that idea. At least one of the guards was always a steady presence as they paced the same route past the cells and around the yard.

Luke spoke in the darkness. "Storm's almost here."

Billy sniffed the air. "I don't smell any rain."

"Glad you don't." Hack walked to the cell door, taking deep breaths full of fresh air. "My mama always said that if you smell rain coming, it won't fall."

"He's right, kid." Luke leaned back against the wall as the low rumble of distant thunder reached their ears. "I think we're gonna get our wish tonight."

Hack studied the empty courtyard and wrapped his big, callused hands around the still-warm bars. "So do I."

Moments later, Perez showed up at their cell so fast it startled them all. Hack took a step back and cursed himself for showing surprise. Taking a key from his pants pocket, the guard glanced around and unlocked the door.

In the dim light, it seemed as if the guard's stained teeth peeked out when the thicket lifted in a smile generated by the thought of money coming his way from the pockets of his *compadres*. "The *comandante* is asleep. I heard him snoring through the door to his room. Come on. It is time, but if you try anything, I will shoot you with this pistol in my pocket."

Keeping his distance, he backed away as Hack approached the door. The mention of a gun was a surprise because the guards who worked closely, one-on-one with the prisoners were unarmed. Those with rifles stayed well away from the hardened criminals who inhabited the cells. That told him that either the man was lying or he was afraid enough of Hack and his guys that he really *did* break the rules by bringing a palm gun to the cells.

Hack stepped into the dark night, and Perez kept one eye on the boys as he closed and locked the gate. Once that was done, he pushed the American ahead, keeping a distance in case Hack had a mind to spin around and attack. He might have at another time, if the opportunity arose, but the big Texan had other ideas.

The lockup young Escobedo shared with two other men was at the far end of the cellblock. The sounds of both soft and loud snoring came from the sleeping convicts as they passed their dark chambers. Others were awake, and Hack saw fingers wrap around the cell bars as they passed. It wasn't unusual to hear footsteps in the courtyard as an occasional guard made their irregular rounds.

When they reached the end of the block, Hack stopped short of Escobedo's door and waited. Though he'd been in dozens of fights in his lifetime, his heart was pounding out of his chest, and that worried him some. This was the minute their lives could change if everything worked out right, and he intended for that to happen.

Perez turned the key in the padlock and then dropped it into the right-hand pocket, where his pistol supposedly rested. With his left hand, he reached into the opposite pocket and took out a pair of iron knuckles that had been hammered out by an untalented blacksmith.

As if slipping a leash on an angry dog, Perez extended the arm and held the heavy contraption between his fingertips and thumb so it was easy for Hack to slide his fingers through that old-fashioned weapon. He stepped back out of reach and glanced down to slip the lock's shackle from the hasp.

Hack took the old-fashioned weapon and made a fist with the semicircular curve's base fitting squarely into his closed palm. The piece of iron felt good. It felt like *power*. "*Bien.*"

Perez nodded, agreeing with him and removing the lock.

Swinging at the guard's temple, Hack gave it all he had. The thick metal connected, and hot blood splattered on his fist. Perez's skull fractured like a dropped cantaloupe. His arms stiffened at his sides, and he slammed into the bars and dropped heavily onto the packed courtyard, as dead as whatever it was those buzzards had been circling earlier in the day.

Afraid the fall had been loud enough to draw attention, Hack crouched and swiveled to see if anyone had heard. Clouds obscured the sky, and the enclosure was pitch-black. Nothing moved. No sounds of alarm rose in the night.

Hack felt anxious to the point of terror, and his throat choked up as he patted Perez's right-hand pocket and found it empty as his dead brain. "Dang it!!" The whisper under his breath was as loud as a shout in his own ears.

Though there was no pistol, the key was there, and he breathed a sigh of relief.

"*Quien es?*" Escobedo's soft, fear-filled voice came through the bars. "Who is it? No *mas*, Perez. Please."

It was so dark that Escobedo thought Perez had brought another man for him to fight. Hack felt sorry for the kid, who was doing his dead level best to survive. "Shhh. It's Hack Long. You speak pretty good English, don't you, kid?"

Escobedo's voice relaxed, and Hack could almost feel the man's tension drain away. "I do."

Hack knelt and yanked the sweat-stained cap off the guard's head and put it on. It was a size too big, but it'd serve in the darkness. "We're getting the hell out of here, and your cell's unlocked."

Hack fumbled at the buttons on the guard's shirt as

Escobedo opened the door with the squeak of rusty hinges. His other two cellmates joined them at the opening like frightened chickens afraid to leave the coop.

"Y'all come with me." Pulling Perez's shirt over his own, Hack winced at the rancid smell of old sweat and unidentifiable body odors. None of them smelled like roses, but that man plain old stunk. He buttoned it up. "Help me get him up."

Escobedo and the others pulled the limp corpse into a sitting position, then kneeling, Hack got a shoulder against Perez's chest. As they lifted the body, he shrugged it over his shoulder like a dead deer.

Escobedo leaned in to whisper. "What are you doing?"

"As dark as it is, they'll think I'm Perez carrying *me* back to my cell." A chuckle of relief rose, and Hack choked it down. They weren't out of there by a long shot, and he needed to remain steady. "I'm gonna lock him in, and when we're gone, they'll think he lost the bet on this fight and ran off with the money."

"Bet?"

"I'll tell you later, if we live through this."

"I'm coming with you."

Perez was getting heavy, and Hack didn't need to waste time talking. "You don't know what kind of men we are. You don't know any of us very well, youngster. Wait half an hour and then slip out with your friends here if you want and go your own way."

"How are you getting out? Are you going over the walls?"

"Nope." He swallowed his rising aggravation. "That little door in the wall beside the big gate. You've probably been too busy staying alive to notice it. That's how the guards get in and out without opening the main gate. Beyond that, we haven't thought that far ahead."

"The other guards?"

Good Lord! He felt like shooting the kid, who wouldn't shut up.

"I'm thinking when they find the door open, they'll think Perez cheated them and went to town with their money. They won't wake up Comandante Mendoza, so they'll either lick their wounds and go to sleep, or some of them'll go into the village to find Perez and settle up. Either way, we'll have until daylight before they realize he's in my cell."

Thunder rumbled closer, and Escobedo spoke in the darkness. "You may have longer."

He and the others disappeared, and Hack headed for his own cell, toting a body that was heavy in death.

CHAPTER 4

Luke was waiting at the cell door when Hack came close. He inhaled sharp and quick. "Oh, no, Perez. Is he dead?"

"No, I ain't."

"Hack! With that cap and shirt on, I didn't know you. I knew you could do it. Who is that?"

"*Was* that. Perez. Here." He passed the key through the bars. "Unlock it and don't drop it. One little ol' skinny key'll be the devil to find in the dark, and this guy's heavy."

The others gathered around as Luke reached through the flat bars and removed the big padlock by feel and opened the door. Throwing a glance at the guard's quarters, Hack carried Perez into his cell and pitched the body on Billy Lightning's quilt pallet in the back corner. It landed with a sickening, meaty thud.

He'd left a lot of bodies behind through the years and dropped plenty more from a distance with a long gun, and they all stayed with him long afterward in dreams and nightmares. Rolling his shoulders to ease the ache, he heard Luke snatch up one of the other ratty blankets and spread it over the body.

The storm announced its arrival with another distant boom, and Hack turned to face Luke, Santana, and Billy, who were vague, indistinct shapes against the open end of the cell. "We gotta get gone."

He choked back the rising fear that one of the guards might come by, all wound up and hoping the fight was already over so they could collect their winnings and maybe sneak off to the village.

Anything was possible with those guys.

He pushed through the fear, patting Luke on the shoulder. They'd been partners since both of them had hit the ground running as kids. Together, they'd survived a dozen battles in the war back East and a long list of serious altercations after that, including more than one shootout with angry townspeople reluctant to give up their bank money and more than a few with stage and train guards.

"This is the only chance we'll ever have. Y'all follow me to the utility door by the gate. Maybe this key'll fit it, too. Once we're out, we scat like rabbits until we can't run no more."

"What about Two-Horses?" Billy spoke louder than necessary, and Santana jabbed a hard finger into his diaphragm. The youngster gasped.

"I am here." The half-breed Comanche's voice came from an even darker shadow, where he was squatting by a pile of firewood stacked in the middle of the prison's courtyard.

Their lives had been routine for the past three years. Go down in the mine and dig out the copper ore in a shaft running beside one worked by free local miners who received barely enough money to buy what few supplies were stocked in their *emporio*, which was mostly empty shelves. Come back to the prison to eat and sleep, then do it all over again.

Soon they would be all on their own, without guards telling them what to do. Born of the plains, Two-Horses was out there enjoying the night wind, and Hack couldn't blame him.

Billy swallowed. "Sorry about that. Just wanted to make sure you were with us."

A shadow passed the open window in the guards' quarters, and Hack knew they had to move. The guards were up and waiting, for sure. "He was the first one I let out on the way here."

Santana's voice came soft and low. "First one?"

"Escobedo and his cellmates are out. Then a couple of others who promised to stay quiet for half an hour. Told them if they made any noise, I'd come back and kill 'em all."

Luke growled low in his chest. "They'll do something stupid."

"You didn't let Morales out, did you?" Hack asked.

Hack pictured the man he'd knocked out earlier in the day. He figured Morales was having a rough night with a broken jaw and teeth. There was no way he'd let him and his cronies know they were escaping.

"Not a chance. They're still sleeping like babies, along with most of the others, and Torres is still in the hotbox. I don't care if they never get out."

A strong gust of wind shoved at the rock and adobe buildings, moving nothing but sand and small pebbles that rattled and hissed against the walls. "This is gonna wake 'em all up, though. We gotta go. The guards in on the bet are probably starting to get antsy. Let's go."

He led the way, moving more slowly into the black night than he preferred so as not to trip or run into something hard. Hack wanted those horses in the corral so bad he could taste it, but they were on the opposite side of the guard quarters, and it was too risky to try to sneak by.

Luke rested his hand on their leader's shoulder as they tramped northward, startling him. That's when Hack realized they'd formed a train to stay together in the darkness and the blowing dust. It reminded him of the time he and Luke had worked on a big ranch on the high plains one winter when a weeklong snowstorm had forced them and the other cowboys to tie a rope from the bunkhouse to the barn so they wouldn't lose their way and freeze to death in the near-unending blizzard that trapped everyone inside.

More than once, they had gone out to tend the stock and had traipsed back and forth with one hand on the rope and the other on the shoulder of the man in front. Luke and Hack vowed right then and there they weren't gonna be trapped in another snowstorm, and when winter set in after that, they'd avoided that part of the country ever since.

Hack realized with a start that once they were outside the prison walls, they'd still have to find their way north through the near-complete darkness. With the arrival of the storm, the only thing that would show them the way was the lightning, which could also reveal their presence to anyone looking for them.

Progress was painfully slow, even though they were all familiar with the prison yard. Advancing with an awkward stride and feeling with both feet rather than walking naturally, the prisoners moved with both arms extended to help feel their way. Though there was no light, the walls and buildings were slightly darker than the sky, and the vague shapes helped register their position. Halfway across, a different rain-cooled wind came through like a refreshing blast of winter that sucked the heat away in seconds.

Behind Hack, the men drew deep, loud breaths of fresh air. "This is gonna bring the guards out," he said. "We need to hurry."

"Señor Hack." Fear washed over him when a soft voice stopped them in their tracks. Hack crouched, expecting an attack, and reached for the pistol that used to ride on his hip. It was habit that took his hand toward a weapon that wasn't there.

Behind him, Hack sensed the others reacting in a similar

way. Luke cursed softly and Two-Horses grunted, either in irritation or understanding.

The voice came again from the darkness. "It is me. Escobedo."

Taking a deep breath to calm down, Hack reached a hand into the dark, empty space in front of him. "You scared me to death, kid. Where are you?"

Again, the creak of hinges reached his ears, and he sensed a lighter shade of darkness. "We are outside."

"What?"

"Come forward. The gate was not locked. We are free."

Mouth dry, Hack headed toward the sound of Escobedo's voice. Maybe someone simply forgot to lock the narrow access door or one of the guards snuck out for a drink or visit with his family, but it made no difference.

Unless it was some kind of trap, they were simply walking out the door, and the coming storm would hopefully wash out their tracks.

It couldn't be that easy.

But that part was.

It was what happened later that became legend.

CHAPTER 5

Eight sets of soggy feet slapped against the hard, unusually wet desert floor as the ragged band of escapees alternately walked and trotted through the storm blowing in from the southwest. As the rain slashed Hack Long's face and washed it clean for the first time in months, the group moved cautiously through the night.

Free for the first time in years, all eight wanted to shout in joy, but that freedom was questionable. As one, they were still trapped in the desert, held at bay by the storm that rose and fell in waves. The others followed close behind Hack, as they had since he'd led them out of the prison after Perez's death.

It kept running through Hack's head that he'd give all the gold they'd hidden under the boardwalk in Barlow, there on the plains of Texas, for five horses. Second-guessing was a fault he'd struggled with all his life, and Hack did it again as they moved through the night and storm, kicking himself for leaving the guards' mounts in the corral back beside their quarters.

Shoot, they didn't have to be *good* horses that he was wishing for, just mounts with enough bottom to reach the river so they wouldn't have to walk. The thrill and near terror of their escape had worn off hours earlier as they strung out across the flat terrain of the desert floor, leaving each man with his thoughts of freedom.

The rain fell only as it can in the desert, alternating between torrential downpours so black and rainy that a man couldn't see his hand only inches from his nose to a lighter shade one grade up from tar pitch. Soaking wet and cool for the first time in months, they pushed northward as the clouds thinned again between waves of rain and indistinct shapes appeared.

It gave them enough hope that they broke into a trot to put more distance between themselves and whoever might be trailing behind. Hack considered their situation as eight sets of footsteps slapped the ground. Unused to running or walking so far, he figured they'd all settle for mules to ride at that point, or even donkeys if they came across such a miracle.

They wouldn't have been running from a Mexican prison outside of Zacatecas in the state of Coahuila if Hack had listened to his mama when he was young. As he was growing up on a dirt farm east of Austin, she'd done her best with a Bible and a peach tree switch to raise the headstrong boy right, but she didn't know that he'd already killed a man by the time he was sixteen years of age and had helped a gang hold up a Lockhart bank a year after that.

It was just the way he was turned out.

It was her final misfortune to feed a drifter who said he was a cowboy down on his luck but instead was a demon in human form. He found her body the next morning in their sad little shack she called home. For what the drifter did to her in the night when Hack was off stringing along with his miscreant friends, he extracted dues when he caught up with the man four days later.

Leaving the barely recognizable corpse swinging from a wide live oak limb, he rode away and stopped by Luke's house to tell him what had happened. By the time he finished the story, Luke had rolled his few belongings in a blanket and joined Hack on the path as a desperado.

Hack had been riding the dead murderer's horse, so they rode double to a settlement consisting of two stores, a church, and two saloons to shop for horses. One of the drinking customers didn't know he'd donated his horse to their cause, and they'd disappeared in the woods.

Months passed, and one by one, Hack had picked up men here and there, testing and weeding them out until he'd formed what the newspapers eventually called the Long Gang, men who rode with Hack because they understood one another and got on like they were made from the same mold.

A good boy, he was not. But neither were the others who followed behind that night to avoid any number of the desert's pitfalls, such as cholla, prickly pear, or the sharp spines of the head-high agave from which the locals made mescal.

The thought of that oily, wonderful liquid rose in his mind, and Hack imagined it would be like sipping heavenly wine. Instead, as the rain intensified, he tilted his head and opened his mouth wide to absorb the much-needed moisture they'd kill for in a couple of days, if any of them lived that long.

In his opinion, they'd make it if the storm continued, and according to the old convict back in Purgatorio, it would for at least another day and maybe another, and the fat drops would wash away any evidence of their passing.

Behind Hack, Luke slapped his wet chest like it was a drum. "Hotamighty! We're free as the birds!"

The girls back in Texas always thought he was pretty, and he might not have been hard to look at if all that dirt and those whiskers were scraped off. He'd loosened up with every mile they'd put behind them, and when there were no signs of pursuit, Luke reverted back to his old self.

"This was the best idea you ever had, Hack! They'll never find us in this."

Moving faster than they had for the last hour, Two-Horses shouted in glee and let loose with a war whoop. Needing freedom and the high plains wind in his face, the half-breed had suffered the most from imprisonment.

Hack had often thought it was knowing how much Comanches valued the breeze in their faces and open spaces that was the reason Two-Horses had a cell to himself. Because of that somehow, Mendoza didn't want Two-Horses to kill or maim other inmates. It didn't make any sense, though, because neither the *jefe* nor any of the guards seemed to care about anyone's life or comfort.

Now, moving through the desert, Two-Horses occasionally sang words no one could understand, but it was obvious his voice was filled with joy.

Instead of answering Luke's comment, their leader concentrated on leading them like a horse heading to the barn. To a man, they knew they had to get shed of Mexico before the prison guards or the Rurales caught up with them. Once they were out of the *frontieriza* and back in the States, it would relieve Hack of the burden he carried since they entered Mexico. If it hadn't been for their leader's *good* idea three years earlier, the gang wouldn't have crossed the river in the first place.

A determined Bandera posse led by Texas Rangers had been on their trail, and after two weeks, none of them could come up with a good way to shake them. No matter which way they turned, the lawmen and determined townspeople stayed right on their tail. Dusty and tired, they rode into Barlow late one night with the hope that their tracks would disappear amid hundreds of hoofprints and wagon ruts.

The half-built town had few saloons, and at that late hour of the night, there were few people about. It was a good thing it wasn't daylight when they arrived. The road-weary gang would have attracted notice no matter where they went.

The sprouting town full of false-front stores was a perfect

place to hide the money. Stashing it in a hollow tree or burying it was always risky. Landscapes could change with the arrival of only a small storm or a settler could claim the land or a hunter might come across fresh-turned dirt beside a unique tree.

That's when Hack decided to hide the loot somewhere in town, and when Gabriel Santana saw the unfinished board-walk in front of the Martin Bar and Restaurant and a stack of lumber in the dirt street, they realized it was the perfect place. The hammers left lying on the pile of two-by-fours and the half keg of open nails made it was obvious the workers would be back the next morning.

As the rest of the boys kept watch on the dark street, Santana reached under the finished walk as far as his arm would reach and stashed the saddlebags out of sight under the newly laid planks. After they shook off their pursuers, it would be easy to come back later and retrieve the gold and silver coins they'd relieved from the Bandera bank.

The gang rode out barely thirty minutes after arriving in Barlow, hoping to outdistance their pursuers, but the next day, a dust cloud revealed the posse was still on the hunt. They'd forced the fugitives south, and there was nowhere else to go. The only escape was Mexico.

It was a questionable idea at best. They'd only been across the river for a few hours and were headed south when a company of Rurales threw guns on them. Surrounded by well-armed men hidden behind boulders and thick brush, Hack and his men knew better than to draw on the professionals who fought bandits and murderers for a living, and they soon found themselves chained up and headed for prison.

CHAPTER 6

The second youngest of the Long Gang, Gabriel Santana was in better shape than the rest of them and was barely breathing hard as they made their way through the rainy darkness. A drifter from New Mexico, he'd cowboyed most of his life. At a young age, he had learned how to talk himself into good jobs, and every ranch hand missed him when he was gone.

He was down to the lint in his pockets the day he met Billy Lightning, who convinced Santana that relieving other people of their money was easier than working for it. With Hack's permission, he joined up while others came and went in the gang. There, he found his place, and life had been good until they crossed into Mexico.

Until then, he hadn't even seen the inside of a jail, and his first experience behind walls made him vow it would never happen again. Only days after soldiers had transported them to the hell-on-earth prison deep at the southern end of Coahuila, Gabe had worked out a suspicious deal with the prison's *comandante*, Raul Mendoza.

Mendoza had called the Norte Americano to his office the moment they hit the yard. The *comandante* stood in front of his quarters as the Long Gang was escorted through the gate by a dozen of President Diaz's well-armed soldiers.

Shoulders back to present his authority, the *comandante* had pointed at Gabe. "You. What is your name?"

Gabe's eyes flicked to Hack, who was being patted down by the prison guard they came to know as Perez. Hack gave a slight nod and Gabe answered. "Santana."

"*Bien.* Come with me."

The rest of the Long Gang watched as Gabe followed the *comandante* out of the hot sun and into the cool interior of the stone building. Almost as if Mendoza didn't care if the man was a violent prisoner, he led the way with Gabe following. More attuned to a prisoner's state of mind, Perez left the others under the eye of his men and followed at a distance.

They reached the second floor and walked down a short hallway to Mendoza's office, which overlooked the prison yard. Beyond the open area was a line of cells that opened toward the building. From the sight of floorboards worn smooth in front of the window, Gabe had figured the man spent a lot of time watching whatever was going on down below.

Mendoza pitched his cap on a rough homemade desk and assumed a position behind it. "What are you men doing in my country?" he asked in halting English.

Not sure what to say, Gabe shrugged.

"You look like us." The *comandante* switched to Spanish. "Do speak our language?"

"I do."

"*Bien.* So when I ask a question, I demand an answer."

Gabe resisted the urge to shrug, knowing it would anger the warden. "We came across to avoid trouble, only we ran into the same thing when a bunch of Rurales threw down on us."

"They are the law here. They were doing their jobs."

"Well . . ." Gabe restrained himself from a smart answer.

"You presented yourself well when you came through the gates."

"I don't know what that means."

The *comandante* turned his attention on Perez. "You may go now."

Surprised but used to the *jefe*'s sometimes strange behavior, the man, who sported a thick mustache and heavy jowls, nodded. "Yessir."

"And close the door behind you."

"*Sí, señor.*" Perez used two fingers to swing the heavy oak door into place.

Mendoza poured two tequilas into dingy glasses and handed one to Gabe. "You did not look to be frightened, nor did you examine the prison, looking for a way out. You absorbed what was around you and no more."

This time Gabe really did shrug.

"Are you an educated man?"

"I am."

"You can read and write."

"Yes."

"You are Mexican."

"Nope. American."

"Your parents were Spanish."

"They were American, too."

Mendoza nodded, thinking. Gabe wondered if the man was considering even more of his ancestors. Instead, he switched subjects. "I have a proposition for you."

Not liking the look in the man's eyes, Gabe sipped at the clear liquor and waited.

"I someday wish to live in your country, but as you can see, my English is not that good. I wish for you to teach me enough that I can speak fluently. If you agree, I will provide you with drink, and on occasion, there will be a woman up here to entertain you."

Surprised at the proposition, Gabe took another swallow.
"On one condition."

"What is that?"

"You don't let my friends know."

Mendoza grinned. "They would be jealous."

"At the least."

Gabe never volunteered an ounce of information to the
other members of his gang, and they soon accepted it as part
of the survival process the inmates struggled through each
and every day.

He wished for some of that tequila as they moved through
the desert, with the early morning hours lit by the near-constant
flickers in the sky that seemed to follow wherever they went.
It was Billy Lightning who suggested long ago that storms
were attracted to him and lightning soon followed.

According to him, he'd been struck four times, and each
one had left significant scars. To prove it, one day behind
Purgatorio walls, he had taken his shirt off, and the inmates
had gathered around to stare in awe at the puckered red tissue
that radiated their own jagged lightning bolts of evidence.

A fracture in the clouds ahead came just in time for Hack
to see he was leading them into a thick growth of head-high
cholla. He stopped as thunder washed over them and waited
for the next pulse to guide them around the bristly cactus.

"I told you I was lucky! That one lit us up just in time."
Billy pointed at the sky. Realizing what he'd done, he yanked
his hand down below his head. "Wow! That's poor judgment
to do such a thing."

Gabe shook his head, wondering how Billy had survived
to that point.

Only a couple of years older than Billy, Gabriel slapped
him on the rotten shirt that barely covered the man's shoulder. "Don't get fried out here. We're almost to Texas."

CHAPTER 7

Hack heard Gabe tell Billy that they were almost to Texas.

"Not hardly." He tilted his head back and placed both hands on either side of his mouth to funnel more water over a powder-dry tongue that felt two sizes larger than normal. Glorious moisture drained in, and those tissues felt natural again.

At the rear of the group, Escobedo and one of his two cellmates, Quijas, squatted not far away. Hack was frustrated as hell that the two young men had ignored his orders to go on their own. He reckoned they preferred to be shot than to spend the next ten years in the hellhole that was one of Mexico's most savage prisons.

Feeling better, though his shirt and worn-out canvas pants were soaking wet and slightly washed for the first time in three years, Hack took a long breath and tried to relax. He'd been tight as a wound watch spring from the moment he'd followed Perez down the line of cell doors and taken the keys from the man's corpse.

All that tension and fear was taking its toll, but Hack needed to keep going.

Rolling his shoulders to ease some of the tension that

made his spine feel like it needed to be cracked, the big man forced himself to relax as best he could. "You boys keep a lookout for fires or window lights. Maybe we can find someone who has horses."

Not a one of them was above stealing mounts.

Santana's voice was soft in the darkness. "It's after midnight, and in this rain, there won't be no campfires, and smart people are asleep and not wasting lamp oil."

Billy matched Santana's tone. "I doubt there'll be a house out here in the middle of nowhere, anyhow."

"You'd be surprised." Another burst of light showed Escobedo standing off to the side, peering north. "My people build houses all over the desert. As soon as a little ridge rises from the flats, somebody will put up a place underneath and try to make a go of it. It is the way of our world."

"No matter, keep watch, anyway." Another flash of light revealed a path around the cholla and through a sea of mesquite. Escobedo held the gang leader's interest as they took a breather, and Hack studied him and his cellmate for a long moment before deciding to allow the two Mexican nationals to stay with them.

What could it hurt? "That way. Let's go."

Refreshed enough to trot once again, Hack led them around the dense thicket and minutes later drew up short when a bright flicker of lightning revealed a man wearing a wide sombrero rising up from behind a tangle of prickly pear where he'd squatted to do his business.

It must have been pretty urgent to have the Guardia Rural out in the storm, and he seemed to have forgotten he was bare from the waist down, with his *pantalones* gathered around his ankles.

"*Alto!* Who are you?" The Rurale called out in Spanish and fumbled to raise the Remington carbine hanging from one shoulder.

For the second time that night, Hack instinctively reached for the pistol that used to ride on his hip. He'd already picked the spot to aim for on the man's chest, the first button above the leather carbine crossbelt draped over his left shoulder.

Again, he slapped nothing but the material of the canvas pants he'd worn for three years, and remembering there was no iron hanging there, he darted off to the side, toward the mesquite thicket. "Spread out!"

The boys who'd obeyed his every word for years reacted instantly. They scattered like blue quail and went to ground.

The darkness had already descended once again by the time Hack dropped to his knees behind the twisted trunk of a downed mesquite. Knowing that any movement would attract the Rurale's attention in the next bolt of lightning, he peered back at the two former Mexican inmates, thinking they'd run at the first opportunity.

Instead, they froze, even though the darkness between lightning flashes would have provided enough time to escape. Another flash showed the national policeman shouldering his rifle and aiming at Escobedo and Quijas's flickering shapes in the lightning.

"Run, you fools. Just because you're Mexican don't mean he won't shoot. They'll kill you for just being with us." Hack found himself whispering aloud, and his jaws snapped shut.

The man jerked the muzzle of his carbine for emphasis and aimed where he'd seen them in the last flash and shouted orders in Spanish. "You two! Don't move!"

Though the landscape went dark again, Escobedo's voice came, full of fear and sincerity. "Don't shoot us. We are lost in this storm and harmless."

Another split in the clouds showed Quijas had moved closer to the Rurale for some reason. Maybe he thought he could plead himself out of trouble, but when Hack saw a dim-witted smile on the man's face, he realized the young man was going to try to reason with the frightened rifleman.

"Please."

The Rurale's voice rose, filled with stress. "Don't *move*, I said!"

The world went black once again, and Quijas's foot kicked a rock that clattered against another. The guard fired, and in the muzzle flash, Hack saw Quijas react from the bullet's impact and fold sideways, a stunned look on his face.

The Rurale quickly cocked the hammer, and Hack heard him thumb open the Remington carbine's breech block to reload. The *guardia* cursed as men shouted from the darkness behind him. From the sound and his cussing, Hack knew he'd tilted the rifle's muzzle too high, and as was the tendency for that rifle, the block had fallen shut, forcing him to waste a valuable second to open it once again.

The rifle's original design, and the man's pants around his ankles, saved Escobedo's life. He darted away amid the sounds of scrambling and snapping twigs, and Hack knew he'd dropped to the ground and scrambled away like a lizard before the rural police officer could reload.

Several men shouted in Spanish. More lightning, and in the cold flashes, Hack saw the man respond as he yanked up his britches with one hand while doing his best to hold the rifle level and point at where Escobedo had been. "Here! We're being attacked!"

Muzzle flashes sparkled between lightning bolts as other panicked Rurales rushed forward and fired at invisible targets.

One of the staccato flickers of lightning revealed Luke not far away, crouched behind a particularly wide mesquite that had been growing and spreading its thin canopy for decades. Resisting the impulse to shout, Hack whispered, "Luke, keep low."

"What do you think I'm doing? I'd get on my belly like a snake if I thought it'd do any good."

"Come on." Making himself as small as possible, Hack moved past Luke and took an alternate route through the mesquites in their original direction of travel.

Luke followed, but his soft voice was full of concern. "They're shootin' over that way, you know."

"They are, and I 'magine they'll have a picket line somewhere close by, too. Maybe on this side of their camp, if we're lucky. Would a horse make you feel better?"

"If I was on it and we were about ten miles from here."

"Then shut up and come on."

A long, thick bolt forked and dropped from the roiling clouds. One of the legs struck a ridge not far away, lighting up Luke's face and scraggly beard. None of them had shaved more than a couple of times in the hoosegow, except for Gabe, who scraped his face at least once a week in the *comandante*'s office.

"I smell horses." Feeling his nostrils widen like a bird dog, Hack stuck his nose into the wind. "They ain't just gonna *give* 'em to us. We circle around behind them and take their mounts. Horses'll get us to the river and out of this godforsaken country. I ain't going back to those cells."

CHAPTER 8

Awakened by the rare storm, Comandante Raul Mendoza sat beside his glassless open office window to catch the cool, moist breeze and watch the rain fall each time lightning lit the line of rock and adobe *celdas* on the opposite side of the courtyard.

It was the only time since he'd been assigned there that the old prison looked inviting, but he knew that was like a dress on a pig, only a costume on ugly reality. He checked the time on his late father's gold pocket watch. Four thirty in the morning, over an hour later than the last time he'd looked.

The first wave of the storm had arrived around nine thirty in the evening, bringing moisture and cooler breezes, a welcome gift for that time of the year. It made for good sleeping, the best he'd had in months, but it had been interrupted by rolls of thunder and crashes of colorless lightning that had seared through his eyelids.

He'd finally risen from the cot in his room and had lit a lamp before making his way into the office. He'd gone there only because the windows were wider than those in the usually airless room in which he slept, and the big window allowed him a more expansive view of the now empty prison yard.

It wasn't the first spinoff storm from a Pacific typhoon Mendoza had ever seen. The last one had blown through ten years earlier, when he was a police officer down in Tlalpán. They'd seen it coming over the mountains from the south-west, and the aftermath of so much rain had transformed the desert into a startling world of color as desert plants quickly bloomed before the heat returned.

An open bottle of tequila sat next to the oil lamp on the table beside his chair. In one hand was a glass half-filled with the slightly oily liquor, and in the other, the English Bible he was learning to read with the aid of Gabe Santana. Normally, he wouldn't be drinking at such an early hour of the day, but the storm required a salute.

He'd seen signs of intelligence in the young man when the rural guard had brought the five to Purgatorio. Looking half-starved and wearing more chains than were necessary, the men had stumbled through the gates behind the line of hard-eyed mounted police who wore distinctive uniforms modeled on traditional charro dress. Bolero jackets, tight-fitting trousers, and a mix of red and black neckties topped by broad-brimmed, high-crown felt hats.

The prisoners were filthy, sunburned, and extremely dangerous. They were all hard as steel, but the way Santana carried himself spoke of cunning and some education. And of course, he somewhat looked like Mendoza, who had olive skin, black hair, and finer features than most of those men under his command.

The others went into the cells with thieves and murderers. The accompanying report said the men were part of a gang that had invaded Mexico and almost immediately killed a number of innocents and *soldados* before running out of ammunition during an intense gunfight outside a small village named San Mateo. Overwhelmed by a large force of experienced Rurales who had learned to fight not long after they cut their teeth, it said, the American outlaws had finally surrendered.

He disbelieved the report. The Rurales always wanted to make themselves to be more than what they really were, mounted policemen who survived on their wits and graft. There might have been a shot or two, but that was doubtful. He suspected they hid in the brush alongside a river or wash until the Americans were in just the right position and then popped out with guns drawn.

However, the federal Rurales were tough as nails and hardened by months in the saddle and battles too numerous to count. They were created by President Benito Juárez to combat the bandits and the murderers who preyed on travelers throughout Mexico. If they were concerned enough to wrap so many chains around the Norte Americanos, then the men who composed the Long Gang were to be feared.

The American prisoners had proved their mettle the day they arrived at the hardscrabble world some inmates called Infierno Secos, and the chains were removed from their wrists. When a group of the most dangerous inmates braced them in the courtyard that first afternoon, the five men fought back with the ferocity of jaguars.

Less than a minute after the ruling inmate Carlos Montiva had demanded their clothes in exchange for the rags he and his *compadres* wore, Montiva and two of his men lay dead on the hard-packed earth. The *comandante* had never seen men killed so quickly in a barehand fight, and though he had them all whipped as punishment, he couldn't help but admire the American prisoners.

Their long-waisted and muscled leader, Long, was a formidable presence and often glared holes through Mendoza, making the *comandante* uncomfortable with the knowledge that though the American was his prisoner, he was still a leader of his men. This was the kind of prisoner a commander handled through men like Perez, so that there was no direct contact that could result in a standoff that would only end in the prisoner's execution.

After that first day, the other inmates mostly left them alone, and when the Norte Americanos had healed from the whipping they received from the guards for fighting, they kept to themselves and there was no more trouble.

Lightning ripped the sky, revealing the low rock-and-adobe buildings housing over a hundred men. Mendoza took a small sip of the liquor and studied the yard. All was quiet and dark inside the cells that opened onto the yard. They weren't allowed any form of light in the small six-by-nine rooms that contained only sleeping pallets and nothing more. The cells were all closed, and not a face appeared at the bars.

Each morning, the prisoners emerged into the hot daylight after the guards unlocked the cells, blinking at the brightness. After they ate their rations in the evening, they were locked in again at six o'clock.

This day they might not work, he thought. It wasn't because of the prisoners. They would do as he demanded and maybe even produce more broken rocks than ever in the cool air, but his guards would have no cover from the storm. Not that he cared about their comfort, but Mendoza knew men, and they'd be miserable, seeking respite from the wind and rain, and eventually not paying enough attention to their jobs.

As the *comandante*, he played chess, not checkers. He planned ahead, considering what he'd do if the circumstances and his life were different and he found himself swinging a nine pound hammer all day. If he were a prisoner, he would wait for the guards to turn their attention to comfort rather than watching the men, and then he'd find a way to escape.

He smiled to himself and took another tiny sip of tequila, satisfied that he was smarter than those down there who would work in the mines until they either served their sentences, plus one day, or died from work and exposure.

The tequila slipped down his throat, warming his gullet. His relaxed attitude evaporated when a shout from the courtyard brought him to his feet. Placing his hands on the windowsill, he listened as a second voice rose. In the next flash from overhead, he saw guards with lanterns running in several directions.

"Escape!"

"The Norte Americanos are gone!"

Mendoza whirled and grabbed his gun belt, strapping it around his waist. He snatched up a double-barrel shotgun at the same time someone banged on his office door. "*Jefe!*"

Not knowing if an escaped prisoner was on the other side of the door, he yanked it open while at the same time leveling the short twelve-gauge coach gun he'd taken fifteen years earlier from the dead hands of a Texan on the opposite side of the river.

The young guard gasped and stepped back, holding one hand out. "Don't shoot. It's Geraldo!"

Mendoza lowered the twin muzzles. "I can see that. What's happening?"

"Capitan Perez is dead. The storm woke me up, and I went out to have a smoke with him. He wasn't on his cot or watching the storm. When I went to look for him, the guard door by the main gate was open, and I went back to check on the prisoners. That's when I found his body in one of the American's cells. They are all gone."

"Alert the others!"

"*Sí, señor.* I have done that, and we're making a head count now."

"Good. Saddle the horses and gather a dozen men and Indio. We'll need him to track, and maybe one other if he knows someone in Nuevo Yucatan. Then send a rider to Saltillo and inform the soldiers."

The tiny settlement of Nuevo Yucatan had grown up around a deep well near the prison, providing people and products that helped support Purgatorio. The town without a single tree to provide shade had a church, a cantina, and a small *cocina* that supplied food for travelers and those with enough money. One small general store sold a few necessities that couldn't be grown or made by hand.

Indio lived there in a shed behind the cantina and was known as the best tracker in Coahuila.

Geraldo turned to rush away and had a thought. He stopped. "Rurales?"

"The nearest troop I know of is too far away. They can join us if we haven't caught the escapees before they make too many miles."

A loud slap of thunder rattled the building, sending a stream of fine sand and dust onto Mendoza's scarred desk. Both men looked upward at the timbers overhead as if expecting the roof to collapse.

When it didn't drop, Mendoza set his hat. "Go!"

Geraldo whirled and ran out the door while the *comandante* gathered what he would need to track down the escapees, then shifted the shotgun to grab the whip hanging coiled by the door.

Comandante Raul Mendoza had already decided that each man would get fifty lashes in front of the other inmates, and if they were still alive at the end of the whipping, the dangerous man named Long would receive a bullet to the back of the head.

CHAPTER 9

Hack knelt beside Luke at the edge of the mesquite thicket with their heads close together, listening to the voices of men searching for those who'd appeared in the storm.

"These guys are Rurales for sure." Gritting his teeth in pain, Hack raised the knee that was on the ground, felt with his fingertips, and removed a thorn as hard as iron. "They kill for a living."

The lightning had moved off, flickering only on occasion. That both hurt and helped. They couldn't see in the darkness, which prevented the escapees from moving ahead and stealing the horses, but it also robbed the troop's ability to see *them*, and that was worth the trade-off.

"How many are there, do you think?" Luke whispered.

Hack wiped water from his eyes. "More than I want to tangle with."

"Let's just circle around them and get gone."

"Won't do any good. They'll wait until daylight and track us. The rain's slacking off, and if it don't start up again, our footprints'll be clear as a buffalo herd."

They'd become fluent in Spanish during the past three years, and the snatches of conversation from several directions told Hack at least one of their members was dead. One of the Rurales thought another had been captured somehow, and that made him grin. The boys were doing what they do best, and it made him proud.

"What do we do?" Luke always deferred to Hack, had even when they were kids.

"Put the sneak on them while we have the chance. It'll start to lighten up soon, and if we listen and move slow, maybe we can crawl up on a couple and relieve them of their firearms."

"The others'll hear the struggle."

Hack picked up a fist-sized rock. "Not if we crack their skulls fast."

"What do you think the other guys are doing?"

"Killing Mexicans, I hope."

Footsteps and the snap of a stick underfoot told them someone was moving around not too far away. A flash revealed a three-foot mesquite limb at their feet, as big around as a man's wrist and dried hard as steel by months, if not years, of baking in the sun.

He heard Luke shifting around and figured he'd picked it up when he said, "This suits me just fine."

Luck was with them and the volume of rain increased, drawing a dark curtain around them that occasionally was lit with overhead fire.

"Stick close." Hack crawled forward on his hands and knees, feeling ahead for whatever might stick, bite, or cut. It was dangerous work in the desert, for rattlers and scorpions inhabited that country, but he hoped the storm had driven the creatures into their dens and nests, leaving them free to creep up on the alert camp.

Knowing the boys, they were likely also working their way around the Rurales, who still kept firing at suspicious shadows in the night. If things continued to work in their favor, the escapees would all meet somewhere close to the picket line and could soon light out on horseback.

It was one of the Rurale's spurs that gave him away. The soft jingle between rolls of thunder told Hack just where the man was. Plucking at Luke's shirtsleeve, he pulled his old friend down low into the deep shadows beside a clump of sagebrush and waited.

The shouting had stopped. If the boys had been close, Hack would have had them spread out in a skirmish line and advance. He learned long ago that most people don't expect an attack. That was something he always did and expected his men to do the same.

Another flicker, and a dark shape with a big hat took form before blackness once again descended. He leaned in and barely breathed in Luke's ear. "See him?"

"Yep."

"Next flash."

Still as coiled snakes, they heard another tiny jingle, and the next flash showed the man only a couple of feet from where they crouched, looking away. Hack dove into the darkness, hoping the guy hadn't moved, hitting him with all the weight of his flying body. The Rurale grunted at the impact, and they landed with a thud on the wet hardpack. Hack swung the rock in his fist at where the guy's head should have been and missed completely.

Shocked by the sudden attack, the man gasped and twisted like a wildcat. Desperate to finish it quickly and as silently as possible, Hack struck again with the rock and missed a second time. The Rurale jammed a forearm against Hack's Adam's apple, forcing him back. Gristle popped, and for one horrified second, Hack thought the man had crushed his larynx.

Grunting with the struggle, he swung the rock still again, but the angle was wrong and the blow proved ineffective. Desperate now and more tired than he thought after running half the night and two fights back in prison, Hack managed to get his thumb and index finger dug into the soft tissue under the desperate man's jaw. Leaning with all his weight, he squeezed as hard as possible while at the same time measuring him for another blow.

The man fought for his life and struggled to draw the pistol on his belt, but the flap refused to yield and he couldn't get it free. He dug one boot into the ground and used all the leverage he could muster to flex his hips and try to throw Hack off. It was all the Americano could do to hang onto the bandolier across the other man's chest, and the next flash showed their faces only inches apart.

The Rurale snapped at Hack's nose like a mad dog, his breath foul from rotting teeth. Hack once knew a man who'd had his nose bitten off in a fight, and the thought of the excruciating pain of his own cartilage crunching under someone's teeth gave him strength.

But then Hack jerked his head back, and the next thing he knew, Rotten Teeth gained leverage and flipped them over, causing Hack to lose the advantage of being on top. Had he been alone, he would've been a goner, but a nearby grunt and a solid pop reached his ears as Luke finally saw an opportunity to swing his limb in a short, powerful arc.

The Rurale jerked and raised his head higher from the sudden pain. Another crack and he went limp. Hack threw the twitching body off to the side and laid back, gasping for breath. "I thought you were never gonna hit him."

Luke jerked a thumb, and the last fading flickers of lightning revealed two bodies lying still not five feet away. "I've been swinging like the devil with a chopping ax while you were rolling around with that guy."

"Where'd they come from?"

"Out of the dark once y'all started rasslin' around. That old boy's spurs sounded like jingle bells the way he was kicking them boots."

"You sure they're out?"

Luke dropped the limb beside Hack, who smelled the blood and tissue.

"More'n out. I didn't want 'em getting up again."

He pressed a knife into Hack's palm. "You can cut his throat if you want to with this."

"Nope. That second swing did the trick." Rising, he felt around the corpse's waist, freeing the pistol belt. While he strapped on the rig, Luke moved away and did the same, raiding the two other bodies. When they were finished, both wore bandoliers of shells for the men's carbines, along with their hats.

"Hope our boys don't shoot us for Rurales." Luke settled the gun belt on his hips.

"I think they've already cleared out, and we need to do the same." Hack went through the man's pockets. "See what else those guys have."

"We don't have time. I'd like to see if their boots'll fit, but those others might show up at any minute. It's quiet over there, and besides, I don't like robbing dead men."

"You're not too particular about banks, trains, and stage-coaches. We're gonna need some cash, and I hoped one of 'em might have a few more coins than what this guy's carrying." He stuffed a small piece of change that felt like a single *peso* into his pocket.

Gunshots froze them in their tracks, but the muzzle flashes were pointed in the opposite direction from where the pair crouched. "No matter." Familiar with Remingtons, Hack checked the carbine in his hands to make sure it was loaded, and he felt fine. Almost giddy. "Let's go find them horses."

CHAPTER 10

When the Rurale had risen from behind the clump of prickly pear and Hack had shouted for them to run, Two-Horses set his right foot and dodged to the left. He sprinted through the darkness without concern of cactus or low-growing mesquites to put distance between him and the rifle that had fired only a couple of seconds later.

Sharp pain shot up both legs, and he realized he'd run into a patch of waist-high cholla. The barbed spines punched through the thin material of his worn-out trousers. Gritting his teeth in pain, he slowed and used the light shown in the sky to find his way through the vegetation that either stabbed, scratched, or attacked in some way.

Now that he was out of range, he paused and waited for the almost continuous flashes in the sky to find his way. When they came, he noted the path through the sticker bushes and wound around as many as possible.

Each step pulled the material up and down against the front of both thighs, wallering holes out of the fabric and working the spines deeper and deeper into his leg. The small wounds were already irritated by the time he put a hundred yards between himself and the rising chaos behind. Despite the steady irritation in his legs, Two-Horses pushed on until the sounds of fighting diminished.

Figuring he was far enough away from the skirmish, he removed the pants, rolled them up, and resumed his journey as bare from the waist down as an Indian toddler. At first, he considered the idea of circling around behind the camp. He knew that Hack and the others would all do their best to either meet up behind the rural police to steal their horses or gather somewhere closer to the mountains.

The sheer volume of continuing gunfire changed his mind. Unarmed, his friends would have no way to defend themselves. The Rurales would hunt them down if they could. By daylight, the experienced fighters would track Two-Horses and the others down one by one, if they weren't already shot and dead.

Comanches were no stranger to traveling by foot, but they preferred horses and were often called the greatest horsemen on the plains. All he needed was a mount to ensure his escape. He intended to find one soon enough.

The storm moved away, and soon the gray, early morning light brought distinction to the land, making travel faster. The dangerous vegetation thinned out, and he was soon trotting across the open, wet desert floor with a ground-eating pace. He was somewhat out of shape thanks to his long incarceration, but it still felt wonderful to exercise and move with freedom.

Anyone who survived would do the same and head for the town of Barlow. From the night they hid their saddlebags full of gold and silver under the boardwalk, all of them had planned to return at some point. The original idea was to arrive as a group, but it looked as if each person would have to make it on their own.

It didn't matter to him. He'd been alone when he'd met Hack Long and the others, and he would make it alone once again when it became necessary. Most of the time, he traveled with the others only for company and safety when they were in hostile territory.

The cholla spines in his legs were a continuous irritation that would soon become serious if he didn't get them out. Some of the larger thorns were deep in the muscles instead of skin, and there was no doubt they'd work their way even deeper.

He had an uncle, High Grass, who had been thrown from his horse when an Apache shot the animal in a battle down near the generations-old crossing by San Vicente on the Rio Grande. That day long ago, High Grass had kicked free of the horse but landed in a thick growth of cholla. Literally covered with spines, he'd continued the fight free of the ambush, killing two of their age-old enemies before the Apaches retreated.

When the battle was over, he'd bristled with large broken joints of cactus jutting from his bare skin. As the story went, High Grass had dropped his weapons and used the blade of a knife to flick the large chunks of cactus free.

Laughing at the sight, the other members of his Quahadi band had gathered around to watch the poor man who was grimacing with pain. Once the largest "limbs" were off, he'd switched to picking out the spines one after the other by hand. They found his situation hilarious enough to change his name to Walking Stick Cactus.

There were so many stickers in his body that Two-Horses' uncle was overcome with fever on the way back, and once they arrived at his village, the women spent an entire day using clam shells to grasp and remove the remaining bristles, and for days afterward, they treated the wounds that festered and oozed thick yellow mucus.

In one way, luck was on Two-Horses' side because the harsh desert sun was blocked by stubborn clouds that showed no signs of dissipating. He typically loved cloudy days, and though summer was the worst time of the year to be in the desert's blistering heat, right then it was gloriously cool.

With his spirits lifted despite the constant irritation in his legs, he also knew there were many challenges ahead. The dry creeks were flowing, and he counted on springs that should have been replenished by the runoff, which also filled depressions in the rock, providing clean drinking water, at least until they evaporated.

Roads were few and far between, and that suited Two-Horses just fine. As a light rain fell from the clouds that seemed determined not to part, he came across a wide deer trail that soon led to a brush-shielded stream running thigh deep and fast.

The cool, clean water refreshed him, and already feeling better, he found a short, fat cactus growing nearby that would ooze a thick sap when cut into or broken. Using a dried mesquite branch, he knocked the cactus into pieces and stuck his hands into the white liquid. Keeping a lookout all around him, he covered his legs with the sticky substance. As the makeshift glue dried, he plucked the remaining larger thorns free. Each one came out hard, and the barbs, which resembled tiny fishhooks, puckered the skin every time he pulled one.

A roadrunner appeared, pausing to watch as Two-Horses removed spines and flicked them away. Feeling safe, the bird sat under a creosote bush and watched the strange activity. When Two-Horses finished plucking out the largest spines, he impatiently waited for the sap to dry. When it felt like soft paper under his fingertips, he peeled the coating away. Each patch came off full of the hairlike stickers, which he pitched into the fast current.

Wearing only his faded shirt, he picked up his rolled pants from where he'd left them on the bank and waded into the cool water, which soothed his irritated skin. Breathing a sigh of relief, he kept a wary eye on the banks. He'd spent way too much time there, and he knew it was too dangerous to remain any longer. It was time to go, but there were still things to be done.

He stepped out of the stream, unrolled the trousers, and studied on what to do. The stickers in the material were all in the front and would take too long to pluck out one by one, so with no alternative, he ripped the leg with the fewest spines into a long strip. That done, he drew the wide ribbon back and forth on a rough rock to remove the little needles.

The waist was so rotten that it came free with a tug. Using it as a makeshift belt, he strapped it on just above his hips and ran the long strip of material through the front, between his legs, then over the back, forming a breechclout like his ancestors wore. Another thin strip of material from the bottom of his shirt became a headband, and he rolled up the remnants for later use.

Though he needed to get out of Mexico and back to Texas, the closest crossings were extremely dangerous for a half-breed Comanche. Growing settlements on the southern border were filled with White men who shot Indians on sight, and to them, one Indian looked just like another, no matter what tribe they were born into. Texas Rangers also rode the Rio Grande, on the lookout for Mexican bandits who robbed on both sides of the river, and they shot quick at anyone who didn't look like them.

The history of Comanche raids against the Mexican people reaching back well over a hundred years was also a death sentence to him. Those same villagers saw most Indians from north of the Rio Grande as enemies. A lone, unarmed man against them would soon be a rotting corpse.

Needing to find territory with as few people as possible, Two-Horses headed northwest, intending to avoid the towns on the Texas side of the river. A wide smile crossed his face.

He'd cross at San Vicente and visit the place where his mother's brother changed his name.

Surely, somewhere between here and there he could find guns and a horse. With surprise on his side, it'd be nothing to kill a traveler, a lone rancher, or even someone living on the *fronterizo*.

Then he'd be free again to either find his people or make his way to Barlow and figure out a way to retrieve the money.

CHAPTER 11

In the soft morning light of a gray, misty day, Hack and Luke rode north on horses stolen from the Rurale picket line. They weren't much, a couple of Roman-nosed, bony carcasses that were in need of a blacksmith or a bullet between the eyes, but sitting high above the ground for the first time in years felt like they were kings on top of the world.

Earlier that night, while the band of Rurales had concerned themselves with those who'd disappeared into the night, Hack and Luke had circled around the empty camp and found the horses watched by only one guard. Luke took care of him with the knife he'd taken from the first man's body. They chose two from the remuda before scattering the rest by slapping their rumps and spooking them with the big, sweat-stained hats.

Hack hoped one or more of his boys would run across some of the horses before the *guardia* rounded them all up. There was nothing else he and Luke could do at that point, and still concerned that those Rurales would be back soon, the pair headed for Texas at a ground-eating lope.

They didn't talk much through the remainder of the night, but with the dawn, Luke's voice returned. "Hey, boss, you know they're gonna come after us when they catch a couple of those ponies."

"They still won't know which ones to follow." Hack checked the low, gray sky. "I'm hoping this rain will keep on for the rest of the day and wash our tracks out, especially on the hardpan."

"That is a wish I doubt will come true. It's slacking off pretty good." Luke pointed at the clouds off in the distance and the streaks of bluish rain that were falling on ground already soaked enough that it was running off in streams. "Do you think the rest of the guys caught horses, too, and got out of there?"

"That's my hope." Even though Hack hoped no one was after them yet, he couldn't help but swivel in the saddle to check their back trail. Sure enough, the hoofprints were visible on the wet ground, but there was no sign of any pursuers as far as he could see in the distance.

"We could swing wide and go back. Maybe cut their trail and pick up some of the guys."

"And the Mexicans would cut ours. The boys wouldn't come back after us, so, no. We push on to Barlow and meet them there to get that gold. Shoot, we can stay in town until one of us gets the chance to get it out from under the board-walk. Then we can stay right there until the boys show up. It'll be a good place for all of us to meet up and rest."

"And divide the money."

Hack nodded. "And divide the money."

"If any of them make it."

"That's true, but they're tough and can take care of themselves. Right now we have bigger fish to fry. We're gonna need some money for clothes and food and such when we get across the river. I don't intend to get shot by some trigger-happy cowboy who don't like Mexicans standing upright." Hack ran a thumb over the butt of the pistol in his holster. "This single-action Colt's not a bad pistol, but I want better rifles."

"Winchesters, like the ones we had when we crossed over down here."

"That's my preference."

Ready to get back to less dangerous territory, they rode for Texas.

CHAPTER 12

Billy Lightning was alone for the first time since he had joined the Long Gang back in Texas. Thankful that the storm was over and any danger of being struck again by another hot bolt was past, he wove his way through clumps of sage, greasewood, and mesquite. Though the rain had stopped, the wind shook any vegetation limber enough to give from the pressure.

Of course, just because a squall was past, that didn't mean he couldn't be struck again. The first time he'd been hit by a bolt, the sky had been relatively clear, though the sharp edge of nearby clouds that day foretold of something worse on the way.

The lightning had struck where the young man's neck connected to his shoulder, traveled the length of his body, and exited through his ankle. One minute he was on a sharp rim overlooking a valley and gazing off into the distance, and the next thing he knew, he was lying on his back in smoldering clothes, staring at the gathering clouds with his left ear almost blown off.

Billy was thinking about that past moment when he stepped into a clear spot in the brush that was occupied by two men, one of whom was busy cutting the other's throat with a dark-bladed butcher knife. It was likely the breeze and the rustling of scrub brush leaves that covered his footsteps and allowed him to get so close to the grisly scene.

The man in a tall, crowned hat straddled the other and dug in his boot heels. "Be still and give up the ghost, hoss. You know what you did, and now's the time to pay the piper."

The stranger on bottom struggled, gasped, and died.

Billy's coming up on foot didn't alert the distracted man, and he finished what he was doing before noticing Billy standing beside a large creosote bush. He whirled, snatched a pistol from the holster on his belt, and cocked it. "Hands up! This is no concern of yours."

"I was thinking the same thing." Billy stared down the bore of that big .44 and held his hands out to his sides. "I'm just here because of unfortunate circumstances."

"I've been tracking this man for a week."

Wondering why the stranger felt a need to explain, Billy shrugged. "I've been on the receiving end of such a trek."

"But not this part." The pistol in the man's hand never wavered.

"No. My head sits on my shoulders just fine." Unsure of what was required of him, Billy hesitated. Mostly unconcerned by the pistol aimed at his middle because many men had done such a thing in the past, he finally noticed a five-point star on the man's dark vest. "You're a lawman."

"Texas Ranger." The Texan's handlebar mustache quivered in the breeze. "My orders were to take him in, dead or alive, for murder."

"It seems to me you've made your decision. I'll be on my way, then."

"Suit yourself." The Ranger studied him from under the brim of his hat. "Never expected to find someone afoot out here, though. You look as if you've been rode hard and put away wet, son." He wiped the knife's blade clean on the dead man's shirt and slid it into a skinny leather scabbard on his belt.

"That's about the sum of it." Billy kept an eye on the pistol aiming at him. He never liked people to point guns at him and was growing irritated with the activity. "I'm leaving with your permission, if you'll lower that Colt."

The Ranger let the barrel drop. "A man walking in the desert has some challenges."

"Those are the truest words I've heard in a good long while."

"I'm a Texas Ranger, and this man robbed and murdered a number of people back in Laredo." The Ranger seemed to find a need for repetition and explanation. "He resisted my attempts to take him into custody, and this is his unfortunate result. Had he submitted, a hanging would have been faster and a sight more painless, I'm told."

"Your preference is a knife?"

"He was asleep, and like I said, the last time I approached him, he drew down with a pistol and shot at me. The attack startled me and put a hole in the side of my shirt before he got away. I'd heard he was a light sleeper, and therefore, I took no chances this time."

"Seems to have been effective."

The Ranger stood and uncocked his weapon but kept it in his hand. "Would you care to ride back with me? Seeing's how I now have two horses, I'll permit you to straddle one of them if you'll help me get this body up over the saddle."

"You're asking me to ride double with a dead man?"

"That pony appears to be capable of carrying two."

"I'm thinking more of the stench. He won't keep in this coming heat. If I'm correct, it's a long way to the Rio Grande."

The Ranger studied on his observation. "That's a fact." He rubbed at a week's growth of whiskers, thinking. "I have a solution. I've a bag of salt. It's the only spice I prefer, though I'll take a pinch of black pepper every now and then, if there's some available. My thought is to sever his gun hand and take it back in that. Does that sound like a better plan?"

Though he wanted to be free of the lawman and continue on with his walk, Billy's curiosity was alerted. "How will your superiors know it's the hand of the man who done the killing?"

"Easy." The Ranger pointed with the barrel of his pistol. "He's missing the ring finger of his right hand. Got it bit off in a barroom brawl by a man who apparently had the affinity to gnaw on a man's appendages when angered, which should have been enough to teach this one to stay out of such businesses, but he was a drinker and therefore drawn to those establishments. I believe it was strong drink that drove him to murder a farmer and his fat wife for their horse, which is what set me on his trail in the first place. A draft horse. Who kills for an animal that pulls a plow, unless a man needs to eat it when grub's low . . . ?"

He drifted off as if pondering such a situation.

That extra horse sure looked good to Billy, and he preferred to travel with a gun for protection, no matter who held it. "How far do you figure it is to Texas?"

The question derailed the Ranger and brought him back to the moment at hand. "About a week, I reckon."

"I don't care to walk that far. I was hoping to come across some road agents and take possession of their horse, but I stumbled upon yourself."

"You fancy yourself capable of such? I see no sidearm nor any cutlery that's visible."

"I'd find a way."

The Ranger tilted his head as if Billy had grown an extra set of ears while they were talking. "What're you doing down here afoot in such a harsh land?"

Billy shrugged as if such a conversation was an everyday affair down south of the border. "Just escaped from Purgatorio, a Mexican prison way over yonder." He waved a hand toward where he'd come from.

"What'd they have you in for?"

"Coming across the border's all."

"I've heard of such. They on your trail? I doubt they let you go, judging by the looks of your clothes. I don't care to get into a gunfight with a bunch of Mexican *guardias* with an unproven boy who thinks himself a gun hand."

"I'm sure someone's concerned by my disappearance, but I got away while it was raining, and I doubt there's much trail to follow as a result." He found it odd that he'd taken the man's speech patterns upon himself.

Patterns and languages were abundant on the frontier. With the constant influx of immigrants, such as Germans, French, Italians, Irish, Mexicans, and Scots, to name only a few, a man often had trouble understanding accents and speech. Those raised in Texas often developed different ways of speaking, and if they were in any way educated, still another ingredient came into the mix, as was evidenced by the Ranger.

Billy didn't want to tell him about the others, just in case he might be curious enough to track them down for some kind of reward. If he knew Billy was part of the Long Gang, he might extract that information by maybe shooting him in the leg and then salting some of Billy's lightning-scarred hide as evidence of his capture and demise. He was wanted back in Texas, and the Ranger might want to collect on it.

"Well, I don't blame you for escaping. I've heard of that prison and how hard it is. Feel free to come with me. What's your name, young man?"

"Billy Lightning."

"That's too uncommon to be real."

"Folks call me that 'cause I've been struck by lightning four times in my life. My mama had a last name I didn't care for because it wasn't my daddy's, and I never liked my first name, neither. A sportin' lady in Las Cruces gave it to me, and I like the way it rolls off the tongue."

"A serious misfortune, the lightning strikes, I mean. I see no issue with a whore giving a man a name, and I've known a hundred individuals who don't go by their Christian names as well. What is it about you that attracts electricity?"

"I have no idea."

"You may have an unusual amount of metal in your body that will call it down. Maybe a bullet or two, or I suspect if a feller carried around a vial of mercury, it might do the same thing . . ."

He paused as a huge rattlesnake appeared between them and slithered past without caring whether the men were there or not. Billy counted the rattles in its tail, twelve and two buttons. They watched until it disappeared beneath a thick scrub brush. Neither were inclined to kill the serpent, who was only minding its business.

When it was gone, the Ranger seemed tense, as if the snake's appearance had put him on edge or reminded him of the danger of everyday life around him. "Just in case you might have a warrant out for your arrest, what's your given name?" The lawman rested his hand on the butt of his pistol. "And don't you try and make one up. I'll know it as sure as I recognized that rattler there."

"Delmar Bailey." It wasn't his real name, but one that had belonged to a man he'd known back in Austin who'd been lynched by mistake. The men who'd done the deed thought he was someone else.

Not finding the name familiar, the Ranger bit his lip. "I prefer Billy Lightning."

"As do I."

"My name's Captain Clarence Hawkins. Your company will be enjoyable, if you can converse in an educated manner."

"I have six years of schooling."

"That's enough." Ranger Hawkins unbuckled the dead man's gun belt and handed it to Billy. "A man ought not be unarmed in this harsh country, but if you dare to draw it against me, I'll leave your body for the scavengers."

"I won't."

"You bet you won't."

CHAPTER 13

Gabriel Santana came across a rough stone house shortly after dawn and raked the hair from his eyes. Hoping he could request some food and water, he squatted in the shade of a lost *huisache* tree and watched for what he supposed was half an hour before a small man the size of a half-grown child stepped outside with a wooden bucket in his hand.

The farmer crossed to a goat pen made of twisted mesquite logs and partially covered by a similarly gnarled brush arbor. Animals in need of milking bleated, and he spoke softly in Spanish. "Patience. I am an old man, and I don't move fast any longer. I told you that yesterday, and it'll be the same tomorrow, only I'll be a day older."

He chuckled at his joke and crossed the bare ground to the gate.

Santana's stomach grumbled, and he started to rise and make his presence known, but the sound of hooves reached his ears just in time. He side-shifted against a creosote bush and was enveloped by the rank odor of its sticky leaves. A roadrunner trotted past without noticing, but it darted away when six men in straw sugarloaf hats walked their horses around the house as casually as going to church and reined up beside the goat pen.

The hats in the shape of sugar packed for sale south of the

border were common wear for men like these, whom he at first thought were *chinaros*, Mexican cowboys. Each man wore a *batero* jacket, *vaquero* pants with buttons from the waist to the knee, and leather *botas* from the knees down, but the gun rigs each man sported, along with the bandoliers draped over both shoulders, quickly changed Santana's opinion of them.

They were professional bandits and dangerous as diamond-backs.

Santana wasn't afraid of anything, but he wasn't stupid. Those men were professionals, like him and the rest of the Long Gang, and they would shoot him on the spot just for drawing air in their presence.

The gray-haired farmer, barely five foot two, almost leaped into the air when one of the men urged his horse up to the pen and called his name. "Flaquito! It has been a long time."

The man threw a terrified look at the house and held both hands out, pleading with the leader. "Refugio, please. Not again. I can't, my wife can't . . . again."

"Ah, your *young* wife. You are way too old for her, as a rock to a sapling, and like the last time we were here, I wonder why she is with a dried-up goat farmer. You must have bought her, because there is no possibility you did something to make her fall in *love* with you."

Two of the bandits dismounted and flashed wide grins at the frightened man. They crossed the bare yard toward the little adobe house, kicking squawking chickens from under-foot.

"Indolent," Santana thought as they pushed inside. Seconds later, a woman screamed in terror.

The diminutive man rushed through the open gate to stop them, but Refugio dismounted and pushed him back. Little Flaquito fell and rolled onto his knees. "Please, we are poor. We have no money."

"You have chickens and a comely wife. She pleased us the last time we were here. That is why we have returned. Men always return to sweet water once they had a good drink at a fine spring."

While the remaining horseman remained in the saddle to keep watch, the other two bandits squatted in the house's shade with their backs to the stones and opened a muslin sack, withdrawing food of some kind that they consumed while watching Refugio torture Flaco with words. His wife screamed again before it abruptly ended.

The mounted man turned his horse to survey the area, giving Santana the opportunity to stay low and crawl like an odd-shaped coyote. He worked his way out of sight behind the thick scrub. Once the house was between them, he darted across the open ground and against the wall to find a back door propped open for ventilation. He peeked inside and saw one of the two bandits with his back to the door and holding a woman down on the bed.

The other man, on the opposite side of the bed and now hatless, held the struggling woman's arms across a corn-shuck mattress. She kicked with both feet, knocking the hatless man's sombrero onto the floor. Laughing, the first man struck her jaw with a fist and unbuckled his gun belt.

He pitched it onto a cluttered plank table with a clink of falling bottles and metal plates. "I will make this as pleasant as the last time."

His *companero*, who was still holding her arms, buried his face in her long black hair. "You are as fresh as the wind, Ynes."

Santana slipped inside so he wouldn't be silhouetted against the door and stepped to one side. The one-room house smelled of scrambled eggs and fry bread. Looking around for a weapon, he saw nothing but a cast-iron skillet on the table where the young woman had left it after breakfast. Hoping the second man would keep his head against hers, Santana gripped the cold handle at the same time the would-be rapist's pants hit the floor.

Intent on the woman, the now unarmed bandit reached for her dress at the same time Santana stepped across the room. Lithe as a panther and with all his strength, he brought the skillet down on the would-be rapist's head. It landed with a crack, and the bandit went limp with a soft groan.

The man with his face buried in Ynes's hair, drawing in her scent, had his eyes closed. The unconscious man still had a long knife with a polished bone handle in a scabbard at the small of his back. Santana snatched the knife as soon as the man went limp, and he leaned across the bed.

"Hey."

The other rapist looked up at the unfamiliar voice just in time to feel the sweep of his partner's sharp blade across his throat. Clasping his neck with both hands, he rose to escape as a gout of blood sprayed across Ynes and the bed. His life spurted away as his mouth opened and closed until he collapsed.

The terrified woman scrambled to the fireplace and huddled with her back against the stones. Santana held a finger to his lips and pointed with the other hand at the door. Glancing back and forth between the corpses, she nodded and pulled her ripped shirt together. Hoping she understood that he was going after the others, he pitched the frying pan onto the bed and turned to the fresh bodies.

Thankful that the first rapist had already removed his gun, Santana snatched it up and threw a glance at the closed front door. No one came rushing through, so he whipped the belt around his hips and buckled it on.

Ynes's face suddenly twisted, and she threw herself over the bed and grabbed the pistol from the man who'd bled out.

"No!" Santana whispered. "They'll hear the shot and I'll lose the surprise."

Throwing him a wild-eyed look, she flipped the revolver

and slammed the butt against the dead man's temple two hard times, then cocked it as she kept an eye on the door. Afraid she was going to pull the trigger and shoot through the door in rage, Gabe held out his right hand, indicating that he wanted the gun. She shook her head, but when he frowned in irritation, holding out his left hand, too, she finally relented and handed him the weapon, bloody butt first.

He nodded his thanks and went to the door. Taking a deep breath, Santana thumb-cocked the unfamiliar revolvers and pushed the door open with his shoulder. The two men were still squatting to the side, and they looked up to see if their *campaneros* were finished already.

He shot the nearest bandit first with the sticky gun in his left hand. The bullet's impact drove the already dying man into the other, who had no time to rise. The falling body knocked him off-balance, and he fell to the side, trying to catch himself while at the same time reaching for his own weapon. Santana's right-hand revolver followed next, the report hammering softer after the first percussion against Santana's ears. The bullet struck the bandit in the head before he could claw his weapon free, and they both fell back together against the wall.

Those two threats settled, both revolvers came up at the same time with the nearest mounted bandit in their sights. Gabe pulled both triggers at the same time, and at least one of the bullets found their mark in the man's heart. Already dead, the corpse draped forward before the sidestepping horse threw it off.

Their leader had plenty of time to drop Santana, but his startled mount crow-hopped for a moment, causing him to grab the high Mexican horn with both hands. He wasn't a cowboy, and the horse unseated him from the saddle. Arms flailing, he fell across the fence, which had been baked hard as iron by the hot desert sun. Ribs cracked, and he flipped onto the goat pen's splintered rails with a cry. Flaco rushed forward with a piece of broken rail and swung it like an axe.

Alternately shouting and grunting, he chopped at Refugio's skull until Ynes's shouts from the doorway brought him back to sanity. Dropping the club, he launched himself up, as lithe as a younger man, and ran to her. "Did they do you any harm?"

She held him close, weeping great tears. "I'm fine."

"They didn't hurt you again?"

"No. This man got there first, and they are both dead." She crossed herself and looked for somewhere to turn away from the sight of the four bodies on the ground. "They are all dead now. He is a saint."

Flaco turned to Santana, who was going through Refugio's pockets. "Thank you, sir."

Unwilling to meet Ynes's eyes, Santana dropped a few *pesos* into his own pants and unbuckled the dead man's gun belt. "You're welcome."

He strapped on the second gun belt and settled it around his hips for a cross draw. Feeling dressed for the first time since they had crossed into Mexico three years earlier, he straightened. "Ma'am, do you have food and water?"

"I do." She turned from her husband and raced into the house, dodging the rider's body and ignoring the two deceased men slumped against the stone wall as if executed by a firing squad.

Flaco's goats started for the gate, but he shooed them back inside as if everything were normal. Slipping a latch made from a piece of whittled wood into place, the old man took off his hat. "Señor, you can stay here the night if you wish."

"Nope." Santana shook his head and looked back toward the south. "I have to go, and I don't intend to bury these men."

He picked up one of the straw sombreros and tried it on. Too big, so he pitched it to the ground and tried on another to find it was a tolerable fit. Though the day wasn't hot yet, the hat's shade fell on his shoulders, immediately making him feel cooler.

"They will not be buried." Flaquito waved toward the east. "I will use one of their horses to drag them away so they might feed the scavengers."

"Take 'em a long way off. If I was you, I'd throw 'em into the nearest creek and let 'em wash downstream. That way, if any of their fellows find them, they won't know who sent them to hell or where they died. What's left in their pockets is yours, and if I's you, I'd learn to use some of them guns of theirs so this kind of thing won't happen again. You did well with that hunk of rail, but it ain't enough against an armed man."

Flaquito ignored the advice. "Water is too precious to poison with decaying bodies. I will find a place for them."

Santana disregarded Refugio's horse due to its skittish nature and caught the reins of the nearest animal that looked to have some bottom. He swung into the Mexican-style saddle and sighed with satisfaction, feeling as free as a bird.

He considered taking the remaining horses and going back for Hack and the others, but that was the wrong direction. Riding into those trailing him wasn't a good idea. North is where he'd go, faster now that he was mounted, to Barlow to meet everyone there. It never crossed his mind that Hack and the boys wouldn't make it.

Ynes came out with a cotton sack full of supplies and passed them up. The bag was tied closed with a piece of rope that he looped over the odd-shaped saddle horn, thick as his forearm. Flaquito put his hand on his savior's leg. "You are a hard man, but a good one. What is your name, my good friend?"

"Santana. And I'm far from good. A long time ago, I sold my soul and gave up all my tomorrows for today. That's not a good way to live for a decent man."

"And why did you get involved, Santana, with two poor people who scratch the earth to live?"

"Horses. I needed food, water, and horses." Santana started to turn away, then stopped. "And I despise men who prey on common folks."

CHAPTER 14

From where Hack stood, fifty miles from the great southern arm of the Rio Grande separating Coahuila from Texas, the high points of the rugged southwestern edge of the mountains were an indistinct profile.

As they grew closer to the river on that clear day, Luke rode stirrup to stirrup with him over the rocky desert floor, sometimes turning to look back over his shoulder, but mostly straining forward, as if leaning in would get them there faster. He reminded Hack of a dog on a rope, pulling as hard as possible to move faster while the owner kept a slow pace.

Seen from a distance, the two scruffy men looked like Mexicans, what with their borrowed hats, clothes, and all. They'd passed a number of small *ranchos* on the way north, but avoided them in case someone talked. If the smallholders didn't see the pair, they couldn't tell the men on their trail.

There were some supplies in the Rurales' saddlebags, but food was running low, and soon they'd have to stop at a hacienda or *almacena* in some little village. Those stores usually had the basics of beans, flour, and chilis. They weren't as well-stocked as merchants in more settled Texas towns, but they were the best to be had in that part of the world.

They knew there was a group of men on their heels,

because two days earlier they had ridden to the top of the highest point they could find in order to check their back trail. That's where Hack saw a plume of dust he first took for a dust devil rising from the desert floor.

The Navajo thought dust devils were *chiindii*, the ghosts or spirits of the dead members of their tribe. Other tribes thought they were demons rising from the ground. In this case, the demons were after the seven escapees for slipping out of that cursed prison, and there was a whole passel of 'em riding hard.

Chiindii are small tornados, and they're mean little devils when they get to spinning hard, generating enough swirling wind to knock a man off his feet. They've been known to rise hundreds of feet in the air, looking as if they were attached to the ground with a long snaking string.

But the dust cloud behind Hack and Luke was spread out and not rising high. Instead, it was the all too familiar rooster tail cloud of men on horseback headed their way, the same thing that chased the Long Gang down into Mexico in the first place.

Even from under the shade of the wide Mexican hat brim, Hack had trouble making out what was down there. "Your eyes are better'n mine. What can you make out? It sure ain't a *chiindii*."

Luke held his hands to his eyes and squinted through his fists as if they were a pair of field glasses. "You're right about that. Riders, and it looks like a lot of them."

"I was afraid of that. Some kind of posse or an Indian raiding party?"

"Mexicans, I figure."

"What's all that with your hands?"

"It blocks out the light, and peering through my fists like this makes things a tiny bit clearer."

"Where'd you learn that?"

"My dad. He was smart as a whip and could figure out things you never thought of."

"Um humm." The news was a surprise, and Hack considered that idea. Luke's dad had been mostly gone not long after the boys took to running together, and it was a surprise to learn he'd come back a time or two. That mention was the first time Luke had ever discussed his dad. "Does that trick make it clear enough to see how many?"

"A dozen, at least. Big sombreros, so it ain't Apaches or a Comanche war party heading home."

"They're following our trail."

"Sure looks that way, whoever they are, and I suspect it's whatever they call a posse down here from Purgatorio."

The gang leader shaded his eyes with a hand, despite the new used hat on his head. "Wonder if they got the boys."

"Can't tell from here." Luke cut his eyes at Hack. "Might be Rurales, too. Can't make out their clothes. Maybe the ones we tangled with back there? I'd suspect they want their horses."

"You think they might've just run across our trail and are trying to figure out who or what we are?"

"There's enough of 'em out in here. Could be a different company. Maybe they all run across one another and joined up together. Wouldn't that be the devil?"

The Rurales were a large corps that numbered about one thousand members. While incarcerated in *las celdas*, Hack had learned they were organized in forty-two squads and primarily responsible for patrolling the Mexico valley region.

While their performance was poor, with charges often made against them to the Mexican government for their rough behavior toward the public at large and slackness in enforcing their responsibilities against bandit groups, the rural guards did make some headway in wiping out a number of the less organized bands of outlaws.

Luke sat back in the saddle. "We could set up an ambush. Kill as many as we can. Maybe they'll turn tail and run."

"Naw, it might work if they're from the prison, but Rurales are professionals. We just caught 'em by surprise the other night. Had they been good and awake, I doubt any of us would be drawing air right now."

"Then we run some more."

"That seems like all we do in this godforsaken country." Just speaking those words made him mad, and Hack felt that tingling at the outside corners of his eyes that always spelled trouble.

"At least we're close enough, if we push it hard, we can beat them to the border."

Hack glanced to the south, then the north. Freedom and a new start with lots of money lay there. He wanted that more than anything he'd ever considered in the past.

That's when he changed his mind, something his boys hadn't seen him do very often, though his mind was constantly weighing their options and second-guessing everything he did. To his men, though, once Hack made a decision, he'd stay with it, but this time his temper got the best of him. "We don't run."

Luke grinned. "What do you have in mind?"

"An ambush."

CHAPTER 15

Comandante Raul Mendoza watched his Apache scout named Indio examine the tracks of two shod horses leading north. "Is it them?"

The man with long hair held back with a wide bandana rose from where he'd knelt on one knee. Leather strings were woven into his hair, and his mouth was a thin-lipped slash. Baked from the sun, his skin seemed dry as leather.

He'd ridden with Geronimo at one time, but a life being chased by the U.S. Cavalry wasn't what he wanted. He was inherently lazy and preferred to lay up with one of his wives and be waited on hand and foot. However, he liked some of the finer things in life and needed money. It wasn't the first time he'd taken out after someone for Mendoza for just that reason. Though he despised the prison's overseer, he valued the money that allowed him to live a little better than the other villagers.

"I do not know who rides these ponies, but they are the ones taken from the Rurale camp."

"For sure?"

Refusing to acknowledge the question, he looked everywhere but at Mendoza. "I recognize one shoe that was made wrong. The blacksmith who hammered it out must have been young and inexperienced. It will probably lame the horse someday. These are the ones we've been following. Those who killed the *guardia* the night your prisoners escaped. That is all I know."

"You sure they're not riding double? Five men escaped, but we've been following only two."

The slit of a mouth became thinner in irritation. "That is the number. You wanted those on horseback and not the others."

"I did." Mendoza figured the man named Hack Long was smart enough to acquire horses. It was him the prison *comandante* wanted the most. The one with him was probably Gabe Santana, whom he'd granted favors in exchange for learning. The young man had betrayed him, even after the *comandante* had promised leniency and a shorter sentence for his services. The others were nothing more than insects to live or die at the whim of the desert.

Mendoza considered the scout's broad face. "You said not the others. Have you seen more tracks?"

"Yes. Men who are walking."

"Why didn't you tell me about them?"

"Because you insisted on the mounted men because they move faster. The others spread out like ravines after these mounted up. I've seen at least two sets that are going north. I believe they are the others."

"We can come back and pick them up after we kill the fastest travelers," Mendoza said, agreeing with himself.

"That is true."

"You can find them after we're finished with these?"

"I have seen tracks of those Norte Americanos, of a band of Comanches, and of horses going all ways. I am surprised you have not seen them."

Unwilling to say he was a poor tracker and had not noticed anything other than the prints Indio had pointed out, Mendoza straightened in the saddle to project an image of control lest his men start thinking he was less of a leader. "How far ahead?"

"A day, maybe, Two at the most."

"Then let's pick up the pace."

Dead men are silent. Dead horses, the same.

Both were covered in flies that buzzed over the corpses in a cloud. The still air was filled with a steady hum of insects drawn by the smell of death.

The scent of coagulating blood was thick in the air when Indio reined up two hours later to ponder the scene. Mendoza hung back as the Apache studied the carnage before them. Suspicious, he held a Springfield rifle ready for trouble as he stayed in the saddle and scanned the ground for sign.

Scattered around the still bodies were hats, guns, empty shell casings, and splatters of drying blood. Satisfied there was no immediate danger from the carcasses, Indio dismounted, working out the gunfight in his mind.

Mendoza's voice came from several yards back. "Is it them?"

"It is a dead man. You will have to identify his face." He pointed at one of the horses. "This is the one with the bad shoe. No worries about him going lame now." His face broke into a smile at his own joke. He looked like a snake smiling at its prey.

It was the first time Indio had ever shown any expression since they had begun and Mendoza didn't like it one little bit. He kicked his horse forward. "That is the one named Luke Fischer. The other? Where is he?"

"I do not see the other. There is a set of prints leading that way and a splash of blood. Maybe he was shot and went off to die out there under a bush somewhere like a dog."

"Staggered away, most likely, from all that blood." Mendoza wanted his men to think he was capable of tracking an escapee. "Only two horses here. They must have run into bandits who took the others."

Indio scanned the area around them and studied their back trail. He sidled closer to his horse and took the reins in one hand.

Mendoza urged his horse closer. "Look around."

"I did. The other is nowhere to be seen."

"How long ago did this happen?" Mendoza waved at an annoying fly. "They haven't swelled."

Indio leaned against his mount and studied the landscape on his side. He raised an eyebrow at footprints between him and Fischer's body. "An hour ago, maybe two."

"We didn't hear the shots."

"The horses' throats are cut. It was banditos with machetes, I think. I cannot say why we did not hear the guns."

"They tend to chop a lot. Why is his body not mutilated?"

"I do not know." Indio shrugged. "I am not a bandit."

Hidden inside a thick tangle of scrub, Hack had listened long enough. It was time. The most dangerous man down there was the Apache scout, and he took careful aim with the unfamiliar rifle and shot him in the chest. The Apache gave out with a groan and fell in the shadow of his horse. He was smart to use it for cover, but Hack had chosen the left side to watch, where people tend to dismount.

Although the rifle in his hands was unfamiliar, he managed to load another round as Mendoza drew a revolver from his belt and twisted around to locate the source of the shot. Hack's next round punched him out of the saddle.

At the same time, Luke Fischer's "corpse" rose, and the gun in his hand barked six times. As if he were at a turkey shoot, Hack squeezed the trigger slow and sure, and he shot at the same time that Luke threw his swarm of bullets down the line of men and horses. Four prison guards slumped and fell limp and dead as the others reined around and fled.

One of the wounded men on the ground gained his knees, and Hack shot him in the chest. The heavy chunk of lead did its job, and the dead man fell forward and remained where he was, still curled on his knees, his forehead against the ground.

When he was sure it was over, Hack rose from his concealment and reloaded the rifle from bullets in his pants pocket. That chore done, he drew the revolver, because if anyone was hurt and playing possum, close work would be necessary.

In the distance, he saw a cloud of receding dust as the survivors lost their taste for fighting or tracking. Leaderless, they wouldn't stop until they'd reached the prison.

A pair of boots crunching on rocks and coming down the shallow slope told Luke it was over. He rose, thumbing fresh shells into his own revolver. Stepping around one of their dead horses, he studied the scene before them.

"You were right." He waved flies away and scratched at the dried horse blood flaking from his face as Hack closed in on the carnage. Luke indicated their pursuers' mounts. "We traded two horses for six."

Pistol ready, Hack checked on the bodies that lay as they fell. "Are they all dead for sure?"

"Far as I can tell."

Despite the bullet in his chest and the amount of blood spreading over his shirt, the prison *comandante* moved a hand toward the pistol lying a couple of feet away, proving the job wasn't done.

"You're wrong." Hack swung the revolver toward the man who'd fed them slop for so long and cocked the hammer.

Mendoza ignored the weapon and raised a weak hand. "Fischer, your friend helped me learn to read."

"*That's* what he was doing up there?" Luke shot him

without pause. "It looks like he wasted a lot of time and effort for you to wind up here."

"Thus endeth the chase." Hack holstered the weapon and went to catch the best-looking horse he'd seen in years, Mendoza's big black stud, standing somewhere near seventeen hands tall. Luke chose a bay that looked to have a lot of bottom, and they struck out for Texas.

Kicking the horses into a lope and leading the others, Luke snorted and spat. "A fly went up my nose back there, and it was all I could do not to gag."

"That's why I wanted you to play dead. I hate flies."

CHAPTER 16

Many days later, Two-Horses drew close to the crossing near the big bend of the Rio Grande, following a centuries old trail from the Chihuahuan desert back into Texas. The White men called it the San Vicente crossing, but his people referred to it as the Mexican Trail.

There were springs near there, and the wandering groups of Comanche bands and other warring tribes called a truce at those watering holes, knowing that survival in waterless country was fragile at best and that no one should fight there. He hoped that truce was still in place and included single travelers.

His feet hurt and hunger gnawed at his belly, but he was alive and would soon find members of his band. It was that time of year for raids into Mexico, and no matter if they were Quahadi, Nokoni, or Tenewa, they'd take him in and feed him, and maybe provide a gun or horse if their raids into Mexico had been successful.

Refreshed by the water, he walked through the rest of the day with a lighter pace. It was late at night when he saw two fires in the distance. Only Comanches were brave and strong enough fighters to build fires. Mexicans and any White men traveling through that territory kept low and made cold camps that wouldn't attract those on murder raids.

He picked his way up to a high point and settled in to watch the activity below. Figures moved back and forth between him and the fires, and more than once he heard female screams. That told him it was Comanches for sure and that the band had taken prisoners who were providing entertainment before they were killed. The Comanches didn't kill every captive. Others might be integrated into their society or left behind like trash to die from exposure as the war party continued on their way back to their homeland.

The night was chilly but refreshing after the heat of the day. He curled up inside what looked like a nest of rocks and slept soundly as warmth radiated off the hard surface. It was only in the early hours of the morning that he felt cold, but he awoke well rested.

When dawn broke, he picked his way downhill to the Indian camp, which was just waking up. A young boy watching a large herd of horses grazing near a stream saw him and shouted in alarm.

"There is a man here! One of the People!"

Two-Horses paused and waited for what would happen next. Six men came rushing out, armed with everything from bows and arrows to rifles and pistols. They stopped in shock when they saw him standing there alone, unarmed and in only a loincloth.

One warrior with a large, hooked nose came forward. "Are you an old spirit?"

"No, I am Two-Horses, of the Penateka band. I am walking back home."

They gathered around him then. One younger warrior reached out to touch him on the shoulder in wonder. "Why are you dressed like the Old People?"

"Because I was in a Mexican prison and escaped."

They moaned as one. The one who had spoken first stuck a pistol into his waist belt. "Come. Eat. We have water and a shirt for you."

Making their way back to camp, the other warriors touched him one by one with their fingertips. Men did that when Two-Horses was younger to draw strength and spirit from strong warriors. He didn't mind now because the smell of roasting meat made his stomach growl.

They settled around one central fire, and the warrior with the big nose cut off a piece of what appeared to be venison and handed it to him on a knife. "I am Kills Them All. Eat."

Two-Horses took the knife's handle and blew on the meat to cool it. He bit into it and almost groaned in pleasure when the rich juices filled his mouth. The men gathered around and watched him chew that and a few other knife-borne slices of meat. It wasn't polite to interrupt a stranger at his meal.

There was silence in the camp as his belly filled. He paused and made the sign for drink.

Kills Them All waved a hand. "*Agua!*"

A young Mexican girl with tangled hair, a bruised face, and a bag of water appeared and approached them like a whipped puppy. Not more than fourteen or fifteen years of age, she sidled up to him and placed the water bag on the ground. A man with a long white scar from his forehead to his jawline slapped her away. She staggered once and hurried back to a scrap of blanket on the ground and watched with wide eyes.

As he ate, Two-Horses glanced around the camp. Since the Comanches were on a raid, there were no lodges, only what they could carry on horseback. Mysterious bundles wrapped in blankets were scattered about, plunder they'd collected from massacred families or travelers. He finished the meat in silence as crickets chirped in the brush around them and desert birds awoke and sang.

Kills Them All waited until he'd finished a chunk of meat and took back the knife. He cut still another piece and again passed it over. Two-Horses cooled it the same as the first few and studied the hard-eyed men.

"You are Penateka."

"We are split from the Nokoni."

"Honey eaters." Two-Horses smiled. "I would like to taste that sweet again."

"So would we." The others around Kills Them All laughed at the joke. Such treats were never taken on a raid.

Two-Horses swallowed and washed his meal down with the water. There wasn't much in the hide bag, and it was bad manners to finish it, so he left a couple of swallows. Holding it out to the Mexican prisoner, he waited for her to take it.

She crept forward and picked it up, but before she could leave, the warrior with the scar gave her another lick, knocking the girl to her knees. He laughed when she struggled upright and almost ran back to her blanket.

It was now polite to talk, and Kills Them All sat a little straighter. "It has been a rough trip for you." He pointed at the scabs on Two-Horses' legs and several areas of angry-looking skin.

"I have been on foot the whole way." He told them the story of his escape but left out the part about Hack and the gang. "I am going back to my people."

"So are we. We will give you a horse. Ride with us and you will be safe all the way to the river. We will kill some more Mexicans. Maybe Whites, and you can have what you want."

"Are you following the Mexican Trail?"

"We are. We have many horses and guns and lots to trade." Kills Them All waved at the girl. "And two slaves that will bear us more children. It has been a good war trail."

"You have much spirit. I haven't seen that in a while."

"It is because Kwana and Isatai have good medicine that makes us all stronger. He is Kwahadi."

"Ah, Antelope band."

"Yes. We have ridden with him this past season, and his men number over five hundred. What band is yours?"

"Waaia." Two-Horses chose that small splinter group because that one small band had camped for a time near his family in the Northeastern Territories. He had no intention of telling them everything about his life, though he'd be free of them quickly enough.

"You are still our brother."

Instead of agreeing, Two-Horses raised a questioning eyebrow. "Why are you down here alone?"

"The White men sent soldiers after us, and we split up for a while." Kills Them All waved a hand left and right. "They don't know how to catch us when we scatter. It is a good joke on them."

The one whom Two-Horses thought of as Long Scar laughed and pointed a finger at the girl. The obvious threat made her cringe, and she looked around as if seeking escape. Such an idea was foolish, because she would either die alone in the desert or the cruel warrior would catch and kill her.

"Girl!" Kills Them All waved at her and again spoke in Spanish, the language they'd long ago learned to communicate with prisoners and those they traded with. The Comanche were great traders when they wanted something. "Get this man a shirt from that bundle."

Long Scar frowned. "You should not give her orders. She is my prisoner."

"I've decided she's mine. You do not treat her well, and she is getting slower from your beatings. I might let you have her back when we get home. We won't have to move as fast, then."

The girl crawled over to a nearby pack and untied the leather bindings. She pulled out a shirt obviously stolen from some unfortunate farmer or traveler and brought it to Two-Horses. The bright blue Mexican shirt was light, and he pulled it over his head. There were no buttons, and it had only a light bloodstain on the long tail.

It was the first piece of fine cloth that Two-Horses had

worn in years. He smoothed the material across his chest. "Thank you for this."

Long Scar rose to go after the girl, who'd already turned away, but Two-Horses held out a hand. "Kills Them All is right. She's no good to you if she's stove up."

"This is none of your business, stranger."

"Just making conversation."

Long Scar looked at him in suspicion. "You sound like a White man."

Knowing he'd given himself away, Two-Horses made a face. "As I said, I have been living in a prison. There are White men in there, also. I talked with them every day."

"Why would they put one of us in prison?" Another warrior frowned. "Men kill us when they can, and true Comanches won't be taken prisoner. I've never heard of our people in prison."

They were getting into dangerous ground. If the band found out he'd taken up the White man's path and ridden with them, they'd kill him on the spot, even though he was a guest in their camp.

"I was chased across the river and a *guardia* captured me." He pointed to an old scar on his forehead. "When you're knocked unconscious and wake up in chains, you have no choice but to submit and wait for a chance to escape, which I did, as you can see."

Nods all around told him most of the warriors believed his story.

Long Scar spat. "I don't believe everything you say."

"It is your right." Two-Horses paused, thinking. "And as a guest in your camp, I have other rights."

Kills Them All nodded. "It is true. What do you want?"

"A gun and knife, and the horse you promised. And the girl." Two-Horses didn't like the way she was treated. He valued women more than the warriors around him. It was a curse placed upon him from living with White men, and Hack Long, especially.

Long Scar stiffened. "You can't have her!"

Kills Them All chopped at the air with the edge of his hand. "Enough! Two-Horses can ask and receive anything he wants. He came to us in the old way, and I think he has an ancient spirit that would be appeased."

He handed Two-Horses the knife he'd been using to cut the roasting meat, then pointed at one of the younger warriors squatting nearby. "Get him a rifle and pistol, and ammunition."

Long Scar spat again and stalked off. The young warrior left to rummage through another pack and came back with a Colt and a lever-action rifle that had seen better days. Kills Them All took the weapons from the young man and handed them to Two-Horses.

Two-Horses relaxed and took the weapons. "Thank you again, my friend, for these gifts."

"I hope you prove worthy of them. There is a hacienda a day's ride from here. Coyote Ears snuck up on it and saw two Mexicans there with fine horses. We will kill the men and take their horses and guns. You being here is a sign that we will have great success, Two-Horses."

Two-Horses shrugged. He broke open the pistol and checked the loads. As the others watched, he shook them out, closed the revolver, and dry-snapped it.

"You can never trust a new gun."

The statement was funny and true. The men nodded and spoke soft words of affirmation. It had been so long since he'd heard so much Comanche that Two-Horses didn't understand half of what they said. Reloading and laying the pistol across his leg, he repeated the procedure with the rifle, shucking out the shells and snapping it as well.

"*Bien*." The Spanish word came unbidden, another result of being in the Mexican prison for so long. Satisfied that it worked, he reloaded the rifle and laid it beside him. Taking up the pistol once again, he thumb-cocked it and shot Kills Them All in the chest.

Shocked at what just happened, the others froze in disbelief. He cocked the pistol a second time and shot the nearest man beside him in the same fashion. The next four bullets killed the others who struggled to rise and react.

Dropping the empty pistol, Two-Horses picked up the rifle at the same time a bullet plucked at his new shirt. It was Long Scar with a stolen Henry .44 caliber. Like the others, he was shocked at the sudden carnage and fired too fast. Seeing Two-Horses come to one knee with the rifle, Long Scar spun and ran toward the horses.

Two-Horses shouldered the repeater, aimed at the middle of the fleeing man's back, and fired. The bullet caught Long Scar between the shoulders, and he fell face-first, hard. In the distance, Two-Horses saw the boy who was watching the horses leap on a roan's back and kick him in the ribs. He was gone in a flash.

One of the men beside the fire groaned, and Two-Horses jacked the lever to load another round and shot him again. The camp was quiet, the silence broken only by a distant bird and horses, snorting and grazing as if nothing had happened.

He looked down at the body of Kills Them All. "I left your kind of life for a reason."

Wide-eyed, the girl stood nearby, as still as a post, waiting to see what would happen. Two-Horses reloaded the pistol and stuck it through the waist belt holding the loincloth under his shirt.

She spoke Spanish. "Please do not hurt me."

"Do you speak English?"

She nodded, hands at her sides. "Yes."

"Good. I'm tired of talking Spanish. And I don't intend to hurt you."

"You killed your people."

"I sure did. It was their misfortune to trust me. I left their kind of life a long time ago because there was no future in it. Go get us a couple of those ponies over there while I load some of this stuff up and skin one of these guys out of his leggings. I don't intend to go bare legged any longer." He looked around. "Kills Them All said there was another slave."

The girl pointed. "She is over there. She killed herself in the night by chewing through an artery in her arm. I am surprised they haven't noticed, probably because you came up."

"She was determined, then. We need to go."

"Where?"

"Texas."

"But my home is Monclova."

"Which way is that?"

She pulled a strand of hair from her eyes and pointed to the southeast.

"Well, we're going the other direction."

"To where?"

"A little town called Barlow. You can stay here or make your way back home, but I'm going to Texas."

She looked south, then north. "I will go with you."

CHAPTER 17

Billy Lightning and Captain Hawkins came over a ridge to find the Rio Grande down below, flowing wide and red on its way to the gulf. The Ranger stood in his stirrups as if the extra few inches would give him a better line of sight. "Well, I'll be hog-tied."

"What do you see?"

"The river."

"Well, that's where we were headed." Billy wanted to kick his mount in the flanks and race down to Texas.

Instead, the Ranger remained where he was. "That's a fact, but it's not supposed to be *here*." He flicked a finger. "Chamizal is supposed to be down there, about two miles away."

Billy looked around them, where the scrubby chamizal plant grew in an inordinate amount. "It's all around us."

"I'm talking about the town. See that smoke over there?"

A faint drift of black smoke rose in the air some distance away. "I do."

"Something's burning down out there. A house or part of the town, I suppose, from the black smoke." He paused, thinking. "Might be a Comanche raid burning out a *rancho* or maybe the whole town, though there's not enough smoke to indicate such a thing."

"I still don't understand."

"The river left its banks up yonder and moved south from all that rain a couple of weeks ago. I bet it left Chamizal high and dry. It'll likely die." The captain thought for a second. "I bet they're burning the town for that reason."

"I've heard about some rivers moving, but not the Rio Grande."

"Unusual, for sure, but rivers are snakes, and they're inclined to writhe under the assault of great volumes of water."

The Ranger studied the muddy river for several minutes as Billy checked over his shoulder. He didn't care to find a company of Mexican *guardias* or bandits coming upon them so close to his escape. "That's still Texas over there, ain't it?"

"There might be some dispute over that claim, but, yeah, when we get to the town, it'll be Texas, if they say it is. Countries, or even states, have gone to war over a mile or two of land reassigned by a river that's up and moved on its own."

"Can we cross here?"

"I believe so, now that the water's gone down. It is hardpack underfoot, and such will remain under the surface of the river. It hasn't had time to cut a bed, so it should be fairly level. The horses will have to tread lightly, but be prepared to slide off and hold your mount's tail if he goes to swimming. You've crossed deep water before, haven't you?"

"I have, but like you said, maybe it hasn't cut much of a channel yet."

"That is my hope, but if the current was powerful long enough, it'll scour out the softer, loose sand and fine gravel. If it's dug out, the bottom might fall out from under us." The Ranger kneed his horse forward, and they found a game trail leading down past a highwater mark ten feet above where they rode. The horses picked their way carefully. When they reached the river's edge, Hawkins pondered the fast-moving water for a moment. "There's no way to know how deep it is, so take care. Let's go, Silky."

The horse sniffed at the surface for a moment, snorted, and took a ginger step forward. "Since the current is so fast, I believe it's fairly shallow here." As the Ranger expected, the ground underfoot hadn't had enough time to silt up and get boggy, so Silky gained confidence and waded across. The water only reached the captain's stirrups, and he was soon on the Texas side, with Billy right behind.

Excited that he was back home, the young man whooped. "Safe at last!"

The Ranger stopped when a faint shout and three gunshots echoed over the river bottoms. "Relatively speaking." He kicked his horse into a lope, and Billy followed.

They soon came upon a wagon stuck hub deep in the mud of what was the old riverbed. Half a mile behind a man and a woman who were struggling with the mired vehicle, what was left of a town burned hot and fast. The water had been high at some point and had pushed a number of structures off their foundations. Smoke and ash rose into the air.

The Ranger shook his head. "There are five elements in this world. Wood, fire, earth, wind, and water. It looks like most of them have gotten together and taken this settlement, all except for those two poor souls standing there."

The man and the woman were muddy up to their waists, and it appeared that they'd been trying to free the rig for some time. In addition, a team of mules were bogged belly deep in their traces, with the wagon they were attached to buried all the way to the bottom of the bed. Their heads hung low in exhaustion.

The Ranger reined up at the edge of what was once the river, but now it was a sea of mud. "Looks like you folks tried crossing at the wrong place. I believe I would have found a better place. Dad blame me. I used the same noun in two places. I prefer not to do that and instead utilize a better sentence structure. Please forgive me."

The man, up to his knees in the muck, tilted his hat back. "We was told this was the crossing." He pointed at three tall cottonwoods that reached fifty feet into the air. "Said right here beside these trees."

"*Was* the crossing." The Ranger hooked one leg over the saddle horn and fished in his shirt pocket for a match and the makings. "It's a mud hole now where the river once flowed, and that presents a problem for all four of us."

"I don't see a problem. I see a solution."

"Pray tell, what is that?" Hawkins sprinkled tobacco on a paper and rolled it with expertise.

The traveler nodded as if Hawkins had confirmed a decision. "Your horses can help pull out my team."

"That won't be likely."

"How come?"

"Because you got yourselves into that mess, and I don't intend to muddy up my clothes and tire these horses to pull a simpleton like you from such a mudhole." Hawkins licked the paper and rolled the cigarette into proper form. "I have a mission to complete and intend to do it with all haste."

"Blast you, man! We need help with this wagon!"

"Sir, I don't appreciate being cursed, and I am a Texas Ranger. I enforce laws and protect the public. If you were beset by outlaws or Comanches, I'd be at your service, but that's where it starts and ends."

The man shifted his attention to Billy. "How about you, then?"

"It's his horse and I'm riding with him." Billy shrugged. "I don't have a say in this matter."

The man's face reddened. "The hell with you both. I'll just take *them* from you."

"I am damned, for sure, because I've shot many men who

needed killing, but you aren't *taking* anything." The Ranger thumbed a match to light and lifted the tiny flame up to his smoke.

He was intent on the small task as the enraged man snatched a repeater from the wagon. "I'll take your life, then!" The rifle rose, and whether it was luck or skill, the first shot caught the Ranger in the throat, and he threw his arms wide and fell.

His well-trained horse shied from the detonation, then stopped only a few feet away from where the body hit the ground.

Not wanting to take on a .44 in the hands of such a good shot, Billy wheeled his borrowed horse around and kicked it in the flanks, but the man was obviously proficient with the Henry. A bullet slapped the saddle skirt just forward of Billy's knee, and the animal stumbled and went down on its side.

Billy had just enough time to kick himself free, and he landed hard behind the horse's body when a third shot thumped into its belly. It groaned, kicked twice, and lay still. Another round buzzed past Billy's head. Relying on the speed of youth, he leaped to his feet and sprinted back the way he'd come, heading for the Ranger's mount, which stood there as unconcerned as if it were merely thundering.

He registered the woman's shrill voice screaming at her husband to stop shooting as another bullet whizzed past. Shooting a man on the run is more difficult than one sitting still or such a large target as a fifteen-hundred-pound animal. Rattled at the miss, the man shot again and jacked another round into the chamber as Billy reached the horse's offside and snatched the Ranger's Henry from the scabbard.

Adding to the melee, the stuck mules jumped and brayed in their harness, only miring themselves deeper in the soft, soupy mud of the former river channel.

The Ranger's horse screamed just as the report of still another shot reached Billy's ears. It staggered sideways and, hit still again, dropped where it stood. With his heart pounding in his ears, Billy fell with the dying animal to present as small a target as possible and braced the rifle across its twitching body.

The gunman hadn't moved from where he stood in the knee-deep mud. He was jacking another round into the chamber when Billy shouldered the rifle, lined up on the man's chest, and fired. Still buried to his knees and hit straight in the heart, the man fell backward in the mud with a wet slap and was still.

The woman, only a few feet behind him, held up her hands. "Don't shoot! Please don't shoot me! I don't have a weapon."

"I can see that." Now that it was over, Billy stood and glanced around as if expecting spectators. "Stay where you are."

"I can't move more than a step at a time in this muck."

He knelt to feel the Ranger's chest, which no longer drew air. "Your husband killed a lawman here."

"He was enraged. He has . . . had a temper that often got out of control."

"I can see that."

"And he wasn't my husband. I work for him. He was my manager."

Now that all the shooting was over, Billy found himself shaking. He approached her and stopped on the dry ground. "I can throw you a rope and drag you out, but that's all I can offer from here."

"I would appreciate the effort."

"Do you have valuables in the wagon you need?"

"Just the coins in his pocket."

"Wade over there and pluck them out and get his rifle. No sense in letting a good weapon go to waste."

Fifteen minutes later, and proving she didn't need a rope, the woman was covered in mud from head to toe, but she was out. He studied her figure for a moment. "You look like you've been rolling around with pigs."

"That was my profession until a few minutes ago." She dropped to the ground to rest. "My name's Gussie by the way."

"Billy."

She jumped when he fired twice into the mules' foreheads. Their heads dropped, and because they were mired up to their stomachs, they died standing up.

"It'd be cruel to leave them there."

"You should have told me you were gonna shoot. You scared the pee-waddlin' out of me."

"I'll give you fair warning next time I need to shoot a couple of mules." He pinned on the Ranger's badge. Strapping on the lawman's gun belt, he looked across the muddy riverbed into Texas. Black smoke still rose from the burning buildings, and he absently wondered where the rest of the people had gone.

She wiped her hands on the only clean part of her blouse. "I reckon we're walking."

He sighed. "I don't intend to carry you on my back."

"I hope we come upon some water so I can wash this mud off. You think we'll find some pretty soon?"

He jerked a thumb. "The river's back over that way, but I 'magine we'll come up on a creek or a wash with a little water. You can clean up then."

She waved a hand. "Well, let's get going. It's coming up a cloud, and I hope it does so the rain'll wash some of this off me."

Billy sighed. "So close and afoot again, with a muddy woman. That's all I need is another storm."

Shocked that he'd possibly called down another lightning

strike, he glanced upward at the cloudy sky, then struck out parallel to the drying watercourse, carrying both rifles level with the ground so as not to attract a bolt.

Head lowered, Gussie followed as Billy searched for a friendlier way back.

CHAPTER 18

Gabe Santana rode into San Felipe Springs without incident. He'd stopped there for water and food before, knowing the next Texas town across the river was much smaller. The last time he'd been there, it hadn't been much more than a few haciendas and a struggling general store.

The little village survived on trade with travelers crossing to and from Texas. They were used to strangers passing through, but the well-armed man with a dark complexion was a significant event.

Knowing those in town who saw him pass would recognize him as a dangerous man, Santana rode with his back ramrod straight and his eyes focused straight ahead on the bare, dusty street. That didn't mean he missed anything going on around him as he passed the first small adobe houses and reined up in front of a cantina. Two hard-looking men sat on a rough bench and noted his arrival from under the brims of their hats.

One had a face lined with sunbaked wrinkles. The other watched with only one clear eye. The other was cloudy as milk water.

After nodding at the pair, he swung down and surveyed the dusty street. Tying the reins to a bent metal post driven into the ground, he slipped his new rifle from the scabbard and stepped through a doorless opening and into the building's cool, dark interior. Planks resting on two barrels served as the bar at the back of the small, dirt-floored room. Two tables hammered together decades earlier defied gravity and remained upright. The chairs were also homemade, and a stump provided an extra place to sit.

A balding man whose remaining hair was oily emerged from a low doorway in the back and brightened when he saw a paying customer. "Come in. Come in!" He smiled, revealing several gaps in his teeth.

Santana moved to the far left and rested against the bar, keeping his right hand free. He leaned the rifle against the wall as the bartender picked up a glass and sat it in front of him. "Whiskey or tequila. I can draw a beer for you, if you're really thirsty."

"All three."

"Well, sir, I can see you're a man not restrained by indecision." The bartender picked up the glass and reached for a bottle. "We require payment in advance. That'll be six bits." He hesitated in pouring the whiskey, waiting to see the color of Santana's money. After a silver dollar rattled on the plank, he poured the drink and sat it in front of his only customer.

Before Santana could pick it up, the man poured a shot of clear tequila into a matching glass and slid it in front of him, then turned around to pull the handle of a beer dispenser as two figures momentarily blocked the light spinning in from the doorway.

Santana kept watch as they crossed to one of the rickety tables in the silent cantina and pulled chairs back to sit facing the bar. The legs and supports creaked under their weight as they settled themselves. The man with the face full of wrinkles drew a long, skinny knife from his belt and began cleaning under his fingernails.

Hands resting on his knees, Cloudy Eye studied the stranger with his only working orb. "Two whiskeys."

The bartender with oily hair raised a bushy eyebrow. "Y'all said this morning you were out of money."

"We plan to come into some cash by the end of the day."

"You can get the whiskey then."

Cloudy Eye glared across the bar, then watched a fly crawl across the surface of their table.

Santana tilted the tequila first, savoring the warm, oily liquid that slowly burned down his throat. It had been so long since he'd had a drink, he made sure to breathe out through his nose before inhaling to avoid the fumes. He didn't want anyone to think he was some kind of weak tenderfoot.

The foamy beer came next, and over half of it disappeared in one gloriously satisfying swallow. Putting the mug back onto the wet ring it had left on the bar, Gabe watched the pair that were watching him.

A contented chicken clucked somewhere just outside the door, then squawked with indignation. The heavy sound of horse hooves outside seemed to be the source of the hen's outrage. Saddle leather creaked as several men swung down.

There were no voices to tell Gabe whether they were American or Mexican riders, but that question was soon answered when they filed in one at a time. The first things he noted were the five-point badges and the heavy iron that pulled at their belts.

Texas Rangers. Mustached and unshaven, they'd been on the trail a long time and, like him, had likely come in out of the sun for a little refreshment. They looked like a pack of wolves.

Santana fought the urge to turn away. He'd been gone a long time, and it was doubtful anyone would recognize him. Five men spread out inside the cantina. Three took a table near the doorway, and two stepped up to the bar.

The original pair at the empty table seemed to find something interesting on the scratched surface. Perhaps they were reading other customers' names and initials carved there.

"Beers all around. We've been out so long I think my goozle needs to be washed down." The Ranger nearest Santana eyed him up and down as he drew a finger back and forth under his mustache in preparation for a drink. He hadn't been near a razor or water for weeks. "Do I know you? You look familiar."

A cold chill went down Santana's back, and he wondered which Ranger to shoot first. He couldn't get them all, but the man standing next to him was as sure as dead if someone opened the ball. After that, it was anybody's guess. "We have not met."

"You sure? Down around Uvalde comes to memory. Blacksmith shop."

"Wasn't me. Never been there."

"Well, I'll study on it. Don't see many Mexicans as heeled as you."

Cursing himself for looking down at the double-strapped guns across his hips, Santana forced a grin. "I'm not Mex, and it's a harsh country."

"You ain't got no accent."

"I don't. I was raised further north, and my daddy left when I was little. My mama's uncle raised me for the most part. Old folks are from Italy. We look Mexican, but we ain't."

"What part of further north you talking about? Not the territories?"

Santana wondered how the Ranger thought he could be from the Indian Territories north of the Red River. "Up past San Antone."

The beers arrived, and the silent Ranger at the bar took four of the mugs by their handles and joined his *compadres*. With him holding two glasses in each hand, it dropped the odds from one against five to two against five, since they'd be the first to go down if Santana took a notion to start shooting.

He didn't want to take the chance.

The closest Ranger studied on Santana for another moment before taking a good, long drink. "How come you look like a Mex?"

"Handed down through the generations, I guess."

"I mean your clothes. Why're you dressed like that? It could get a man killed down here this close to the river."

"I've thought about that, but this is what I wound up with."

"You got a name?"

"Not one I spread around much."

"How about you do a little spreading now?"

"Is that an order or a request?"

The skin around the Ranger's eyes tightened, then relaxed. "A request. We've been riding so long I must have outrun my manners. Name's Captain Royce Bookbinder."

It was a frontier request at that point. Once he'd identified himself, he expected Santana to follow suit. "I'm Virg Preston." He used the name of a banker up in Paris, one they'd robbed years earlier.

He remembered the name because it had been his first bank and the manager had been indignant when he and Luke showed their guns, stating, "Why, I'm Virg Preston!" As if the mere mention of his name would make them rethink their intent.

Bookbinder considered the name. "That's a White man's handle on both sides."

"Like I said, my mama was White, and I was raised by her family, the Prestons. Left off the 'i' when they came to America. That's what they hung me with. What'd you expect? Garcia, or something mixed like Joaquin Murietta?"

Bookbinder grinned at the mention of the famous, and long deceased, California outlaw. "Noted. We're looking for a missing Ranger who went out after a bad outlaw by name of Cole Shelton. Had a propensity for bushwhacking folks, and we intend to hang him."

"There's a lot of that going around."

"Had a price on his head and a paper on him out of Laredo for killing a handful of folks."

"Your friend have a name? Though I haven't talked to many people lately, I might remember it down the road, if I run into him."

"Captain Clarence Hawkins. A good, solid man, though a little overeducated for the job, in my opinion."

"Takes all kinds, but I don't know him." Santana surveyed the four at the table, who were watching the pair of men at the other table, who'd put away their knives. "I thought y'all worked alone."

"We do, when it's possible. We have a lot of territory to cover down here, so we split up and ride alone and come together every few days when we can. Trade information and whatnot."

"Like today." It was just Santana's luck to be in the one cantina within fifty miles when they rode in.

"That's right. Since you look like a gun hand, I doubt you live here."

"I'm not, and I don't."

"You sure don't offer up much in the way of interesting conversation, unless you're prodded."

Santana sighed, which was what the Ranger might expect. "This is harsh country, so I carry guns against Apaches, Comanches, and those like you're looking for. I'm heading up toward Santa Fe 'cause I ain't never seen it before and I hear it's a sight cooler there than here."

Absorbing the information, Bookbinder took another swallow. He glanced over his shoulder at the pair of men who'd been cleaning their nails, then back at his fellow Rangers. Something passed between them that Santana didn't understand. One nodded and rose and went outside.

"Been in the heat, huh?" Bookbinder thumped an index finger against the bar to get the owner's attention. "How about another beer all around, and one for Mr. Preston here."

"Much obliged." Santana threw off the shot of whiskey that remained before him and drained his beer mug. It was a delicate dance, this back-and-forth conversation, one that made Santana nervous. "It's been hot, all right."

"You traveling alone?"

"I appreciate the offer of a beer, but why don't you go ahead and ask what you want to know."

"Fair enough. I have a memory for faces, and you look familiar, but I can't recall the circumstances, and that makes me nervous. When I get nervous, I get angry. To keep me from becoming incensed, I want to know where you've been and where you're going and anything else that might help my recollections. Your guns are in pretty good shape, but them pants and that shirt's near rotted off of you. I'm looking at two different tales."

"Virg Preston, like I said. I don't have any roots, and I've been in a Mexican prison for the past few months because I was stupid enough to go across the river. I got these guns from some men who were trying to rape a woman down there, and I killed 'em and I crossed back a couple of days ago, and that's all the story I have."

"Now that's more like it." The beers came, and Bookbinder waved to one of the three Rangers with big hats who were still at the table. One rose and picked them up for the others. The fifth was still outside, maybe tending to the horses, Santana thought.

Bookbinder raised his beer, took a swallow, and in one smooth motion put the mug down and snatched his revolver from its holster. Santana almost drew down on him, but the Ranger spun toward Cloudy Eye and Wrinkles at the same time his associate stepped through the door with a double-barrel scatter gun leveled at the pair. The strangers froze in open-mouthed astonishment with still not a word between them.

The three remaining Rangers sat as relaxed as if they were

in a bordello's parlor. The smallest of the group chuckled, still sitting at their table. "I saw it right off. Ol' Royce recognized those two the minute we walked in. Kinda stiffened up, and that's how I knew."

Keeping his pistol on the pair, Bookbinder crossed the cantina. "You two put your hands on the table where I can see 'em. Hank, get what weapons they have on them and tie their wrists."

As Hank leaned his shotgun against the Rangers' table, Bookbinder thumb-cocked his pistol. "You two are under arrest for horse thievery. We stopped by the livery on the way in and saw four horses there, all wearing the Bar L brand, that you stole two nights ago."

Cloudy Eye finally found enough spit to answer. "They ain't our'n."

"Liveryman says they are."

"He's a-lyin'!"

"Man don't have anything to lie about." Bookbinder watched as Hank located two knives and the same number of hidden revolvers. "And besides, I recognize y'all from a paper I saw here a while back." A small hideout gun came from Wrinkles's boot, as well as a straight-razor from the stovepipe of Cloudy Eye's knee-high boot top.

Wrinkles spat on the floor. "We bought them horses from the Bar L."

"Where's your bill of sale?"

"Don't have one. The owner said give anyone who asks his name and that was good enough."

"What's his name, then?"

Wrinkles licked his dry lips, eyes darting around the cantina as if looking for an escape, or even a wide rat hole. "I forget. Lane something? Relates to the Bar L."

"What's gonna relate to the Bar L is a high limb outside of town and a short rope."

"You ain't hanging nobody without proof, are you?" It

was the first time the bartender spoke, and his voice came high and reedy.

"We have stole horses and an eyewitness that saw these two put 'em up in a corral behind the livery. That's proof enough to us, along with your familiarity. I have a good memory for faces, and I can see your likeness on a wanted poster."

Quickly draining their beers, the Rangers pushed the pair outside, leaving only Bookbinder and Santana. He nodded toward the bartender and placed a gold coin within reach.

"Justice is swift here on the Rio Grande." He turned away from Santana and then back. "I still don't recall where I saw you, but it'll come to me. Like I said, I have a mind for faces."

"Hope it does so you can rest easy at night." Santana raised his beer in a salute and took another sip. "Don't mind me if I stay here instead of coming out to watch the hanging."

"We won't, but I can tell you now, those two were about to lay for you. They're a bad pair."

"I don't doubt it."

The Ranger disappeared through the door, and the sound of horses' hooves receded into the distance. Santana finished his beer. "Gotta go," he told the bartender.

Minutes later, he was on the way to Barlow, hopefully leaving the Rangers behind before Captain Bookbinder could recall a wanted poster from three years earlier.

CHAPTER 19

The people in Escarino thought Hack and Luke were Rurales when they first rode into the little no-name village. It wasn't much, mostly sunblasted adobe overseen by a tall, plain Catholic church recognizable only by the crude steeple and cross on the left. Everything opened onto a wide courtyard centered around a well.

An old wall of melting adobe circled most of the town. It might have been constructed to repel attacks by Apaches or Comanches, but it had long since crumbled until much of it was less than waist high. The Texans followed a wagon trail through the widest part and let the horses take their time on the flat street.

Each little house was shaded out front by brush arbors built to filter the sun that speckled through them and onto tables and benches. What Hack took for a little stable had a crooked pole corral sitting between two buildings with open windows.

It was hard for the villagers or anyone else to tell they were Anglos from the sun and the clothes they wore. Kids shouted and pointed as they drew near. Women rushed out to scoop the kids up and disappeared like wisps of smoke. A dozen men appeared and spread out, holding a variety of weapons from axes to machetes.

A bent, wrinkled old man in loose, light-colored clothes and *huaraches* on his feet emerged from a stone house with a thatched roof. Holding a single-shot rifle, he also wore an unusually wide-brimmed hat.

"That one." Luke pointed. It was his way of saying the old man was the most dangerous because he held the only gun they could see.

There were others closing in, and from Hack's experience, a knife was just as lethal in the hands of a determined man. He readied himself to shoot the nearest villager carrying a long, sharp knife after he put down two others who were too close.

They stopped a few feet away from the villagers.

Hack had the pistol riding on his offside and kept his right hand on the horn with the reins in the other. "If I go down, you take up my revolver and clean them up. It's better than the one you have."

More men came from the buildings and surrounded them. Ignoring the gunman, Hack turned his horse around to face the gathering bunch. "Don't get behind us. We don't like being corralled."

One of the townspeople, a man with a face full of scars, lifted one corner of his mouth in a mean grin. "You do not ride in here and tell us what to do." He stepped closer and raised a machete. "This is our town, and we have a way of dealing with outsiders."

"Don't crowd me, I said." The big Texan drew the pistol and thumb-cocked it, not pointing the muzzle at any one person but holding it in a way that they knew he meant business. "And I don't issue orders twice."

Facing the other way, Luke snapped at the gunman. "Keep that rifle lowered!"

Hack heard Luke cock his pistol, and he thought about how fast things could happen.

"Alberto!" A woman's voice rang out. She was pregnant, with a baby on her hip. "They are not *guardia*!"

"Alberto. You speak English?" Hack addressed the older man with the rifle, whose face was a map of arroyos and canyons of varying depths.

"Elena, hush!" The old man gave the woman a sharp look, and in any less dangerous situation, Hack would have laughed at the notion that grandpa there wanted to shoot *her* for being so bossy.

Alberto nodded, but there was a different look in his eyes that made Hack relax. "I do. I speak English. You should learn to speak our language since you are in our country."

Hack grinned at the statement. "Good. To tell the truth, we do, but I think faster when everyone's talking American."

"Maybe I do not want you thinking fast."

"I suspect you don't. Look, it wasn't our idea to be here, but listen to me. This man and I are not like *gringos* you've met before. We'll not be frightened or threatened. We've killed for a living, but we're fair. So if you don't put down that rifle, I'll start with you and my partner will shoot the nearest man to you, and then we won't stop triggering these weapons until they're empty."

Grandpa shifted his weight and didn't look convinced.

"Listen to me, dad. We got these clothes and gear from some Rurales who weren't much inclined to give them up. If we start in on y'all, we'll kill every man in this village before we're through. Or you can put that down and we'll eat and get water and maybe a bite to go. It's that simple."

"Listen to him." The woman's voice was softer. She was the voice of reason in that standoff, and Hack figured she had the good sense to run the whole village if they'd let her, but that sure as hell wouldn't happen in their Mexican culture.

He wanted to turn his attention to her, but right then there was a situation to deal with. The old man needed to listen to the voice of reason.

Luke gave them one of his grins that tended to disarm folks. "She's right. We're just passing through."

The guy lowered his rifle a few inches. "Why did you need the *guardia*'s clothes?"

"We escaped Purgatorio and are going home to Texas. Traveling in those rags they had us wear wouldn't have helped against this sun."

More than a few seemed to understand English, or it might have been the name of the prison that they recognized, but the people gathered around and spoke in a low murmur of either surprise or excitement.

Elena finally came into Hack's view from the side, and she put her hand on Alberto's arm, pushing the rifle lower. Like Alberto's clothes, her blouse and dress were sewn from light-colored material. She also wore a wide-brimmed hat, and the little one riding her hip with one chubby arm wrapped around hers was one of the prettiest babies he'd ever seen.

Everyone relaxed when the tension went out of the man. Hack understood how her presence was so important to him and Luke, because she reminded him of his dead wife, who was in that same condition when she was murdered, and any time she put her hand on him, any tension Hack felt was instantly gone.

Alberto waved a hand, and the others lowered their weapons and moved back. "How many did you kill?"

"How many *what* did we kill."

"*Guardia.*"

Standing in the sun and heat, they were suddenly in a conversation. "Four."

"I wish you had killed forty."

"Didn't have the strength or the time."

Alberto grinned, exposing several gaps from missing teeth. "Do you see this smile?"

"It's a big one. Hard to miss, though I've seen better."

"The *guardia* knocked these out, for resisting their orders."

Luke holstered his revolver, though he stayed where he was, watching the men around them. He'd never been a trusting person. "What kind of orders?"

"Many times while on patrol, they come here for supplies and make us provide for them. Sometimes, it is only water, which we give freely." He flicked a finger at the well, fifty feet away. "We have plenty, and it is deep and cold, but we do not have enough grain or hay for more horses than the few we own, or much food to feed ourselves."

So they were exploited by the very people Porfirio Diaz, the president of Mexico, had created to guard them against bandits and renegade Indians. It wasn't any big surprise. Hack and Luke remembered what Quantrill did to civilians in the not-too-distant War between the States, and more than once they'd seen Texas Rangers exceed their authority against those they could easily push around, or didn't look like them.

Alberto rested the stock of his rifle on the ground. He touched the woman's arm with his fingertips. "This is my daughter, Elena, and my granddaughter and one as yet unknown. Get down and come into my house. It is cooler in there, and we have frijoles and tortillas for you to eat."

"You said y'all didn't have much food here." Ever suspicious, Luke spoke the words they'd both been thinking.

"We have enough for friends."

That was a quick turnaround from a few minutes earlier, when they were all about to kill each other. "I'm Hack, and this is Luke. Much obliged for the food."

It was surprisingly cool inside, and the little family had good quality, polished furniture that didn't match the rough surroundings. Elena saw them looking around and appeared pleased.

She ran a hand along the top of a smooth sideboard. "This belonged to my great grandparents, who got them from a rich Spanish ship captain. When he died, no one wanted the furniture, and they brought it here when they fled Mexico City and Presidente Nicolás Bravo."

Alberto leaned his rifle against the doorframe and hung his hat on a single peg on the wall. Hack and Luke took seats on the opposite side of the waxed table so they could watch the door. In direct opposition to the fine furniture, a couple of the crude chairs had been hammered together from scraps or repaired so often they'd lost their original shapes and seats.

Hack and Luke had been expecting packed dirt floors, so the wide, wooden planks, sanded smooth and even, were a luxury. Nothing crunched underfoot, proof of Elena's frequent use of a broom. She went to the stove and filled two crock plates for the men who'd been eating jackrabbits, roadrunners, and one small doe that had wandered too close.

Hack thought the spicy food smelled wonderful.

"Eat," she ordered gently.

Remembering their manners, the hungry men dropped their hats to the floor beside the table and dug into the first good food they'd seen cooked by a woman in years. Hack used the edge of his fork to cut into a corn tortilla rolled around seasoned chicken and covered in a rich tomato sauce. It was rich and full of flavor. One bite and chilis exploded in his mouth like fire. He tore a tortilla in half to use as a scoop and shoved in another forkful in self-defense. Luke did the same, chewing with his eyes closed.

Elena picked up a pair of metal cups. "I have goat's milk, if you want?"

Hack glanced at the little girl, who likely needed it more than two grown men. "No, thanks. Water will be fine."

As they ate, Alberto poured cups of clean, clear water from a dented metal pitcher and sat them nearby. "I have a request for you."

Before answering, Hack drained the contents of his cup, and Alberto filled it again. Knowing what was coming, he shook his head. "We're not for hire."

Alberto frowned. "But you haven't heard me."

"We're heading for Texas as hard as we can go."

Luke was interested, though, and Hack wanted to shoot him for it. "What is it, bandits?"

Alberto shook his head as Hack glared at his partner, which the other man either missed or ignored. "It is for Elena." Alberto paused and ordered her in Spanish to go outside. Angry at the order, she readjusted the little girl, who watched the men with wide eyes, and stepped into the bright sunlight.

"There are some men living not far from here." Alberto rose and went to the stove. He rolled a tortilla into a long, skinny tube and dipped it into the bubbling pot of green chili stew and bit half of it off. He dipped it again and returned to the table. Hack figured it was hard to eat with so many teeth gone. "They are American, but come down here to rob and steal from poor people."

Hack ate in silence for a minute. "They rob y'all because you're easy pickin's."

Alberto stopped chewing and worked the food into his cheek. He raised an eyebrow. "I do not know what that means."

Luke chimed in. "It means guns beat tools and machetes in a fight."

"In some ways. When the men in our village go out to work in the fields, they are often alone. Most of the time, it is safe because the Comanches and Apaches raid farther to the west these days, pushed that way by the *guardia*, but in the case of Elena's husband, he was tending his peaches down by the creek and did not come home one night. We found him the next morning, beaten to death."

"For what?"

Alberto shrugged. "He had no money, no possessions on him besides a silver cross around his neck. We suspect they wanted his food or the little piece of metal."

His attention on the half empty plate, Hack could feel Luke swell up beside him. His old partner always loved a good fight. "That pretty little gal's husband was beaten to death for a couple of pieces of fruit or a drop of silver?"

"It is the way Ignacio read the scene. Now, no one goes out alone, but that causes problems because some tasks go uncompleted."

It sounded as if he'd said "nacho" for the feller's name, so Luke repeated it back to him the same way. It wasn't until a couple of years later that Hack saw how it was spelled on a wanted poster outside of Uvalde. "Who's Nacho?"

"The best hunter in the village."

"Where is he?" Luke asked. "I'd like to talk to him."

Alberto grinned. "When you entered the village, he climbed up on the roof of the church with his rifle. He is probably still there, though maybe not because I believe Elena told him all is well when she went outside."

Luke's eyes widened. They'd been concentrating on the men gathering in the street and were so rusty neither of them had checked the flat rooftops, which would provide a perfect place for an ambush. The clay-colored church had been on their left, and when Alberto had stepped outside to draw attention to himself, their backs were to the rifle in an experienced shooter's hands.

A chill went up Hack's spine as he scooped up a bite of beans and meat. "I *thought* you had some kind of ace up your sleeve besides that single-shot rifle in your hands."

"We had our best marksman behind your back." Alberto chuckled. "I see you are surprised."

Luke scratched the back of his head, as if trying to remove a target. "I bet your priest has something to say about using his church to fight."

Alberto's face fell. "He is dead. Went to sleep one night and didn't wake up. We sent word to the monsignor in Mexico City but have not heard back. The doors are open for prayers, but there are no services."

Hack scraped his plate clean and glanced over at the hot woodstove and a loaf of hard bread. "I have better manners than this, but can I have a piece of that bread and a little more of whatever it is we're eating?"

The look in Alberto's eyes told them he'd been hungry before. "Of course." He turned slightly in his chair and addressed the open door. "Elena, please serve our guests again."

She must have been sitting on one of the hard wooden chairs beside the door and came back inside, without the little one this time, and hurried to the table to take their plates. Her smile and dark eyes were soft. "I like to see men eat. My husband was good with a knife and fork."

The trio of men sat there in silence as she refilled the plates. She set them back on the table, and the little girl came inside with tiny, uncertain steps. Elena scooped her up with a grunt because it was difficult for her to bend over in her condition, and she left again.

Though he was starting to like the family, Hack didn't want to get involved in their problems, but the thought of Americans coming down across the river and robbing and murdering innocent people was starting to raise his ire.

Luke talked around a cheek full of food. "How far away are these men, and how well armed are they?"

Hack shot him a glare that he chose to ignore.

Alberto drummed the tabletop with his fingertips. "Four, and they have many guns."

Luke drank water around the bite in his cheek and went back to chewing. "Are they in a camp or what?"

"They took over an old *casa* that has been empty for years. The roof is mostly gone, and it sits alone not far from a low *mesa*. They stay there and drink all day. At night, they leave to raid the farmers and small *ranchas* nearby, then buy more whiskey and come back."

"You know a lot about them."

"Ignacio watches them from a little butte not far away. He has a nest in the boulders and stays hidden when he's there."

"If he's a good shot, why don't he just pick them off?" Luke nodded at his own question. "That's what I'd do."

"He is afraid. He is a hunter, not a fighter. None of us are prepared for war or battles."

Hack forced down a grunt. "You were ready to fight out there."

"We will defend our homes when necessary."

"Do they ever come into the village?"

"Sometimes, but it is swift, like Indian raids, and always at daylight when we are fighting up from sleep."

"Set up an ambush. Wipe 'em out."

"I have only a handful of ammunition for my rifle, and Ignacio can't shoot them alone."

"Y'all looked like you'd chop us to pieces."

That's when it all came together. Alberto's eyes filled, and he threw a look at the door to make sure Elena wasn't standing there, listening. "They said if we fought back, they would become ghosts outside our village and watch, and kill every child we have. We can't fight against that kind of a threat."

Hack's head filled with a high keening sound, and red flickered at the edges of his vision. Luke's eyes went hard and flat, and they didn't have to acknowledge each other.

A white-winged dove flitted to the ground just outside the door with a peep, and it pecked at the grit twice before something scared it away with a flutter of wings. Hack sopped at the rich liquid on his plate with the piece of bread and paused. "We know how to fix that, but I'd like to talk to this Ignacio, first."

CHAPTER 20

Two-Horses was aggravated with himself by the time he and the captive girl reached the Rio Grande. He would have made better time, but the youngster, who finally told him her name was Gabriela, wasn't much of a rider and he had to go slow.

Her horse sensed that she didn't know what she was doing up there, and the animal spent much of the first day ignoring her attempts to make it respond to her wishes. At one point, an extremely frustrated Two-Horses was several hundred yards ahead when he heard her shout.

"Two-Horses! Please! Stop! This animal will not do as I say."

He turned to see her too close for comfort to a thicket of tall ocotillo cactus. His bad mood broke, and he grinned as the girl's horse sidestepped closer in an attempt to scrape her against the sharp spines. Wondering exactly why he cared, he rode back and stopped nearby. "Do as I told you earlier. You have to be his master."

She thumped it with her heels, and the horse threw its head back, scaring her so bad she nearly fell from the saddle. "We did not ride horses in our village. We had burros and mules. Only rich men rode such horses as this, and they did it in big saddles decorated with conchos and high cantles and large spurs. I wish I had spurs to make this animal mind me, and I do not think it likes me, anyway."

"He thinks he can do as he pleases. Make him obey. Squeeze with your calves against his rib cage. It will remind him of his lessons."

"I saw a woman once ride sidesaddle. Maybe that's the way I should try it."

"You are riding like a man, so make him think that's what you are. Do as I say, or I will leave you here stuck on that cactus like those shrike birds that pin their prey on thorns."

With a sound of frustration in the back of her throat, she did as he said, and the roan pricked its ears forward. The horse took two steps toward Two-Horses, and she met his gaze with surprise. "It worked."

"Of course it did."

The horse stopped again, and she slapped its rump. It took another step and waited for Two-Horses' mount to move. She crossed her arms. "I would like to get down and walk."

He looked up at the blue sky. "It is too hot, and we do not have much water. If we do not get to the river soon, we will die."

"But I'm not feeling bad."

"You will only feel hot when it's too late. Have you been drinking the water I gave you?"

She reached down and patted a hide bag. "Some. I've been saving it."

"You have to drink often. It is bad to wait and only drink when you get thirsty. It will be too late then. Already, when you make water, it is too yellow."

Eyes wide, she gasped in shock, pressing one palm against her chest. "You looked!?"

"Yes. I see everything."

"That's . . . that . . ." Her face and neck reddened. "You can't . . . you shouldn't do that."

"I see no reason why not, and I also watch the horses to be sure they can continue. It is the way out here."

She hid her mouth with both hands, not knowing what to say. When Two-Horses didn't add anything else to the conversation, Gabriela changed the subject. "What about the horse? What color is his water?"

"He can go longer, but we cannot travel much farther without finding water. Now, drink, as I said."

She moved a flap from the top of the bag and drank in several long swallows. Finished, she lowered the bag and gave it a shake. "There isn't much left."

"The river is ahead, but we have to push forward. We might get lucky and find a spring or seep, but there is no promise in that." He turned and retraced the tracks he'd left, and she squeezed again with her bare calves.

Her horse followed.

It was near dusk when they came upon the crumbling remains of a mud and stone house. Leading the way, Two-Horses circled the structure, which was surrounded by catclaw and mesquite, making sure no one was hiding in ambush. When he reached the offside, which was partially shaded by a tall cottonwood, he reined up and snatched the revolver from his belt at the sight of a gnarled old man with a shovel.

Long gray hair standing up on his head, the man looked up from a deep hole he'd been digging. His rheumy eyes focused on the mounted Indian. He spoke English, though his voice was high and soft with age. "Well, that's just my luck. Water is about to run dry, I'm out of food, and I was hoping for a White man, and now here I'm looking down the barrel of a gun in the hand of an Indian."

Keeping his pistol trained on the man, Two-Horses ignored

the comment and tilted his head, reading the scene before him. "That looks like a grave."

"Well, you speak English at least." The old man dropped the shovel onto the mound of slightly moist dirt beside the hole. "You'll understand what I need."

"What does that mean?"

"That means that I can tell you what I want, since you talk pretty good English."

"Where is the body you intend to bury?"

"It's standing right here." The stranger with a gray beard wore baggy pants held up by a pair of expensive-looking suspenders. They were the newest item of value on his body, because the sweat-stained, salt-encrusted shirt was almost thin enough to read through. His broken-down hat hung on a weathered wooden cross only feet away.

Two-Horses studied the scene before him, looking for weapons or signs of others. The man was on foot, because there were no hoofprints in or around the area. A small bundle of personal items lay against the wall, not far from the ashes of a campfire. He'd been there for a while, because evidence of former meals, such as the bones and hides of rabbits, was thrown nearby, along with scattered feathers of various birds.

It was the tree that most interested Two-Horses, not the old man or his hole. Cottonwood trees need water, which meant there was probably a spring not far away. That was the reason the original builders had placed the house where it was, near such a continuous source of life, but it hadn't kept them there.

The house's ridge pole was cracked in two and sticking into the air in a wide "V" that pointed to the ground inside. Mesquite poles that had served as rafters had collapsed inward and were tangled with rotting canes gathered from a distant river to turn the rain. Mud wrens darted in and out of the gaping windows and doors. The builder was long gone.

He and any others who'd been with him might have given up on ranching in such hostile country, or Comanches had taken their toll, or the settlers had been the victims of any sort of a thousand accidents.

Two-Horses heard Gabriela's roan stamp its feet and snort when she joined them. She quickly took in the scene and the old man, who scratched at his whiskers as if pondering the new predicament he found himself facing.

Gabriela had missed the first part of their conversation. "Who are you going to bury?"

"Myself." He squinted at her with one eye. "Why're you riding with a Comanche? Ain't you afraid he's gonna kill you or worse? Looks like he's already beat you considerable. If I had enough bullets, I'd shoot him for you."

She looked back and forth between them. "He's not like the murderers who had me. He saved me from a war party, and we're going back to Texas."

Two-Horses shot her a look.

"I never heard tell of such a thing." The old man appeared to weigh her statement. "Was that the war party I saw come by here a few days ago?"

Two-Horses shrugged. "How would I know. It was a band who had her and another woman. I did not like them, so I took their guns and horses, and this woman-child came with me."

"Well, those old boys were painted up for war, but they rode past me like I wasn't here. Maybe they thought I was a ghost, and right now I feel like one."

"My name's Gabriela." She pulled a strand of black hair behind one ear. "Who're you?"

"Boston."

"You have a last name?"

"Not that I know of. It's been Boston since I was a kid. Grew up on the streets there before I came west. Worst thing I ever did. I should have stayed where I was hatched, and I'd probably be a rich man now, instead of digging my own grave."

Two-Horses was growing bored with the discussion. "Well, get in it, then, and be quiet. I want the water you were talking about."

"Over behind the tree. It's not much of a spring, more of a seep, really, and the tree takes most of that. One seep, one tree. It's how this terrible country works."

Gabriela dismounted and went to the edge of the fresh grave. "Why do you think you're going to die?"

"Ran out of food. Ate my horse when it rolled over and died here 'while back. And I've never been any good at making snares." He pointed at the bones and hides not far away. "Ran out of bullets for my rifle, and there's only one cartridge for my pistol. Can't make myself use it, so I figured I'd just wait until I got too weak and then get in the grave there. Planned to rake in as much dirt as I could over my legs and body, and then hope my idea works that's supposed to finish burying me, but now that you're here, you can do it."

"No." Two-Horses also dismounted and stepped over to Boston's pile of belongings. Sure enough, there was a rusty revolver lying on top. He opened the cylinder and found one unfired round. "You are telling the truth."

"Of course I'm telling the truth." Boston's face reddened. "I don't like to be called a liar. Everything I done told you is a fact."

Gabriela angled herself to better see the grave. A framework of sticks held back much of the dirt Boston had dug out. A piece of rope with a loop at one end dangled from two thin supports. "What's all that?"

Boston squatted and lowered himself into the empty grave, as if he'd practiced that move a hundred times. He stretched out with his head toward the mound. "See, I's gonna lay here and cover my legs, and then raise my arm up and put that loop around my wrist. When I die, my arm'll fall and pull those two little sticks out, and the whole thing'll collapse and cover me up."

Two-Horses snorted and dropped the pistol back where it was when they first got there. "Well, get on with it while I water these horses."

"Can't right now. I'm feeling a little better with y'all here. You have anything to eat?"

Gabriela nodded and reached for a bundle riding behind Two-Horses' saddle. His sharp voice stopped her. "No! He is dying and we need that food."

She jumped. "But you helped *me*."

"That's different."

"But aren't we almost back to the river? We can get food there, and sharing a little with Boston won't hurt."

Two-Horses felt his chest tighten in anger. His face flushed, and that was a dangerous thing for those around him. "You are alive only because I killed those annoying men. I don't like annoying men, and this one here is making me mad." He pointed at the contraption beside the grave. "I might kill you now and put you in that hole."

"That's what I wanted in the first place. Shoot me and let's get this over with. I'm tired of standing here and talking about it in the sun."

"No!" Gabriela snapped. "We aren't killing Boston. He can go with us."

"I'll use your last bullet on you." Two-Horses turned back to the pistol lying nearby.

"No, you won't!" Gabriela's voice rose. "He can ride behind me, and when we get across the river, we'll go our own way."

"That won't work." Boston's voice grew soft. "It's a ways to a town. Just because we get back into Texas, that don't mean we're in the clear."

Two-Horses threw up a hand in disgust and turned away. "I should kill both of you, and then I could have some peace."

Gabriela crossed her arms. "Boston, can I have your possessions after you die?"

He looked surprised at the strange question. "I reckon. They won't be no use to me."

"Then I want them now."

"Okay."

She stalked over to the pile of gear and snatched up the pistol. "This is mine, now. Two-Horses, you're not shooting anybody, and we are riding with you."

He reached for the revolver in his belt and hesitated. He'd always liked strong women, because his mama was as tough as they came. He grinned, then threw back his head and laughed. "Save your bullet. You can use it to kill yourself if we run into another band of Comanches and they kill *me*."

Boston looked down into the grave. "All that work for nothing."

"Look on the bright side." Two-Horses repeated the statement he'd heard Hack Long use more than once. "I have your shovel to dig out that spring and catch more water. You should have thought of that in the first place, old man. We'll water up, and then go on. I'm tired of Mexico and all the people in it."

Boston sighed and sat in the shade of the old house.

Two-Horses hated the idea of using a hand tool, but it was the only way to find water. He noticed Gabriela holding the revolver in an unsafe manner and grunted. "Maybe that pistol will go off and kill old Boston here and we'll be over this mess. There's already a hole for him."

Waving one hand at the grave, Boston leaned back and closed his eyes. "That was the idea in the first place."

CHAPTER 21

Captain Royce Bookbinder led his men into the small town of Edinburgh on the northern bank of the Rio Grande. A single street stretched the length of a thirty-wagon mule train, lined on both sides with a mix of adobe, plank, and log businesses.

The little frontier town had one main street, running west from a dry wash on the eastern side, and was big enough to boast a drugstore, a dry goods store, a tin shop, a blacksmith, two eateries and a pie shop, and eight saloons. The largest was the Crystal, which was a full-fledged gambling house. A couple of other buildings down the street were also dance halls.

It was one of those towns where if two men disagreed on a subject, they agreed to settle up with guns and pushed outside to start shooting. Typically, the one who made the first draw was the one who told the tale, while the town's undertaker buried the other.

The Rangers stopped in front of the Crystal, and Bookbinder swung down and tied his horse to a mesquite post. "Mr. Wilson, would you please go and find the town marshal's office? See if they've seen Captain Clarence Hawkins, and if not, the man he was after."

Ranger Wilson remained on his horse and stared down the busy street. "Cole Shelton."

"Glad to see you have a good memory." Bookbinder gave Wilson's leg a pat above his knee-high boots. "Go on now, and we'll be waiting inside where it's cool. Beer's on me when you get back."

No cowboy or Texas Ranger worth his salt mare-shanked to a destination when they could ride, and Wilson was no different. He urged his mount forward and settled back into the saddle as it picked its way down the busy dirt street, weaving around covered schooners, buckboards, stacks of logs, pedestrians, dogs, and one hog who'd found a muddy spot and refused to move despite all the traffic.

Bookbinder and the others pushed through into the dark interior and separated just in case someone inside wasn't pleased with their presence. It had happened once in San Antonio, and when the smoke had cleared, two of his men were wounded, and the shooter, who was on the run from the law in the first place, had bled out on the floor from half a dozen bullet wounds.

It was early in the day, so only a few customers were scattered about. Grit crunched on the raw boards under their boots. As was their custom, the others took seats to the side of the door, and Bookbinder stepped up to the bar to find a short Irishman waiting with a rag in one hand. He was surprised to find the bar was made of polished mahogany, as were the shelves framing a large mirror topped by a painting of a reclining nude woman of some girth.

"How may I help you, sir?" The bartender's brogue was thick, but not unusual in a frontier town. His nose, which was slightly off-center, battered and deformed ears, and old scars over his eyebrows revealed he was also the bouncer, or had been at one time.

"I'll require beer for me and the boys, and some information."

The short redhead raised an eyebrow. "What may that be you're looking for?"

"Looking for a Texas Ranger named Hawkins. Clarence Hawkins."

"Yep, he was through here sometime back."

Bookbinder turned to be sure his men had heard the exchange. Too many times, his excellent hearing made him think others had received the same sounds or news, sometimes with near disastrous results. Now that they knew the saloon was safe, for the moment, they gathered around one table to the right of the door. His heart sped up with the news, but he refused to show emotion, as was his custom. "How long ago?"

"Weeks, four or five, but I disremember. It could have been longer, but I remember him because he talked like a schoolteacher, and we get few educated lawmen here, present company excepted, of course. Our own marshal can read, but he talks with a heavy British accent that's irritating, to say the least."

"Was Hawkins alone?"

"He was." The Irishman turned to draw the beers from a keg perched on a shelf behind him. The wide mirror allowed him to see the Ranger as he filled thick, heavy glasses. "Said he was going across the river after a murderer. Man with nine fingers, as I remember."

"That's him. Sounds like he didn't come back through."

"Never saw him again." The bartender put the beers on the bar, and Bookbinder slid a gold coin across. "I figured he found his man and either strung him up or took him in to wherever y'all lock up miscreants."

One of the Rangers came forward and picked up the drinks. It was a repeat of every saloon they'd ever entered, for they all believed in maintaining order. He returned and distributed the drinks before settling down where he could see both the bar and the door.

Bookbinder remained where he was, with one boot propped

on the long brass rail. "You reckon he brought his man in to y'all's jail?"

"Nossir." The bartender took a rag from his shoulder and polished a glass. "We have a single cell made of real brick and bars. Sits o'er there beside the marshal's office. We all know who's in there, and it's easy to see inside, so, no, other than a few drunk cowboys and one horse thief, there's been nobody in there."

"Horse thief?"

"Tree fruit a couple of days later. He won't be stealing any more horses, nor anything else for that matter."

"This looks like a quiet town. Wouldn't expect much trouble."

"Quiet enough. Depends on how you define the word. Every now and then, some fool gets shot, but it's usually settled pretty quick. Stage comes through every day, and sometimes it brings trouble, but most of the travelers behave themselves.

"Not too long ago, a feller came through here driving a herd of turkeys, though. Caused quite a stir, and a friend of mine had to draw down on a feller who wanted to rope one of 'em. That man changed his mind pretty fast when that big .44 was aimed at him. Darndest thing I ever saw."

"Turkeys, you say?"

"Yep. Hundred or so. He'd clipped their wings so they couldn't fly and herded 'em with a sheep dog."

"What for?"

"Why, taking them to market, he said." The Irishman wiped the bar top. "M'name's Cafferty, by the way."

"Captain Bookbinder here. So do you have any idea where Ranger Hawkins might have gone once he left?"

"Well, sir, he got to talking with a rancher here who has a place a few miles west of town. Jeremy Thatcher's his name. He has good grass down near the river, and they left together. Thatcher told him he'd hired a new man a month or so earlier with only nine fingers, so he took the Ranger out to see."

"They come back?"

"No, and that was the last time I saw him. Thatcher's been back a few times. Has a taste for good whiskey, and not what you see on the shelves back there. I keep his under the counter here."

Another customer pushed through the batwing doors and took up a position at the far end of the bar. Cafferty moved down, and Bookbinder considered their discussion. He was pleased that he'd thought like Ranger Hawkins and had been able to follow him to this town, but the trail would likely grow cold on the other side of the river. They'd visit Thatcher's ranch, of course, for the cattleman might have more information, and the possibility existed that he'd hired the man Hawkins was after, but there was a distinct likelihood that the outlaw had disappeared across the river.

The others were finishing their beers and Bookbinder's glass contained nothing more than traces of foam when Ranger Wilson came through the doors with several folded papers in hand. He wiped his mouth when he saw the others and their glasses, but he joined the captain at the bar.

His face broke into a wide smile as he spread the papers beside Bookbinder's glass. They were wanted posters and two of them immediately soaked up rings of water. Wilson tapped them with a forefinger. "Lookee here what I found down at the marshal's office."

Bookbinder drained the rest of his glass and studied the picture of a face he recognized. "That's the man we saw back in San Felipe Springs who called himself Virg Prestoni."

The detailed black-and-white likeness of Gabriel Santana on the wanted poster might have been taken from a photograph. The outlaw created in pen and ink stared into the Ranger's eyes with a hint of amusement.

"Wanted for robbery, murder, and other crimes against the people of the state of Texas." Bookbinder read the copy for the others to hear. "Gabriel Santana. Believed to be a member of the notorious Long Gang. Robber of banks and trains. Contact your nearest sheriff or marshal. Five hundred dollar reward." He paused and stroked his thick mustache. "I knew I'd seen that man before. And I had him dead to rights back there in that little one-horse town."

"He got away, but we hung two horse thieves. That counts for something."

"We did that."

Ranger Wilson slid another page over. "When I saw his picture and read this poster, I went through all the papers at Marshal Dudley's office, looking for anything that mentioned the Long Gang. I found these. Hack Long, Luke Fischer, Santana there, Billy Lightning, and some half-breed called Two-Horses. You ever seen a wanted poster for a Comanche?"

"Not 'till just now. I remember seeing a couple of these, but it was a long time ago."

"Over three years. The marshal remembers when they came in. He keeps records of everything. Says he used to be a banker, and he wrote the dates on the back. Said they stopped here to cool off, but there was a posse on their tail, he heard later. They skinned out pretty quick and haven't been back."

Bookbinder flipped one over to read the date, confirming the last time the Long Gang had been seen. "So it looks like at least one of them is back in business."

"We don't know that, sir. He was a man getting a drink in a saloon."

"He was a wanted outlaw in a saloon with a paper and price still on his head. He's a fugitive from the law, and it is our honor and duty to bring him in or hang him at our discretion."

"These men look tough." Wilson pulled at his earlobe in thought. "It might behoove us to just shoot this Santana on sight, as well as the others."

"If we can run this one to ground, he might lead us to the others."

"They've been keeping low."

"Men like that always turn back up." Bookbinder folded the wanted posters and slipped them into the inside pocket of his coat. He spun on his heel and headed for the door as the other Rangers stood to join him. "Let's get after it."

CHAPTER 22

Billy Lightning and Gussie paralleled the Rio Grande in a driving rain, hoping to find a shallow crossing with a good bottom. That wasn't likely, because rain was falling at such a high volume that he felt he could see the water rise.

They were soaked to the bone. The dead Ranger's hat was a little large for Billy, but he was proud to have it because water poured in steady streams from the brim both in front and back.

Disgusted, he shook his head at their situation and the woman's laughter. She'd already stopped several times to sluice water from her clothes, and fifteen minutes earlier had done the unthinkable when they had come upon a steady runoff from a rocky arroyo into the muddy river.

She'd walked upstream a few yards and stripped down before he knew her intentions and sat naked as a jaybird in the waist-deep water as if it were a hotel bathtub. Shocked at her unusual behavior, he'd turned his back on the scene, remembering an admonishment from his mother when Billy was only ten years old or so.

"There's a difference between being nekked and naked. Naked is when you're doing something you're supposed to do with your clothes off, like taking a bath. Nekked is when you have your clothes off and doing things you ought not be doing."

His face had flushed with heat as he waited for Gussie to finish her impromptu bath. It had taken longer than he expected, because once she was clean and her hair washed, she'd insisted on rinsing out her clothes.

"You're a crazy woman, you know that?" He continued to face westward.

"Just because I want to be clean?"

"Naw, but it's the way you're doing it. Why don't you just let the rain do its job and come on. You've got me standing out here like a drowned possum, and lightning's likely to strike me at any minute."

"I'm not hearing any thunder. Why're you worried?"

"Because I been struck before. That's why they call me Billy Lightning. And besides, you realize that water you're settin' in could turn into a flood at any minute. You're out of your mind sitting in there like a big old turtle."

"A big old turtle out of her shell." She laughed and wrung out her blouse. "So that's not your real last name?"

He tried not to peek. "No, it ain't."

"What is it?"

"I'm not telling you."

"'Cause you're wanted for something."

"How'd you know?"

"You forget my late profession? I knew all kinds."

"Well, I'm a Texas Ranger now, so I'm not wanted anymore, and I think you should address me in that way if we come up on travelers or a town."

"That's a bunch of hooey. The first real Ranger you run into is gonna know you ain't been sworn in. He'll shoot you for just wearing that badge."

"Won't happen. I happen to know that there's a goodly amount of Rangers on the job with nothing more'n papers in their pockets saying they've been sworn in. They have to pay for their own badges 'cause the state won't do it, and most of 'em don't want to cough up the money. This badge is gonna get us some horses so I can get out of here, and then you can do what you want, as long as it's far away from me."

"What makes you say that?"

She was waist-deep in that water while it was raining buckets and having a conversation as if all that was going on was as normal as a church service. Billy had to bite his lip. He considered going on without her, but though he was good at robbing trains and banks and killing folks who needed it, he felt a strong sense of responsibility toward the former lady of the evening.

"Well, I usually ride alone."

"Like with that Ranger."

"That's different. I was afoot, and he gave me the loan of a horse."

"That's just fine." Finished with scrubbing her clothes, she stood and tiptoed out of the water. Sitting back on a big, flat rock, she ran her fingers through the long brown hair that stuck to her neck and cheeks. "You just go on, then."

He couldn't help but peek as she struggled back into her wet clothes and leaned back over to rinse out her shoes. Grunting in an unladylike way, she got them on and tied.

A crack of thunder rolled over the land, and Billy jumped. He hurried down to a low spot in the arroyo and crouched, as if it were possible to hide from the weather like one would duck from a war party.

Gussie did the opposite and rose to her feet. Tilting her head, listening. "Did you hear that?"

"I sure did. Where there's thunder, there's lightning, and I'm staying down here until this storm passes."

"No, listen. I think I hear a woman's voice. Sounds like she's hollering."

Billy cocked his head. "I don't hear anything but the rain."

"Over there. I have excellent hearing, and that's the sound of a woman and she's crying. I've heard it enough times in my life."

"I thought you said she was calling someone."

"Well, she's wailing right now. That way!" Gussie shielded her eyes with one hand and struck out in the direction they were headed when the storm arrived. Billy watched her go until the rain prevented him from seeing her anymore.

He remained where he was, crouched against a head-high ridge of rock until the rain ended and the storm moved away. Rising from his low spot, he struck out and wondered what had happened to Gussie. In one way, he was relieved because she was gone, taking his responsibility for her away.

There were no tracks to follow on the hard ground after the steady rain, but the air was cool, and that made walking pleasant. His good mood vanished later when he came upon Gussie and another completely drenched woman who was pacing back and forth beside a burned-out wagon with charred hoops and black canvas strips hanging down.

Arms folded under her breasts, Gussie was just standing there, watching the woman who was talking to herself. Billy stopped a few feet away. "What's she doing?"

"Being crazy."

The woman waved her arms, as if emphasizing some important fact she was explaining. Her eyes widened, then narrowed as her expressions varied from fright to bewilderment to a series of frowns.

"I can see that." Billy absently touched the handle of the pistol in his belt with light fingertips. He felt there was a distinct possibility that she'd charge them, and he intended to be ready. "Why?"

"I don't rightly know, but she's talking to the wagon. I

can't understand a word she's saying. I think it's German or Russian, maybe."

Billy considered the scene. "There's bullet holes in the sides of that schooner, looks like to me, and I think I see what's left of an arrow sticking out of that spoke."

Gussie seemed to fold in on herself. She hugged her middle with both arms and leaned forward as if suffering from a stomachache. "That's what I was afraid of."

"What's that?"

"She lost her mind after Comanches came through."

"How do you know such a thing. All I see is a crazy woman."

The wind shifted for a moment, bringing the gagging odor of burned flesh. "That's how I know."

Billy raised a hand to pinch his nose, then let it drop when the variable breeze took the stench away.

Gussie approached the German as if she were a skittish horse. The woman didn't look at her and moved away to maintain a safe distance between them. When Gussie reached out a hand, the woman took another step away.

However, Gussie's presence pushed the woman toward the wagon tongue, which lay straight out in front. Billy didn't have to wonder where the team was, because Comanches would have taken them to ride or trade if they were horses. If they were mules, they would have driven them with the other stock to eat later.

The woman's wails increased as Billy drew closer to the wagon. It was as if her cries of inner pain could push him back and she wouldn't have to think about what had happened. They grew in volume when he reached the blackened wagon. She still didn't look at either of the pair of strangers, but it seemed to him that she sensed his intentions and didn't like them at all.

Once there, the air reeked of burned coal oil and charred flesh.

Billy knew what he would find.

Keeping one eye on the woman, who was shouting and gesturing toward the south, he held his breath and stepped close and peered over the tailgate to see the bed was full of blackened corpses and pieces of charred wood. The rain must have put out the fire she'd set, depriving the woman of what she'd wanted, a burial by fire.

The bodies were burned so badly that he recoiled. "I swear. I've seen some sights."

"You don't have to describe it. I can smell what's in there. It's a funeral pyre."

"Was."

The woman shrieked, this time in English. "I wasn't finished! God wouldn't even let me do for them after what them savages done to my family!"

Billy backed away from the sight and scent of such horror. Though he knew the Indians were gone, he scanned the horizon in case they took a notion to come back and finish with the woman.

Gussie moved back to Billy, and the woman resumed pacing beside the wagon, pulling her black hair and rubbing her head. "What are we gonna do with her?"

"I'm thinking about putting her out of her misery."

"You. Will. Not shoot that poor woman."

"It'd be a kindness."

"She's just out of her mind from grief and what she's seen. It'll come back."

"How do you know that?" Billy had never understood women, and this was a situation well beyond his experience.

"I've heard of such things."

"Well, we can go on and tell someone in the next town to come fetch her."

"The marshal?"

"Sure."

"Then he'll ask you why you didn't bring her in with us, since you're a Texas Ranger."

He glanced down at the badge on his shirt. "Well, I can take this off until later."

"They'll still ask questions. Let's just take her with us. Once we're finally back across the river, we can find a town and maybe a doctor who knows what to do."

"They'll put a posse together to go after them Indians and want me to go with them. I don't intend to ride after a bunch of Comanches who're a hundred miles away already. Let me just shoot her and we can go on."

"No!" Gussie's shout silenced the woman, who stopped wailing and stared at them as if they'd just arrived. Gussie gave her a smile. "There. Hey, hon. Can you hear me?"

"Of course I can." Her voice came clear and steady.

"Well, good. How about you come with us."

"I can't leave my husband and kids. They need me. I need to finish up."

Gussie looked back and forth between her and Billy. "Not anymore, honey. You need to go with us to tell someone."

"What?" The woman's face twisted, and she slipped closer to madness again. "Tell someone what?"

"Billy." Gussie's eyes welled. "Help me here."

He raised the rifle, and she slapped the barrel away. "That's not what I meant. Help me talk her into going with us."

The woman fell over the edge of her mind again and pulled her hair out in great handfuls, wailing at the top of her lungs. Billy reached the end of his patience. He crossed the distance between them in a handful of steps and took her arm with a firm grip, as if grasping the reins of a recalcitrant horse.

"That is enough. You're coming with us," he said. "Come on."

Giving her a yank, he struck out, nearly dragging her off her feet. The woman struggled for a moment, nearly pulling away, then all the fight went out of her and she stumbled alongside him. Gussie rushed up and took her other arm. Then, holding her between them, they set a pace through the driving rain that would accommodate the three of them.

CHAPTER 23

"We're going about this the wrong way." Ridge Tisdale turned his head at the sulfurous odor of burning hair. After branding for so long, he expected to get used to the odor, but it hadn't happened.

His brother, Oscar, stepped back to admire the clean BENT T burn on the longhorn's hip. It was the tenth one they'd finished that day, and they were both worn out from chasing the wild cattle down in the brush, dragging them fighting all the way to the fire, throwing them down, and slapping on the brand. A quick cut to remove the *cojones*, and the young bull was a steer.

Ridge yanked the pigging string loose and stepped back as the shocked animal regained its feet and considered charging. Ready to spring into the saddle if the steer showed fight, Ridge watched it hurry away before they could heap any more abuse on its body.

Oscar dropped the iron back onto the mesquite fire. "How do you mean?"

"We need to build a corral, run 'em in, and then do all the branding at one time."

"That'd mean taking the time to build that big corral, and then the two of us having to herd 'em in. This is faster."

"It seems piecemeal to me, somehow." Ridge stepped

back into the saddle and checked their surroundings. It wouldn't take but a moment for a Comanche war party to pop up out of the creek and come a-running. "I'd rather we cross the river and steal cows. That'd be easier."

"It would, but then you'd be doing something against the law, and that ain't your way, no matter how you talk right now."

Starting a ranch had been Oscar's idea, and he'd talked Ridge into joining him. They'd been working for old John Hastings down in Dimmit County, riding for the Rio Ranch, when Oscar got married and realized he didn't want to work for someone else his whole life. After his twins were born, he'd talked his drifting brother into joining him and starting their own ranch.

Tilting his hat back to display a white forehead, Oscar drank lukewarm water from his canteen, which was covered with a piece of old trade blanket sewn on by his wife, Ruth. Each time he crossed a stream, he soaked the material to keep the water cool.

Ridge waited, and when Oscar had finished, he took the canteen and drank. "You know as well as I do that I wouldn't steal," Ridge said. "I'm just talking. That's all."

"I'm surprised you're still at it."

"Still at what?"

"Cowboying. You only got into this because I needed help. I figured you'd have gone by now."

"I couldn't leave my baby brother to do this all alone. One man can't run an operation like this." Ridge grinned. With their wide-set eyes, cleft chins, and similar dimples when they smiled, he and Oscar favored each other so much there was no doubt they were brothers. "I figured I'd wait until you had enough cash to hire someone on to help, then I'd drift on."

"To what?"

"I don't know for sure. I've been itching to travel. They

say up in North Texas, there's some rolling country that's thick with trees and lots of grass, and I'm tired of this heat. I might stay there awhile, then head for Colorado and do a little prospecting."

Oscar laughed. "I can't see you panning for gold."

"There's other ways to prospect."

"That ain't you, neither."

Somewhat irritated, Ridge coiled his rope. "Then what would you have me do?"

"Stay here and run the ranch with me, for one thing, but if you've got it in your head to travel, I figure you'll wind up throwing in with the law somewhere." Oscar nodded at the well-oiled .44 Ridge wore on his hip. "With your sense of right and wrong, you'll likely get a job as deputy or even marshal in some cow town or gold camp."

Most Texas waddies carried guns, but mostly for coyotes, varmints, or to put an injured horse down. Men always had a gun close to hand, though, because there were two-legged snakes as well that they were sometimes required to dispatch.

"I doubt you'll ever see me standing behind a badge. Sometimes, my temper gets the best of me."

"You've gotten better through the years." Oscar always enjoyed teasing his brother, though Ridge didn't like it much. "Used to, you'd fight a grizzly, but now you just have a slow burn, like a stick of dynamite."

"I don't know if I like that."

"Like it or not, you've simmered some. I can tell you've been anxious to do something else, and you know your part of the ranch will always be here, even if you go string off somewhere for a while."

"I know that, but I doubt I'll leave until the kids get a little older to help, and especially until the cavalry does something about those Comanche raids. They say they're riding with

White men now, and I don't like the idea of you out here without a second gun."

"You've always worried too much about me."

"I had to. Saw that since the day I had to fish you out of the Guadalupe or you'd have gone straight to the bottom."

"And that's why I don't swim today."

They laughed and went back to building the Bent T herd.

CHAPTER 24

Gabriel Santana followed a distinct wagon trail heading northwest. It felt good to be free, and his horse sensed the good mood. Santana knew horses, and he always said a sad or tired man rode heavier, while someone happy or excited sat lighter in the saddle. As if affirming his thoughts, the Mexican gelding bobbed his head and broke into a short lope for the sheer joy of it.

Scissortails dodged and darted above the mesquite and cedar trees that surrounded him, chasing the flies that were their main source of nourishment. Mockingbirds went through their list of other birdsongs, then repeated them again and again. Javelinas grunted in the brush, followed by the thunder of small hooves as they ran away.

Not wanting to tire his mount, Santana pulled the gelding back into a walk and sat back to enjoy the ride. His mood vanished when the rhythmic clack of hooves from behind told him that someone was loping in his direction.

Always cautious, Santana made sure the pistol was free in his holster and reined off the trail behind a thick cedar only moments before a young cowboy appeared. He had almost passed Gabe's hiding place before his head snapped around and he pulled back on the reins.

The buckskin he rode dug in and stopped on a dime, a sure

sign it was a trained cow horse. The cowboy adjusted his seat in the saddle and threw up a hand. "Howdy!"

The greeting annoyed Gabe. "You can't see me. How'd you know I was here?"

"Felt you." The cowboy tilted the sweat-stained big-brimmed hat up on his forehead and threw a leg over the saddle horn, a sure sign he'd settled in for a nice long chat. "I can do that."

One hand resting near his pistol, Gabe urged his mount out from behind the cedar. He studied the man, who had a lock of long hair dangling from under his hat and down on his forehead.

"I don't believe it. You likely saw me step off the road, or maybe there was some dust hanging in the air. That's how you did it."

"Believe what you want, but you can stay clear of that iron on your belt." He flashed a smile full of perfect white teeth. "I'm harmless."

"I don't know that." Gabe fiddled with the reins in his fingers. "You were moving pretty fast. Running from or *at* something?"

"From, though it's no fault of mine. A couple of old boys who dislike me for making the gals back there in town fall in love with me. Women do that, you know. They say I'm, what'd that little redhead call me . . . irresistible. Name's Barnaby. Most folks call me Barney, once I get to know 'em."

Gabe found himself liking Barney for his grin and easy disposition, but he had no intention of letting him know that. "Irresistible when it comes to women, maybe. I doubt I'll call you much at all after we're done here." He leaned forward to check out their back trail, expecting to see a posse thundering along the road. "I figured you were outrunning that company of Rangers I ran into back there."

Using one end of the bright red scarf tied around his neck, Barney wiped at the sweat running down his jawline. "Saw 'em. But I'm not worried about those guys. I ain't done much to draw their attention. Aw, maybe I've used a runnin' iron a time or two back before I turned twenty, and I have to admit I stole some stick candy from Old Man Henry's store over in Uvalde last year when I was running short of funds and needed something sweet, but nothing serious. How 'bout you. You're on the dodge for sure, since you ain't told me your name yet."

The accusation irritated Gabe, and he kicked his horse into a walk. Barney fell in beside him, and Gabe sighed. "I'm not running from anything. I'm heading toward a place is all."

"That's the same thing you just asked me. Where to?"

"That's my business."

"You're pretty surly for a well-heeled feller on such a nice day. You must have a sour stomach."

"Getting one right now."

"How about I ride along with you?"

Barney's grin was infectious, and despite Gabe's attempts to end the conversation and possibly ignore the cowboy, Gabe felt himself drawn in.

Barney glanced over his shoulder. "Two guns are better than one, if we run into Indians or road agents. I hear tell there's been a couple of robberies and shootings here on this road. Stage was held up not long ago, but the last few weeks they've hired a couple of extra shotguns because of the Comanches, though they don't usually bother stages, as far as I know."

"I figure you can say that for most roads well-traveled."

"What're you doing out here alone?"

"Like I said, I was heading this way to meet some friends

in a little town called Barlow." The second those words were out of his mouth, Gabe cursed himself for talking.

"You didn't say that, but I heard of it. Barlow's a boom-town right now. They say the Comanches ride around it these days because soldiers are there, putting up a fort just west of there. Them Indians don't like cavalry much. Folks are moving in, and the town's spreading out. Heard tell they're already talking about running a rail line through there. Once a train arrives, a place gets civilized pretty quick."

Gabe studied on that bit of information as they rode side by side. It hadn't occurred to him that the town would have grown so much, and his stomach dropped. What if they'd already torn down that building and boardwalk to put up something bigger. If they had, the money was gone like smoke.

He could barely remember what the store looked like, since it was dark when they rode through and every one of them was worn plumb out. What if it all looked so different they had no idea which boardwalk it was? They came in from the north, and it was on the left side . . . or did they arrive from the east?

A pair of doves peeped into view and shot across the road. He was about to comment on the growing town when two men in their late twenties and holding pistols suddenly rode out in front of them and stopped on the twin tracks. They were dressed as cowhands, with flop hats and riding britches under leather chaps. One had a thin blond mustache that curled down over his upper lip, and the other wore a red scarf and a three-day beard.

Their horses were winded and lathered up from a hard ride. Blondie grinned, forming deep dimples in both cheeks. "I told you we'd get around in front of him."

"You did that." Red Scarf gestured with his pistol and spoke around a chew in one cheek. "Barney, keep your hands away from that pistol on your hip, and you, stranger, do the same. You done got yourself in trouble, taking up with this feller."

Sitting easy in the saddle, Gabe rested both hands on the saddle horn. Even though they were pointing pistols at them, neither looked to be a gun hand. Gabe had experience and a trail of dead bodies behind him, and they had no idea what they were bracing.

"That pretty blond feller's Wade. The ugly one who's trying the best he can with the red scarf that's supposed to help his looks is Elmer. You won't like to hear him talk much 'cause he's pretty juicy around that chew he always has in his cheek."

Santana's voice was cold and filled the air like a whipcrack. "You boys are making a mistake, pointing them guns at me. I haven't taken up with anyone, and I don't know you, so move aside and let me pass."

"We'll move when we're ready." Wade's voice hardened, showing he didn't like being ordered around.

"Y'all have a grudge against him." Santana nodded the brim of his hat at Barney. "Not me. I was riding by myself here, and he just rode up."

"Don't matter. Men've been hung just for drinking with outlaws." Elmer's words squished around his chew, and he spat. "You're with him now, and we have a crow to pick with Barney there."

"If you go to pickin', somebody's gonna get hurt, Wade."

Santana watched Wade when the man's eyes narrowed. "Don't threaten me, boy. You got my sister in trouble, and you're gonna pay for it."

Raising an eyebrow at Barney, Santana looked disgusted. "That's what you meant when you said you were irresistible?"

"It's a matter of chosen words." Barney's eyes flicked back and forth between the two blocking their way. He was afraid, and it was obvious to Santana that the cowboy was no fighting man.

A feeling of dread washed over Santana. He'd seen men act that way, weighing those in front of them and judging the odds. None of the three were killers, and all three suddenly found themselves with their backs against an imaginary wall. None wanted to crawfish. The altercation had already gone too far, and any man worth his salt would stand up instead of backing down. That sense of pride had buried a lot of boys who could have simply turned around and left.

But it was coming, and there was no way to stop what was already in motion.

"You boys need to let me pass." Santana desperately wanted away from an altercation that was no business of his. "This is the last time I'm gonna tell you."

Those pistols had been waving around too long, and the blond cowboy named Wade was holding his too low, more or less aimed at Barney's horse and not the man himself.

Barney licked his dry lips, all the former humor gone from his eyes. His face was pale. "What do y'all want?"

Wade almost shrugged before collecting himself. "Our pound of flesh, for my sister. Elmer, hand me your whip. We'll get this done and over with."

"In for a penny, in for a pound, huh?" Barney shifted his weight, and Santana nudged his horse with his left knee, making the gelding step to the right. It seemed as if it were the horse's idea, and the two bracing them didn't notice.

The other men's attention was on Barney's face, which had lost all expression.

Santana threw a glance to his right, judging the obstacles that might be there. Thick grass and rocks promised a hard fall when he pitched off that way if Barney drew down on them. Doing so would put his horse between them, giving Santana a little edge.

He hoped Barney would keep his wits about him for a few more minutes and they could talk it out. He once saw a man of slight stature talk his way out of a beating in a Colorado saloon. A gang of miners took offense to his presence, and the little man convinced them it would be embarrassing for the four of them when it was over, looking as if it took them all to whip one guy who weighed no more than a hundred and thirty pounds.

That little feller talked himself out of a sure beating, and Gabe bought him drinks all night for demonstrating such a useful talent.

Maybe Barney had that gift himself. It was suicide to draw on two men holding pistols, even though they didn't appear to be gunmen. The tension between the men built, thick as molasses.

"Back away, Elmer." Barney's voice quavered as he addressed the other man. "You ain't beating on me or whipping me, and I won't be shot at."

Elmer spat a long brown stream onto the dust that rolled it up and made it look solid. "You don't tell us what to do. I do believe I'd rather string him up, now that he's made me mad."

"He's right. Y'all just leave him alone and let everything work out." Santana felt sorry for Barney, who'd given in to every young man's dreams and was about to pay the price for sowing wild oats. "I'll take him with me, and you'll never have to lay eyes on him again."

"This ain't no schoolyard argument, Wade." Wild-eyed, Barney was doing everything he could to get out of trouble. "You and Elmer just let it go. I didn't do all that by myself. Libby was there, too, and agreeable to what we did, but she's the one who run me off, saying she couldn't take it and would go back East to have the baby."

It was exactly the wrong thing to say.

To suggest that the man's sister was a willing participant

to their tryst was too much. Wade squeezed the trigger, and his Colt barked. The slug slapped the pommel of Barney's saddle and cut through the top of his hip. He grunted and yanked the pistol from his holster as his horse jerked sideways.

Not wanting to fight with a chew in his cheek, Elmer spat it out and proved he was no gunfighter by swinging his pistol back and forth, not sure of who to shoot.

With their attention on Barney, Santana decided not to bail off his horse. Instead, he drew his pistol and thumb-cocked it. "Hold it! Stop shooting!"

Wade swung on him, and Santana fired. The big .44 caught Wade in the stomach, and he grunted and folded over the saddle horn. Santana always shot a second time to eliminate the threat. The next slug punched through one lung and struck something that angled the chunk of lead back out the upper part of Wade's right chest.

Hit hard, Barney finally got his pistol free and shot. His bullet hit Wade's horse in the forehead, and it dropped in its tracks, throwing the man's limp body onto one of the bare wheel tracks. Fine sand flew from the impact.

Fighting to control his horse, Elmer thumb-cocked his pistol and finally got to fighting, shooting Barney in the upper chest and knocking him off his horse.

Barney landed hard and rolled to his side. "Stop it, Elmer!" Those were the last words the soon-to-be father ever spoke.

Unwilling to continue the fight that wasn't his, Gabe spurred his horse, and it charged forward, brushing against Elmer's mount. Elmer swung on him, and almost point blank, Santana's pistol barked as he rode past, and the bullet puffed the man's shirt right over his heart.

Silence followed as Gabe leaned over his horse and rode for all he could ride to get away from the murder scene behind him. It would be his tracks a posse would follow, likely thinking he'd killed all three himself.

There was no getting away from the color of his skin and the fact that they'd string up a Mexican in a heartbeat to solve the murders of local boys.

CHAPTER 25

Hack and Luke followed Ignacio down a deep arroyo. The Mexican hunter rode his mule with a well-worn Remington rolling-block rifle across his thighs, ready to raise it and fire in a second. He sat straight in the saddle, head constantly swiveling right and left.

Neither of the Texans liked being down in the winding watercourse where bandits or Indians could pop up over the rim at any moment. It would be a turkey shoot if someone started shooting down on them, but Ignacio looked as comfortable as if he was sitting in a rocking chair on someone's front porch.

He was too comfortable, and that spot on the back of Hack's neck started tickling.

Luke turned to watch their back trail. "I sure hope this guy knows what he's doing."

Hack felt the same way but tried not to show it. "He appears to."

"Funny, the two of us going after a gang that any one of us could have fallen in with."

"We're bank and train robbers, not men who prey on people like wolves."

"Your mama wouldn't agree."

That statement hit the gang leader hard, and his face

flushed. Only one person in the world could talk to him like that, and it was Luke, who'd become closer than a brother.

"Well, first off, I lost the right to call her Mama a long time ago, and she had a stronger sense of right and wrong than I'll ever have."

"You know the difference, though, same as me."

"We just slice the truth a little different than most folks."

Luke thought about that for a minute and took the conversation back to Ignacio. "He acts like a hunter, but not like us. I had my druthers, I'd get out of this canyon where we can see what's coming."

"I believe this old boy's followed this trail more'n once. Alberto back there said Ignacio keeps an eye on those guys from what he called a nest of some kind. He gets in and out pretty often, so I reckon it's all right."

"But look." Luke pointed at a trail in the sand. "These are his mule tracks we're following, and he takes the same route in and out every time. Don't you figure those guys we're after have come across them? If it was me who saw all these hoofprints, I'd set up around this next bend and wait to see who's going back and forth all the time."

A chill went up Hack's spine because he hadn't thought of that. Three years in Purgatorio had taken their toll, and he'd missed something as big as the moon. He kicked his horse and hurried up beside Ignacio.

"Hey." He didn't shout, but Ignacio heard him coming.

"*Que?*"

"Let's talk English."

Ignacio shrugged but allowed his mule to plod onward. "Talk."

"You're going up to that lookout point of yours on the same trail you use every time."

"So?"

"So you might be a good hunter and a good shot, but you don't know nothing about men who ride the owlhoot trail."

"Owls?"

"American outlaws. We need to find a different way to your lookout. The men we're after might be waiting for us up ahead."

Ignacio stopped his mule and thought about what Hack had said. "This is the long way in. They are usually in a hurry and ride a straight line to wherever they are going."

"Usually." Hack was getting that twitchy feeling that something wasn't right or that somebody was watching from cover. It had saved them more than once. The sun was low, and the scrub was casting long shadows across the ground.

Ignacio considered his words. "You are right. Most of the time, the wind wipes out the trail in this soft sand, but there hasn't been much coming down this wash."

"It only takes one man to find a trail and sit up on it like you do when you're hunting. You know as well as I do that's the way to shoot a deer or rabbit, setting up on their trail. It'll be dark soon. Let's hold up and take a different way in. Think you can find where we're going in the dark?"

"Of course. This country is my home."

"Then let's wait."

The full moon gave them more than enough light to see. They rode single file, following Ignacio, who trailed around catclaw, ocotillo, and the rest of the vegetation that either scratched or stuck. No one spoke until they came to a low rise backed by a tall *mesa*.

Ignacio turned his horse and came back. "Their camp is just over there." He pointed into the darkness. "There is a higher point to our right. You can see the shell of a house from there."

"Lead on."

Neither of them expected the sharp drop that fell off once

they reached Ignacio's nest. His hideout was located about ten feet down a slope, preventing them from being backlit. Cedars grew thick there, tall enough to conceal their mounts at the base of the *mesa*. Tying them to a gnarled mesquite stump, the trio settled down to face south. Wishing for a pair of binoculars, Hack scraped several rocks out of the way and sat cross-legged, the way they did in prison.

"See that glow?" Ignacio spoke in a soft voice.

A fire reflected off the interior walls of a dying house, defined by the darkness on the outside.

Luke stood behind them. "Three hundred yards. Maybe four. Do they ever leave by themselves?"

"No. There is power in numbers. It is always the whole *pandilla* . . . gang."

"How often do they go out?"

"Every two or three days. It is always in a different direction. They hunt, as I do, but their prey is different. The innocent. The old. The weak. Those who are afraid, which is my village."

Luke drew a long breath. "So you're telling me you watch them ride past here and into town and threaten to kill every living thing and you nor your people won't do anything?"

"They are afraid. When children are at risk, my people think is better to submit. It is a good thing, too. I haven't told Alberto or the others back in the village, but they have been joined by four more. Now there are eight gunmen."

Hack felt Luke looking at him and knew what he was thinking. "Why didn't you tell us before we got here?"

"Because you might not have come." Ignacio squared his shoulders. "But there are three of us against them, so that is better odds, do you not agree?"

"You say you're not a fighter." Luke rubbed his forehead.

Ignacio shrugged. "I will fight if I have to, but until you

came, it was just me against them, with an old rifle that takes a long time to reload."

"The odds just got worse." Luke's voice sounded distraught.

"Not for us." Hack had to adjust his seat against a stone that was digging into the back of one thigh. "They're not expecting the fight to come to them."

"That is why we are here, to kill people." Ignacio gave his rifle a pat. "I have killed many animals, but never a man. You will do this thing."

"Because that's what we do." He didn't like talking about it, but Hack was working his way through the idea and a good part of it rested on getting the villager to cover for them.

"Your confidence will see you through, with this." Ignacio kissed a small wooden cross hanging around his neck and made the sign. "God will help us."

"I hope you're right." Hack stood and returned to the horses. He was far from confident about anything. He needed time to think. Loosening the girth on the black, he slid the rifle from the scabbard.

Luke joined him. "It's too far for these guns."

"I don't plan to use the rifles. I'm putting this one over there in case we have to fall back to fight."

"Fall back from what?"

He spoke at the same time an idea occurred to him. "I intend to ride right up there all slow and easy about an hour before dawn and shoot every one of them sidewinders with my pistol."

"That makes sense. Twelve shots. Eight men."

"See, we're thinking alike. Surprise and sleep will be on our side. That should work, but if it don't, we hightail it back up here to Ignacio's nest. I can't imagine more'n one or two would still be alive to chase us, but if they do, he'll have the sun on his left side and can pick them off with that rifle of his. This'll be a good place to fight from."

"If he's that good a shot."

"We have to hope."

Ignacio's voice came to them. "I can hear you, and I am a very good shot when I can take my time."

"I'd like to cut down on the odds. It's too bad they don't raid in pairs." Hack was thinking aloud and Ignacio heard.

"I never see them alone, except, of course, when they walk away from the house to do their business."

Luke started laughing.

Dawn was a dim glow as the Texans made their careful way down to the roofless adobe. Hack had spent the last few hours working out a more detailed plan, but changed his mind only minutes before when he and Luke were saddling the horses and one stomped a hoof. The sound was loud as a blacksmith's hammer on an anvil, for the desert air was still, with not a breath moving.

"This won't work." Stopping what he was doing, Hack put his forehead against the saddle, thinking. "We're gonna have to walk in there and kill 'em like I said at first."

"We do it that way and things go bad, we won't have any way out without the horses. We'll have to run like driven rats back up here."

"We still have an ace there in Ignacio."

The hunter joined them, rifle resting in the crook of his arm. "What will you have me do?"

Hack pointed at a dark spot about a hundred yards from where the house sat. "You ease down there and wait in those bushes. If they manage to fight us off, we'll fall back, acting like we're on the run. They'll want us dead, after what'll happen when we first start shooting. If any of them are left, they'll chase us and you pick 'em off. A hundred yards ain't much of a shot, for a shooter, when somebody's running right at you."

Ignacio grinned, his teeth white in the dim light. "I like your plan."

"I don't, but I can't think of anything else."

A slight breeze came up, and Hack changed his mind again. There was something wrong, and he couldn't put his finger on it. His thoughts went back to riding the horses most of the way, not wanting a long run on foot back to the rifles if anything went wrong. And there were a lot of possibilities with the unknown.

The breeze was in their faces, and he hoped it would push the sounds of the horses' hooves away from the long-abandoned hacienda.

The three of them separated, picking their slow way toward the quiet camp on horseback. When they reached the cluster of cedars not a hundred yards from the encampment, they gathered once again. Ignacio checked his rifle and knelt with the greenery at his back. The sun would rise behind him, rendering their ace in the hole nearly invisible if he didn't move.

Luke took the horses and tethered them with slipknots behind the cedars, ready to jerk the reins free if the fight went bad and they had to retreat in a hurry. He and Hack had two pistols each, with pockets full of extra bullets.

Luke hung his hat on the saddle horn, but Hack took it off and put it back on his head. "I know these things are too heavy, but we're gonna need 'em to keep the sun out of our eyes so we can shoot."

It's impossible to set a hat on another man's head, so

Luke adjusted it and sighed. "When we get back, I'm gonna get me a decent Stetson instead of this heavy old thing."

Hack grinned at him. "Boss of the Plains. We'll both get one, but right now, these'll do."

It was a typical desert morning, smelling of damp dust. Quail called nearby and sleepy doves sang to each other from a number of unseen locations as the two outlaws picked their way down the slope as quietly as possible. They reached the quiet adobe shell without incident.

Walking softly, Hack pointed with his pistol to the right of the front entrance and whispered. "I bet there's a back door or a window on the side. Go around and set up a cross-fire. Pour it on 'em from there when I go in through the front, but don't shoot *me*."

"Not in the mood today." Luke grinned and made a wide loop around to the offside.

They approached the old house place one slow step at a time, thinking the bandits might have set someone out to watch. When they grew close, Hack saw he needn't have worried about those guys hearing their horses. Their own restless mounts were stomping their feet and snorting in a pole corral on his left. There was no water in there, so he figured they were thirsty and waiting for someone to come lead them to drink.

A cold chill went over Hack when he saw the eight saddle horses waiting. The odds suddenly seemed insurmountable, and he almost turned around to regroup and think about the numbers that had doubled. Eight gunmen didn't sound like so many up on the slope, but the horses were proof that the odds weren't in Hack's favor.

Snores came from behind the walls, and he caught the odor of mesquite smoke rising from the inside, the remainder of their evening campfire. Someone coughed, a thick phlegmy sound of a waking smoker.

Despite the increased odds, there wouldn't be a better time.

His nerves settled and the butterflies in his stomach vanished, the same way they did when it was time to pull a job. He knew what he had to do.

Hack's slow approach gave Luke enough time to make his way to the other side, and staying close to the exterior wall, Hack crept up to the vacant, doorless entry. The big sombrero kept bumping the wall, so he took it off and dropped it in the sand. Taking a deep breath, he drew both revolvers and cocked them.

The dance started when a bearded man appeared suddenly, stepping into view only two feet away and fumbling with the buttons on his pants. His eyes were closed against the rising sun.

Hack stuck the muzzle of the pistol against his chest and shot him dead as a doornail.

The outlaw collapsed back with a sharp groan, and Hack followed his falling body inside. Overhead on the far side of the shell of a house was a loose arbor of alternating mesquite limbs to provide some shade in the heat of the day. Had there been a real roof, it would have been dim inside, but light spilling over the walls and through the open door and window reflected against the light-colored walls, illuminating distinct targets.

Startled men rose in a rippling wave from pallets scattered on the dirt floor. The nearest man was barely awake and rose on one elbow to see what was going on. Hack shot him with the pistol in his left hand at the same time Luke fired at someone else from the rear. Hack's target fell onto his back, looking as if he went back to sleep, but the one Luke shot flew forward, slamming face down on top of a huge beast of a shirtless, mustached man who rose with a roar.

He flung the corpse off and came to his feet faster than a human should. The man's chest and back were so hairy that it seemed like a bear was loose in the room. With such imagery in place, Hack shot him twice, and he went down.

Gunfire hammered their ears, blocking out shouts of alarm that rose from the other outlaws. More than one struggled awake, snatching guns from holsters or where they lay beside them on their blankets.

Muzzle flashes lit the scene as men who were yanked from a deep sleep fired at the first thing they saw, and more than once it was their own men in the chaos. There was motion everywhere as men shot at friend and foe alike, all mixed with shouts and screams, but Hack was looking for immediate threats with iron in their fists.

A terrified voice rose from the roar. "Indians! Rise! We're under attack!"

"Not hardly," Hack said to no one and saw a figure rise to one knee. The glint of morning light on his pistol caught Hack's notice, and he fired with the right-hand pistol and gave him another slug with the left.

From the corner of his eye, Hack saw Luke rushing through the melee, sticking the muzzle of his revolver against the closest side, back, or stomach. He ran like a dervish in Hack's direction, pulling attention toward himself and away from Hack, giving him time to cock, aim, and shoot as steady as target practice.

Lead from their guns filled the air, pulverizing the adobe walls and throwing dust into the air to mix with the cloud of gun smoke hanging low in the house.

A shrill voice full of fear shouted. "Devils among us! Devils in the camp!"

Before Hack had left home at fifteen, the horror in that young man's voice would have made him feel sorry for the guy, but that kind of sympathy had been wrung out long ago. These were wolves who preyed on the weak, and most of all, they'd threatened kids.

Hack Long could never tolerate any meanness toward children.

A shape still screaming about devils rushed at Hack from the side, knocking him off-balance and against the wall. A fist slammed into the side of his head, almost crossing the Texan's eyes.

Both pistols were dry, and he used the one in his left as a club, slamming it against the forehead of an outlaw standing taller than him. They must have recruited gang members by the pound. The blow didn't faze the giant. The next thing Hack knew, he was using the empty hunks of iron as hot, smoking clubs, pounding his opponent with rights and lefts like a windmill.

The giant must have thought there was more than one person swinging empty pistols as he dropped, still hanging onto Hack's waist. "Y'all stop hitting me."

Hack finally had the angle and hammered him one last time with the force he'd used breaking rocks in the prison. The giant hit the floor and was still.

The hacienda was silent except for the groan of a wounded man. Luke stood in the middle of a sea of bodies like an oak tree absorbing nourishment from all the blood soaking into the ground, calmly reloading and looking around for the next threat.

The groans were coming from the hairy, shirtless guy Luke had shot first as he killed his way inside the hacienda's four walls. Wounded twice and still capable of doing damage, the man gained his feet with a knife in one hand and a pistol in the other. Hack was too far to fight him and out of bullets.

Luke was still stuffing fresh rounds into his cylinder. The Bear planted his feet and saw Luke's back. He extended his gun arm as if taking careful aim to shoot at a tin can on a post. Things moved slowly in the morning light coming through the glassless window. It filtered through the gun smoke filling the room and shined on the Bear's long, tousled hair.

The glow seemed almost peaceful in the carnage.

"Luke!" Hack threw the empty pistol in his right hand and missed.

His partner's head snapped around, but it was too late. The cords of muscle in the Bear's forearm swelled as he squeezed the trigger on a double-action Colt, but the hammer never fell. With a loud gasp, he staggered to the side from the impact of a heavy bullet. A thunderclap followed as the unfired revolver in his hand dropped and the Bear's eyes died at the same time as his body from a big slug sent by Ignacio's rifle.

CHAPTER 26

Billy Lightning and Gussie crossed the Rio Grande easy as you please, with the crazy woman between them. They stopped on the Texas side beneath a thick stand of mesquites, and ignoring modesty, they stripped down to their underwear and draped the wet clothes across the bushes while the crazy woman sat in the dirt with her head in her hands.

Finding a broken limb sticking out of the main trunk, Billy hung his pants by one loop and tended to his guns. "She's sitting right there in the dirt in that wet dress. It'll be a muddy mess if she don't get out of them clothes and let 'em dry."

Gussie'd been in the presence of men without her clothes so long she didn't pay any attention to her condition. "I'm gonna take her back into the water and give her a good scrubbin'. That Ranger didn't have any soap in his saddle-bags, did he?"

"I don't know." Surprised that he hadn't thought of that, Billy dragged the bags close and rummaged inside. "Sure enough did!" He held up a thick cake of lye soap. "When y'all get finished, I believe I'll wash up, too. Just make sure you don't peek."

Gussie rolled her eyes. "Nothing to peek at I ain't already seen." She took the now quiet woman's arm. "C'mon, honey. Let's get cleaned up."

They were both surprised when the lady grabbed the soap from Billy's hand. "Wash it all away. That's what I'll do. I'll wash it all away. Clean it right off."

The women pushed through the mesquites and back to the shallow river crossing. Billy heard them splashing and went back to the saddlebags. Digging through the contents, he found waxed lucifers, jerky and hardtack, a small wooden box containing a surveyor's compass, a book of poetry, handcuffs, a sheathed knife wrapped up with a whetstone, a small leather bag with fishhooks and a small coil of line, a small tin of oil, and a straight razor.

He rubbed the whiskers along his jaw that felt like thick bristles. "Y'all hurry up. I have a thought to shave."

Gussie's voice came through the lace of green leaves. "You'll get your turn."

Wearing nothing but his hat, long johns, and boots, Billy finished oiling the Colt and gathered dry sticks to make a fire. They didn't need one, really, and had no food that required cooking, but a fire was always welcome, even when it was hot out. He struck one of the lucifers and applied the small flame to a pile of tiny twigs, dry grass, and papery leaves. It quickly caught, and he added larger sticks until he had a small bed of coals that wouldn't soon go out.

Cicadas complained about the heat from the trees. A soft breeze brought the scent of cedar, dirt, and birds calling in the trees. Feeling the need to get the lay of the land and enjoying the scent of burning mesquite, he looked around to check their surroundings.

He walked a ways from the drying clothes and made a circle. Halfway back to the river, he stopped at the sound of a buzzing rattler. Not wanting to engage a serpent he couldn't see, he retraced his steps and returned to their camp, where he discovered the girls sitting by the fire.

Gussie was ringing out her long hair. The crazy woman simply sat there, water draining down the back and shoulders of her camisole. For the first time, Billy saw she was a handsome woman, with almond eyes and olive skin.

"You look to be feeling a little better."

"Her name's Annabelle."

"How do you know that?"

"She volunteered it while I was scrubbing the filth off her."

"Well, Annabelle, I'm going down there to scrub up some, too, and if we're lucky, I might catch us a catfish or two." He held up the packet of hooks and string.

The woman didn't respond, just stared into the flames.

Gussie twisted the ends of her hair. "Use grasshoppers. My daddy always caught big grasshoppers for catfish."

Billy rose. "There's jerky in there, if you need something before I get back. It might take a while, so I might set a snare close by, too."

"Do what you want." Gussie plucked her shirt off a bush and turned it over to dry evenly. "Get to it, then. I'm starving."

Clean, shaved, and bearing three catfish, Billy Lightning returned to the camp to find the women dry and dressed. Annabelle sat against a gnarled mesquite tree, head on her knees and sound asleep.

Hair curled down past her shoulders and legs stretched out before her and hidden by the long gingham dress, Gussie occupied herself with the surveyor's compass, turning it one way, then another. "Thought you'd never get back. I figured you'd cleared out and left us to fend for ourselves."

"Wouldn't leave my clothes, dummy."

He hung the fish from a low limb and pulled on his pants

and shirt. "Soon as I get these fish cleaned, we're gonna eat high on the hog tonight."

"The Ranger had three bars of soap. It was stuck down in a corner."

"Missed that."

Billy was cleaning the fish when Annabelle awoke and looked around. "I had a dream about my mama."

He stopped to listen. Gussie rose and knelt beside the woman, who showed no expression.

"My mama had me and all my sisters sitting on the front porch of our house over in Tennessee. Didn't have any brothers. They both died when they were babies. She was reading from the Bible and quoting the deacon of our church. Said, 'The wicked among us continue to multiply, while the dead are the only ones to find peace.' Then a little boy and girl took her hands and led her away to be baptized in the river."

She looked into Gussie's eyes. "Do you know what that means?"

"I don't know, hon."

"I do." Annabelle rose and smoothed her dress. "I have to go and tend to my business."

"Don't go too far." Gussie gave her a pat on the shoulder and went to help Billy finish with the fish.

Annabelle nodded and gathered the front of her dress so she wouldn't step on the hem. She was soon out of sight, and they were finished cleaning the fish when Gussie gave a start.

"Now I know what Annabelle was saying!"

She spun and raced toward the river. "Hurry!"

Billy followed closely behind, and when they reached the muddy water, the woman was nowhere in sight. Gussie pointed at a single set of footprints down from where they'd bathed that led into the river. Annabelle's clothes hung on a mesquite. Her shoes were neatly placed beneath them.

Billy sighed. "You should have let me shoot her. It would have been faster than drowning."

"She did what she had to do." Gussie wiped a single tear, the only one to be shed for the tormented Annabelle.

CHAPTER 27

"There were only seven bodies." Luke's head was on a swivel as they rode back to the village. "Eight saddled horses in the corral, and I counted only seven."

Uneasy about the uneven numbers of bodies and horses, Hack chewed his bottom lip in thought. Unable to sit still in the saddle, he twisted back and forth, searching for hidden threats. "They might have lost a man on the trail somewhere and brought in his horse."

Ignacio led the way back on his mule, rifle once again across his thighs as if he didn't have a care in the world. "That was a good shot, no?"

"You did well." Luke was better at praising accomplishments than Hack, who expected men to do their jobs without wanting a pat on the head every time. Luke kept fiddling with a hat he'd taken from one of the dead men, forcing the crease into a shape he preferred.

When the smoke had cleared back at the ruins and Hack was sure the dead men were all talking with each other in hell, they'd gone through the outlaws' belongings, finding shirts and pants that came closest to fitting their frames. He and Luke were tired of looking like Rurales, and there were enough clothes and boots to make re-outfitting easier.

They came up with over fifty dollars in mixed American

coins and *pesos*. Luke saw a buckskin he liked better than the one they'd taken from the Mexican posse and used that first one to pack what they wanted to take with them. Ignacio still rode his mule, but he led a string of ponies to distribute to the other people back in his village. There was no sense in leaving behind good Henry rifles, Colts, and ammunition, so they outfitted themselves as well as when they'd first crossed the Rio Grande into that hell on earth.

"I feel more like an American for the first time in years." Luke ran his fingers down the side of a vest containing a small bullet hole only a fraction of an inch from the middle button hole. Only a tiny spot of blood stained the garment. He wore a light blue shirt that one of the dead outlaws had rolled up in his saddlebag for when he wanted to dress up. "And these boots feel like they were made for me."

Removing his own newly procured hat, Hack read the maker's name in the lining and replaced it, tilting the brim low over his eyes. "Those the ones you found in that pack?"

"They are. Those guys had some style at least." Luke worked on the hat brim some more. "They were kinda picky about what they stole. Kinda reminds me of us."

His statement was a surprise. "What does that mean?"

"It was like that little town west of Carrion Springs. Remember, there was that rancher out there who was building his herd by rustling other people's cattle. He hired those gunslingers to pick off a few of their hands, saying it was Comanches who killed them, but we all knew better."

Hack remembered that town. They were just passing through on the way west and stopped for a whiskey. Santana heard about a freight company that was hauling silver from New Mexico to a rail line in Dallas, and they decided to lift some of the weight from them.

When they rode into town, the whole place was in an uproar because one of the gunmen had killed a deputy in town, and they were gearing up for a hanging. Then someone broke him out of the jail, and the whole town picked up guns and went after the fugitives.

Everything quieted down, and the Long Gang realized there were more of them than the men left in town. Calm as church ladies, he and Santana strolled into the bank and took every penny they had while Billy Lightning, Luke, and Two-Horses kept watch in the street. They rode out the opposite way of the posse and never did rob that freight wagon.

Marveling at how Luke thought those men back there were like them, Hack found himself aggravated. "They were scum, and I'm glad we killed 'em all."

"Well, we did what we had to do, and I reckon the same end'll come to us at some time or another, but we didn't kill all of 'em, I don't believe." Luke looked around at the *mesas* on both sides of them. "That missing man is making me nervous."

"I don't like it, either, but he might have been out of pocket and run off, or it was just a spare horse." They rode along and thought for a minute as Hack worked things out in his mind. "You know, there's a good chance he was on the lookout and went to sleep. When he woke up and heard all the shooting, he might've lit a shuck for somewhere else. Most of these guys aren't shootists. They're murderers and won't face a man when things get rough."

Luke sat up a little straighter. "That makes more sense than anything I was thinking. I'da run if I heard that kind of shooting. We hit 'em hard and fast, and they never knew what happened. I wish the rest of the guys had been with us. It would have gone smoother."

"It was the only way to win." In Hack's mind, there was no such thing as a fair fight, even if it was two men facing each another in the street. Nothing is equal, so one of the two in a shootout will always be better than the other. That's what makes it a contest, though it's always one-sided, no matter what people might think.

It was the first time he'd wondered where the boys were in a couple of days. He fully expected to find them once they reached Texas, but their progress was frustrating. He vowed to himself that once they were through Alberto's village, he and Luke would make a beeline for the river and get across as soon as possible.

He'd even swim the deepest part of the Rio Grande to make the trip shorter. It had been a long time since they'd been free, and Hack wanted to gather the boys up, pick up that loot, and go find a clean cathouse that offered real baths to their customers where they could hole up for a month or two.

He rested his palm on the butt of a Walker Colt riding in a cross-draw holster. Those boys they left back there had good taste in guns, though. Walkers were usually carried by Texas Rangers, and Hack figured they'd taken it from some lawman's dead hand.

There was also a Colt Paterson on his right hip and a Henry repeater in the scabbard under his right leg. Two more loaded revolvers rode stuffed in the saddlebags behind him. Those guys were better outfitted than a good mercantile.

Luke had also pitched the rusty guns they'd taken from the Rurales and kept the better sidearms. Two of the men they'd killed had carried Winchesters, and he had one on his own saddle. Though their new clothes and weapons were used and bloodstained, they felt like kids at Christmas. It was a great sensation after so many years.

The noon sun beat down, and Hack was looking forward to a long drink of cool, clear water from Elena's bucket when they got back to her place. Now that she and the other villagers could live in peace, he figured she'd be glad to cook up one more supper before they left the next morning.

It was so hot the birds were silent. The only sign of life was a lizard sunning on a rock.

After the past few hours of fear and tension, all three were exhausted and almost dozing in their saddles. The rocking pace of the horses lulled Hack into a nap, something he'd learned to do years earlier while riding. Every good cowboy he'd ever known had learned to sleep in the saddle, and both he and Luke had done their share of cowpunching when they were younger.

Ignacio's abrupt shout jolted Hack back into consciousness. "Oh!" Ignacio dropped off the side of his mount and landed heavily.

The report of a rifle shot swept across the land. Some men's first instincts might have been to drop off and check on the hunter, but he was dead when he hit the ground. The ponies he was leading just stopped, unconcerned.

Other men might have pitched off their horses to hide, but there was nothing but vegetation around them, which a man with a rifle could shoot through. Hack and Luke weren't new to the game and reacted through sheer instinct. Luke yanked his horse's head to the right and put the spurs to it.

Seeing his move, Hack did the opposite, kicking the black into a dead run to the left, pulling on his packhorse's lead rope. Lying low over the saddle, he raced away from the ambush to make a second shot more difficult. Another crack followed, but he didn't hear a bullet strike.

Giving the horse his head, Hack hung tight onto the lead with his free hand, reluctant to lose the extra guns and equipment. The young gelding kept pace, and they ran.

As mesquites, cactus, and ocotillo flashed past, he thought back to how Ignacio had reacted when he was shot, figuring the angle of the bullet. Whoever it was that had ambushed them wasn't very creative and not sure of his own marksmanship. He'd taken the easy shot, straight into Ignacio's body as he rode directly toward the shooter's hiding place.

That simple fact gave Hack a plan.

Putting enough distance between them to get out of sight, Hack reined up in a thicket of mesquite trees. Grabbing the

Henry from its scabbard, he swung to the ground and tied the black to the thickest trunk he saw. It took another few seconds to secure the packhorse, and he dashed away, hoping they'd been trained well enough not to fight free.

Time was important, and he hurried toward where the shot had originated, working his way around to come in behind where the man had been. It became clear as he ran. The backshooter was the missing outlaw, and the man was on foot.

At least, he'd been on foot until he'd shot Ignacio out of the saddle. Hack changed his angle again, heading straight for where Ignacio had fallen. In his mind, the shooter made a beeline to the dead man's mule after he and Luke ran. A man on foot in that desert was as sure as dead. With the mule, the last remaining outlaw could ride out anywhere, even to the village.

Another shot came to Hack's ears. Though it was close, there was no telling whose weapon it was, but from the sound, it was a rifle.

He ran through the heat, dodging obstacles and watching for movement.

Another rifle shot came, then a pistol cracked twice, right on the echoes of the first.

Nearing where he figured the fight was taking place, Hack slowed and moved forward in a crouch from cover to cover. The next rifle shot was louder, closer. So close, in fact, that he heard the man shuck in another round.

Unsure if he was coming up behind the bushwhacker or Luke, Hack adjusted the Walker Colt on his left side to keep it out of the dirt. He dropped to his stomach and crawled forward, peering from under the brim of his hat. Someone fired, and a round intended for someone else buzzed past a few feet overhead and to his right.

Moving forward a few inches at a time on his stomach and elbows like a lizard, Hack held the Henry off the ground and crawled along a shallow runoff only a few inches lower than the surface of the desert. A rustle from up ahead reached his ears, coming from beyond a low, bright green creosote bush. The sharp odor of the sticky leaves filled his nostrils, along with the smell of disturbed dust.

A shape partially hidden by a young mesquite tree moved, and he made out a pair of striped trousers and a boot. The figure raised up on one knee and shouldered a rifle. In all the action, he'd forgotten how Luke was now dressed. He blinked the sweat out of his eyes and studied the back of the man's vest, but for the life of him, Hack couldn't remember what color his partner had on.

He needed to get closer.

Planting his boots and digging in with the edges of the soles, Hack pushed on ahead to get around behind the man, who remained still, looking down the barrel of his rifle. One foot. Two. He was still fifty yards away when he finally reached a point where the scrub vegetation thinned out enough to get a good look at the man's face. He had a thick mustache that draped down both sides of his mouth to his jawline. It wasn't Luke.

Slowly shouldering the Henry, Hack thumb-cocked the hammer. Beyond the rifleman, Luke saw a chance and fired. The slug struck a rock instead of flesh and whined off over Hack's head, making him duck.

He rose to a knee, aimed again, and froze when a rattler buzzed with a dry sound that was becoming all too familiar.

CHAPTER 28

Finished after a long day of working cows on their small ranch, Oscar Tisdale and his brother, Ridge, rode up to their cabin at dusk, looking forward to a hot meal and a good long night of rest. Instead, they found Oscar's wife, Ruth, pacing in front of the door and wringing her hands. Her face was white with worry and fear.

"Oscar! I thought you'd never get home."

He hit the ground quick, throwing his hat back so the stampede string caught it to hang behind his shoulders. "What's the matter?"

"The kids. They're gone, and I've called and called and looked everywhere."

Unable to grasp what she was saying, he looked around their little cluster of buildings, as if expecting Art and Arlene to come running out, laughing that they'd scared their mother. "What do you mean? How long?"

"They left to go play this morning. I was airing out pillows and blankets, and they were underfoot and I got frustrated and shooed 'em outside. They went off down to the creek and didn't come back for dinner. They're usually in and out all day, but I haven't seen them. I went looking for them, but they weren't in their usual places, and now it's almost dark and I don't know where they are."

Fear frosted Oscar's spine. "Indians? Did Indians take my babies?"

"No, at least, I don't think so. I looked everywhere and there were no hoofprints. I've been looking ever since, making circles around the place, but there's no sign that Comanches have been here. What I did find was wagon tracks down close to the creek, but I expected that."

Still sitting on his horse, Ridge frowned into the distance. "Indians don't use wagons. Who else has come across the spread?"

Ruth didn't seem to know what to do with her hands. They fluttered around her dress, up to her hair and neck, then back down again to the belt around her waist. Thinking, she pressed them against the sides of her face.

"A traveling preacher came by, saw the smoke, and stopped for a minute. Him and his missus wanted to talk, but I said I didn't have time. Told them they were free to camp in that little glade down by the creek if they wanted and could come up and have supper with us tonight, but they kept going."

Grim-faced, Ridge dismounted and went into the lean-to shed on the side of the barn where he slept. Emerging with a Winchester and two boxes of shells, he stuffed the ammunition into a saddlebag and stuffed the rifle into its boot.

Swinging back up, he looked down at his little brother, who had a family man's disposition and seldom angered or lifted his voice. Oscar was the steady hand, while Ridge had his own code of responsibility that often led him to violence.

"Oscar, I'm going after that wagon."

"We don't know it was them."

"Ruth can read sign as good as any man I've known. Heck, she tracked y'all's milk cow four miles right before the kids were born and brought it straight back here. She says it was the two of them in that wagon, then it was."

Ruth steadied. "It was three. They had a boy with them,

maybe thirteen or fourteen. He didn't seem to be feeling good and didn't say a word, just sat there and almost went to sleep while they was here talking. It worried me, and I didn't want the twins to catch anything from him, so that's why I sent them away."

"You said they was invited to supper."

"I figured to set a board table out here, and we could eat outside in the cool when the sun went down. I didn't want to be inhospitable."

Ridge looked down at Oscar. "You can stay here if you want. I'll go get the kids."

"They're mine."

"They are."

Like Ridge, Oscar went inside their notched log cabin and came back out with a rifle. He got back on his horse and said, "Ruth, you set tight. We'll be back with the kids."

"I'll go crazy just sitting here."

"Go over to the Roberts's place. Tell G.W. what happened and that you need to stay with them. He'll come milk and let the chickens out in the morning."

"It'll be full night in a few minutes. You can't follow tracks in the dark."

"There ain't no way I can sleep with Ridge on the hunt and me doing nothing. A wagon is easy to find, and with that moon as bright as it is, it'll be like riding with a lantern."

She touched his knee and they were gone, leaving the worried mother standing in the spill of light coming from their open cabin door.

CHAPTER 29

Humans are born with the fear of snakes, and Hack was no different. He didn't move other than his eyes, which flicked from side to side, looking for the irritated diamondback. At the same time, he hoped the murderer wouldn't turn his head at the sound and see him.

Either Luke or the outlaw fired again, the sound straining through the mesquites, but this time Hack didn't react. That snake was close, and any sudden movement could cause him to strike. Two more shots followed in the space of half a second.

Lying at the bottom of the twenty-foot-wide shallow wash, Hack knew the snake was within striking distance. Floods kept the wash swept clean and undercut the shale bank of flat rocks that was the likely place for it to lay up. That's where he finally located the thick rattler, coiled in the shade of a thin rock at eye level. Had it been any other situation, Hack would have backed away or waited until it took the opportunity to crawl away, as most snakes do.

But time was short, and he didn't like staring into that serpent's eyes.

Bitten once when he was a kid and with a wide scar still

on his ankle from the flesh rot that came later, Hack hated snakes.

They say a rattler can strike half the length of its body, and that big feller was the longest he'd ever seen. Another shot came, and it sounded like Luke was working around to get an angle on the guy. All the harsh slaps of gunfire made the rattler even madder, and that big triangular head pulled back to strike.

Odd things happened. A roadrunner trotted past as if on an errand. A dove landed on a mesquite limb and stared down as if wondering why a man was lying there as still as death. At the same time, he saw the shadow of a buzzard that passed directly overhead, emphasizing Hack's situation.

Clearly mad, the snake rattled again, Hack was done with it. Having no other choice, he pointed the Henry, figured out where the bullet would strike without putting the stock to his shoulder, and pulled the trigger. He flinched at the resulting explosion of lead against rock, shards, and snake blood that splattered his face.

He rose on one knee and jacked the lever to load another shell into the chamber, not for the now-dead no-shoulders, but for the other kind of snake who was trying to kill him and Luke.

The startled man with the rifle swung around, and Hack registered his brown skin and a long black mustache. The shooter in a floppy horse-thief hat found the Texan, threw the rifle up, and swung the muzzle around.

The distance was too far for a snap shot like Hack had used on the rattler. This time, he aimed and was pulling the trigger when Luke shot the outlaw in the back at the same time the Henry roared. Luke's slug must have cut through the man's backbone, for his chest thrust forward at the same time his head snapped back from Hack's shot. He landed face-first and didn't move.

Wiping snake matter off his face, Hack stood. Luke

appeared, nudged the body with the toe of his boot, and grinned. "How'd you get bloody from that far away."

"Snake."

In pure Luke fashion, he took the statement without question and studied the dead man. "Just like we planned it."

From where he stood, Luke didn't see the dead snake's body uncoil and flow out from under the flat rock like it was alive, until the weight changed and it rolled over with its white belly toward the sky.

Hack shivered as, overhead, the buzzard circled back around.

Luke rested the rifle in the crook of his arm. "Well, that was the eighth one."

Readjusting the Walker Colt on his belt, Hack watched the bird floating on the air currents. "I hope there weren't nine."

"Let's take poor Ignacio back."

"Nope." Hack was done with that part of the country. "We're gonna load him up across that mule of his and send it home."

"Then what?"

"Then we're going straight north to the river. I plan to be back in Texas by dawn."

Luke grinned. "Think we can make it?"

"If we don't get hung up in that village. Let's get the horses and get out of here."

"You don't have to tell me twice."

CHAPTER 30

Crossing back into Texas should have been more significant for Hack and Luke, but it was nothing different than fording any other stream. They found a spot with a hard bottom, and the horses made their slow way against the current. With boots barely wet from the muddy Rio, they were back on Texas soil.

Luke turned around to look back into Mexico. "Well, there ain't no Rangers waiting for us, and no Rurales on our tail."

Though it wasn't possible, the air seemed cooler on the north side of the river, and cleaner. "Let's get as far away from here as fast as we can." Hack kicked the black into a run for the sheer enjoyment of feeling the wind against his face.

"I'll never cross that river again!" Luke's buckskin matched the black's speed, and they raced each other across the flat river bottom toward an intersecting line of trees alongside a tributary leading away from Mexico.

They eventually hit a two-track freight trail leading northwest and spent two days following it to a small town consisting of one busy street. The first thing Hack noticed was a bar named the Crystal. "Looks like we're home."

"You don't have to tell me twice."

Leaving the horses at the rail out front, they went inside.

Cool darkness thick with cigar and cigarette smoke welcomed them back to civilization. As one, they headed straight for the bar. Luke dug out a few coins he'd taken off the outlaws back in Mexico they'd killed and slapped them onto the smooth top. "Bartender, we'd each like two beers, and along with those, I'd like a tequila and my friend here drinks Old Forester, but if you don't have that, anything with a kick will do."

While Cafferty the bartender poured the drinks, Hack turned around and squinted through the smoke to get a good look at the saloon. It was fairly busy for an afternoon, so by dusk it would be full of thirsty men looking for fun and dancing. They'd already seen saloons and two dance halls farther down, and any town with that many drinking establishments could always expect good crowds.

As if he'd been watching for strangers, the town marshal strolled in with a double-barrel twelve gauge in the crook of his arm. He walked straight up to the space between them. "Howdy, boys."

Trying not to look startled, Hack took a sip of beer as the marshal grinned from under a wide handlebar mustache. "Surprised to see me?"

"Surprised to find a lawman standing up right against me."

"Hard to draw a weapon when you're this close."

"I don't intend to draw on you."

"That's good to know. Go ahead, boys. Drink up, and then tell me how come one of you is riding Hank Bohart's horse."

Hack picked up the beer and took a long, deep swallow. "Don't know the name."

"You must have run into him within the last few days. That's his bay out there, next to the black. He was in here a while back with a few other men. Hard cases who make a suspicious living down across the river. You boys ever go to Mexico?"

Hack nodded. "Just got back."

"Why were you down there?"

"Running from a posse."

The marshal digested that answer for a minute, and it was a good thing he couldn't see Luke's face, because his eyes widened as big as silver dollars. The marshal frowned and then threw his head back to laugh loud and long. "Dang, son! That's the best joke I've heard in a year. Posse."

Hack grinned along with him and took another swallow of beer that tasted as good as honey right then. "Sorry, couldn't help myself."

"Marshal Dudley's the name. You go by any handle I'll recognize?"

"Hank." Hack chose a name that was easy to remember. "That's Richard White."

Luke frowned at the name, though they'd ridden with a man by that name some years earlier, before that man found himself dead from a shot in the back after a drunk cowboy'd taken offense to an offhand remark in a San Antonio saloon.

"But you *were* in Mexico. I can smell it on you."

Wondering what Marshal Dudley meant, Hack shrugged. "We were, and ran into Bohart, if that was his name. Him and some other hardcases were threatening kids in a little village down there, and we crossed swords."

"By that, you mean you killed him."

"We did. And them others, but it was a fair fight."

Dudley was silent for several long moments, absorbing the story. Coming to some conclusion that satisfied him, the lawman gave them a half grin. "Well, that's in Mexico, and I don't have any jurisdiction down across the border. Hell, there ain't no law down there nohow. But Bohart, there was four of them in here last week. Y'all killed four in a stand-up disagreement." The sheriff looked at Luke and then back at Hack.

"More'n that, but pure luck is what it was. There was a Mexican down there who took up with us, and he evened up the odds. Got killed in the fracas, though."

"Good story. I have a feller that goes back and forth between here and Escarino. I believe that's probably the town you're talking about. Heard there was a gang operating down there and Bohart and some other men whose names I recognize might be involved in all that."

He watched Hack watch him and shrugged. "What happens on that side of the river is no concern of mine. Bohart was no-account anyway, and it made me nervous every time he came into town."

The marshal flicked a finger, and the bartender brought him a bottle of Scotch whisky. Hack never had a taste for the stuff, but Dudley poured his own shot and sipped on it. "Why, you boys are the second interesting thing that's happened in the past few days."

"An acting troupe come through, or some singer?" Luke always liked a good stage show, and he looked hopeful.

"Naw, nothing like that. A company of Rangers rode in and talked to some old boys who were in here. Those guys left, and not long after, the Rangers took off after 'em."

Neither of them liked hearing that Rangers were so close, but they'd been gone a long time, so surely they weren't after the Long Gang anymore.

The marshal took another light sip of scotch, taking in as much air as liquid. Hot coffee was typically consumed that way, and louder, but neither of them had ever seen a man drink whiskey like that.

Dudley tilted his hat back in a question and looked directly into Hack's eyes. "Y'all been here before? You look familiar."

Hack shook his head, glad those twin twelve-gauge

barrels in the crook of the marshal's arm were more or less pointed into the air. "This is all new territory for us."

Marshal Dudley looked over at Luke. "You don't talk much, Mr. White."

"Not till I've finished my drinks, had a beef steak and a bath. I'll be more talkative tomorrow." Luke tossed off the tequila and closed his eyes in pleasure.

Another sip of scotch. "Where y'all headed after here? You don't look like cowboys, nor men who like to work. You're gun hands, I'll wager." Marshal Dudley reached out as quick as a snake and grabbed Hack's hand that wasn't holding the beer and turned it. He saw the calluses from three years of prison work. "But on the other hand, so to speak, you ain't opposed to it."

"Grew up on a farm in East Texas." He told him the truth, which folks usually realize. "Never liked it, so I left and got in some trouble. Moved on and cut timber for a while, then got a job chasing down outlaws out in the Big Thicket."

"Rough country, that." Dudley sipped more scotch. "I heard tell that more'n one grown man stepped off a trail out there and was never heard from again. Panthers, bears, or starved to death."

"Or wolves, cut to death by wild hogs, killed by renegade Indians or outlaws, or put in a shallow grave by some that don't like to be found." The part of East Texas Hack was talking about ran in a twenty-mile-wide, forty-mile-long strip where people who didn't want to be found could disappear forever if they wanted. The Thicket was also full of Confederates who never surrendered nor agreed with Lee's decision.

"Took a job as a logger for a while, hauled freight, and took work as a lawman."

He didn't mention forming his gang at a young age or robbing banks and an occasional train.

The marshal finished his scotch and studied on Hack's

story for a minute. "Well, good to meet you two, but I'm gonna say this as friendly as I know how."

"What's that?"

"There's something familiar about y'all, but I can't put my finger on it. You might be who you say you are, and I doubt those names are the one's y'all were christened with, so get the hell out of my town when you finish those drinks and don't come back."

Luke raised an eyebrow, and Hack answered for the both of them. "Good advice."

They were out of town, following the freight road once again, when Luke finally broke the silence. "He knew who we are."

"No, he didn't." Hack adjusted the lead on the packhorse. "But he knew *what* we are. That old boy's tough as whang leather, and we need to get away from this place."

"I sure wanted a bed and a bath."

"Those are waiting for us in Barlow."

"That's a ways from here."

"So's everything else right now. There'll be another town up ahead, and probably friendlier than that one." Though it was hot, the air was dry and the ride wasn't as miserable as it could have been.

Despite the tense situation back in town, Hack was just glad to be back in Texas, and he was lost in thoughts of getting that bank money back when they came up parallel to a creek lined with cottonwoods. It was getting late in the day, and the drinks they'd consumed back in town were making him logy because they'd become unaccustomed to liquor in the past three years.

"Let's get back off this road and make camp for the night." He waved an arm toward a thin track leading to where water gurgled. "Sounds like a spring over there, and I'd like a good night's sleep."

Without answering, Luke peeled off the road toward a large thicket of cottonwoods. Hack's good mood faded when he saw the cool, inviting shade was marred by the presence of a canvas-covered schooner. A team of hobbled horses grazed on rich, green grass not far from a small campfire, over which a bubbling pot hung suspended from an iron tripod.

Luke sighed. "People, again."

"We'll just ride on past and find another place upstream. Just wave as we pass."

They rode up slowly, so as not to frighten a young boy and girl squatting by the fire and spooning what looked like stew into their working jaws. Faces dull and without expression, they forked in the hot meat and chewed.

Luke being Luke, he slowed and waved. "Howdy, kids."

A man stepped out from behind the wagon. "You ain't got no call to talk to my kids."

Hack held up both hands. "He's just saying howdy. We're passing through, that's all."

"Me and my woman don't have nothing for you."

"Didn't ask for anything."

The man with a soft, slouchy belly hanging over his waistband had long silver hair pulled back from his forehead. It curled past the collar of his loose white shirt. "The Lord provides for those who help themselves."

Hack never liked for a man to quote the Bible at him, and this one was one of those men who spiked his conversations with Psalms and such as a way to hammer people with religion. He was about to say goodbye when a severe-looking woman also came into view, adjusting her long dress, which swept the grass at her feet.

Luke was close enough to Hack and far enough away

from her to whisper. "That's the most spiteful mouth I've ever seen, all pursed up like a cat's butt."

Hoping she hadn't heard Luke, for she looked like the kind of woman who carried a weapon in her dress, Hack whispered back, "Careful there, boy. She's probably got a straight razor there in her apron." He addressed the man again. "Don't mean to bother you. We're just passing on through."

"Hermann." The woman spoke without revealing her teeth. "These men are in need of enlightenment. They are just the ones I've been praying for."

"You're right, mother." Using his free hand, Hermann unbuttoned his dingy white shirt just above his waistband and did something in the vicinity of his stomach, which moved in a disturbing way that bodies shouldn't. He slipped the hand inside the shirt, and the next thing they knew, a huge triangular head poked out.

Hack almost had a rigor at the sight of a rattler in another man's shirt. Hermann slipped his hand underneath the snake to support its head and pointed it at them in an obscene manner. He wagged it and smiled. "See, the devil himself resides on my person, understanding that I have a power over the unholy."

"Good Lord." Luke stiffened, eyes wide.

The kids quit eating and watched the exchange. Ignoring the horror that was going on just above her head, the girl, who looked to be about five or so, made her unsteady way over to a piece of grass beside the wagon wheel and laid down and immediately went to sleep. It was the strangest thing they'd ever seen, until the boy, who was the same age and looked exactly like her, keeled over on his side, almost falling into the fire, and slept himself.

"Your kids all right?" Hack pointed at the boy, trying to ignore the snake that seemed to be looking right at him and hoping the woman would come over and pull the boy a ways from the hot coals.

"They will be soon." Hermann remained where he was, the snake in one hand and the pistol still pointed at the ground. "Their bellies are full. Would you like to eat with us? We have plenty, don't we, mother?"

The last thing Hack wanted to talk about was food. Being way rougher with the snake than one would have thought with a reptile in his shirt, Hermann stuffed it back inside.

Luke swallowed with a loud, gulping sound.

Seeing the sleeping boy so close to the fire, the woman reached down and pulled him away by one gallus on his overalls. She'd ignored the rattler as if it was the most common thing in the world to handle such a serpent in that way.

"The deacon Hermann Bierhals is right and true in everything he preaches. Just this morning, he said, 'If among you, one of your brothers should become poor, in any of your towns within your land that the Lord is giving you, you shall not harden your heart or shut your hand against your poor brother, but you shall open your hand to him and lend him sufficient for his need, whatever it may be.'"

Luke surprised the hell out of his partner. "That's Deuteronomy. Heard it more'n once growing up."

For the first time since they'd stopped, the man's face lit up. "That's right! You must be a believer." He closed his eyes and rubbed the snake's coils inside his shirt. "'Take care lest there be an unworthy thought in your heart and you say, "The seventh year, the year of release is near," and your eye looks grudgingly on your poor brother, and you give him nothing, and he cry to the Lord against you, and you be guilty of sin, as we are.'"

Luke's head snapped toward Hack. He'd heard something alarming as the man continued to drone on in an unexpressive voice, repeating by rote what he'd memorized.

"'You shall give to him freely, and your heart shall not be grudging when you give to him, because He will bless you in all your work and in all that you undertake. Therefore I command you, you shall open wide your hand to your brother, to the needy and to the poor, in your land.'"

Hermann opened his eyes. "That's why Mother and I are here. This evil land has been fallow for too long, full of cutthroats and savages, likely such as yourselves, and we are here to accept any tithes that might be offered so that we can fertilize and water this country in our God-given way and make this inhospitable frontier a place as close to the Garden of Eden as we can."

For the first time since Hack had known him, Luke surprised him so much that he didn't know what to think. "Proverbs. 'Do not say, I will repay evil. Wait for the Lord, and He will deliver you.'"

Hermann's eyes narrowed, and his knuckles whitened on the grip of that little pistol. Hack didn't know what was going on, but he didn't like it. He leaned forward and rested his right arm on the saddle horn, putting his gun hand near the butt of that cross-draw Colt.

The woman knelt beside the sleeping boy and dipped her hand in the pocket of her apron. "A year ago, Brother Hermann had a vision. He has been blessed with the charge to make this world a better place. An angel appeared to him one night as the fire burned low and said, 'Therefore I tell you, whatever you ask in prayer, believe that you have received it, and it will be yours.'"

Hermann nodded in agreement. "And I'd asked for a vision and it came. Romans 12:1. 'Therefore, I urge you, brothers and sisters, in view of God's mercy, to offer their bodies as a living sacrifice, holy and pleasing to God—this is your true and proper worship.'"

Luke drew his Colt. "You got that wrong, friend. You've twisted it around."

Hermann smiled. "How so, brother?"

"It reads *your bodies*, not *theirs*."

Hermann's pistol came up, but Luke fired three times in a roll of thunder, the slugs taking Hermann in the chest. Red bloomed on his white shirt as he staggered sideways, knocking the kneeling woman off-balance.

A butcher knife flew from her hand as she fell sideways and caught herself. Screaming like a panther, she scrabbled toward the gun Hermann had dropped and Hack's big Walker Colt roared. The bullet ripped through both sides of her chest and she fell and lay still.

They saw the horror of that snake moving in Hermann's shirt at the same time and emptied their revolvers into that nasty, unseen thing that writhed and twisted in death.

Kicking his horse, Hack raced to the back of the wagon in case there was someone in there with a gun, but it was only full of boxes. Seeing it was all clear, he turned to Luke. "What'n hell was that all about? I didn't understand a thing y'all were talking about."

"They were going to sacrifice these kids for some crazy idea that nut came up with. I wouldn't be surprised if they've done it before. These kids are drugged. Laudanum, I bet, or some such."

"What was all that Bible talk? You make that up?"

Luke holstered his pistol and swung down. "Nope. My uncle was a preacher, and mama made me learn Bible verses when I was little, instead of making me go to church."

"I didn't know that."

"You didn't need to know."

Movement caught Hack's attention. A pair of mules hobbled on the backside of the wagon stood almost on top of two people lying on the ground, bound back to back. One was a man with a badge on his coat, the other a woman who was sleeping as soundly as the kids on the opposite side.

They both had scarves tied around their mouths, but Hack recognized the man when he raised his head and looked at him.

"Well. Howdy, Billy Lightning."

His head dropped back to the ground and his eyes closed.

CHAPTER 31

The company of Rangers kept up a steady, ground-eating lope on their way west, Captain Bookbinder leading the way. His men were smart enough not to ride directly behind him in the dust kicked up by his horse's hooves and were scattered to the sides, keeping ever-watchful eyes on their surroundings.

Their pace was intended to catch up with the man they were after and therefore to take him to the nearest strong limb for an oak hanging, but their progress was impeded by two men walking their mounts slowly, studying the ground below.

Hearing the hooves and likely fearing Comanches, the two whirled their horses and dropped down behind them, leveling Winchesters at the company of lawmen. Noting their expertise and quick reflexes, Bookbinder raised a hand and stopped as his men spread out in a well-practiced skirmish line.

"Hold your fire, men. We're Texas Rangers." He spoke loud enough for the company to hear. "Easy, boys. Don't shoot the civilians unless we're fired upon."

One man, slightly taller than the other, spoke down the length of his rifle, which was aimed at Bookbinder's chest. His eyes were hard as stone, and the creases in his face told of years in the sun, despite the big hat with the curled brim on the right side.

"Move closer so I can see that badge!"

Empty hands still out, Bookbinder kneed the horse forward. "I'll take this only so long, sir. I am Captain Bookbinder, Texas Ranger, and don't intend to stare down that rifle any longer."

The stranger exchanged glances with the other man, who favored him to a T. His blue eyes were full of distrust and had the cold look of fury. "We're not outlaws nor road agents. You're holding us back."

Bookbinder rode closer, noting their demeanor. "Holding you back from what?"

"Going after my kids." The man with blue eyes lowered his rifle. "Name's Oscar Tisdale. This is my brother, Ridge. My children have been stole, and we're going after them."

"Stole by whom?"

Ridge stepped around his horse and lowered the Winchester in his hands. "We don't know for sure, but they were taken from our ranch two days ago. His are twins. A boy and girl. Six. And we suspect a traveling preacher."

"Preachers don't steal kids."

Oscar joined his brother. "This one did. Crazy as a Bessie bug."

Bookbinder noted they had the presence and demeanor of men who'd done killing before. "Have you found their tracks for sure?"

"We have." The Rangers gathered around them as the two ranchers explained. "The preacher's horse led us to a low-water creek up north of our place, and it took us a day and a half to work out he'd gone first one way, then doubled back and went the other. He's experienced in criminal behavior and has evaded people before, and we lost his tracks in rough country. We found that he didn't have the kids, and that's

why he could move so fast, so we circled back to a camp
where we first heard of them.

"That's when we found a grave." Oscar gathered himself
and swallowed. "Thought it was the kids, but when we dug
down, it turned out to be a boy about fourteen years old.
Field dressed and cut from throat to gizzard."

"You sure it wasn't Indians?"

"Comanches don't take time to bury. This was a grave not
expected to be found, but it was our luck to stumble across
that bare patch of disturbed soil. Now we know what kind of
people have my kids, and it gave us a new starting point with
a set of wagon tracks."

"You sure it's the right one?"

"I am. The right rear hub is bad, and the wheel wiggles.
We learned that back in Wattstown, where he'd stopped to get
it fixed. That's how we know he's the right one. A preacher.
Got it from the blacksmith."

"That's a lot of suspicion." Bookbinder didn't disbelieve
the man, but he always wanted all the information he could
gather before going after an outlaw.

"Ridge worked it out and suspected that his wife had the
children and was hightailing it west while we were off stringing along behind a decoy. We're about two days behind them
now, but come hell or high water, we'll find 'em."

Bookbinder considered the ranchers, who looked perfectly capable of the trials in front of them. He couldn't abide
the idea of people stealing and murdering kids. He addressed
the youngest Ranger with them.

"Mr. Gatewood, please return to town and post a telegram
to Austin telling them we have temporarily abandoned our
pursuit of the Long Gang and have taken up an urgent mission after a murderous preacher who has stole children. We
will send further information when we have captured and
hanged this evil man and his . . . wife."

The Ranger hesitated, looking at the angry ranchers.

"Go on, now." Bookbinder waved a hand, slightly annoyed that the youngster hadn't immediately done his bidding. "A good Ranger such as yourself can catch up to us by tomorrow."

The Ranger spun his mount and took off back toward the last town they'd passed through.

Without another word, Oscar and Ridge Tisdale swung back in the saddle and kicked their horses into a lope, followed by Captain Bookbinder and his men.

CHAPTER 32

Now Hack and Luke were saddled with two kids who were lost in the dreams usually implemented by opium. It wasn't the kind normally peddled by the celestials in those smoking dens. This was the patent medicine that could be purchased from any apothecary or dry goods store.

Luke looked down at a bottle in his hand that read CREST BRAND. "I've seen this poison sold by those charlatans who go from town to town, calling themselves doctor this and doctor that."

"Lots of times, it's sold for female troubles." Those familiar bottles were common, and Hack remembered an old aunt when he was a kid who drank the stuff like it was water. Out back of her house was a ditch where she pitched empty cans and bottles she couldn't reuse, and there were dozens, if not hundreds of the little flat bottles out there.

They'd put the kids on a quilt pallet beside the wagon, hoping the fresh air would help them sleep. The bottle Luke held was almost empty, and Hack was worried about how much that crazy preacher had given them.

They'd untied Billy Lightning and the woman, who were as disoriented as drunks. Carrying them around to the shade, they laid them on quilt pallets and waited. The activity woke Billy and he puked onto the ground.

He spat and crawled a distance away from his regurgitation. "Good to see you boys are alive and kicking."

"We're better'n you at the moment." Luke watched the woman breathe heavily in her sleep. "What happened to y'all?"

"Had some coffee those two made." Billy started. "Where are they?"

"Shaking hands with the devil." Hack went to the fire and picked up the coffeepot. Giving the contents a sniff, he poured the coffee onto the edge of the fire and refilled the pot with fresh water after rinsing it out. He came back and went about rebuilding the fire. "I'd suspect you'd have tasted it in the coffee."

"We did, but I thought it was something like chicory they added." Billy swallowed as if keeping his stomach down. "It was enough to take our senses, then they held our noses and made us drink that nasty stuff. Saw 'em spoon it into the kids, too. I think they have a case of it in the wagon."

The woman snored softly, and now they knew why. "So the kids didn't get all of this."

It took a moment for Billy's eyes to focus. "Not if that's the bottle they used on us. I remember seeing it was half empty when they poured it into Gussie."

Hearing her name somehow made the woman familiar. "Why're you wearing a Ranger badge, and where'd you two get together?"

"Long story." Billy retched again and spat.

"We have time to hear it."

"Where'd you say those two are who did this to us?"

"Killed 'em and drug 'em off a ways."

"Smart work." Billy was coming back to himself. "Did you kill that pet snake of his? I don't want that thing crawling around here. He could let it go and call it, and it would come back like a dog."

"It's dead, too."

He laid back and closed his eyes. "What a nightmare."

A pot sitting to the side of the fire contained stew that smelled good when Hack lifted the lid. Not trusting what might have been in it, Hack tipped the little cast-iron bean pot over into the fire and took it over to the water barrel on the side of the wagon. Taking a dipper from its hanger on the side, he poured water into the pot and took it back to the smoking fire to boil for a minute and steam out what was left.

Luke came out from under the tight canvas. "There's ten bottles of Dr. Edward Depew's poison in there, along with enough provisions for half a dozen people. Flour, beans, beef, and best of all"—he held up a cloth bag—"about a hundred dollars squirrelled away."

He weighed the hard cash in his hand. "Oh, yeah, there's this, too." He reached back into the wagon. "Arbuckle beans and a grinder. Fresh coffee, boys!"

While Billy regained his wits, they cooked some supper and caught up, trading stories about their trek to Texas after being separated by the Rurales back in Mexico. It hadn't been that long, but it seemed like a year to all three men. The kids were still asleep, but Gussie finally stirred, looking like she'd been on a two-week drunk.

She groaned, struggled to her feet, and moving slowly, made her way out of sight for a few minutes. Returning, she settled down between the little ones, who were still asleep on their own pallets by the wagon, first rubbing the boy's head and then the girl's.

Her voice through the long dark hair hanging in her face came soft and low, like the old women Hack grew up around. She even had the same accent. "How could anyone be mean to sweet little things like these two?"

"It's an evil world." Hack sipped at the first cup of hot coffee he'd held in years. A drop ran down his ragged whiskers, and he wiped it away. "We're all lucky to have lived past their age."

Billy Lightning rubbed his head. "Lordy, this is worse'n a whiskey drunk."

Luke sat by the fire, cleaning his guns. "I'm looking forward to a whiskey drunk."

"That'll be after Barlow." Hack hadn't meant to speak the town's name aloud, but he was tired and forgot Gussie, who hadn't seemed to hear. He covered it up as best as possible. "Ma'am, I know you've been traveling with ol' Lightning Rod here, but once you and these kids are back on your feet, you can't keep going with us. Next time we come close to a town, we're gonna drop all y'all off, and you're on your own."

She blinked slow as if it hurt to think. "I'm not their mama."

"No, but if you show up with them and find the town marshal, he'll know what to do. You sure they didn't belong to them two we shot?"

"No." Billy moved slow to the coffeepot. He picked up a china cup with flowers on the side. It looked out of place there in the woods, but he poured himself a cup and sat back, holding it in both hands after finding the handle was too small for even his slender fingers.

"I roused up once and heard them talking about getting away from a ranch back there a ways." He inclined his head to the southeast. "They'd stopped by a spring creek for water, and the kids came along, looking for frogs. They sweet-talked them, and that scorpion of a woman tricked 'em into drinking something sweet and they went to sleep.

"She took off with them in the wagon while Hermann wiped the tracks and made an easy trail to follow in the other direction, then he turned back and caught up with her the next day. They were laughing about how easy it was and that it was all because the Lord wanted blood sacrifices."

He stopped and looked into his cup, as if seeing the past in the surface of the steaming coffee. His eyes were dark and haunted. "They've done this before, and from what they were saying, there's a trail of little bodies from here all the way back to Natchitoches." He pronounced the Louisiana town the way native Texans and Louisianans do, saying "Nak-a-desh."

Working out the problem in his head, Hack scratched at the underside of his jaw, wondering if there was shaving gear in the wagon. "Gussie, you know that if we showed up with you and those kids, they'd think it was some of us who stole them. But if you went in, telling them the truth about what happened, they'll be more inclined to believe you and not come after us."

"I don't like to be used."

"None of us do." Hack took another sip, savoring the rich taste. "But that's the way it has to be."

"I don't know how to drive a team."

He pondered her statement. Not everyone could handle a team, and if a pair of horses realized there was an inexperienced person behind them, they'd take the bit in their teeth and run, possibly killing her and the kids.

Billy came to her aid. "Look, we'll all ride together until we come to a town big enough for a marshal. We tie my horse to the back of the wagon, and while you boys wait a ways off, I can go in at night and tie them up in front of the jail and ride back, and we can get back on the road.

"After I'm gone, you and the kids can sleep in the wagon, and when the town wakes up in the morning, y'all can talk to the marshal. If it's a big enough place, they can wire back down the line and find out who those two belong to, and if not, they'll send a post."

Wrinkling her brow, Gussie continued to rub the little girl's forehead. "What happens to me, then?"

"You make your way. Find a husband, settle down, have kids."

"I never had a husband. I was a prostitute when I met

Billy. The Ranger he was with killed my boss, and I took up with him."

Luke and Hack turned their attention to Billy. Luke grinned. "So that's how come you have that badge. You're the only person I know who can kill a Texas Ranger and wind up in the presence of a good-natured whore."

"I didn't kill the Ranger," Billy said.

Gussie didn't blink at the harsh word. "That's what I said I was last month. Now I have a chance to do something different."

"Sure." Billy was enthusiastic. "I bet you can get a job in town. You're pretty, and anybody who needs help will be quick to take you on."

She gave him a sad smile. "You don't know nothing about being a woman. That was my idea when I first came west, but nobody wants to hire a woman who isn't married or a schoolteacher. A woman shows up unescorted in a town, and the local tongue wag start in from the first day. Single women have it hard, Billy."

He looked confused. "Well, you can't ride with us."

Gussie cocked a knee and rested her forearm on it in an unladylike way. "Why not?"

Hack didn't want to hear that kind of talk. "Because you can't, and you ain't been invited. We're not men you'd want to ride with."

"What kind of men are you?"

"Ones that won't be sucking air in ten years, or likely even five. We don't have houses or farms or ranches or jobs. Miss Gussie, you have fallen in with thieves. That's what we are and what we'll always be."

Luke carved a mouthful of beef off a spit over the fire. In addition to being kidnappers and murderers, the so-called religious couple were also cattle rustlers who butchered their beef as they traveled. The meat was wrapped in an old flour sack, and it was like finding a Christmas present. They'd forked a roast over the coals and had been working on it as it cooked, cutting off the done parts on the outside as the thick meat continued to cook toward the middle.

Luke chewed for a minute and swallowed. "You know, Hack, I wouldn't mind riding with a woman."

"Whoa now, I know what you have in mind, and it's not gonna happen."

Gussie chuckled. "Luke, I just said I was out of the business. I don't want to have nothing more to do with men in that way for a good long time. I'd like to go with y'all for a while just for something to do."

"We stay in the saddle for hours, days even." Hack wanted to cut that line of talk off as soon as possible. "We rob and sometimes shoot people, and we aren't the James or Younger gangs."

He was referring to the penny dreadfuls that made the bank robbers out to be modern-day Robin Hoods. In those pages, the two families stole and gave the money to the poor, but the truth was they rode and stole for nothing but vengeance and the gold. Those on the owlhoot trail knew the truth, because they were all the same.

Hack had the bad feeling that he wasn't getting through to her. "We sometimes have to shoot our way out of situations, and I wouldn't want a woman to get hurt."

"So you're fearful of me getting hurt. What else are you scared of?"

"Nothing." Hack's voice came soft, but hard. "If I'm afraid of anything, I kill it. That solves the problem."

He considered the shocked look on her face as she pulled a strand of dark hair behind one ear. "Think about this," she suggested. "No one expects a woman to rob banks. I can walk in while y'all watch the street and stick a gun into a teller's face as slick as you please, and then with the cash in hand, I can stroll right out that door, and we can all ride away together."

The idea sounded appealing in a strange way, but there were foreseeable problems. He was taken with her in a strange way but was doing his best to avoid those entanglements. "That'd work once, twice maybe, before word got around about a woman robbing banks."

"There are trains, too. There are lots of scenarios where a woman can be of use."

Hack shook his head. "I know men. Before long, there'd be some he-ing and she-ing, and then somebody'd get shot or cut over you. We've been fine with it being just us."

Billy's stomach must have settled down because he looked much better. "Hack, if I get a vote, I wouldn't mind her riding with us. She's been a good partner up to this point."

"Which brings us up to where we are right now." Hack wanted to lead them off that line of discussion. "Just how did you two end up knotted together and unconscious?"

Billy looked ashamed. "It was easier than you think. We came up on those two butchering a cow. Said it was their milk cow that broke a leg on the trail and had to shoot her. I'd worked with a butcher when I was a kid and offered to help, and they took me up on it. We'd finished, and they asked us to eat with them. That was two days ago, and this is where we've been since."

The little boy stirred, mumbling nonsense.

Gussie laid her hand on his shoulder, and he went back under. She brought them back to the conversation Hack was getting tired of. "Look, I don't beg for nothin'. Never have, but I don't have anything to go back to. I'm good with a pistol . . ."

"What?" Billy's mouth fell open in shock.

"You never asked if I could shoot, but I can probably hit better than you, and maybe even Hack and Luke." Dimples appeared at the corners of her mouth. "I'll be a great asset, and if you decide I'm not, then y'all can ride off and leave me. How's that?"

Frankly, Hack liked the look of those little dimples and the way her bottom lip rolled out in that grin. But that fact alone told him what kind of trouble might be waiting for them all down the road.

Nevertheless, he shrugged and gave in. "On two conditions. You're Billy's responsibility, and if he gets killed, and there's always that possibility, you're done. You understand?"

She nodded and started to comment, and he cut her off. "And if things change between y'all, or us, and we ride off, you'll stay behind like you're told."

She laughed. "I've never been good at doing what I'm told, neither."

CHAPTER 33

Halfway to his destination in Barlow, Gabe Santana walked out of the blacksmith shop in Sweeten and stopped at the sight of his old friend Two-Horses and a young woman-child assisting an old man down a busy, covered boardwalk.

Sweeten was close enough to the frontier that the sight of a half-breed assisting an elderly gentleman didn't seem too out of place. Further west, any man on the street would shoot the Comanche on sight, and back East, he'd be gazed upon with interest but little understanding. In the busy, growing town, anything was to be expected.

Instead of rushing over, Santana backed against a board-and-batten wall to watch and see what might happen. Few turned on the busy street, as if the sight of an Indian and a comely woman helping an old man walk might be common.

But it only takes one person to stir up trouble, and that came from a bearded, drunk hide hunter who staggered out of a saloon across the street. Dressed almost in rags and probably stinking to high heaven, he somehow saw them through bleary eyes and crossed the street on unsteady legs.

He drew a revolver from his belt. "I'm tougher'n any man on this street! My mama was a panther and my daddy was a grizzly, and I fought my way to where I'm standing with just my knife and pistol, and I can prove it drunk or sober!" He squinted. "I believe I'm gonna shoot me an Indian."

Another hide hunter with greasy hair down past his shoulders came out behind him. His beard was tangled and clotted with unthinkable material nasty enough to make a buzzard gag. "Come back in here, Blackjack, and let's finish this bottle. I'd rather drink inside than out here on the street, and besides, I ain't in the mood to kill nobody today!"

"Indian!" Blackjack focused on Two-Horses and stopped and waved his pistol. "Step away from that old man and girl. You savages don't belong in a civilized town. I've killed a passel of y'all and don't intend to stop until all you murderin' savages are wiped out!"

As people on the street stopped to watch the exchange, not caring if anyone shot the half-breed or not, the woman pulled the blind man to the side and put herself between them. Two-Horses stopped and faced the drunk in the middle of the street. Men and horses fell back to give them room, fully expecting a shooting.

"I'm only half Comanche, and you should stop this now." Two-Horses spoke clearly and crossed the street in a steady walk, heading straight for the hide hunter. It was always his way to confront trouble. "Leave me alone!"

"Don't address me in such a familiar manner!"

A different voice came from an onlooker in the crowd across the street. "Shoot that Indian so I can pass! I don't have all day to wait for y'all to palaver out in the middle of the street."

"I believe I will." Blackjack cocked his pistol and raised it, but Two-Horses was too close. He swung with all he had while maintaining his pace, and his fist cracked against the hide hunter's jaw. The man staggered back and swung at Two-Horses with the revolver, instead of shooting.

Two-Horses grabbed the man's wrist and twisted it back

against the tendons until the drunk grunted in pain and the pistol dropped. Not angry, but determined to end the conflict, Two-Horses hit him again square in the nose. Blood spurted, and the Indian followed up with a third punch in the same place.

Blood pouring from both nostrils, and with his nose lying against his cheek, the hide hunter's eyes rolled back and he collapsed.

Two-Horses kicked the unfired pistol away and turned back to rejoin his companions. Blackjack's filthy partner snatched a pistol from his waistband and leveled it at the Comanche's back. "You won't be fighting dirty like that again, Indian!"

Santana had enjoyed the action until then, but he didn't intend to let some skinner shoot his friend in the back. Shooting him in the front in a standup fight was different, but he wouldn't tolerate a bushwhacking.

He drew his own revolver and was about to pull the trigger when the woman produced a weapon from the folds of her dress and fired. The bullet missed, but it startled the buffalo hunter so much he stumbled against the saloon wall.

Two-Horses whirled and charged across the street, hands outstretched. The skinner pushed himself away from the wall and fired. The first bullet missed, but he was drawing down on Two-Horses, who was still too far away.

Santana drew the pistol he'd taken from the Mexican Rurale and fired. The slug whistled across the street and struck Blackjack's buddy in the right side of his chest, punching through the dirty material of a vest and shirt and deep into one lung. He staggered, raised the pistol a second time, and Santana shot again.

Seeing his opponent fall, Two-Horses paused at the boardwalk and looked over his shoulder at the woman across the street. "I thought there was only one round in that pistol!"

The dark-haired gal held it up. "There was. I missed with it."

As men gathered around to check on the still bodies, Two-Horses looked around and spotted Santana thumbing fresh shells into the cylinder of his revolver. "Why, lookee there."

Santana snapped the cylinder back into place. "That does it for this town. We need to go."

Two-Horses nodded and waved at the girl. "I got you this far. Good luck in finding a place to die, old man!" He trotted back across the street and jumped on a horse that was presumably his.

She put a hand against Boston's chest to make him stay against the wall and out of the way, then stepped out in front of a wagon so suddenly the driver had to rein hard and his team reared. "So help me, if you leave us here, I'll hang your hide on my wall!"

Two-Horses laughed. "You don't have a wall to hang anything at all. Find your own balance with old Boston there, and your scale will weigh true for you both!"

She screamed in anger and frustration. "What does that mean?"

"I don't know." Two-Horses saw Santana ride out of the livery on a big bay. "I just heard Hack say it once. Adios!"

Two-Horses rode to the livery and joined Santana to race out of town before the citizens of Sweeten could gather their wits.

As townspeople gathered around the dead body of the bearded hide hunter on the boardwalk, his friend who started it all rose with a groan. The girl flipped a hand at the wagon driver who was giving her the business for spooking his team and turned to Boston.

"It's just you and me now."

Boston rubbed his forehead. "He wasn't gonna stay with us nohow. What town are we in?"

"Sweeten."

He grinned and spoke in his old, weak voice. "Let's go to the bank."

"Why?"

"'Cause I used to live here before I sold my store and went to Mexico. There's enough money in that vault to take care of us for a good, long while. That is, if no one's robbed it in the last ten years."

CHAPTER 34

Billy and Gussie's plan turned out to work better than they'd imagined, although in an entirely different way. With the groggy kids still suffering the effects of the laudanum and dozing in the back of the wagon, they rode into the town of Sweeten at midnight to find it was buzzing with excitement.

Their plan to get in without being seen went out the window when a street full of people saw him driving the wagon and Gussie sitting in the seat beside them. They pulled to a stop in front of the marshal's office to find a crowd lit by torches dipped in coal oil and demanding a hanging.

Billy wrapped the reins around the wagon's brake and stepped down while Gussie remained high in the seat, watching the activity. He circled the group of liquored-up men in the street and knocked on the marshal's door.

A gruff voice came through loud and clear. "Get out of here! Y'all ain't hanging nobody tonight. We'll have a trial in the morning, and then these two'll hang!"

"Don't matter none to me." Billy raised his voice to be heard and stepped back from the door. "Hang who you want, but I have a pair of dead bodies in the back of this wagon, along with a set of twins they stole."

Those nearby quieted, and a hush fell over the crowd as

they stopped to listen. Billy shifted his stance to see the men who were studying him and Gussie. A low whistle came from one of them, and several mean chuckles followed.

Billy rested his hand on the pistol in his holster and met the gaze of a man holding a torch. The looked that passed between them caused the stranger to back up a step, and Billy nodded.

Several heartbeats later, the crowd parted to reveal a marshal peeking through the cracked doorway with the muzzles of a short coach gun leveled at the crowd. "Back up another step. You there on the wagon. Is there anybody close to you?"

"Depends on how close you mean. There's a bunch of armed drunks in the middle of the street and my wife here with me."

The door opened wider, and it was a good thing, because the marshal's mustache needed the space to pass. "Hands up. Disarm yourself and come in."

"Nope." Instead of doing as he was told, Billy turned and handed the pistol to Gussie. "Shoot the first one who bothers you."

She took the weapon and nodded, marking the crowd with her gaze. Sensing she was more than capable of using the revolver in her hand, they milled around and then drifted a few feet away.

Climbing down, Billy held his hands up. "I'm unarmed and not with this bunch out here. I have business with you that don't involve a rope, not yet, at least."

"Come on in, then." The lawman backed away, and Billy stepped inside the closed-up jailhouse, which reeked of coal oil fumes from half a dozen lamps turned as bright as possible without smoking up the chimneys.

The next thing he knew, the bore of a pistol was against the back of his head. Someone had been behind the door, and Billy cursed himself for not checking.

"Pat him down, Daniel."

The man Billy assumed was a deputy did just that. "Nothing else. Felt a folding knife in his pocket."

"I ain't worried about no jackknife." The marshal's mustache jumped as he worked his lips, thinking. "All right, boy. What's your story? Who you got dead in that wagon out there?"

"Some crazy feller who called himself a preacher and his wife." Billy jerked a thumb at the door and lowered his hands. "Like I said, they kidnapped two little kids and were gonna kill them in some kind of sacrifice, I'll allow. Us, too. They fed us all laudanum, but I come out of it and shot 'em both and now we're here."

The marshal lowered the shotgun and squinted at him with one eye. "How do you know they was gonna kill anyone?"

Billy told him the story, what they'd heard from the crazy couple, all their preaching, the snake, the trail of bodies back to Louisiana, and the kids they took. He left out the part where Hack and Luke arrived and did the shooting.

Putting the shotgun in a rack behind his desk, the marshal went over to his desk. "You're making sense. I got a telegram from a Texas Ranger somewhere southeast of here, saying they were on the trail of a couple who took some rancher's kids." He stopped and stared up. "Hey, you might be that couple they're after."

"Could be, but we ain't. When them kids wake up, they'll tell you the truth."

Billy hoped they'd be long gone by then, for the kids might fill in the rest of the story if they could recall what went on around them.

"The ones you want are cold in the back of the wagon. If you want proof, why don't you go out there and open old Hermann's shirt. His pet snake is still in there, but it quit moving an hour or so ago. Snakes don't die as quick as they ought to."

The marshal watched Billy for several long moments, then nodded. "All right. Says here in the telegram it was an older couple, so that leaves you out. So what do you want me to do?"

"Take those kids off our hands. We aren't parents. And do something with those bodies before they start to stink."

"You expect the county to pay for their burial?"

"I don't expect anything. I'd already drug them off for the buzzards, but then decided we oughta bring them in and explain what happened so no one'll think we're traveling murderers. We're headed west, not east, so you can keep them kids here until the Rangers or their parents show up."

"The kids' dad is riding with them, along with an uncle."

"Good. Then we'll bring the twins in here and be done with it."

"Don't you want to wait and see if there's a reward?"

The thought of money made Billy pause, but that would take too long, and if Rangers showed up, they might remember wanted posters from long ago. "No, thanks. I didn't do this for the money, but to do what's right."

"Harry, go out there and bring those kids in. Then run over to the Reverend Hart's house and wake him up. Him and Miss Pearl'll take care of the twins until their daddy gets here." The deputy started for the door and paused when the marshal kept issuing orders. "After that, go get the undertaker and have him come fetch the bodies. Tell him about that snake in the man's shirt, so he don't have a heart attack when he sees it, but I want to come over and see them people at daylight."

The deputy set his hat and cracked the door. Seeing the crowd was still well away from the jail, he went out and closed the door. The marshal came along behind and dropped a thick two-by-four across two hammered brackets to lock them in.

He turned. "Name's Marshal Black."

Billy nodded. "Brenner. Matt Brenner." He cursed himself for the name. Hack had always used an alias that was a real person, so it would be easy to remember, and here he was coming up with a name that came out of nowhere that he'd be hard-pressed to recall come daylight.

"Well, Mr. Brenner, how about you set down and we visit for a while."

"I'd rather not." Thunder rumbled outside, announcing a coming storm. Billy glanced up at the plank ceiling and changed his mind. "On second thought, maybe my wife could come inside until this rain passes. I don't like lightning."

"That'd be fine."

A knock at the door was followed by the deputy's soft voice. "Got the kids and the missus."

Marshal Black took down the bar lock and cracked the door. The deputy came in, leading the scared little boy. The girl had Gussie's hand in a strong grip.

Billy put an awkward hand on her shoulder. "Gussie, come on in . . . honey. We need to wait out this storm."

She nodded and pointed at two chairs beside a door across from the front, inset with a small, barred hole at face level. "Come on, kids. Y'all sit over there. Marshal, you oughta crack a window or something to get some fresh air in here or somebody's gonna fall out from all these fumes."

"I would, but the old boys out there might stick a pistol in to shoot one of us."

"Either way, you'll be dead by morning." Gussie crossed over to a boarded-up window and opened it up, fanning the shutter to move the air. "They won't shoot a woman, and get me a pair of scissors to trim these wicks."

Not knowing what to say, the marshal opened a desk drawer and rummaged around for her required instruments.

Obedient and silent, the kids went to the chair and sat. Only a second later, the boy spoke up. "Can I have a drink out of that water bucket over there?"

The deputy left again to do Marshal Black's bidding, and he answered the boy. "Go ahead on." He found the scissors and handed them to Gussie as he returned to drop the plank back across the door again.

The water bucket sat on a high shelf, making it difficult for the boy to reach the dipper. Billy crossed the room and filled it for him. Instead of coming over, the boy remained where he was. Billy passed the door leading back to where he presumed the cells were located and glanced through bars covering the one-foot-wide opening.

He was right. There were two cells within view, containing one prisoner each. One was Two-Horses, and the other, Santana. They were standing at the bars, holding on with both hands and watching the door. When they saw Billy's face peering at the opening, both men grinned, and it was all he could do not to show his surprise.

CHAPTER 35

Sweeten should have been a town asleep at that time of the night, but to Hack, it looked like they were having some kind of celebration. He and Luke sat their horses at the end of the street, which was lit by yellow light spilling out from several watering holes. The two packhorses snorted and bobbed their heads, not liking all the activity.

It was after midnight, and lightning flashed not far past the treetops. Even though they expected to see the saloons open and slowing down in the early morning hours, they were surprised by the agitated people carrying torches who milled around the middle of the street.

Halfway down the drag, Billy pulled the team to a stop and exchanged words with someone in the crowd before they parted to provide a clear path to the marshal's office. He stepped down from the wagon, but from where Hack watched, he couldn't see what was going on.

Luke tilted his hat back as he did when thinking and scratched his ear. "Is this July fourth or some local holiday?"

Hack was as confused as his partner. "I have no idea what the date is, but I don't see any bunting or decorations, so I reckon not."

"Well, something's going on, and them torches spell trouble if you ask me."

"They're in front of the marshal's office, so it looks to me like they're not happy about whoever he has in there." The crowd calmed for a minute, and Luke adjusted the pistol in his holster. "Wonder if Billy told them about those bodies in the back."

"Maybe, but no one seems to be interested in him." Hack nudged the black forward and Luke fell in beside him. By the time they closed in on the Silver Dollar saloon, directly across from the wagon, Billy was inside.

Dismounting, they left the horses at the well-chewed rail in front. Hack was just finished with his slipknot when the marshal's door opened and a man came out and went directly to the wagon. He spoke to Gussie and helped her down.

"Deputy," Luke said.

They circled around to the back of the covered wagon, and Gussie saw them by the rail. She didn't let on she knew them and leaned in to the back of the wagon.

A pale face appeared in the darkness, and then another. She helped one of the twins out, while the deputy lifted the other over the rail. He then followed her and the kids to the door. He knocked, and it opened and they went inside.

Lightning flashed closer to town, and the wind freshened. Luke set his hat. "Storm coming."

"I can feel the rain. Let's get inside and see if we can find a place to watch the street."

Luke chuckled. "Billy won't be back out until this cloud blows over."

Watching the crowd disperse in response to the coming rain, Hack laughed. "Let's see if we can get a table before all those guys fill this place up."

They pushed through not a moment too soon. Wind gusted down the street, blowing grit in behind them. Several tables scattered around the big room were filled with card players, but two beside the fly-specked front window were empty, probably because no one wanted to sit so close to where passersby could look in and see the game and the cards they held.

Luke pointed. "Four chairs there. I'll hold a couple if you'll get me a beer."

They'd already agreed to forgo the hard stuff, just in case they needed to keep their wits about them. Luke sat facing the door, where he could see out. Two bartenders were busy keeping up with the demands of those coming in from the weather, but the youngest one, who didn't look much older than fifteen, saw Hack find a place at the end of the bar and came over. "Whiskey?"

"Two beers."

"Four bits apiece."

He dug the coins from his pocket and placed them on the bar. The barkeep's gaze ran from his waist up. "You hire on with the Double J, or another place?"

"Just passing through."

"There's a lot of that, but more folks are staying since the railroad's coming through. You might find a job with one of the crews."

"I don't intend to swing a hammer for a few pennies a day." Hack picked up the beers, remembering three years in Purgatorio with no pay at all. "Done that."

"You wear that pistol like it's familiar. I heard the marshal is looking for another deputy."

Hack almost laughed, but he bit it off when the older bartender came over and spoke to his associate. "Son, I know you're trying to be friendly to our customers, but there's certain things you don't bring up to a man. Go over yonder and pour J.W. a whiskey."

The youngster he presumed was the older bartender's

son raised an eyebrow. He wiped at an invisible spot on the bar top and moved down to serve the men bellied up there.

"Sorry about that." The older man gave Hack a friendly smile. "My boy there, he don't have a lot of bark on him, and he's way too nosey for his own good. I really don't want him in here slinging whiskey, but I got caught short tonight. I'm sending him over to the Double J tomorrow and see if they'll hire him to muck stalls until he can learn to cowboy."

He nodded. "No harm done, and that's good honest work. He better get to working out there pretty soon, though. Most of those old boys who're riding the grub line started working cows when they was still hanging onto their mama's skirts."

The barkeep leaned in. "That's the problem. His mama won't hardly turn him loose. She's madder'n an old wet hen right now as it is, since I pulled him in tonight." He slid the coins back across. "Beer's on the house for the impropriety."

Hack slid them back. "Many thanks, but I pay my way."

The barkeep bobbed his head, and the change disappeared into a big hairy hand. "Good luck."

Hack joined Luke at the table and passed him one of the mugs. Lightning flashed outside, and raindrops rattled on the saloon's roof. Thunder followed, shaking the rafters.

"That deputy's running around like a chicken with its head cut off." Luke sipped his beer. "Came and went. Got the undertaker, who looks like he just crawled out of bed. They loaded the bodies in another wagon and hauled them away. Didn't act like it was much more than just another job."

"Good. If it wasn't for this storm, we'd be gone already, but I bet Billy's probably hiding under the marshal's desk right about now, until this lightning gets past." He sucked down half of the beer, which tasted better than honey. "I still want to get gone before daylight."

"We really taking Gussie with us?"

"I guess, but it's probably a mistake."

"Well, I like that little gal . . ." Luke stopped short when the door opened across the street and Billy stepped outside. "What'n hell? Billy Lightning's out walking in the open big as you please in this kind of weather?"

"Something's wrong."

Billy made a beeline across the street, casting worried glances overhead. Something was up for him to be out with lightning sizzling overhead. Hack wondered if they'd arrested Gussie for something, maybe from her old days as a prostitute. Those kinds of things can follow a person for years, and he really didn't care, for that would take care of her joining up with them.

Billy pushed through the doors and saw them sitting there. He sat at the table and leaned in on his elbows. "We got troubles."

Luke slid his beer across to Billy. "Gussie?"

He took a long swallow and wiped his lips. "Naw. She's fine and we're free to go. Marshal said he had somebody to take care of the kids, and we don't have to worry about them two carcasses anymore, neither."

Hack watched the marshal's office through the wind. "Then what is it?"

"Two others ain't free to leave."

Hack sighed at his predisposition for not getting right to the point. "What *is* it?"

Billy whispered so low they could barely hear him over the voices and laughter in the saloon. "They got Santana and Two-Horses locked up in there."

Hack's stomach sank. He didn't like his boys to be in jail, for one thing, but the other thing was more worrisome. He wasn't sure they could find the right business and boardwalk where Santana had hidden the gold in Barlow. Any reasonable person knew a town grows and changes, and in the past three years, any one of a hundred things could have happened to change the looks of that town.

Santana would remember, though, because he had an excellent memory and had stashed the saddlebags himself. While they were in Purgatorio, he'd told them he'd used his knife to mark one of the planks already in place, but he'd never said which one or how.

Hack made sure no one was listening in. "What're they in for?"

"A hanging. They beat up a hide hunter and killed his partner yesterday."

"How come?"

"Made 'em mad, I reckon."

Hack sighed. "Well, at least we know where they are now."

"How're we gonna get 'em out?"

"I'll have to study on that for a while."

"You can't study long. Traveling judge is gonna be in town tomorrow, and Marshal Black says it'll be a short trial and a shorter rope an hour after the judge bangs his gavel."

Lightning cracked and struck something in town with a loud bang that sounded like cannon fire. Billy ducked and looked around. "Lordy, that was close." He took another swallow of Luke's beer while Hack ran a finger around the wet ring on the table, thinking.

"We can't let them do that to our boys."

"All those guys out there want them dead. They been trying to get the marshal to turn them over so they can take them down to the cottonwoods on the creek."

Luke said, "Ahhh. That explains all these people this time of the night, and the torches."

"That's right." Billy glanced over at the bar and caught the young bartender's eye. Hack turned and waved him off.

"They're all stirred up like a nest of ants, and those boys want blood. No more beer until we can all drink together."

Pulling at one ear to think, Luke pursed his lips. "Say, how'd you get out here without making that lawman suspicious."

Billy grinned, looking like a schoolboy. "Told the marshal and his deputy I'd come over here and get us a bottle of whiskey to wait out the rain, if they was thirsty. Said I needed a taste to calm my nerves after everything that happened, and he allowed that was a good idea."

The conversation ended when a shout came from the street. "Fire!"

The saloon grew silent. Fire in a town built entirely of wood was one of the worst things that could happen. A customer went to the batwing doors and looked out. "Where is it?"

A voice called from the darkness. "A.D.'s General Merchandise. Let's go!"

The customer charged out, leaving the doors flapping behind him.

The bartender shouted at his son, "Boy, go get them buckets out back and fill them with water." He shouted across the saloon, "That store's only six doors down. Y'all get out there and help them!"

The saloon emptied in a rush, leaving only the professional gamblers to rake their winnings and a few forgotten dollars off the tables. Watching them move as calm as a preacher in church, an idea formed in Hack's mind.

"Billy, did you see a back door to the marshal's office?"

"Nope. The back is solid, and the whole thing's made of real bricks and iron. Two cells back there and that's all. The front door's barred, though, from the inside. Every time somebody goes in or out, they bar it behind them, too."

"Your job'll be to open it up, then. Run back over there and get inside. Do what you can to get that lawman and his deputy to help fight that fire. We'll be there as soon as we see them leave."

Despite the lightning, Billy took off, running back across the street bent almost double, and they couldn't help but laugh at the way he was dodging horses, people, and the weather.

Luke gave Hack a grin. "We gonna get the boys out?"

"You bet we are."

CHAPTER 36

Two cowboys at the end of the Crystal Bar had positioned themselves near the batwing entrance for one good reason. Eli Maxwell was missing his left ear, the result of losing a fistfight when he was working for the Two-Bar ranch up on the northern range in the New Mexico territory five years earlier.

The bad ear worked fine when a speaker was up close, but his right ear had tuned itself to make up for the other and was especially sensitive. When two men he recognized came inside, he turned when they sat at the table beside the door so he could hear their conversation.

On the opposite side, Rudolph Polk saw his partner tense. "What's the matter?"

Maxwell stared forward, down the length of the bar, as if unaware of the newcomers. "You remember when we were signed onto Oarlock ranch out of Bandera about three or four years ago."

"Three and a half."

"Right. That bank robbery we heard about that had the whole country up in arms."

"You're talking in circles, Eli. Of course I remember, we joined that posse for something to do." Polk laughed. "That's how we wound up down here, working for the Bar J, the sorriest outfit I've ever run across. We had a good job and threw it all away to go chase bank robbers all the way down here, and now we've been damn-near broke in this godforsaken country ever since."

"We might've caught 'em."

"What do you mean?" Polk leaned closer in case Maxwell was having trouble hearing him over the noisy saloon. "Caught who?"

"The Long Gang."

Polk shook his head. "They vanished into the wind."

"Well, I believe they just reappeared right here beside us."

Polk leaned back to look around his old partner. Two men sat alone at a table, talking quietly. "Those two?"

"Yep." Maxwell sipped at the whiskey that he could scarce afford. "If I'm not mistaken, that hard-looking guy nearest to us is Hack Long."

"I figured he was dead."

"So did everybody else, including the sheriff of Bandera County who gave up."

"We'd all given up. Those boys were fast, on good mounts, and there was no way to catch them on those wore-out nags we were riding."

"But here they are, big as the sky."

"So what?"

"So, we can draw down on them and take them in. There's bound to still be a reward on their heads."

Polk shook his head. "You see how they wear those sidearms? Those boys probably still rob and kill for a living."

"Then why are they here?"

"Maybe to rob the bank?"

Maxwell was interested. "That makes sense. Maybe we could wait outside with our Winchesters and shoot them when they come out. We'll get a reward then." Thunder rumbled in the distance and blew rain that cooled things down.

Polk cut his eyes back to the pair of outlaws sitting and

talking as if they didn't have a care in the world. Seconds later, a younger man came in and joined the other two at the table. All three leaned in and spoke quietly.

Polk nudged Maxwell's arm with a finger. "Can you hear them?"

"Some. Just words. Heard one of them say bodies, jail, and undertaker." Maxwell took a sip of whiskey. "Then a name. Santana."

"That's familiar."

"It should be." Lightning flashed outside, and Maxwell broke into a smile. "Hack Long. Santana. Lightning. I remember hearing after we got on with the Bar J those were the names of men in the Long Gang. I was right. They're here and planning something."

"Planning what?"

"I don't know yet, but if I was a betting man . . ."

"And you are."

"You're right. I am. That sheriff we were with, what was his name?"

"Williams."

"That's it. Sheriff Williams was of the mind that gang hid or buried the money somewhere, then scattered so's we couldn't catch them. Said they'd probably come back and get it sometime."

"I remember him saying that, but we didn't come through here. We were what, thirty or forty miles west."

"What's out that way?"

"Not much. Fort Stockton. Odessa further north. Barlow. Lots of other towns struggling and dying between here and the territories."

The young man at the table rose and went outside.

"I have a notion that after all this time they're back after the gold."

"Fifty thousand or so, if I remember right."

"Or more. How about we keep an eye on them and see

what they're about. If they leave town, we follow, and when they retrieve that gold from wherever they stashed it, we just use those Winchesters out there on the horses and take it."

"The two of us ain't enough to take on the Long Gang."

"How about four of us?"

"Four? Who?"

Maxwell nodded at the card table in the far corner of the saloon. Two more Bar J riders had hands in the game. "Dub and Jimmy Dale. They're as tired of punching cows as I am. They've crossed the line a time or two, and I bet they'd throw in with us."

Lightning struck nearby, causing everyone in the saloon to jump, then laugh. Maxwell tossed off the rest of his whiskey. "That struck close."

The crowd went back to talking, and half a minute later someone rushed into the saloon. "Fire!"

CHAPTER 37

The main street in Sweeten was full of people darting in all directions. By the time Hack and Luke stepped outside under the cover of the boardwalk, only a small amount of water was dripping over the edge and mixing with a little stream running down the street. It was one of those storms with more bark than bite.

At the other end of town, A.D.'s General Merchandise was burning through the roof, despite the bucket brigade of frantic men throwing water into the fire. Tall orange and yellow flames reached almost to the low clouds, making them look a sickly green. Even worse, the heat had punched a hole through them, and the smoke seemed to be sucked up in there to disappear from sight. It was something Hack had never seen.

The saddlery shop next door was also burning, and the eatery farther down called Rice's Place was also on fire. The MEALS SERVED AT ALL HOURS sign out front was already smoking in the heat, and the glass in the front windows shattered and rattled onto the boards. With the whole town in danger of being consumed, every eye was turned toward saving what they could.

They couldn't have planned it any better. Thick smoke hung heavy on the ground, making vision even more difficult in the darkness. It drew a veil across the town, and it was difficult to see more than twenty yards or so.

Down the street, men were releasing horses from the corral next to the livery, and others led stock out of the stalls, slapping them on the rumps to get them out of town, then rushing back inside. Other terrified horses yanked themselves free of their hitching posts and raced down the street, forcing people to avoid their dangerous hooves.

Billy dodged and darted his way through that mess and reached the other side of the street without getting stomped into jelly. He banged on the jailhouse door with a fist and shouted to be let in. It opened a crack and he edged inside. Standing in the pool of light coming from the saloon, Luke waited beside their nervous horses. Coughing, he pulled his bandana over his nose to filter the thick air.

Not nearly as concerned about the lightning as Billy, Hack waited until there was a gap in the traffic and trotted across to the horses Billy and Gussie had brought in behind the wagon. He didn't like having their cayuses split up when things were about to start happening, so he brought them back across to the closest tail. They pulled at their leads but settled some when Luke joined them with the other two.

Hack was barely back across when a riderless, terrified stallion raced past, his hooves thundering on the packed road. A man running toward the fire with an empty bucket wasn't paying attention, and the panicked horse ran him down. He hit the ground and rolled and was still. A pair of cowboys rushed from the boardwalk and picked up the man's limp body. He looked dead as they threw him into the deacon's empty wagon and essentially stole it and the team to take him somewhere to find a doctor.

Presently, the door to the marshal's office opened as they'd hoped, and he rushed out. It didn't take but a second for him to absorb what was happening, and he hurried down the street, pulling up his own bandana and taking charge, ordering a milling crowd of interested observers to help.

The door closed behind him, and Hack waited for several minutes until he felt the time was right. He and Luke mounted up and, leading the spare horses, rode over to the barricaded office because being on horseback was safer than crossing on foot.

Billy was right, the strong oak door was banded with strips of iron. It was the only one built so substantial. While Luke held the horses, Hack knocked, listening to the shouts of frightened men not far away and the roar of dried wood going up in the inferno.

Thinking his knock wasn't heard, he used the butt of the knife from the sheath on his belt to hammer again. A thump on the other side told of a heavy bar being removed from its brackets. It was followed by a sliver of light and the odor of burned coal oil.

Billy opened up and peeked out, rubbing at a bloody nose. His eye was swelling shut, and he looked like he'd been through the wringer. Hack pushed inside to find the deputy on the floor, blocking the door leading into the cells out back, his head a mass of bruises and bleeding profusely from a scalp wound.

"Wouldn't leave to go help, even though I told him I'd watch the prisoners." Billy waved a hand. "Told him he wasn't in charge anymore then, but he came at me when I said to turn around so I could tie his hands."

The man looked as if he'd been beaten with an ax handle, although Hack didn't see one or anything like it. "What'd you use on him?"

Billy reached into his pocket and dropped a ten-inch cast-iron stove lifter designed to remove and replace the circular stove lids that covered the hob. "I didn't want to shoot the poor feller."

Through the small open door leading to the back, Santana

and Two-Horses stood upright in their cells, taking it all in. The office was lit bright with several lamps. "Be right back," Hack said and pulled the unconscious deputy out of sight around the wall separating the office and jail.

Not far from the desk, Gussie watched him drag the deputy across the floor. She had the kids on either side, holding their faces against her skirt. "That man wouldn't give up. Every time Billy would knock him down, he'd get back up and come at him. I thought he'd have to kill him to make that fella quit."

The groggy deputy looked tough, but he'd been no match for a man who'd been swinging a sledge hammer for three years. Coming back into the office, Hack searched the walls for a nail or something to hold the key ring. "Some folks won't quit and take their job serious. You can't fault a man for that. Where're the keys?"

From where he stood, Hack saw Santana shrug and point. "They'd lock us in here and then go out with 'em."

Opening the top drawer of the desk, Hack found papers and a little pocket pistol. Everyone stopped what they were doing when someone pounded on the door.

"Deputy! Open up and let us in. I'm Reverend Hart and Pearl's with me. We're here to get the kids, and there isn't much time! The fire's jumped the street!"

Hack slipped into the back where the cells were and closed the door, leaving it cracked so he could peek into the office.

Billy reached into the pocket of his coat and withdrew the Ranger badge. He pinned it onto his lapel. Making sure all was right behind him, he wiped the blood from his nose with the back of one hand and opened up to find a man and woman. "Hurry and get inside."

The couple rushed in and took note of the badge. The reverend hesitated. "Where's the marshal?"

"Out fighting the fire with his deputy," Billy answered. "I'm in charge until they get back."

Pearl waved a hand in front of her face. "The fumes are strong in here."

"Had to have it closed up against that lynch mob." Billy pointed at the front of the building.

Pearl went to the children sitting on either side of Gussie and knelt. She smiled at the stranger who'd helped rescue the kids. "We're here for you, sweet things. The fire's coming, but we'll take you to our house out back of the church. The fire won't reach there."

She addressed Gussie. "I hear you helped save them."

Gussie swallowed and her eyes darted around as if searching the walls for something to say. "I was there."

"You're a good woman."

"I wish everyone thought so." Gussie looked at each of the twins, who bore blank expressions.

The looks on those young people's faces were familiar to anyone who'd seen similar expressions on young people who'd suffered through Indian attacks and murder or any other violence their little minds couldn't cope with.

Gussie gave them each a squeeze. "Y'all go with this nice lady. She'll make sure you get home to your mama and papa."

Pearl rose from one knee, and the kids, who still hadn't said a word since they woke up, allowed her to take their limp hands, probably ready to be away from so much misfortune. Gussie gave them each a quick hug, and the little girl looked up at the reverend and his wife.

She whispered to Gussie. "People like them took us and was gonna eat us."

Tears welled, and Gussie knelt beside the kids. "Those people who took you weren't like the reverend and Miss Pearl. They're good folks and will get you back to your papa and mama."

"Why can't you do it?"

Gussie wiped at the tears on her cheeks, and she whispered in the girl's ear. "Because I'm not as good as they think I am." She pulled the side of the kids' heads against her legs and covered their ears so they couldn't hear. "Things might have been done to these babies. Y'all better take care of them."

The reverend and Pearl read volumes in those two sentences. He nodded, patted Gussie's arm, and opened the door, filling the room with the scent of woodsmoke. "We'll get these two to their parents."

Billy smiled as if he didn't have a care in the world, playing the part of a confident Texas Ranger. "Y'all be safe."

The reverend paused. "Are you all right, sir? You look to have been recently accosted."

"I'm fine. Those two back there tried to get rough with us when we fed 'em, but they settled down after we thumped on their heads for a while."

Two-Horses snorted like an aggravated mule, and Santana gave out with a soft chuckle.

"Thank you for what you've done, and God bless you both." The preacher took the boy's hand, and his wife urged the little girl outside. The children waved tiny goodbyes, and they hurried down the street, away from the rising conflagration.

Billy closed the door and dropped the thick wooden bar into place as Hack rushed to the desk. The second drawer he opened contained the keys to the cells, and they soon had the boys out.

Santana came into the office and pointed at what Hack first took to be some kind of cedar chest or quilt box. "Our guns are in there."

It was secured by a small, keyed latch. Gussie picked up a piece of stove wood and smashed the brittle cedar around the lock. She opened the lid to reveal more than one holstered gun and several boxes of ammunition.

Santana flashed Gussie a grin. "Looks like we have a new partner."

Two-Horses selected a gun and holster, then dropped them back and picked up a new-looking Colt in a hand-tooled holster. "This one looks better." He strapped the guns on and settled the belt around his hips. "Lady, you're gonna have a hard time riding in those clothes."

Gussie undid the buttons on her dress, and their eyes widened at the sight. She dropped the long garment, revealing a man's shirt and pants tucked into boots. She gathered up the dress in a bundle and tucked it under her arm. "I'm ready to ride."

Billy chuckled and took the bar down. "Boys, meet Gussie."

He let Two-Horses and Santana go outside first, probably to see if lightning would strike anyone. Gussie followed, with Hack and Luke behind. They stepped out into the light rain and smoke, finding most of the town was fighting the fire.

Acting as innocent as babies, they mounted up. Santana and Two-Horses swung up into saddles that didn't belong to them, and they all rode out of town and into the darkness.

The Long Gang was back in business.

CHAPTER 38

Eli Maxwell and Rudolph Polk tucked themselves in the alley between the Silver Dollar Saloon and J.D. Grimes's tax office, where those responding to the fire wouldn't see them. While men shouted and ran, hauling water and moving stock away from the flames, the pair kept an eye on the marshal's office, where the Long Gang had disappeared.

Polk pulled his bandana up to block the smoke. "It's odd that outlaws would rush *into* a jail."

"They ain't going to visit." Smoke caused Maxwell's eyes to tear up. Using his own scarf, he wiped them dry. "I bet those two murderers who're awaiting a hanging are part of that bunch. I suspect they've gone to break them out."

Tucked back in the shadows, Polk waved a finger across the street. "That's the reverend and his wife. They ain't in on no jailbreak."

The door opened and the pair disappeared inside. Farther down the street, the flames spread, and Maxwell wondered if the whole town would go up before Long and his men came back outside. He leaned out to see down the street when someone spoke his name.

"Eli? What'n hell you doing ducking around corners while Rome burns?"

His head snapped back the other way, and he saw Dub

and Jimmy Dale watching the excitement in the street. "What does that mean?"

"Nothing." Dub hooked both thumbs in his chaps' belt. "Y'all hiding from somebody?"

The jailhouse door opened, and a crowd of people spilled onto the boardwalk. Only one looked around. Hack Long, but he took little notice of a few cowboys loafing in front of a saloon and paying more attention to the activity around them than anything else.

They saddled up, turned their horses, and calmly rode away.

Maxwell nudged Polk. "We got to go."

"Where you going?"

It was time to see if Dub and Jimmy Dale were looking for a little adventure. "Boys, we're done cowboying. See those people riding off? They're the Long Gang, and I believe they're going to collect some gold they stole in Bandera and buried three years ago. We're going after them."

Dub rubbed his mouth in thought. "You're leaving the brand?"

"We are, and when those guys get the gold, we're taking it away from them."

"You think you're that tough?"

"I believe so." Maxwell couldn't wait any longer. Following them in the dark was risky, but waiting too long might result in them disappearing forever. "We got to go. You with us or not?"

The two young cowboys looked at each other for direction until Jimmy Dale shrugged. "Why not? It's something to do."

CHAPTER 39

Captain Bookbinder and his company of Rangers rode down the muddy main street of Sweeten, Texas, in the late afternoon sun. The damp air stunk of wet charcoal, manure, and burned meat, which came from the livery and under the burned-out pier-and-beam buildings where a wide variety of animals had denned up.

Over half of the town was gone, and many of the remaining structures that still stood were scorched on one side. The town was a beehive of activity as people sifted through the still-smoking ruins or loaded wagons with burned planks, timbers, and destroyed possessions to be hauled out of town.

Other wagons filled with newly sawn lumber were already lined up in a narrow train down the wide street, waiting for saws, hammers, and nails. Bookbinder rode ahead of his column of men, taking in the activity with a stern look on his face. Riding well back from the Rangers, Oscar and Ridge Tisdale sat straight and seemingly ready for trouble.

One of the untouched buildings on their left bore a wide sign proclaiming it was the marshal's office. The heavy oak door leaning against the outside of the building was a splintered mess, and it looked to Bookbinder as if a lynch mob had chopped their way in.

He swung down. "You boys go find out what happened here."

They did as they were told, but the Tisdale brothers followed them inside. It annoyed Bookbinder that they acted as if they had the authority to stick right in his back pocket, but he understood they were concerned with the safety of Oscar's twins.

He entered the marshal's office without knocking and found one man lying on a bunk, nursing a head wrapped with a white bandage stained with blood. The other man, who was wearing a badge, was going through a sheaf of papers on his desk. He looked up with a startled expression.

"Marshal, I'm Captain Royce Bookbinder. What'n hell happened here?"

"What'n hell happened to knocking?"

"I'm sorry. I'll remember my manners next time, but my question still stands."

"Lightning a couple of days ago."

"Sorry to hear that, but hard times can come from the heavens, the same as from the devil's mischief."

"It's the same thing, as far as I can see. Cap'n Bookbinder, I'm Marshal Black. How can I help you?"

"Got a first name?"

"Marshal."

"You seem to be feeling ill this morning, sir."

"I'm aggravated is what I am. In addition to half of this town burning down, the two prisoners I had locked up back there escaped after whacking on my deputy, and I have no idea which way they went. We had to chop through a perfectly good door to get inside. They somehow balanced the brace so that it fell into place when they slammed the door. Pretty smart, if you ask me.

"Furthermore and all that, some stranger came in here after killing a murderous man and woman and left us with a set of twins to look after and two people for the town to bury.

I barely have enough funds to fix that door, and Calhoun down at the undertaker's office is wanting money to pay a carpenter to build two coffins, and the price of wood just went sky high because all of it's going to rebuild the town."

When Oscar heard the mention of children, he pushed up to the desk. "Where are they?"

He'd endured the exchange with a frown until the mention of the twins. Bookbinder learned early on the man was determined and unused to letting others have control. He'd urged them to ride faster and later than the Ranger had intended, and more than once, bad-tempered words were exchanged.

The marshal immediately stood, for such inappropriate action and tone of voice often required violence. "Who're you, sir, and back off."

From beside the door, Ridge crossed his arms and chuckled. "That's the kids' daddy, Oscar Tisdale, and I'd recommend you answer him pretty quick. He can be fractious when his dander is up."

"Why, I will, then. The boy and girl are named Art and Arlene. They yours?"

Oscar clapped his hands and turned to Ridge. For the first time in days, Oscar's chiseled face broke into a smile. "I knew we'd find them!"

Marshal Black relaxed for the first time since the Rangers had come in. "They're safe and in good health over at the parsonage with the reverend and his missus."

Oscar ignored the marshal's question. "You hear that, Ridge? They're safe." Half a second later, the cloud returned over his features. "Now, where's the people who took 'em. I intend to shoot them where they stand."

Bookbinder looked pained. "Damn, you are, indeed, an ambitious man, Mr. Tisdale, but I intend to hang them myself."

"Neither of you will get your wish." Marshal Black thumped

a finger on a page lying on his desk. "They're the ones we have to bury on the town's ticket. This is a note from our local undertaker describing for the town councilmen the two bodies brought in with the children.

"They were laid out by a traveling man and his wife, who killed them when they attempted to harm them and your twins. They brought them in and left when the town caught fire, along with a couple of hundred other people who fled the conflagration." He paused. "Well, why didn't I think of that earlier. They had a wagon when they came in, and we can sell it to provide funds for their burial and a little something to the reverend."

Oscar started for the door. "Where's the parsonage?"

The marshal waved a hand northward. "Up behind the church. Go past the wagon out front and what's all burned out. You can't miss it."

Oscar turned to his brother. "Let's go get them."

Ridge pushed out his bottom lip, thinking. "You know, I bet there's a stage that comes through here. Why don't you and the kids take it and go on back home. I need some time on my own, and if the captain here'll take me on, I'd like to ride as a Ranger for a while."

Bookbinder tilted his head, thinking.

Not looking a bit surprised, Oscar nodded. "You never much liked being a rancher in the first place, did you?"

"Not much, but it got you and Ruth started. I'll send her a telegram that you're on the way with the kids. You just go get them, and I'll be by later."

Oscar stuck out his hand, and they shook. He pushed outside, leaving his brother with the Rangers, but popped back inside after only a second. "For your information, marshal, there ain't no wagon out here."

He left and Marshal Black went to the door. "Somebody's done stole the wagon from right out front. This is turning out to be a helluva town."

Ridge remained where he was and realized they expected him to say something. "Don't look at me. He's going to get the kids, but I want to hear what y'all have to say. Besides, I'm kinda tired of branding calves."

Bookbinder seemed to see Ridge for the first time that day. "You'll make a fine Ranger, I suspect. Glad to have you in my company. Monthly stipend, when we can get it, and you provide your own weapons, horse, and cartridges. I'll get you a badge out of my saddlebags directly."

The Ranger dismissed his new man as if he typically took on Rangers as a matter of course. He turned back to his previous conversation. "Well, it seems that someone took justice into their own hands to settle up with that pair of murderous abductors, and it was justified. Now, tell me about those prisoners who escaped."

"One was a half-breed Comanche. Wouldn't give me his name when I asked, nor would his associate, who had some Mexican in him."

"I assume he was reluctant to give his name as well."

"That's correct. We were gonna have to try them under some alias."

"Names aren't required for proper justice to be administered. I've hung more'n one nameless rustler and outlaw."

"There are others, we believe." The marshal kept watch on the open door, as if someone might come in and steal something else from under his nose.

"How come?"

"Because when those two killed the hide hunters in cold blood, one of them was heard to say another man's name, and I figured it was the boss of their outfit, though I doubt he was in town at the time. Quoted something that makes me think he'd been a lawman at some time or another."

"Quoted what?"

Black rubbed his chin whiskers in thought. "Something about balance with an old man and weighing scales. Sounds to be concerned with litigation or something similar. Anyway, spoke the name Hack."

Bookbinder paused, thinking. He reached into his coat pocket and removed a sheaf of wanted posters. He shuffled through them and studied one page. A slight smile curbed the corner of his mouth before he passed them over the desk. "Have you seen any of these men? We're looking for them now. Called the Long Gang."

Marshal Black studied the face on the top poster, then the next. "Never seen these two." He turned them face down on the desk and paused at the next. Reading it as carefully as if it were a bill of sale for an expensive horse, he looked up at the Ranger and then revealed the next page.

Again, he seemed to be memorizing the face and description. His expression changed. "Hack Long."

When he reached the last one, his mouth dropped open. "It was them. These three." He held up two pages. "It was them in my jail, Two-Horses and Gabe Santana. These likenesses are close."

He passed them over to the Ranger and turned the third sheet so they could all see. "This was the one who brung them kids in. Billy Lightning. But that's not what he said his name was, Matt Brenner."

"An alias." For the first time that day, Captain Bookbinder smiled. "Well, boys, it looks like the Long Gang was here, and we've come in behind them."

Marshal Black frowned. "But he brung them kids in, him and some woman, and killed them that stole those little things."

"They're still wanted for other heinous crimes, though. One right don't make up for years of lawbreaking. We'll cuff them all and let a judge decide what to do."

CHAPTER 40

They could have taken the freight road to Barlow, but Hack wanted to avoid contact with as many people as possible. Unfortunately for them, civilization was expanding west, and it seemed that everywhere they went, it was wagon tracks, trails made by horses, or river and creek crossings that had been used so much the boys expected to meet people each time they dropped over a bank.

Despite the heat and sun, it was good to ride with the gang again and felt like the old days. Unlike the last time they were together, running across the dark desert from Purgatorio, they were mounted and rode easily in saddles that had been reluctantly or unintentionally donated by their former owners.

With Hack once again in the lead, they made good time after leaving Sweeten, pushing hard to put the town and any pursuers far behind. The day was uneventful until Two-Horses, who'd been hanging back, rode up and slapped him on the shoulder and threw his head back to laugh big.

That wasn't him.

Hack tried not to show any reaction as the rest watched to see what was about to happen. "Let me guess. Trouble, and somebody's watching us."

"More than a few, and I believe that means trouble."

"Where?"

"I saw a glint of something behind us. Rifle, maybe. Mexican concha on a hat or saddle, but they're not only there." He jerked a thumb. "You're losing your skills. Did you see that little wisp of dust over to the east?"

"No. Horses?"

"Probably. It wasn't much, and it didn't last long."

They were on a long slope so gradual it was hard to realize, leading down to a wide, shallow arroyo. There were no high ridges around the band on the slightly rolling land, and few trees managed to exist in such arid country, except for thin lines of green surviving on little streams.

It was all Hack could do not to look around. "You thinking raiding party?"

"Could be, but this ain't their usual country. These days, I'd expect them further west, but there's a lot of easy pickings out here with so many settlers and homesteaders moving in."

"The big ranches push them this way, too."

Two-Horses drifted back. "They do, but the ants running up and down my spine tell me there are a lot of them around. You'd better laugh, or we're gonna fight them out here in the open and not on ground of our own choosing."

Hack forced a laugh and waved for the others to come close. They kept riding and he flicked a finger at nothing. "We got troubles. Two-Horses thinks there's a war party watching us, though I didn't know they were raiding down here these days."

"They are." Billy Lightning flicked his fingers at Gussie, who looked and rode like a man in her clothes and a big hat she'd slapped on her head back in the marshal's office. "Comanches. They killed most of a White family down on the river, left the mama who'd lost her mind. Me and Gussie came across what was left of 'em, and it wasn't pretty."

She nodded in agreement and adjusted the reins in her fingers as if thinking about making a run for it. Hack shook his head. "Don't. We'll just keep this pace until we find a better place than this to fight."

She met his eyes. "What are you looking for?"

Hack shrugged. "I have no idea."

The place they found was a burned-out homestead not far from a trickle of water some might have called a creek. There was a chest-high square of stacked rocks some ambitious settler had planned to use as a barn but never finished, probably because his bones lay within the house or scattered around in the brush and scrub.

Luke looked around. "What a miserable place."

Hack made a face. "To these folks who tried, it might have looked like paradise."

While the others kept an eye out for the approaching war party, Hack took the opportunity to look over their surroundings. It reminded him of a time many years ago in East Texas when he'd come upon an old house place not far from a collapsing notched-log barn.

A young man with a bloody hole in his chest that day had been lying on his side and slowly digging with the head of a broken iron hoe. When Hack had ridden up, the cowboy pulled a rusty metal box from the ground and laid his head on one arm to rest. When Hack had dismounted to see if he could help, the boy, who wasn't much older than he was when he started down the outlaw trail, had pulled a well-oiled pistol from its holster and aimed it at him.

"Don't shoot me no more."

"I didn't shoot you in the first place, son. Put that pistol down."

He needn't have issued that order, because the barrel dropped to the dirt as the life ran from the youngster's body. "Wish I'd listened to mama." He dropped an ambrotype back into the hole he'd been digging.

Hack had knelt and reached in to pluck it from the dirt. The glass plate that came from the rusty box contained the likeness of a solemn-faced woman dressed in dark clothes. He'd studied her features as if memorizing the woman's face.

"We all should have listened."

He'd tucked it into the boy's shirt and ridden away. Now, standing in the ruins of what could be the site of their demise, Hack remembered that day and how choices stuck with a man throughout his lifetime. "Not my idea of the promised land I heard about in church as a kid."

Gussie checked out the home place, riding close and then turning back quickly. "We can't use the house for protection. The whole place is a rattlesnake den. I bet I heard half a dozen warning me away."

Billy swung down and drew his pistol, but Hack held out a hand. "Don't. We'll need the ammunition, and there's no way to shoot all them diamondbacks, anyway. They'll keep coming out all night, and one of us'll get bit. We use the walls of this barn for cover."

"Not much protection." Santana nudged his mount around the exterior of the enclosure, looking it over. "Now, I wonder why snakes took up over there, not fifty feet away, but not here."

"I don't even try to think like a snake."

Billy called in surprise, "There's a good spring here. Pool's big enough for us and the horses."

"Good to know." On the ground, Hack led the black inside what was to be their makeshift fort and slid the Henry from the scabbard. "Leave your saddles on, but take down your bags and rifles."

Doing as he said, Luke turned his horse out into the confines. The rest of them did the same while Gussie looked around for snakes. "What about the packs?"

"Get out what we need for the night, but leave the rest."

Hack looked toward the stream and the short willows growing on the banks. "We need to fill up everything that'll hold water."

As they rummaged around for canteens, Hack turned to Two-Horses. "Why'd they let us get here. They could have killed half of us out in the open like that."

"I do not know. Maybe . . ."

Gunshots back the way they'd come from cut him off. The shots were far away but close enough to be distinct. They tensed as the sounds of a fight rose and two groups unloaded on each other. The rattle of shots increased, then slowed and stopped.

"That's the reason, maybe." Two-Horses leaned his Winchester against the wall and placed a box of ammunition nearby.

"Sounds like those Comanches tangled with folks who know how to shoot back." Standing in place, Luke turned a complete circle, looking for trouble. "Maybe they'll lose their taste for fighting, and that's over with."

"Or they might be riled up enough to sweep over us, depending on how many there are."

"Riders coming!" Santana pointed.

Four men leaning low over their horses raced in their direction, throwing up clods of dirt back toward the biggest band of Comanches Hack had ever seen. The war party chased them with war cries that raised the hair on his neck.

"Rifles! Push 'em back!"

His men, along with Gussie, rushed to the rock wall and shouldered their guns. When Hack fired, they followed and five chunks of hot lead whipped past the cowboys heading toward their barricade. Three of the rounds found flesh, but only one warrior fell. The other two reacted, slumped, and turned their horses back.

Luke shucked a fresh round into his Winchester. "That'll make the rest of 'em mad."

Pistols and rifles in their hands, those boys heading for

safety rode for all their horses could ride and closed the distance at a dead run. Santana waved them around to the opening that served as an entrance, and they wheeled around and inside.

Three of them dropped out of their saddles. Two rushed over to the wall with rifles ready while the third helped a wounded man down and under the cover. Gussie and Billy ran over to get him down and tucked him up against the wall to stay out of the line of fire.

Gussie ripped his shirt open, and Hack saw a hole in the big muscle against his ribs, just under his armpit. She pressed her hand on the wound. "Billy, there's an old shirt in my saddlebag. Get it and tear me a rag."

She looked up at the cowboy who Hack assumed to be the leader and who was missing his left ear from some long ago incident or altercation. "It's bleeding pretty good, but he'll live."

The one-eared cowboy gave her a curt nod, and Hack noticed his hat was tilted to that side to hide his disfigurement. "Thanks. Name's Dub that's shot there. And thanks y'all for keeping them savages off our backs."

"Glad to have you. We can use the extra guns."

"So can we." He looked back across the now empty landscape. "You wouldn't know there were so many of them behind us just a minute ago."

"They're good at what they do. How many did you see?"

"Most of the Comanche nation, and they weren't alone. Half of 'em were Comancheros."

It was bad news. Comancheros were once Whites who traded with the Comanches and had been part of their success in ruling the Llano Estacado. During the Civil War, things had changed, and they'd joined up with the roving bands of warriors, supplying them with guns and supplies.

In the years since, the worst of the traders were adopted by the tribes and became part of the tribes. They turned out to be meaner and more bloodthirsty than the warriors themselves. Hack ran into them once and barely got away with his hair.

He looked over at Luke, who hadn't been so lucky when they were younger. He was missing a small circle of scalp from when an Indian had shot him unconscious up on the Brazos and had cut the gold dollar–sized piece down to his skull and yanked it free before Hack shot that savage in the eye.

He shoved fresh cartridges into his rifle. "Was there a red-head warrior with them? White man with long red hair and beard?"

"I believe I saw a guy like that. Why?"

"I was afraid of that. They make these strikes down the Llano all the way down to Mexico, and then fall back to their retreat up beyond the Canadian and Red River. Led by that fella who goes by the name of Carl Haoka. He's the devil they stole from the Pawnee. He was taken by the Penateka and raised as their own. Far as I know, he's the meanest human being on earth."

The cowboy looked even more worried than he did when they arrived. "Forgot my manners. Name's Eli Maxwell."

He didn't offer a shake, and that was fine by Hack. "Hack Long."

"I *thought* that was you. This here's my partner, Rudolph Polk. Like I said, the one with the hole in him's Dub, and over there's his buddy Jimmy Dale. They'll introduce themselves when things calm down in a little bit."

While Hack pondered his comment about knowing who he was, Billy put down his rifle and picked up a rock the size of a watermelon. He stacked it on top of the wall and hefted another. "I want this wall higher."

The rest of them did, too, and joined in raising the wall.

CHAPTER 41

The gunfire was so faint Captain Royce Bookbinder had to turn his head like a puppy listening to its master to be sure of what he had heard. He pointed northwest. "It's coming from out yonder."

His second, Gil Wilson, stared into the distance as if he could see far enough to determine what was going on. "More guns than we have here."

"I don't believe that ever made any difference for us."

The other heavily armed Rangers sat their saddles in silence, listening. They answered to Captain Royce Bookbinder and awaited his orders. To a man, they operated at the behest of the captain when he was around, but once on their own, they performed their duties independently and without oversight.

Each was a hard-shelled man who tolerated no nonsense at any time or in any situation and would ride into hell alone if the situation warranted such aggression.

Ridge Tisdale reached up and touched the new badge on his coat. He'd been wearing it only a few hours, and here he was already in action, leaving his brother Oscar to catch the stage and make his way home with the kids. Holding his revolver pointed at the sky, the newest Texas Ranger waited for orders.

Bookbinder didn't take long to make a decision. "Limber up them guns, boys. Somebody's in trouble. Let's ride." He noticed Ridge was already holding his pistol and nodded.

They thundered toward the gunfire, which had already tapered off. There was nothing but birds singing and carrion birds hanging in the air when they approached the source of the gunfire. A single horse without a saddle startled an armadillo that crashed off into the brush.

Coming over a low rise on lathered horses, they were met with a small band of Comanches tending three men on the ground. It looked as if they were administering to their wounded.

Without slowing, Bookbinder put the heels to his horse and fired at a warrior on the ground before charging into the middle of the war party, shooting left, then right. The company of Rangers followed closely, firing as well.

Two Comanches fired back and went down in a swarm of Texas lead and smoke from the Rangers' guns. Bookbinder shot at another while a warrior raised up from behind a thick bush and unleashed an arrow at one of the men behind him. A White man in Comanche dress shouldered an old rolling-block rifle and drew a bead on Bookbinder.

The sight of a White man with the Indians almost took Ridge's breath. He shot the man in the torso, and the man spun away, the rifle flipping end over end. Ridge reined right, directly over one of the wounded men lying on the ground. He fired straight down into a bleeding Comanchero who still had enough steam to raise his own pistol. The slug caught him in the chest, and he dropped the pistol and closed his eyes like a man dozing off.

Bullets whizzed through the air as the Rangers split up and returned fire from their running horses. They'd learned that technique from the same men they'd fought, and that's what made them so dangerous to Indians, bandits, and other miscreants roaming the state.

The Rangers' charge broke against the onslaught and split to the right and left into two groups, circling back to meet a couple of hundred yards from their point of origin. Bookbinder counted heads and, seeing they were all accounted for, reloaded his pistol.

"They'll break on this one!"

Silent and serious, the others thumbed shells into their rifles and pistols. Looking as cool as if he were in church, Ridge slapped empty casings from his pistol and shoved in fresh rounds from his belt. A bullet whizzed past, then another. Bookbinder looked up, and his blood chilled. It looked as if a hundred men were descending on their position.

One of the Rangers shouted, "Where'd *they* come from!"

Bookbinder's horse screamed and went down, throwing him onto the hard ground with a grunt. Gaining his feet, he reversed and took cover behind the big body. The world was full of charging Comanches and Comancheros riding and firing as fast as they could pull the triggers. Another of the Rangers' horses squealed and went down.

Ridge saw another pony fall. "They're shooting the horses!"

Wilson stuck the muzzle of his pistol behind his mount's ear and pulled the trigger. It went over on its side, and he dropped behind it.

"Save your ammunition!" Bookbinder shouted. "Don't kill your horses! We're gonna need them bullets."

One of the less steady Rangers broke and fled, lying over his horse's neck. His back was an easy target, and he pitched off his horse and landed in a puff of dust. Another pony screamed and went over on its side.

Bookbinder fired accurately and steadily. Holding his reins in his left hand, Ridge knelt beside his own mount and aimed, lining up on a man, shooting, and jacking another round into the chamber. His horse, trained to stand fast, proved his worth, showing the whites of his eyes and trembling.

Mouth dry and heart pounding, Ridge held his ground as warriors and White men dressed as Indians went down under the onslaught of bullets. As they dropped, he hoped Bookbinder and his men would remain solid under the onslaught. Ridge had no stomach for running.

The terrain worked against the attackers, and it funneled them into a field of fire from the Rangers' advantage. Ridge's vision seemed to narrow down to only what was in front of him on the wash. When he felt the Rangers could hold out no longer, the Comanches fell back, followed by the flowing gun smoke as the Rangers reloaded from rounds thumbed from their gun belts or from containers made from old boot tops hanging from their saddle horns.

Wilson shuffled over behind the captain's shelter of cooling flesh. "I've never seen so many Comanches."

"Comancheros. White men riding with Indians."

Bullets smacked into the ground, throwing up gouts of dirt and rocks.

"They're gonna overrun us." Wilson dug into his pants pocket for fresh ammunition. "If they get smart and get around behind us, we won't have a chance."

Ridge saw the captain consider their situation for a moment. It was Ridge who spoke up. "I have a better idea." He reached into one pocket and located a small box of matches in a metal container. Lying on his stomach, he crawled around Wilson's dead horse and struck one of them on the rough end of the box designed for such.

The long tickle grass was dry as old hay. He jabbed the little flame to a thick clump, and when it caught, he moved to another spot and lit it. Bullets whacked into the dead horseflesh between Ridge and Bookbinder, and his men returned fire. The match went out, and Ridge scratched another to life.

In minutes, the fire, pushed from behind them by a steady breeze, blew life into a conflagration that rose up in a roar and swept toward their assailants. The Indians' return gunfire slacked off, and Bookbinder waved his men forward. "Behind the flames, boys. Push 'em back!"

One of the Comancheros shouted in English for them to fall back. The flames chased the routed Comancheros and grew larger, feeding on the downed, dry wood that had been lying there for years. Thick, green cedars virtually exploded and burned hot and fast, creating an inferno.

Figures moved through the smoke, darting back and forth, and in moments they were gone.

Bookbinder stood and was joined by Ridge Tisdale. "That was some quick thinking there, son. Where'd you learn something like that?"

"Me and my brother was burned out by just such a fire a couple of years ago, but it wasn't set by no Comanches, but a fellow named Kreeger who wanted our place."

"I'd bet he didn't get it."

"He got six feet of land, and we took his place to go with ours."

CHAPTER 42

The newcomer had quit bleeding, and Hack settled down beside Gussie just to talk with a woman for a while. After so long with nothing but men, her soft voice reminded him of songbirds in the trees.

She didn't appear to be afraid, as he'd expected, at the possibility of an Indian attack, and that impressed him. "You're tougher than you look."

"You don't know the half of it."

She cut her eyes at him as she tore up the cowboy's neck rag for more bandages in anticipation of more wounded. The sounds of a pitched battled came to those bottled up inside that half-finished rock barn. They listened, tense as rabbits in a thicket and waiting for the Comanches to show themselves.

In the past, Hack had seen them appear out of nowhere in a full charge or send in a warrior or two crawling like lizards on the ground until they reached bow or rifle range. "Keep an eye out, boys. They could pop up like grasshoppers at any time."

Instead, all the defenders saw were mesquite leaves and grass moving in the wind.

It was mind-rattling.

Hack pulled a saddlebag close and reached inside,

producing a little revolver. "This belonged to some men we ran into down in Mexico."

"Ran into as in how?"

"Killed 'em all." He watched for her reaction, which was nothing more than the tiny flick of an eyebrow. "They had it coming."

"I didn't ask."

"Well, they did." He opened the cylinder and saw five loads. Closing it, he handed it to Gussie. "This is for you if they get past us. Shoot four times. The fifth is yours."

She took the pistol and weighed it in her hand. "I don't know if I can do that."

"It'll be your decision." The corner of his mouth ticked, and she saw it.

"You don't like that advice."

"Not one bit."

He wanted to slide over and tell her about the last time he gave a woman his old Navy Colt. A young man of barely two decades, he'd married and taken his blond-haired wife, Betsy, up to the Red River bottomlands, where floods often twisted the river out of its banks and deposited fresh land that was rich in nutrients.

There, grass grew thick and belly deep to a horse. Game was abundant, and several fresh springs welled with sweet water so cold you'd think it came from ice down deep below. He was building a little cabin and had started a horse herd, intending to be the best breeder in that part of the state.

But they hadn't been there long before a Comanche moon rose bright and clear. Bad luck came with that silver disk, and they found themselves behind the half-finished walls of their cabin, just like those around them, with a war party firing and moving in close, one foot at a time.

Running low on ammunition, he'd given Betsy that Colt and the same instructions about how to use it. It had been a sleepless night, with them discussing their predicament and possible outcomes. She'd withdrawn into herself as the hours passed, speaking less and less until they'd both grown silent with their thoughts.

At dawn, the war party'd come in a rush, and Hack had his hands full defending their position, shooting and reloading as the Comanches caught the newlyweds in a pincer movement, coming up on both sides.

One warrior had flown over the wall, and Hack killed him with his pistol. Another'd jumped over on the other side, and Betsy's pistol barked twice. The man had fallen, and Hack had whirled to see others on the opposite side of the wall, preparing to breach their position.

He'd killed another and saw a red-headed man with a short beard flashing past. He'd snapped a shot that knocked him spinning and turned to see Betsy with a horrified look on her face when she'd realized Comanches were within the walls. As he'd watched, she put the revolver to her head and fired.

Someone outside the walls shouted in English, and the whooping band had vanished as if they'd never been there. The next morning, he'd buried her and looked for the redheaded man's body. In the light, he'd seen a blood splatter, but the man who Hack had figured was a Comanchero leader was gone.

Hack looked at the pistol in Gussie's hand as those memories came flooding back. They were the wellspring of his self-doubt and the internal struggle with decisions that no one suspected. Had he not given Betsy the gun, she couldn't have shot herself, but she'd taken at least one of them with the revolver, possibly saving Hack's life in the first place.

On the other hand, late at night when everyone else was sleeping, he often wondered if he'd killed her with the knowledge of what could happen. It was something he'd never know, but ever since then, he'd asked himself, "What if?"

He tapped the butt of the Walker Colt on his belt and

pointed at the little pistol in her hand. "Think before you act. That will be your last act, but only if they're about to put their hands on you. Understand? Only if they're about to touch you."

Solemn, she nodded, and he realized he had other things to do. Leaving her to go back to making bandages, Hack stood and peered over the chest-high wall. "Y'all be suspicious of anything out there. If you think it wasn't there a few minutes earlier, draw a bead on it and shoot."

The wounded cowboy lying nearby looked pale, but he gave Hack a teeth-gritting grin. "I can fight when they bring it to me."

"Have you ever fought Indians?"

"I've never fired at anything but game to eat, but if they intend to shoot me again, I'll take more'n one with me before I go. Name's Dub. Would you put that on my grave marker?"

"Try not to die and shoot 'em all." Hack pointed at his chest, making sure he caught Gussie's eye, too. "Aim right here."

The pale cowboy nodded and winced as a lance of pain shot through his body. "And I thought this was gonna be easy."

"What was gonna be easy?"

The expression that crossed Dub's face was unreadable. It was something between shock and embarrassment and regret. His eyes slipped over to Maxwell, who was talking to Polk, and he changed the subject, pointing at the fourth cowboy, who was oiling his guns from a little metal container. "That's Jimmy Dale. We've ridden together for five seasons."

"Well, when we get out of this, y'all go back where you came from and go back to working cows where Indians ain't raiding."

"That's the best advice I've heard in months." Dub closed his eyes, providing an abrupt end to the conversation.

Hack stood and Polk nodded, his face grim. He wanted to go over and pick at the cowboy's thoughts for a few minutes in order to find out what Dub meant, but the odor of smoke reached them before the flames roared into view.

Luke and Santana joined Hack at the wall.

Luke wiped a hand over his mouth. "This could be bad or good."

Santana set his jaw. "They're gonna try and burn us out."

There was an ocean of dry grass and vegetation as far as they could see. The homesteaders had cleared the land out fifty yards all around, probably with a plow and sweat, so most of the taller cedars and mesquites were gone, but the grass was still knee-high and had been growing and dying ever since the settlers had been gone. It was a tinderbox.

"Here they come!" Billy stepped in front of Gussie, as if to protect her from whatever was coming, but she pushed around him and rested the forepiece of her rifle on the wall.

Horsemen appeared in the distance, dodging scrub and cactus and riding hard. Comanches all right, riding with the scruffiest White men Hack had ever seen. The Indians were painted for war and rode as if they were part of the horses between their legs.

They broke out of the smoke and headed for the breast-works at a dead run. The defenders hit the wall, rifles ready, but just before the raiders got into rifle range, a rider with long red hair and a beard that reached down to his chest led them off at an angle. "Later!"

That one word sent a shiver of fear down Hack's spine, for he'd heard that voice years earlier. But they thundered past, riding hard as if the devil was on their heels, and Hack wished he could see what was after them. Jimmy Dale fired and missed.

"Hold off!" Hack watched the war party pass without hardly throwing them a glance. "They're running."

A wave of fire threw heavy, oily smoke into the air, and

it rushed at them from behind a line of fleeing animals that exploded into the open after the fleeing Comanches and Comancheros. Deer, rabbits, armadillos, and birds of all kinds rippled the grass that would soon be consumed by the firestorm.

The horses behind Hack and the others snorted at the thickening smoke, nervous and ready to run like the wildlife that swept around them like water.

Eli Maxwell and Rudolph Polk, the two cowboys who seemed to be ramrodding the foursome, straightened and broke into grins. Maxwell slapped Polk on the shoulder. "Their plan backfired! They done set the world on fire, and it got behind them."

It was something Hack had never seen, and he wondered how they'd miscalculated the results of the fire. Seemed to him like they would have set it at the edge of the thick brush, waiting for the smoke and flames to blind the defenders before coming in from any of the three other directions to wipe them all out.

The big war party rode due west and was soon out of sight.

It didn't make any sense at all.

Neither did the change in wind direction when it seemed to have been swept with a giant hand toward the fleeing Comancheros.

CHAPTER 43

Captain Bookbinder and his men made camp in the same spot where they'd planned to fight to the death. Everything to the west was still hot and burning, and the horses made it clear they wouldn't be in any way enthusiastic about going in that direction until the fires died out and everything cooled off.

Several of the Rangers went out on foot to make sure the Comanches who remained were well and truly killed. Bookbinder had no intention of ordering his men to give those godless barbarians a Christian burial. Instead, they led their remaining horses out into the ashes to throw their ropes around the corpses' ankles and dragged them a good distance away from the charred ground before the carcasses started stinking.

"Gentlemen, we will establish a picket line around the perimeter of this camp. However, I suggest you all sleep with the horses attached directly to your own bodies. Mr. Wilson, we will require guards throughout the night."

"Yessir. Charlie, you and Bill take the first watch. Web and Richard will take over after midnight. This will be a cold camp, gentlemen."

Relieved and fighting the fatigue that followed terror and excitement, the Rangers dug out hardtack and jerky from their saddlebags and the odd chunk of cheese and moldy biscuits. They settled in for what would probably be a sleepless night.

The full moon rose, huge and silver, and the sky was so clear they could see the craters in detail. Ridge Tisdale watched it come over the trees. He spread a blanket and rested on one elbow. "I'm glad we have this light. It would have been an unfortunate occurrence had it been a night black as a tomb."

Liking the man more and more every day, Bookbinder sat next to him, his back against a cottonwood log. He was an excellent judge of character and could read a man within minutes of first meeting him. This Ridge Tisdale came across honest as the day was long and had already proven to be someone to ride with in any engagement.

"I've never heard anyone describe a dark night with such words."

"I read a lot. That was in a book."

"It's good to ride with an educated man. Most of these boys can cipher and maybe sign their names, but I doubt more'n one will have a book in their possibles."

"Reading teaches us a lot and makes a man think." Ridge bit off a tough strip of venison jerky and chewed. "My brother doesn't like to read, but he makes a solid rancher."

"And you abandoned him to ride with us."

"I wouldn't say that. I heeded to the siren call of adventure and decided to pursue a new life fighting outlaws and Indians. I've lived my whole life doing what's right, and when I heard y'all were after murderers and thieves, I wanted to help. If good men do nothing, then the wicked ones will take the world, leaving the weak and the dead."

Bookbinder removed his hat and scratched his scalp under the thick mat of sweaty hair. "You do talk, sir. So, what are your thoughts on our mission."

"I have no thoughts. I'm just here to serve justice."

"Well spoken!" Bookbinder slapped his knee. "Tomorrow we get back after those wanted men."

"What about the Comancheros?"

"It will be useless to go after them. They have war trails a thousand miles long and can travel a hundred miles in a day. I'd bet they've split up already to make it harder to catch them or to divide our forces so we'd be easier to kill. I will not fall into their trap. This band we just tangled with is too big for us to handle. We will come across them again, but right now, I intend to track down this Long Gang."

"It'll be slow without horses for everyone."

"We will ride double to the next town, where I will procure new mounts."

"They might all be dead over yonder somewhere." Ranger Wilson squatted down with them. "I heard a shot or two from that direction."

"A shot or two won't kill very many men." Bookbinder felt in his vest and drew out a briar pipe. The captain stuck it in his teeth and puffed as if it was lit, which he wouldn't do in a cold camp. He knew better, because even the light of a match had resulted in a man's death back when he'd first become a Ranger. "My guess is those miscreants rode hard as they could when they heard the shooting. That's what I'd do."

Not far away, a pack of coyotes tuned up, yipping and barking in pursuit of their prey. Ridge listened. "They'll find those bodies we drug off pretty quick."

"It's the way of this land," Bookbinder said. He did not care what happened to the bodies. They were no use to their former owners or himself. "The living feast on the dead."

"Speaking of that." Ridge adjusted his seat on the hard ground. "When we get to the next town, I'm gonna buy the biggest beefsteak they have in the first kitchen we come across. Anyone know how far it is to the next town?"

"Thirty miles or so." Captain Bookbinder rose.

Ridge watched him set his hat. "Where's that?"

"Place called Barlow."

"Ever been there?"

"About two years ago, right after a cyclone strolled straight down their main street. They were rebuilding, and it looked like a boom town."

"What could be there to keep 'em going?"

"Water, and a railroad coming through."

CHAPTER 44

The wind shifted before the fire reached the edge of the wide clearing surrounding the defender's haphazard palisade, and the fire rushed north and away before it came close enough to be dangerous. One minute they were in danger of being killed by the war party, dying from the smoke, or being burned to a crisp, but instead, they found themselves with challenges.

It was a letdown, but Hack told everyone to stay alert. That many Comanches in the area was a nervous thing, and they needed to be ready. The night passed peacefully, and most of them got at least a little rest while they took turns on watch. Sleep was impossible for Hack, so he moved from place to place, watching and listening.

Dawn was a glow on the horizon when he made the rounds to shake everyone out. "Wake up, folks. We need to get gone."

Luke rose quickly and went to check on Dub and his wound, and the rest of them tightened girths and packed their gear. Gussie had already roused the skinny cowboy up, but he was groggy and groaning from the pain.

Horses stomped and snorted, wanting water. Two-Horses gathered up the reins of four ponies. "I'll let these drink and come back for the others."

"Good thinking." Hack picked up the Henry leaning against the wall and shoved it into the scabbard under his saddle's skirt. "Billy, you want to help him so we can get out of here a little quicker?"

"Sure enough."

Santana stretched and walked to the wall to keep watch. "Y'all are acting like this is over all of a sudden. I'll keep watch, because I don't think it is."

Jimmy Dale helped his wounded partner up, and they leaned against the partial wall for a moment for Dub to get steady on his feet. The other two who'd ridden in with them stayed separate from the rest, and Hack figured that was because they knew each other better than his men and were more comfortable with each other.

Two-Horses led the ponies down to the spring and waited as they ducked their heads to drink. One snorted to clear the surface of the water like they'll do, and the others did the same. The spring was close enough to the breastworks to hear them suck up the water.

They were also close enough for the sound of a wet *thunk*, followed by a soft *snap*. Billy and Hack turned to look for the source of the strange sound at the same time that Two-Horses swayed like a tree in the wind. He steadied and dropped to his knees.

Seconds later, the wounded cowboy grunted and fell against Jimmy Dale, who grabbed him, and they both hit the ground. From where he stood, Hack hadn't seen what had hit Two-Horses, but the arrow in Dub's back told everyone what was happening.

"Indians!" Billy shouldered his rifle and fired at someone Hack couldn't see. He jacked the lever on his repeater and squeezed the trigger again, and the next thing they knew guns were going off all around.

The Henry was too far away, but Hack snatched his Colt from the holster and looked for something to shoot. There was no return fire from any attackers, and the air grew quiet enough to hear crickets starting up again with their morning song.

Yellow light filled the world and illuminated the four horses that'd been watering. They'd shied away, but still thirsty, they had returned to finish drinking beside Two-Horses' still body. Hack rushed across to the black, grabbed the Henry, and jumped over the wall. Other footsteps joined in to pound across the grass as he rushed to Two-Horses.

Billy, Santana, and the two cowboys were right on his heels and scattered out to cover their boss with long guns at their shoulders. Hack dropped to one knee beside Two-Horses, who was lying on his right side. The skin on his back bulged against the tip of an arrowhead that hadn't punched all the way through his chest.

Not wanting to turn him over on that frightening prominence, Hack gently lifted Two-Horses' head. Blood flowed from his mouth, and the dying man's eyes rolled in his head. Hack turned his head so he wouldn't choke and grasped the dying man's shoulder. "Hang on."

Two-Horses coughed and a gout of red followed. "My own people killed me," he said softly, and went still.

A rifle went off only a few feet away, and Hack jumped. Whirling to face an oncoming threat, he saw Billy shucking another round into the chamber. "I got him!" Billy's voice was sharp in the silence. "Saw him lying there trying to fit another arrow." He and Santana crept forward, ready to shoot again if necessary.

Eli Maxwell joined the party, pistol in hand. "Dub's dead. Boy had some bad luck, shot yesterday and then an arrow in the back this morning, but where'd it come from?"

"Looks like there was only one." Billy pointed toward the tall grass at his feet. "Right there. He was already shot to pieces and half cooked when he killed Two-Horses.

Somebody put three holes in him, and he still crawled up here in the dark."

"He probably crawled here for water, after that fight we heard in the distance," Hack said, reading the ground. "Scuff marks where he drank and then worked his way back over there to wait for somebody to come down."

Santana shook his head. "That's determination. Dying himself, he curled up like a water moccasin by the water to wait for daylight. He still had enough in him to loose two arrows."

"Bad luck. Let's get back and saddle up." Hack stood. "We need to go."

Jimmy Dale approached the dead Comanche warrior. Rudolph Polk followed, looking pale as a ghost. "He's not much more'n a boy. I bet he ain't sixteen or seventeen."

"He's old enough to kill two men in less than half a minute." Hack could never understand anyone who was shocked that a young person could kill. Cain was only fifteen when he bashed out Abel's brains with a rock, and things hadn't changed one whit since then.

Polk pointed at Two-Horses' body. "What about him?"

"We'll take him back up to the barn and stack rocks on him. That's the best we can do, and all he'd expect. We'll do the same for your friend." Hack didn't say the dead man's name because he couldn't remember it.

Maxwell swallowed. "You're hard men."

"That's what's kept us alive." Hack looked down at his old friend. "At least until now."

CHAPTER 45

It was late afternoon when the Rangers spread out around the ruins of a ranch and a half-finished barn. Ridge read the ground. "Lots of prints, inside and out."

Ranger Wilson made a slow loop around the collapsing house until his horse went sideways and sunfished underneath him. Grabbing the saddle horn, he hung on as the gelding bucked and did its best to run away. It took several long moments for him to get the frightened animal back under control.

He took off his hat and waved at the surprised Rangers. "Get away from that house! It's a snake den full of rattlers. One of 'em barely missed its strike."

The horses smelled the spring, and the Rangers let them drift down to drink, knowing they'd all need water before they continued. Ridge gave the collapsed structure a wide berth and rode around the unfinished barn, wary of serpents.

When he didn't hear any warning rattles, he dismounted and led his horse into the chest-high enclosure. There was evidence that several people had been there, and piles of horse droppings proved it to be true.

A layer of rocks on top of the walls had been placed there recently, and he studied the scene with an eye toward what had happened. It was two stacks of new, large stones against the west wall that caught his attention. They looked like graves.

Ranger Wilson waved a hand from the grass. "Body over here. Comanche boy. Burnt and shot to pieces."

Bookbinder rode over and backtracked the marks on the ground. "Well, at least they drug him away from the spring so's he wouldn't poison the water. Good for them."

While the others tended to their horses, Ridge chose one of the graves at random and moved a few of the smaller stones that were carefully placed to fill in the gaps between the larger ones. He stopped when the toe of a boot appeared.

Moving to the opposite end, against the wall, he uncovered a body that was fresh enough to have not yet swelled. He removed enough rock, dirt, and gravel to reveal the fletched end of an arrow in the body's chest. Moving up, he exposed the wide face of a man with long black hair and high cheekbones, marveling that he felt nothing at the sight of such recent violence.

"Half-breed."

Ridge jumped, for he was so intent on his work that he hadn't heard Captain Bookbinder come up behind him. "Good Lord! You darn near scared me into this man's condition."

"It was an arrow killed him, not fright, though that might have had something do with it at the end." He removed the folded pages from his pocket and shuffled through them. "Thought he looked familiar. That man's name, I suspect, is Two-Horses. Former member of the Long Gang."

"Comanches did for him, looks like."

"Saved us the trouble." Bookbinder replaced the wanted posters and opened a packet of tobacco and filled his pipe. Packing it with one thumb, he struck a match and puffed it to life. "We'll need to open that other grave."

His tone irritated Ridge for the first time. "You ordering me to do it?"

Bookbinder shrugged. "Not so much, just thinking aloud." He seemed to ponder Ridge's tone. "You don't take to such orders, do you?"

"Not used to it."

"None of us were, at first. Took me a while during the war to get used to younger men telling me what to do, but I got over it."

Some men would be inclined to ask what side Bookbinder had fought on in the War between the States, but Ridge never cared one way or the other. He'd been too young to serve and had always figured that when something was over, it was done.

Since he hadn't been ordered to do so, this time Ridge made quick work of uncovering the upper half of a young White man whose face was covered by his hat. "This one of them?" Ridge asked, removing the hat.

Bookbinder tilted his head to look square down on the corpse. "Nope. Another outlaw, I suppose, took up with him and got himself killed for his troubles."

"Those Comancheros lowered the odds for us."

"That leaves how many of the original gang, four?"

"Yep. Or three, if they didn't get to bury another one of their men."

"Doubtful. They seem to take care of their own."

"Well, it looks like they have some new members, less this one here. More than five or six horses, and lots of boot prints in here."

Bookbinder watched his men finish up with the mounts. "Let's make a few more miles before we camp. Too many spirits here, but we're close, and I don't want to run up on them in the dark. We'll get 'em tomorrow."

CHAPTER 46

The roofs of several buildings rose on the horizon. The Long Gang stopped and considered what they'd found. Billy Lightning slapped his leg. "By God, we made it. I'll wager that's Barlow."

Santana rested one fist on the top of his thigh. "What a deal. Thought we'd never get here."

"Almost didn't," Luke said.

"What's the big deal about this town?" Maxwell and his friends stopped with them.

Hack warned the guys quiet with a look. "It's just that we've been on the trail for a long time. We've been talking about laying up here for a while and resting."

The look Maxwell gave Hack rested on his face way too long. Hack felt that hum inside his head and swallowed it down, for the moment.

Santana understood they couldn't talk about the gold in front of strangers. "I'm gonna buy me a steak, a bed, and a woman." He cut his eyes over at Gussie. "Sorry about that."

She shook her head and smiled. "It's the way of the world."

Hack wished Two-Horses was there with them. His friend had earned the right to feel what was welling up in their chests, and he already missed him. He turned to Maxwell, Polk, and Jimmy Dale.

"I guess that's it for us, gentlemen. It's been good riding with you boys and thanks for forting up with us back there. I'm sorry about your friend, though."

Something passed between the three cowboys before Maxwell settled deeper into his saddle. "Well, we were kinda thinking about joining up with y'all. Maybe doing a little . . . work, with you, if you know what I mean?"

The high hum in Hack's skull turned into a familiar rush of heat that washed through his face. It all fit together then. The three cowboys knew who they were. "Thanks, but we're not taking on any new people right now."

"We're not new." Polk laughed. "We all just . . ."

"The man said no." Santana's voice cracked flat across the space between them. "Hack chooses who rides with us, and it ain't y'all."

No one drew a breath for several heartbeats. The air grew still, and nothing but the snorting horses broke the tension. Saddles creaked as the men adjusted their positions, ready to draw.

The cowboys saw the positions of the outlaws' hands near the guns on their belts and got the message. Maxwell sighed. "Well, then. That's it. Y'all don't mind if we stop in town for a drink or two, do you?"

"Don't mind at all." Hack kept his hand near the Colt. "I figure we're gonna take rooms here, so we might see you in a saloon. I'll buy y'all a drink to say thanks."

Rudolph Polk was finished. "Suits me just fine."

Maxwell turned his horse toward the roofs in the distance. "Come on, boys. Let's go have a drink for Dub."

Walking their horses to prove they weren't being run off, Polk and Jimmy Dale followed him, and they rode away in single file.

When they were out of earshot, the surviving members of the Long Gang relaxed, at least a little.

Billy poked at Santana. "He liked to've made you mad, huh?"

Eyes narrowed, Santana kept an eye on their receding backs. "I didn't like those guys when they showed up. Especially Eli Maxwell and that missing ear. They'd been following us pretty close until them Comancheros showed up. It was like they were trailing us."

Hack had felt the same way. "You didn't show it when they rode in."

"We needed the guns, and besides, I had my eye on them, especially the way Maxwell kept turning his head to hear. His mannerism was irritating."

Gussie spoke up for the first time in a while. "I don't know what you mean. They seemed all right to me."

"They smelled gold, Gussie." He didn't know why, maybe it was because Two-Horses was gone, but Hack felt like she might have earned a little of the money for just putting up with them. He hadn't wanted a woman with them at first. In his experience, they were hardheaded and usually more trouble than they were worth, but Gussie brought something different to the table.

He decided to tell her, even though he figured Billy already had. "We left a set of saddlebags full of stolen money hid there in town. That's why we're here, to get the gold, and somehow those guys suspected what we're doing."

She glanced from him to Billy. "I figured. Nobody handles themselves like y'all without walking the wrong side of the law from time to time."

Luke was still watching where the cowboys had disappeared, as if expecting them to come riding and shooting back at them. "What do you mean?"

"Billy. One minute he's this cute kid in trouble, then he shoots my manager and takes the badge off a Ranger and puts it on, and the next thing I know, you guys show up. Honey, I was *raised* in a cathouse, and I've seen my share of good and bad men. Y'all didn't fool me for a minute."

It was as if a pall had been lifted off the men. Santana threw back his head and laughed, followed by Billy. Luke caught his eye and chuckled.

Grinning through his beard, Hack shook his head. "Well, we might be in the money pretty soon, boys, but we don't have it yet. We still have to find where we stashed it and figure out a way to get those saddlebags out from under that boardwalk without people seeing."

Luke's laugh dissolved in a long coughing fit. "I can't wait to get my hands on that gold."

"We can't just go up there and start pulling up the boardwalk in the daylight." Santana drew a long breath. "The only thing I can think of is to wait for a dark night, like the one when we came through, and do it then."

Billy made a face. "That'll be a couple of weeks. This moon's been bright as a dime at night."

Hack gave the black a little nudge and started forward. "It's been three years. A few more days won't matter."

"It will if we run out of money."

"We won't. Y'all quit fretting about this and let's just enjoy some time in a town without people shooting at us."

They cut onto a wagon road and came upon a hand-painted sign just outside of town.

BARLOW.

CHAPTER 47

Ridge Tisdale inhaled the aroma of fresh-milled raw lumber, cooking meat, and the waist-high pile of horse manure out front of the Barlow Livery. W. A. Harbinson's Mercantile had barrels and boxes stacked out front. Piano music floated in the air, coming from some mysterious location down the rutted dirt street.

At the far end of town, a windmill creaked and spun in the breeze, pulling water from deep underground and depositing it into a large wooden trough the size of a one-room schoolhouse. It overflowed on one edge and sent a stream winding down the edge of the street against the boardwalk.

Halfway down the abnormally wide street, a boxy two-story saloon operated under a sign reading JACKRABBIT. Painted in black with a rough brush was a hideous rabbit with abnormally long legs and a disfigured head. Waving from behind a rail on the balcony above, three painted ladies waved at potential customers and blew kisses. When they saw the badges on the Rangers' coats, their smiles vanished and they went back inside.

Ridge rested both hands on his saddle horn and took in the busy street. "Hard to believe all this civilization is going on around us, and yesterday we were being shot at by renegades."

"Different kind of renegades are here." Bookbinder eased himself to the ground and tied his horse. "More than a few savages, too."

Ridge dismounted, too, then loosened the girth and raised the saddle up and down to get some air underneath and rest his buckskin. The horse appreciated it by throwing his head up and down several times.

"That's what'll make you a good Ranger," Bookbinder said. "I like to see a man take care of his horse before thinking about himself." He turned to his men. "Y'all fend for yourselves. Get something to eat and drink. Mr. Wilson, would you see to it that everyone regroups back here at the"—he looked up at the hideous sign—"Jackrabbit, in a couple of hours, please?"

They dispersed, heavily armed and silent men under black hats and coats and behind distinctive badges that brought immediate attention from everyone in town.

Bookbinder loosened his own saddle. "Ridge, there's a kitchen over there. How about we get something to eat?"

"Fine by me."

They expected to find a riot of noise and rowdy men inside. Instead, Butterworth's Restaurant was a bright, clean establishment lit by two wide windows made of many panes. It contained eight individual tables and two long ones that stretched the length of the building. The establishment was only half full.

Bookbinder flicked a finger at a table with three chairs against the wall. Its position allowed them to see the entire room, including the doors both front and back.

The closest table contained three dusty cowboys who looked as if they hadn't eaten in a year. Bookbinder noted one of them was missing his left ear as they passed. "Poor fellow. I feel sorry for the man, or for anyone who can't hear as well as I."

Ridge wondered at the comment, wondering why the

captain had vocalized what he was thinking loud enough for others to hear. Several sets of eyes found the men and their badges, then went back to their own conversations and food. Minding their own business, no one even turned a head as they passed.

A skinny Frenchman appeared at their side, wiping his hands on a towel. "Let me guess. Steaks and potatoes."

Ridge watched Bookbinder's face break into a grin. "You have coffee, too?"

"Just boiled a fresh pot."

"That will do!"

The Frenchman disappeared through a swinging door, and Bookbinder smoothed the red checkered tablecloth with his hands. "I haven't seen a covering like this in years."

Ridge scratched at the material with a fingernail. "First one for me. My mama had a white cover she used for special occasions, but it stayed folded in a drawer most of the time."

"After we eat, I'll track down the local constabulary." Bookbinder laced his fingers on the table. "Then we'll ask if anyone's seen our quarry."

"Can it be that easy?"

"Probably not. I usually make my arrests out there somewhere." He pointed toward the outside. "We've taken most of them on the run, or in camps, the woods, or somebody's house. The majority of our arrests in town are by happenstance."

"Which is what?"

"Oh, walking into a saloon and recognizing someone from a wanted poster, hearing that a criminal has been hanging around a particular town or county, or in the case of Ty Hankins, I was on a train he tried to rob, to his misfortune."

There was something about the eatery that funneled sound over to Bookbinder and Ridge. Unable to comprehend the conversations going on around him, Ridge chose to ignore them and concentrated on his new captain.

The cowboy with the missing ear on the opposite side of the room hacked at the steak on his plate. He spoke louder than necessary, likely due to his missing ear. "This hunk of overcooked bull is mostly gristle."

It was not the news Bookbinder wanted to hear after ordering a steak from the same kitchen. He grew silent for a moment, listening.

The one-eared cowboy kept adjusting his seat, turning his head so his good ear was toward the customers surrounding them. "Rudolph, next time I tell you and Jimmy Dale to let me sit first, you do that. Y'all know I don't hear well out of this bad side and need to set with my good ear out."

They chuckled together. Rudolph Polk waved his knife toward the other tables. "It's a good joke on you. There's nothing to worry about in here with all these townies."

"And besides." Jimmy Dale tucked a bite into his cheek and spoke around it. "Two Rangers just came in and set down. This is the safest place in town right now."

Still irritated, Maxwell sipped at a mug of hot coffee. "How much money you boys have left?"

Directly across from him, Polk chewed for a moment. "Two dollars. Jimmy Dale said he had a dollar."

"Dammit, Rudolph. That's my lucky dollar. I'd druther not spend it if I don't have to."

"What makes it lucky?"

"Because I say so."

They chuckled at the weak joke. Maxwell examined the edge of his knife. "Maybe this utensil could use some sharpening." He forked a bite into his mouth. "I oughta hone it to a razor edge and cut that Hack Long's throat with it for treating us like he did."

Polk lowered his voice. "Those are hard words from a man who intends to rob them at the first chance."

Maxwell frowned. "Quiet down with that."

Ridge, who hadn't heard the name or any of the conversation, opened his mouth to speak but stopped when Bookbinder raised one hand for quiet. Ridge held his tongue and rested both elbows on the tabletop.

Bookbinder gave him a grin. "Continue speaking, but lower, please. Something going on over there interests me."

Obviously not understanding, Ridge bent a little closer. "Am I hurting your ears? What I was saying is there's a lot I have to learn about this business, and it seems that you don't want your men to speak very much."

Bookbinder turned all his attention to the conversation and glanced over to see One-Ear cut his eyes across the restaurant. The man was obviously upset, and his voice showed it.

"Keep your voices down. Those are Texas Rangers over there, and they don't need to hear what we have to say."

"Oh, hell, Eli, they can't hear us way over here with all these people talking." Polk tore a piece of bread from a chunk on his plate and sopped at the juice. "So shouldn't we be somewhere we can keep an eye on those boys while they look for that money?"

"I was planning to do just that, but then they run us off. Those rats will pay for that when the time comes."

Jimmy Dale pushed his empty plate away and sat back. "How about we split up and keep an eye on Hack and them.

One of 'em'll eventually go out after that money, if what you say is true and they hid it on the way into town."

Maxwell put down his utensils and grinned. "That's exactly why we brung you along, Jimmy Dale. Who do you want to watch?"

"Gussie!"

They laughed and stood to leave as the Frenchman came out with two steaks for the Texas Rangers on the other side of the room.

Bookbinder cut into the steak that steamed on his plate. "Looks to me like we just walked into one of those coincidences I was telling you about.

Ridge raised an eyebrow. "Such as?"

"Those gentlemen just unintentionally informed me that Hack Long is in town looking for money they squirrelled away somewhere around here."

"We should go talk to them." Ridge made to stand.

Bookbinder grinned and carved on his steak. "We shall, but first I intend to finish the first good meal I've had in weeks, then we'll go arrest them all."

CHAPTER 48

The best place to get information in a town is either the
barbershop or the saloon. The boys with Hack weren't
interested in haircuts and baths right then, intending to use
the dead deacon's hard cash to buy beer and wash down their
troubles of the past several days.

Smelling like billy goats, they pushed into the dark saloon
and stepped up to the bar. A couple of girls occupying a table
in the rear stood up at the sight of potential customers, but
Hack waved them back down. Number one, they didn't want
to do any business right then, and two, folks needed to stay
clear of Gussie right then so they wouldn't find out she was
a woman.

He wasn't sure why she wanted to keep her sex a secret,
but Hack knew a reason would reveal itself at some point.
She trailed in behind them and stepped over to the nearest
empty table, sitting with her back to the room like they'd
planned. That way no one could see her face or her lack of
facial hair. Billy sat with her as the others lined up at the bar.

A barkeep with a face full of deep smallpox scars waited
on them. "What'll it be, gents?"

Santana must have been thirsty. "Beer."

"All around?"

Hack jerked a thumb. "Yep, for those guys over there, too."

The beers came quickly, and Santana carried his and the other two across for Gussie and Billy. Staying at the bar, Luke and Hack were down to half a glass when the barkeep came back around.

Business was light, and he leaned on an elbow to talk. "First time in town?"

He opened with a common topic of conversation, along with the weather and women. It was why Hack had remained at the bar to talk. "Came through about three years ago. There was a lot of building going on, but things look different than what I remember."

"Not surprised. Cyclone came through here two years ago. Woke up one morning and the sky was green as bile. I knew what was gonna happen the minute I stepped out the door. I was raised over in Denton County, and we had our share of twisters.

"I went down in my friend's cellar, and it sounded like that train we've been waiting for was coming through early and without the tracks. That whirlwind came out of the west and went straight down Main Street. Sucked up most of the buildings and half of the people and horses."

He pointed at a painting behind the bar with a jut of his jaw. A voluptuous woman with her nether regions covered by a scarf reclined on a fainting couch, smiling at the customers below. "That's Maggie. She's new because we had her sister up there when that cyclone came. Blew her off the wall, and some old boy found her about a mile from here, leaned up against a tree like somebody'd just set her there to admire the art outside.

"Only problem was a stick jutting out through her belly button. We would have had it fixed, but that guy who found her refused to bring her back to us. She's hanging in a barn over a bunch of milk cows. Guys says he looks at that painting every time he's milking, and you know, I can't blame him for that."

Finishing his beer, Hack exchanged glances with Luke, who was caught up in the story. Hack waited until the barkeep stopped for a breath and changed the subject. "I remember the Martin Bar and Restaurant. Had a drink and ate in there."

The barkeep picked up Hack's mug and hesitated, weighing the empty. "Blew Martin's place away and him along with it. Just across the street and sucked him up in the air. Found what was left of his body half a mile out of town, not far from that painting, but the coyotes had been there already, and he didn't look like himself. Should have asked. You want another one?"

"Sure enough."

The barkeep adjusted the garter on his arm and reached for the beer tap. Luke drummed his fingers on the bar top. "Well, that's a wrinkle we didn't expect. Right about now, I think I need a whiskey, too."

The beers came, along with Luke's whiskey, and a customer farther down waved for service. The barkeep made his slow way down, served him, stepped out from behind the bar, and disappeared through the back door. He was back in a couple of minutes.

Hack wasn't finished with questions. He waved him back over. "So exactly where was Martin's, there on the street?"

The man wiped at the bar's surface with a damp rag. "Directly across from our front door. Sat right there where W. A. Harbinson's Mercantile is now."

Luke positioned himself to look out the door and grinned. "Right there."

"Yessir, right there. Must've been a fine drink in Martin's to bring that smile."

"Enough of one."

"Funny thing. You must be misremembering. Martin's never opened. He didn't have the cash to finish the inside. The storm was good news for his wife, though. Killed him dead."

Hack's face flushed at the realization they'd stepped into

a bear trap. Stalling for time, he took a sip of beer and was able to form words again. "How was that good for her?"

The bartender's eyes were bright with knowledge, or mischief. "Well, about a week later, she got news that a rich uncle back East had died and took a train to go tend to his business. She came back a rich woman from all that inheritance and rebuilt the building. Made it a mercantile and then opened the Jackrabbit, here, and half a dozen other places in town. That brick bank down there? It's hers, and she's the bank manager. She's a rich woman now, and getting richer, because it was her who brought in the railroad."

"Rich, huh?"

He laughed. "Sure enough, and you can tell every place she owns because she had the blacksmith make her a bunch of little cyclones. Look over every door that's hers, and there's an iron twister nailed up there."

Hearing that, Luke went outside to look up above the batwing doors. He came back with an odd look on his face. "Sure enough. About a foot tall. One up there, and now that I knew to look, I saw one over the mercantile entrance." He tossed off the whiskey and closed his eyes.

The bartender moved away again to serve other customers. Luke drew a long-suffering breath when the talkative man was far enough away. "You know where she got that money to buy up this town, don't you, and it didn't come from no rich uncle, neither."

"I suspect not."

"Well, damn." Luke tilted the empty glass again to get the last drop.

CHAPTER 49

Wearing a star high above his protruding abdomen, the red-faced marshal of Barlow stepped into Butterworth's Restaurant with a double-barrel coach gun in his hands. He looked over the room and, seeing the Texas Rangers eating at a side table, approached them.

Captain Bookbinder straightened. "Marshal, I'd advise you to point that street sweeper at the ceiling, instead of waving it around like a kid with a stick gun."

Instead of doing as the captain suggested, the marshal looked confused for a moment and lowered the barrels toward the floor. "Sorry, I, uh, I'm Marshal Tub Patterson."

The captain fished out his pipe. "Good to meet you, Tub. You look like you need something."

"Well, I do, mister . . ."

"Captain Royce Bookbinder. This here's Ranger Tisdale."

"Good to meet you, too."

"Marshal, I simply offered our names."

Tub stopped. "Well, what I mean, Captain, I just got word that there's a couple of suspicious fellers in the Jackrabbit."

"Well, you're hanging behind that tin badge. Do your job for the good folks of Barlow and go see why they're suspicious."

"I, um, I figured that since there were so many of you

Rangers in town and thought you might want to go with me, seeing how there's three or four of 'em."

"You said a couple."

"Well, I misspoke. There's upwards of five, maybe six."

"And who proclaimed them suspicious, may I ask?"

"The bartender. He's usually a steady man and don't lean toward excitability."

Bookbinder considered the information. "You know, now that I'm full as a tick, I'd like a drink. How about you, Mr. Tisdale?"

Ridge put on his hat. "Suits me just fine."

CHAPTER 50

Hack bought a bottle and Luke another beer. They joined the others at their table. Luke carried five shot glasses on his fingers and distributed them about. Hack poured everyone a drink and brought the others up to snuff with the information they'd just learned.

The news took their spirit, and everyone sat there in silence as customers came and went. The first round disappeared fast as a snowball in a fireplace, and even Gussie swallowed her whiskey without a cough.

It was Santana who finally broke the wake. "Well, now what do we do?"

Gussie reached for the bottle and refilled all the glasses. "Shouldn't we at least look?"

"We'll have to figure out how." Hack sipped at his whiskey. "We can't just go start pulling up planks off the boardwalk. Gabe, what do you remember about that night?"

"It was dark." Santana chuckled, despite the bad news. "Half-finished boardwalk and lots of buildings going up. I counted, it was four posts from the corner, if that helps."

"They'll likely have been pulled up or replaced after the whirlwind came through." Billy was closer to Gussie than when they first sat down.

"Yeah, but I'd expect a good carpenter to measure about

the same distance for support posts." Hack rested his chin on one hand. "I did a little building with my old daddy when I was a kid. Gabe, you said you made a mark somewhere."

"I did." Santana used his thumbnail to cut indentations in the soft tabletop. "It was a crucifix with another smaller cross under the top one. I put it above the last plank they'd nailed down. Used my knife and carved it on the trim board about two inches high on the outside of the joists. That's the part we can see across from here."

"You think you can find it?"

"If I get down on my hands and knees, but that might look suspicious."

Billy laced his fingers on the table. "We're here because of that money. It's all I thought about while we were in Purgatorio, and now we find out it's all gone."

While they were feeling sorry for themselves, Hack's mind raced with ideas. The widow built an entire town with their money that was obviously no longer under the boardwalk. There was only one way to leave town with their pockets full.

"Boys, that money's gone as yesterday, and we don't need to waste our time trying to look under the boardwalk. With that said, I have an idea."

The boys quieted, waiting. Gussie raised both eyebrows in question.

"This town is booming, and all because of the gold we left under the boardwalk. That money funded all these businesses, and there's one place it all funnels into." Hack lowered his voice. "We do what we're good at. We're gonna rob the bank first thing in the morning."

Luke and Santana exchanged grins and clicked their glasses. When they did that, Hack suddenly remembered the look on the barkeep's face when he'd lied and said they'd been drinking in Martin's. If it hadn't yet been open, they couldn't have been in there.

He stood. "Get up now. We have to go."

Knowing him, Luke, Billy, and Santana left their drinks and rose as well. Hands on the butts of their pistols, they searched the room for trouble.

Gussie, on the other hand, acted as most women he'd ever known. "What? Why? I'm not finished with my drink."

Billy grabbed her arm and yanked her to her feet. "When the boss says move, we move."

Hack was already walking straight past the line of cowboys at the bar and out the back door. The boys came out behind him, and they broke into a trot, heading around behind the line of businesses.

Stopping at the first alley, Hack ducked around the corner and waited for them to gather. "We messed up. That barkeep knows we were lying, and I'll tell you why later, but right now we need to get the horses and scatter again. Don't have to leave town. It's a busy place and we can blend in, but y'all find somewhere to hole up 'til the bank opens in the morning. We meet back in front of the bank at nine."

Gussie started to ask another question, but Hack cut her off. "You get out of them man's clothes and back into a dress. You and Billy just got married. That should make the two of you invisible. It's all I can think of right now, so y'all go!"

They scattered like sheep, and Hack ducked around the corner and back onto the street. Ahead of Hack when he stepped back out of the alley, two Texas Rangers followed a fat man with a shotgun into the Jackrabbit.

CHAPTER 51

Captain Bookbinder and Ridge Tisdale trailed Marshal Tub Patterson into the Jackrabbit saloon. Tub walked straight to the bar, where the barkeep met him and started talking a mile a minute.

Shaking his head in disgust, Bookbinder directed Ridge to address the left side of the establishment while he covered the rest. He'd already figured out that Tub didn't know his butt from a hole in the ground and wouldn't know what to do if a line of outlaws was standing at the bar with a sign around their necks.

Tub laid the shotgun on the bar. "I hear there's trouble."

Once he was sure the room was safe, Bookbinder joined Tub and cut in. "Mr. Server, the good marshal here says you sent someone to come get help. I see no disturbance here."

The bartender explained what had happened, and Bookbinder listened. When the man was finished, the Ranger withdrew the sheaf of folded papers from his coat and opened them up. Spreading the wrinkled sheets toward the barkeep, he asked, "Were any of these likenesses the men you're talking about?"

His answer was immediate. "All of them. How'd you know?"

As Tub turned his head sideways to look at the likenesses,

Bookbinder declined to explain what he'd heard in the restaurant. "We're on the trail of these desperados. They appear to be in town."

"They just left." He pointed at the table covered with glasses and bottles. "Went out the back door."

Hearing that, Ridge dashed the length of the establishment and drew his weapon. He yanked the back door open and disappeared outside.

Leaving Tub, Bookbinder spun on his heel and pushed back through the batwings they'd just entered. The wide, busy street looked normal as a wagon rattled by. Men on horseback and on foot traversed the boardwalks on both sides.

Across the street, a photographer behind a camera mounted on a wooden tripod ducked under a black cloth. He reached around to adjust the lens aimed toward the saloon. Seeing the Ranger, the man uncovered his head and straightened.

"Would you stay right there without moving for a moment. You add an extra interest to this image Mrs. Martin commissioned."

"No." Bookbinder saw Ridge come around the corner of the saloon and relaxed.

"Nothing around back."

"They're gone." Bookbinder read the street.

"They've cleared out. I'll round up the boys."

"No need. They won't leave town."

"Why do you say that?"

"They're here after money."

"You know that how?"

He gave the new Ranger a grin. "Because I listen."

CHAPTER 52

"There they went."

Eli Maxwell gave Rudolph Polk a light slap on the chest with the back of his hand. They'd been loafing in front of a wheelwright's business, watching him work on a damaged wagon wheel, when three members of the Long Gang popped out from between two buildings.

Jimmy Dale saw the trio disperse and vanish in several directions. "They split up."

"That makes it easier for us. Those two ducked down over there." Maxwell pointed at an alley halfway down the street.

"Wonder where the other two went."

"No matter. That was Billy and Gussie. They'll be the easiest to work on." He struck off toward where they disappeared.

Polk and Jimmy Dale trailed close behind.

Hack was watching through the window of the Brown Brothers Meat Market and saw Maxwell and those cowboys only a few feet away. They seemed to be looking for something and moved on out of sight. There was no one at the counter, and the sounds of a cleaver chopping through a cut of meat came through loud and clear.

Strings of sausages hung in the window, both raw and smoked. Hack shifted to see through them and caught a glimpse of Billy and Gussie crossing the street in the distance.

Carrying what looked like a rolled-up dress under her arm, she'd already removed the hat she'd taken from the Sweeten marshal's office and taken her braid down. She looked softer and more feminine than when he'd first seen her. Billy wore the hat and broke the brim down, and he'd removed his own hat and guns. They were unidentifiable as the two who'd come into town only a couple of hours earlier.

They crossed the street twice, as if they didn't know where to go. The couple appeared and disappeared in the mob of horses, men, and wagons, and finally emerged from the throng in front of the White Owl Hotel. Billy took her elbow, and looking like a married couple, they stepped up on the boardwalk and into the hotel.

They were doing what Hack had said, and he wouldn't have been concerned, but one-eared Maxwell and his boys were following close behind like bird dogs on a covey of quail.

"Can I hep you?" The heavy German accent coming from behind was deep and rich.

Hack turned to see the butcher with a meat cleaver in his hand. "What time do you open tomorrow?"

The man wore a stained apron, and his hands were greasy with fat. "Not long after daylight."

Reaching up to squeeze one of the fat sausages strung together, Hack built a stiff smile. "I'll be back for some of these, then."

"I make them myself. They are very good."

"I'm sure they are." He set his hat against the sun and stepped back outside to follow those who followed his friends. "Thanks."

* * *

Billy and Gussie crossed the simple lobby that contained a few chairs and a round, horsehair stuffed settee. He took her arm and they approached the desk.

A woman with a wide part splitting her dark hair to both sides adjusted the register before her. "Would you like a room, folks?"

"We would." Billy took up a pen and dipped into the inkwell. "Mr. and Mrs. Gus Lane."

Gussie gave him an inquisitive look, and Billy smiled at the desk clerk. "We were just married and decided this is the place where we intend to settle down and have kids."

The door opened behind him, and three backlit figures entered. It was impossible to make out their features, and the men took only a moment to look the lobby over and go back outside, as if they were giving the couple room to finish their business and were waiting on service themselves.

The desk clerk watched the door close behind them and glanced at the signature. "That'll be two dollars." Billy slid two coins across, and she handed him a key. "Y'all been traveling, by the looks of your clothes." She addressed Gussie. "Would you like a bath? I can have one brung up to you by my daughter. The mister will have to step out, though, while she assists you. Have y'all put up your horses yet?"

Taken aback at so many orders and questions, Billy frowned. "Uh, no. They're down in front of the Jackrabbit."

"Figures." She sniffed. "The livery is down that way. Can't miss it. Your room's up the stairs. Last door on the left at the far end of the hall. It's what we call the honeymoon suite, but that's just because we have bright wallpaper in there and the rest of the hotel is just plank walls. We're gonna be painting next year, though."

"I could use a bath." Gussie hugged him as a new bride

would. "Find something to do for an hour and then come on up." Still toting her rolled-up dress, she took the key from his hand and went up the stairs.

Confused and unsure of what to do, Billy started to take a seat on the uncomfortable looking settee and changed his mind as the desk clerk opened a door behind her and called out back. "Jewel, we need a bath toted up to the bridal suite. Get Buck to carry the tub up."

Billy waited until she was finished. "I'll be back in a few minutes."

The woman turned the register back around. "I'd take my time, if I was you."

He went outside and glanced back down the street toward the bank. The red brick building rose two stories into the air and looked like a fort to him. They'd robbed more than one bank in the past, but this one looked foreboding. He preferred stagecoaches, which limited the number of pursuers. Here, they'd have to elude half the town in the morning.

A shaded wooden bench under a window painted with the words HOTEL looked inviting. He had no intention of going back to the Jackrabbit to get his horse, not with the law looking for them. He'd pick up the gelding after dark.

He settled onto the bench with a sigh, and only a minute later, Eli Maxwell dropped heavily beside him. "Howdy, Billy."

Surprised, Billy gave him as much room as possible, though only a couple of inches separated them. "Didn't figure to see y'all today."

"Well, here I am."

Maxwell adjusted his seat, and Billy felt something press against his side. When he looked down, the point of a Bowie knife was poking at the soft spot just under his ribs. "What'n hell are you doing?"

"Getting ready to walk with you out there past the windmill. There's a little foot path over there leading down in that arroyo. Rudolph and Jimmy Dale are waiting on us. We're going to meet them and have a little talk."

Beyond the structure was a plank bridge over a deep arroyo. Cottonwoods shaded the drop-off that was invisible from the town.

Confused, Billy looked down at the blade between them and backed up. "What do you want to talk about? And why are you poking me with that pig sticker?"

"That money y'all came to get."

Billy snorted. "I don't know how you found out about that, but brother, I got news for you. That money is gone. We just found out a little while ago a widow woman used it to build this town."

"I don't believe you."

"We didn't believe it ourselves, but it's the truth. We're leaving in the morning."

Maxwell thought for a moment. "Well, I don't intend to discuss this any further here. Get up."

"That's where it'll end. I'm gonna sit here for a little while longer, and then I'm going inside and sleep in a real bed. You need to put that knife up before you wind up with it sticking out your ear."

"You got a room?" Maxwell's eyes glinted. "That explains it! Y'all already have the money. That's why you're not together anymore." He grinned, nasty and wide. "Y'all split it up, and you and Gussie are gonna celebrate in one of those rooms up there."

As Maxwell's eyes glinted, Billy Lightning's expression went flat and dark. Fear was making a lump in the pit of his stomach as he realized he wasn't armed and his pistol was rolled up in Gussie's dress in their hotel room.

Done with talking, he grabbed for Maxwell's arm and missed. Maxwell leaned in with all his weight and thrust. The razor-sharp blade slit through Billy's vest and shirt and deep into the soft tissue under his rib cage.

Grunting in pain, Billy recoiled and folded against Maxwell, doing his best to push the murderer back and reach for his pistol at the same time. The knife plunged again and again. The shock took everything out of Billy, and he curled in unspeakable pain before something gave away inside and a bolt flashed behind his eyes and the man who'd survived four lightning strikes drifted into the darkness left by the storm of life.

Glancing at the busy street, Maxwell watched to see if anyone had noticed, but it had happened so suddenly and silently they were invisible. Billy's limp body slumped against his shoulder, and Maxwell slid the bloody knife back into its sheath and pushed away from the dying man. He stood and lifted Billy's feet onto the bench to make it seem as if he'd curled up to sleep. Tilting the outlaw's hat down low over his head, the one-eared man studied his work.

To those passing by, a tired cowboy in need of money had made himself comfortable in front of the hotel to take a snooze.

Maxwell wheeled and went to give the news to his men. The money was there. Now they'd have to come up with a new plan to get it.

CHAPTER 53

It was the first time in years Hack didn't have one of the boys close by. He was on his own, but he couldn't take the chance of the marshal or a deputy seeing them together. One man in town was a common sight, and two might be familiar, but anyone looking for them wouldn't expect those who rode together to be alone.

He left the meat market and ducked down the street after pulling his hat down low. He considered going back for his horse, but then the marshal came out with the Texas Rangers and they split up on the opposite side of the street.

One part of his mind was working out a way to avoid the lawmen, while another part was planning what would happen in the morning. Right then, he needed to stay out of sight. Keeping his head turned toward the windows and businesses along the street, Hack passed men and women going about their business without noticing an increased number of lawmen on the street.

He came to the bank and pushed into the brick building, the best place to hide with so much going on outside. An armed man who looked like an everyday cowboy occupied a stool beside the door. He nodded at Hack, who gave him a smile in return. Two tellers behind bars at the far end of the room served twin lines of customers.

A fat man and an extremely short woman sat behind two different desks on the right. She looked up with a bright smile and spoke with an English accent. "Help you, stranger?"

Hack had intended to spend a minute memorizing the room, but he responded with an equally bright expression. He had an idea. "Just hit town and was wanting to open an account."

"Well, sir, Fred here is in charge of accounts. Fred, look up from your work and get his paperwork started." She saw Hack's raised eyebrow. "I know you didn't expect this accent nor a woman from the sceptered island, did you?"

Baffled, he searched his memory for that reference. "I beg your pardon?"

She laughed. "What I said was, you didn't expect a woman from Brixton, England, to stop you in your tracks, did you? Mr. Jackson there's my accountant and second in line as the bank manager. I'm just the owner."

"I've heard of you, Mrs. Martin. The bartender over at the Jackrabbit says you own half the town."

"Old Bob loves to talk." She laughed and stood, raising up only a few inches above her original sitting height due to her petite stature. "Not really half, but a business here or two."

"Those cyclones above your doors."

She shook her head in mock disgust. "I wish he'd quit telling folks that. I like twisters. They're beautiful and deadly, the one I've seen. It brought me bad luck, and then good, so instead of hanging horse shoes above doors like superstitious people, I nail up iron cyclones."

"I never heard of such." Not knowing if it was proper, Hack neglected to hold out his hand. "I'm Abe Hendershot."

"Glad to meet you. Ruby Martin, and like I said, that's Fred Jackson. Fred, would you please accommodate this man?"

Obviously tired of hearing the same thing, Fred waved at

a chair across the desk. "Have a seat, Mr. Hendershot. Let's get an account opened for you so you can be on your way."

From the corner of his eye, Hack saw the marshal and a Ranger pass by the window. The door opened, and he angled himself so his back was to the entrance. Ruby looked up and smiled. "Tub, how are you?"

He glanced around at the customers and Ruby. "Just checking things out."

"Okay?" She waited for an explanation, and Hack watched her puzzled face.

"Fine then."

The door closed and Hack relaxed.

Paying attention to the job at hand, Fred took up a pen. "How much would you like to deposit?"

Hack stuck a hand in his pants pocket and pulled out a small leather bag. He shook a handful of American coins and Mexican *pesos*. "Fifty bucks. It ain't much, but it's all I got."

Fred frowned at the amount and shrugged. "Well, once a feller came in here and paid for a deposit box with his last dollar to keep his daddy's pocket watch safe."

Taking up a printed form, Fred scratched out the amount and date. As he worked, Hack kept an eye on the window instead of memorizing the interior like in the old days. It was a straightforward bank design with the tellers in the back. They finished their business, and Hack stood to shake with Fred. "It's been a pleasure doing business with you."

Ruby flashed him a smile. "We hope to see you soon."

"You will."

Running footsteps on the boardwalk and the sound of racing horses caused them to turn. A man rushed through the door. "Is the marshal here? Somebody said they saw him."

Eyes wide, Ruby shook her head. "He just stuck his head in the door and went on. What's the matter?"

"Somebody's just killed the outlaw Billy Lightning outside the White Owl Hotel!"

CHAPTER 54

In her room on the second floor of the White Owl, Gussie heard the commotion in the street. Stepping out of her bath, she wrapped herself in a towel and went to the window. Men gathered below, drawn by something below and hidden by the boardwalk overhang.

Excited voices shouted, and people ran both to and from the entrance. The marshal and another man wearing a badge came running, and behind them, several other similarly dressed lawmen converged.

Turning her attention to the north end of the street and the livery, which was clear from the second floor window, she looked for Billy Lightning. Not finding him, she turned back and dried off.

A knock came, and Gussie called through the door. "Who is it?"

There was a long beat before the answer came. "It's me. The desk clerk. Are you decent?"

"Not yet."

"Ma'am, you need to get your clothes on."

"How come?"

Silence again. "Ma'am, I'd rather not talk through the door."

"I'm just in my towel."

"Please open the door."

Exasperated, Gussie twisted the knob and yanked the door open to give the desk clerk a piece of her mind. Instead, she stopped when she saw the woman's face. "What is it?"

"I don't know how to . . . I'm sorry . . ."

"What!"

"Your husband."

Gussie's breath caught at the woman's distressed expression. "What about him?"

The woman swallowed. "He's been killed. Out front. I'm sorry . . ."

Suddenly numb, Gussie returned to the window. Now she knew why there was a crowd below. She looked out again and her eyes welled.

Four men carried Billy's body from under the overhang and roughly shoved it into the back of an empty wagon. Down the street, a photographer carrying a camera mounted on a tripod hoofed it in their direction, shouting something unintelligible and waving his free hand.

She turned back to the woman, who waited for a reaction from the new widow. Gussie took a deep breath and knew she couldn't trust any of the other members of the gang to stand up with her. Hack had made it clear only hours earlier that she was with them only because of Billy, and now he was gone.

She wiped at a single tear trickling down her cheek and drew a deep, shuddering breath. "Who runs the cathouse in this town?"

"Why, a madam named Victoria Jeffers does the hiring, but Mrs. Ruby Martin owns it, I'm told."

"That figures."

CHAPTER 55

Not knowing where Luke or Santana were hiding out, Hack had to find a hole somewhere. Robbing the bank was now out of the question with all the excitement going on. They just needed to get out of town and come back later.

There were still a few coins in his pocket, and Hack needed time to think. He'd seen a barbershop when they came in through the south end of town. Doing his best to not hurry, he turned his back to all the action and made against the current of people headed to the north end of town, excited about the murder, and that would work in his favor.

Making his way past several doors, Hack kept his hat low over his eyes until he reached the shop. The interior smelled of soap and witch hazel. The barber, with a waxed mustache, was alone beside his chair, looking into a mirror and clipping the hair in his nose with a pair of scissors.

He put down the looking glass. "How can I help you?"

Hack needed to change his appearance as much as possible. He waved a hand toward the street. "See those horses over there in front of the Jackrabbit?"

Interested, the barber went to the window and positioned himself to see. "Lots of horses there."

"The buckskin beside a roan, and then the packhorse?"

"I see them."

"They're all mine. I'll require everything you offer, and when we're finished here, I'll write you out a bill of sale for the roan and packhorse, after I get a few things off him. That should pay for a bath, haircut, and powder." He looked the shop over and read the sign nailed to the wall that offered other services. "Some new clothes and a few sprinkles of that smell good you have on the shelf there will do, too. You have someone who can get over to the mercantile?"

Eyes bright with the thought of so much money, the barber grinned. "The boy who works the baths out back."

"Good. Tell him to hurry over there. New boots this size, and maybe a hair over so they won't pinch my feet. Fresh clothes." Hack paused, thinking. "A new hat, too."

The barber went to the back door and then returned. He waved at the chair, and Hack took a seat and closed his eyes as the man covered him with the cape. That done, he leaned Hack back and poured steaming water over a towel in a dishpan before wringing it out. Hack closed his eyes as the barber waved the towel to cool it some, then wrapped it around his face to soften his beard.

"I'll have to scissor them whiskers for you, then I can shave you clean."

"Whatever you want."

"You've been traveling some, I reckon. You haven't been in here before. I remember every head of hair I've cut."

"Um humm."

"Lots of new folks through here because of the growth and the railroad. Miss Ruby's done a lot for this town."

"Um humm." Hack opened his eyes to see the barber whipping up foam with a brush and cup.

"We'll get you shaved and then get after that hair."

"Take your time. I'm in no hurry."

"Miss Ruby now, she's something. Owns the safest bank in Texas."

Hack kept his face impassive under the hot towel. "How so?"

"Why, if you go in there, take a look around. There's ports in every wall and a man back there with a double-barrel ten gauge. They're watching from the time the doors open to when they close. Won't nobody be robbing *that* place."

"Umm humm."

"She did it for the railroad. That's one of the reasons they're running that line through here, because they can store silver from the Arizona and New Mexico mines on its way back East."

The back door opened, and Hack's hand slid to the pistol on his belt. Seeing it was the boy, he relaxed and closed his eyes again. The kid sat in a chair against the wall. "Water's hot when you're ready, mister. I'll go get your clothes while you soak."

"That'll be fine."

"You hear about the outlaw was killed out front of the White Owl?"

A great sadness washed over Hack. "What do you know about it?"

The boy stood and adjusted the only working gallus on his overalls, as if it was necessary to take a position to relate the information. "Lightning was his name. Somebody stuck him half a dozen times with a big ol' knife. He'll be coming by here directly, since they're hauling his body over to the undertaker, that is after the photographer takes a death picture."

Pausing in his work, the barber went to the window and looked out. "I don't see nothing."

"He'll be by directly." Finished dispensing his information, the boy took his seat again. When the barber came back, Hack's Colt was in his hand, hidden by the cape.

CHAPTER 56

Like all Western towns, the prairie or frontier began at the immediate edge of Barlow. Once past the last building, there was nothing but grass and vegetation. In Barlow, the Cedar Post corral, only a few yards from the windmill, was the last structure on the north end of town, and that's where Luke Fischer sat on an empty nail keg, talking with a group of loafers with nothing better to do than spend time talking or drinking.

The corral was adjacent to the railroad depot that was under construction, though the rails still hadn't been laid. Since most of them didn't have the money for such indulgences, they gathered to discuss the weather, Indians, the coming railroad, or any number of subjects that did, and didn't, have anything to do with them. The subject had evolved to pondering the wisdom of building a depot so early.

On the way there, Luke had seen Billy talking with Eli Maxwell in front of the hotel, and he was thinking about putting some distance between them and the other gang members like Hack had ordered. Being so close to his partner might cause problems, and he wanted to avoid any entanglements with nosy townspeople or the local constabulary.

Though it was nothing out of the ordinary, Luke had

wondered why Maxwell and Billy were together. It could have been anything, so he dismissed the scene and listened for a while longer, enjoying the sounds of free men exchanging ideas and stories.

Luke always liked to listen when people talked. When he was young, he'd lie on his pallet in their little cabin, listening to his mother reading aloud from the Bible beside the fire until he went to sleep. It was a comforting sound that still echoed in his head.

Facing the outer edge of town, Luke was about to get up and leave when he saw Maxwell moving at a brisk pace to a hitching rack near the windmill. The one-eared cowboy swung onto his horse and kicked it into a lope. Instead of crossing the bridge, he turned and paralleled the dry watercourse.

From where he sat, Luke saw Gabe Santana strolling down the street toward the corral. Finding Luke sitting comfortably with the group, he apparently decided to ignore Hack's orders and rejoined his friend. Maybe it was because they were at the outer edge of all the action or because the no-accounts hanging around at that end of town wouldn't notice the two men who'd ridden into town together.

They hadn't been out of sight from one another for years, and it felt natural to stay close once they came together again. Santana nodded a quick hello and settled down with his back to a cedar fence post. The conversation meandered for a few minutes more before a shout came from the White Owl fifty yards away. Others took up the alarm, and in minutes excited citizens raised a cry that a man had been killed.

Conversation dried up like spilled water in the desert, and many of the loafers crossed the street to see what was going on. Luke watched Santana cross the street with several others to see what had happened. He came back with a shocked look on his face and jerked his head for Luke to follow. They drifted over to a stack of lumber beside the framed depot.

Santana positioned himself to see the gathering crowd. "Billy's dead. Murdered."

Luke's face fell. "He was just there a few minutes ago."

"Yep, and someone killed him."

Anger flushed Luke's face. "Yeah, and I know who did it." He pointed. "Let's take a little walk down that arroyo."

"Walk? I'd rather ride."

"We'll ride back." Luke lifted his Colt to loosen it in the holster.

"Hack doesn't want us together."

"He will for this."

CHAPTER 57

Freshly barbered and in new clothes, Hack looked into the mirror to find a stranger staring back. Even his eyebrows had been trimmed. The only thing familiar was the white forehead provided by his ever-present hat, which was the mark of every cowboy who ever forked a saddle.

Rolling the brim of his new hat to set the crease, he crossed the street to the Jackrabbit. Untying Billy Lightning's horse, he led it over to the barbershop and left it there. Waving at the window where he was sure the barber was watching with the fresh bill of sale, he went back and untied the black.

The change in his appearance was evidenced before he got halfway down the street. The town marshal and two Texas Rangers with grim looks on their faces passed without giving him a second glance.

Resisting the strong urge to turn and watch them on their way, he kept going. The rattle of gunfire came from somewhere to his left, distant and out of town. The sound was as common as birdcalls, but the cadence told him those shots were fired in anger or defense.

More than one man stopped what they were doing and

turned their heads, but no one went to investigate. Interest was only generated when people fought each other in town.

Feeling safe and hungry, he went to Butterworth's Restaurant, where the barber said he could use some of the money from the sale of Billy's horse to get the best steak west of Fort Worth.

CHAPTER 58

Bookbinder and Ridge Tisdale left the scene of the murder in front of the White Owl and were walking down the middle of the street, where they could keep an eye on everything around them. The crowd that had gathered at the scene of the murder had dispersed, and people were going about their business now that the photographer was finished with his pictures.

Ranger Wilson saw the pair and joined them. "That was murder, pure and simple."

"It wasn't someone after the money on Lightning's head. The killer wouldn't have left him there. It was something else, and maybe revenge." Bookbinder clamped the stem of his cold pipe between his teeth. "Gather the men. We need to talk about this."

"Where do you want to meet?"

"The marshal's office will do."

"I'll find them and meet you there." Wilson peeled off in search of the other Rangers.

Still maintaining their pace, Ridge turned to look behind them. "Tub has his hands full."

"I don't need *him*. I need his office."

"What're we gonna do?"

"Consider this matter, is what. There's more going on here in this town than meets the eye."

CHAPTER 59

In the arroyo outside of town, Eli Maxell, Rudolph Polk, and Jimmy Dale sat in the shade of a rustling cottonwood tree. Their horses were tethered to a downed log, swishing their tails at flies.

"That was a foolish thing you did, Eli." It was one of the rare times that Polk was angry with his partner.

"I didn't intend to kill him, there. I wanted to walk him down here where we could work on him a little bit and find out where that gold is. Then he started fighting with me, and it got out of hand."

"Whether you intended it or not, he's dead. Did anyone see you do it?"

"Nope. We were just sitting on that bench outside the hotel, talking. If anyone noticed, it was just two people passing time. It was his fault, though. He's the one that grabbed my arm, and I couldn't let him start hollering."

Sitting on the edge of the steep bank, Jimmy Dale stared at the ground between his feet. "This ain't turning out like you said, Eli. There's folks dying all around us, and Dub's dead, and we don't have a plan for what to do next."

"Our plan is to find them others and make one of 'em tell us where that gold is. The whole thing's pretty cut and dried, in my opinion."

A new voice made them start. "You don't have to make us tell you anything. I'm right here with everything you want."

As one, the three cowboys stood in shock, staring down the barrel of the Colt in Luke Fischer's hand. Polk stepped back, ready to draw, but he froze when someone spoke behind them.

"Nope. Hands in the air, boys."

Polk swung to see Gabe Santana pointing his own revolver. He smiled and spread his hands. "Hey, Santana. What're you boys doing pointing guns at us?"

Maxwell hadn't moved, stunned by the big bore pointed at his chest. "Easy, Luke. Don't point that gun at me."

"What's that on your side?"

Maxwell glanced down and drew a sharp breath at the sight of drying blood on his left side. "Hey, I was talking to Billy and he got mad."

"Y'all messed with the wrong people." Luke's gun spat fire, and Maxwell spun around when the slug ripped through his shirt. He took two stumbling steps and fell like a tree.

Polk and Jimmy Dale slapped leather, but their disadvantage killed them both. Caught in a crossfire between Luke and Santana, their guns barely came free as a swarm of big .44 slugs punched holes in their contorting torsos.

Smoke drifted over their bodies as Santana quickly knelt and rifled their pockets, producing a few coins and one pocket watch. Luke chose a bay that looked to have some bottom. The next best was a chestnut mare. He untied the third and slapped its rump. Snorting, it loped off down the arroyo.

Luke spat. "That was for Billy."

Leaving the bodies sprawled on the rocks, they mounted up and made a meandering way back to town.

CHAPTER 60

Grim-faced Rangers filled the marshal's office. Tub started out behind his desk, but when Captain Bookbinder came around behind and crowded him out, Tub found an open space beside a rack of shotguns and rifles with the blue worn off.

Ignoring him, Bookbinder picked up a box of cartridges off the desk. They would fit his Colt. "Here's what we're gonna do. Mr. Wilson, you take half of the boys and I'll take the rest. We go back down the street to the south end of town, gun up, and start a sweep all the way to the other end."

Ridge didn't understand. "Just scatter out and come down the street?"

"No. We scatter out and each man checks every building and house. We knock, we talk, we look, and then we continue on. Don't get ahead of the rest. This is a roundup, men. When we move, we'll be sure none of these desperados are behind us."

"What if folks won't let us look?" Ridge had never heard of such a thing. "I can bet you there're a couple of old boys who'll say no with a shotgun in their hands."

"We are the law. Tell them what we're doing, and then do it."

"I ain't drawing down on a citizen." Ridge couldn't believe what he was hearing. "That ain't right."

Bookbinder's eyes flashed. "You'll do as I say, or you can take that badge off."

Ridge plucked the badge from his shirt and dropped it on the marshal's desk. "Won't do it."

"There are men who will, and men who won't. Now I know which side of the fence you ride."

"I ride the side with the law."

"We *are* the law."

"These are American citizens."

"We're after American outlaws who threaten their peaceful existence."

"This ain't right, and let me tell you something. Every man in this town has a gun, and if you poke them enough, they'll gather and shoot every one of you, badges or not."

Captain Bookbinder's eyes flashed. "Don't argue with me, boy. You don't know what I've seen. What these men around you have done. Those outlaws have robbed and murdered their way across this state, and we have 'em holed up here somewhere. I bet you wouldn't open your head if I said we were going after those Comancheros who shot at us, to kill every last one of them we find."

"Well, of course not."

"This is the same thing. These men are savages, and I intend to either shoot them down like the dogs they are or take them to the nearest convenient location and hang them."

Ridge Tisdale shook his head. "I don't see it that way."

"You will, when you gain enough life experience to see the truth!"

Instead of arguing further, Ridge slammed the door behind him and ended his short tenure as a Texas Ranger by walking out the door.

* * *

Tub watched, open-mouthed. "Are you really going to do what you said? These people won't stand for it."

"That young man left before he realized that once these people see we're Rangers, they'll comply. It'll always be that way."

A man in a dusty suit and equally dirty bowler rapped on the door and stuck his head inside. "Marshal, uh, you Rangers might want to know there's been a shooting outside of town. Three men dead. You want me to get the undertaker?"

Tub swallowed. "Uh, yeah, I reckon. Who was it?"

"Don't know yet. Strangers."

The man left, and Bookbinder spread the wanted posters on the desk. "They're here. Memorize these faces if you haven't already. Each is distinctive, and you should have no trouble recognizing them. If you see anyone who reminds you of these likenesses, get your gun ready and watch their eyes. Let their fear reveal their guilt. Let's get to work."

The Rangers filed past the likenesses like mourners taking one last look at the deceased in a coffin. When the last one went out into the street, Bookbinder reached out to take the short coach gun lying beside them. "Marshal, I'm gonna borrow this scattergun for a little while if you don't mind, and I suggest you stay right here so people can come to you for advice."

CHAPTER 61

An hour later, Hack finished his steak in the near empty restaurant, and the Frenchman poured a little more coffee into his mug.

Two men came in and took a table. When the owner went to take their order, the older, with salt-and-pepper hair, took his hat off and hung it on the back of an empty chair. "Benoit, did you hear what's happening?"

"No." Obviously friends with the two men, he pulled up a chair and sat at the table with them. Benoit's accent was heavy. "What's going on?"

"The town's full of Texas Rangers, and they started at the south end of town, going door to door, looking for some outlaws that have wanted posters on them."

Pausing with the coffee halfway to his lips, Hack put the mug down, listening.

"There's been four killings today."

"I heard about the knifing in front of the Owl, but what else has happened?"

"Three men were shot down in the arroyo out past the windmill. Murdered, they say."

"Who are they?"

"Strangers in town. Look like cowboys. Shot to pieces."

Hack took a sip of cooling coffee. "You said three?"

The older man nodded and ran fingers through his long hair. "That's what I heard."

Not knowing whether to be relieved or worried, Hack did his best to look merely interested. "Was one of them a Mexican-looking guy?"

"Not that they said. Why do you ask?"

"I saw a Mex starting trouble earlier today. Thought somebody might have had enough and did for him."

They laughed, and Benoit rose and went into the kitchen. The younger man finally spoke up. "They were just cowpunchers is what I heard. One was already missing an ear. He probably lost it to an Indian or a mad wife."

"Hard times."

They laughed, and Hack finished his coffee and left a dollar on the table. He went outside, wondering if Luke and Gabe were all right.

CHAPTER 62

It was late afternoon, and as Bookbinder expected, most business owners and homeowners alike welcomed the Rangers when they knocked or came through to check out each building. A couple of old soreheads complained and were persuaded to comply.

While two Rangers posted themselves near the middle of the wide street, the others swept down the sides and alleys like they were on a rabbit drive. They didn't allow anyone to head north to pass from behind, and southbound individuals were cleared as they went about their business.

Mounted on his gelding, Bookbinder sat directly in the middle of the thoroughfare and waited for his prey to pass or flee. Men both riding and walking passed by, and he studied their features, dismissing them as if flicking away cards from a deck.

A rider approached with his hat set square on his head. The man kneed his horse away from the three Rangers. Bookbinder's eyes locked on him, noting by the lighter shade of his upper lip and jawline that he'd recently had a shave.

Behind him, two riders appeared in a wagon lot and yanked their horses to a stop at the sight of the lawmen. Their suspicious behavior caught Bookbinder's attention, and he dismissed the stranger.

CHAPTER 63

Unaware of what was going on in town, Luke and Santana rode right into trouble. Many of the businesses along the street were built shoulder to shoulder, but there were the occasional empty lots and more than a couple of alleys that led to corrals, scattered houses, sheds, tiny shacks, and dozens of outhouses.

Riding side by side through a wagon lot, they came out in front of a mounted Texas Ranger with two others flanking him on each side. Events and the situation conspired against them as the one on horseback reacted with the speed of a copperhead striking.

"Fischer!" The stubby twelve gauge came to his shoulder. "Hands up!"

The Rangers on foot drew and cocked their weapons with the ease of constant practice.

Wheeling his horse, Gabe Santana snatched up his Colt and fired, missing everything except the wooden building behind them. Hearing the order, Luke started to raise his hands, but saw three weapons rising against him as a man on horseback ducked and put the spurs to his mount.

He drew and fired, hitting the mounted Ranger's horse in the shoulder. It reared at the pain, throwing its rider, who hit the ground with a solid thud. The shotgun landed beside him and went off, catching the hard-looking man in the chest with both barrels. The Ranger jerked as if hit with a chopping axe and stilled in the next second.

The rattle of pistol fire filled the street. Struck by a hot chunk of lead directly in his heart, Santana went limp in his saddle and fell, dead before his corpse struck the ground.

Luke snapped two shots at the nearest Ranger on foot, spinning him around. He thumb-cocked his Colt again and shot at the other lawman, who was saved when the dead Ranger's horse bolted. Like an angry bee, a bullet from an unknown weapon buzzed down the street and caught Luke in the throat, and he dropped the pistol and clapped one hand over the wound.

Wheeling the horse, he kicked it in the flanks and used the other hand to grab the horn and stay in the saddle. Blood spurted, and he barely registered still *another* lawman with a protruding abdomen who stepped out from behind an outhouse and shot him in the chest with his pistol.

Luke spilled from the saddle as his stolen horse loped away.

CHAPTER 64

Gunshots all around him caused Hack to glance over his shoulder to see Luke and Santana reach for their guns. Kicking the big black into a run, he looked again and saw Santana fall in a hail of bullets and what seemed like everyone on the street shooting at Luke.

The echoes of gunfire followed Hack Long as he raced out of town, back the way they'd come so recently with the hopes of finding their money. Ahead of him, the road swept in a big arc through the scrub, hiding him from the town and any pursuit that might come.

There were times to stay and fight and times to run. Leaning over the black's neck, he ran the stud until lather flecked and flew back against his face. For mile after mile, there was nothing but the sound of thundering hooves and the harsh breathing of the horse doing his job.

When the black began to falter, Hack allowed him to slow and then walk to cool down. Dusk came, and with it the night birds awoke, along with crickets and other creatures that lived by the moon and stars.

When the stud's breathing steadied, Hack dismounted and walked the big horse. They both needed water, but that would have to wait until they reached the spring beside the crumbling house and half-finished barn.

He alternately walked and rode the stud all through the night. The gray light of dawn revealed the same abandoned ranch and the sight of a man saddling a buckskin. Hack was walking again by that time and raised both hands. "Hello!"

The cowboy walked around to the back side of his horse as calm as a man going into church and spoke over the saddle. "I bet you need the water."

"I do."

"Come on in, but I'd stay clear of that old house. It's a rattlesnake den."

"I will." Hack pretended to look around, as if he'd never been there.

The cowboy stayed where he was as Hack led the stud past on his way to the spring. They stopped, and Hack mirrored the cowboy's posture now, with the two horses between them. The black dipped his head, sucking up water with loud gulps.

"Go ahead and get you a drink." The cowboy tightened his girth. "I don't bite."

"Everything out here bites."

The cowboy chuckled. "I've learned that, too. I'm Ridge Tisdale."

"Good to meet you." Something was familiar about the man, though Hack was sure they'd never met. "Call me Jack."

"Which way you going, Jack?"

"No particular way. Just drifting and looking for the next job."

"The last one must've paid good. Fresh shave, haircut, new clothes."

"It didn't last." What was it about Ridge that was familiar? Hack reached up to adjust his new hat. When he touched the brim, it reminded him of another brim curled up on the right side. Where'd he see that? In town?

The cowboy stayed where he was, with nothing but his

head and shoulders above the curve of the saddle. He turned his head again when a quail called. Hack did the same, because Comanches communicated by bird calls and coyote yips. A jackrabbit hopped out of a thicket and watched them interfere with his time at the spring.

Experienced men, they looked for anything out of the ordinary, but the cool morning was quiet and normal. The rabbit waited patiently, for all animals drank from the same watering hole.

Hack wouldn't let the black drink as much as he wanted because he'd founder himself. Pulling him back by the bridle, Hack knelt on one knee and dipped his hand into the small pool, filling his palm. Lifting it to drink, he swallowed, and that small action reminded him of that last swallow of beer in the Jackrabbit.

Jackrabbit.

Two men following the marshal of Barlow into the saloon. Texas Rangers.

One of the men had a hat with the brim turned up on the right side, just like the cowboy watching him over his horse and Hack's horse had stepped to the side, leaving him wide open. "You're the law!"

"Was. Turned in my badge."

"Once a Texas Ranger, always a Ranger." Hack's wet hand reached for the Colt and the butt slipped.

"No!"

Something hammered him hard in the chest, and he staggered back. He grabbed the revolver again, and this time it cleared leather, but the hammer slipped under his thumb at the same time another slug struck him in the chest, then a third.

Feeling incredibly tired, Hack rested on his back and stared upward at the blue sky. A face appeared in front of them. "Howdy, Hack."

Mouth suddenly dry as the desert, the leader of what had

been known as the Long Gang stared at the man who'd killed him. A hot metallic taste of copper filled his mouth, and Hack coughed.

The face spoke, sounding far away. "Name's Ridge Tisdale, and I guess I still *am* a Ranger. I believe I'll have to take you to Angel Fire and pick up that badge again."

Hack worked up enough moisture to speak. "How'd you know?"

"I saw the wanted poster that looks exactly like you. A shave and a haircut don't change a man's eyes, nor the man inside."

"Shouldn't have second-guessed myself." His voice was a whisper.

"I don't know what that means, but it looks like you got what was coming to you."

"Not hardly" was Hack's last thought as darkness replaced the dawn.

**TURN THE PAGE
FOR A RIP-ROARING PREVIEW!**

**JOHNSTONE COUNTRY.
BACK IN THE SADDLE. AGAIN.**

**In this rip-roaring new series,
the bestselling Johnstones present a character
who's sure to be a favorite with Western fans.
He's a once-famous Texas Ranger who's given up his
badge and gone fishing'. But when trouble strikes, he's
ready to get back in the saddle—with guns blazin' . . .**

MEET "CATFISH" CHARLIE

As a former Texas Ranger, Charlie Tuttle
spent the better part of his life catching outlaws.
Happily retired in Wolfwater, Texas, he's content just
catching fish—namely Bubba, the wily old catfish
who lives in the pond near Charlie's shack and keeps
slipping off Charlie's hook. He also likes hanging out with
his trusty tomcat, Hooligan Hank, and tossing back bottles
of mustang berry wine—maybe a little too much, to be
honest. Sure, his glory days are behind him. And yes,
maybe he's let himself go a little in his "golden years."
There's no reason for Charlie to even think about
coming out of retirement . . .

Except maybe a double murder and a kidnapping.

It starts with a jailbreak.
Frank Thorson and his gang ride into Wolfwater
to bust Frank's brother out of the slammer.
First, they slaughter the deputy. Then, the town marshal.
Finally, they run off with the marshal's daughter and no
one's sure if she's dead or alive. The townsfolk are
terrified—and desperate. Desperate enough to ask
"Catfish" Charlie to put down his fishing pole, pick up his
Colt Army .44, and go after the bloodthirsty gang.
Sure, Charlie may be a bit rusty after all these years.
But when it comes to serving up justice,
no one is quicker, faster—or deadlier . . .

Once a lawman, always a lawman.
Especially a lawman like Catfish Charlie.

National Bestselling Authors
William W. Johnstone
and J.A. Johnstone

CATFISH CHARLIE

On sale now, wherever Pinnacle Books are sold.

LIVE FREE. READ HARD.

www.williamjohnstone.net

CHAPTER 1

May 2, 1891

"Bushwhack" Wilbur Aimes, deputy town marshal of Wolfwater in West Texas, looked up from the report he'd been scribbling, sounding out the words semi-aloud as he'd written them and pressing his tongue down hard against his bottom lip in concentration. He knew his letters and numbers well enough, but that didn't mean he had an easy time stringing them together. He almost welcomed the sudden, uneasy feeling climbing his spine, stealthy as a brown recluse spider. He frowned at the brick wall before him, below the flour sack–curtained window, the drawn curtains still bearing the words PIONEER FLOUR MILLS, SAN ANTONIO, TEXAS, though the Texas sun angling through the window every day had badly faded them.

The sound came again—distant hoof thuds, a horse's whicker.

Silence.

A bridle chain rattled.

Bushwhack, a big, broad-shouldered, rawboned man, and former bushwhacker from Missouri's backwoods, rose from his chair. The creaky Windsor was mostly Marshal Abel Wilkes's chair, but Bushwhack got to sit in it when he was on duty—usually night duty as he was on tonight—and the marshal was off, home in bed sleeping within only a few feet of the marshal's pretty schoolteacher daughter, Miss Bethany.

Bushwhack shook his head as though to rid it of thoughts of the pretty girl. Thinking about her always made his cheeks warm and his throat grow tight. Prettiest girl in Wolfwater, for sure. If only he could work up the courage to ask the marshal if he could . . .

Oh, stop thinking about that, you damn fool! Bushwhack castigated himself. The marshal was holding off on letting any man step out with his daughter until the right one came along. And that sure as holy blazes wasn't going to be the big, awkward, bearded, former defender of the ol' Stars an' Bars, as well as a horse-breaker-until-a-wild-stallion-had-broken him—his left hip, at least. No, Miss Bethany Wilkes wasn't for him, Bushwhack thought, half pouting as he grabbed his old Remington and cartridge belt off the wall peg, right of the door, the uneasy feeling staying with him even beneath his forbidden thoughts of the marshal's daughter.

He glanced at his lone prisoner in the second of the four cells lined up along the office's back wall.

"Skinny" Thorson was sound asleep on his cot, legs crossed at the ankles, funnel-brimmed, weatherbeaten hat pulled down over his eyes.

Skinny was the leader of a local outlaw gang, though he didn't look like much. Just a kid on the downhill side of twenty, but not by much. Skinny wore his clothes next to rags. His boots were so worn that Bushwhack could see his socks through the soles. The deputy chuffed his distaste as he encircled his waist with the belt and soft leather holster from which his old, walnut-gripped Remington jutted, its butt scratched from all the times it had been used to pulverize coffee beans around remote Texas campfires during the years—a good dozen. Bushwhack had punched cattle around the Red River country and into the Panhandle—when he hadn't been fighting Injuns or bluebellies and minding his topknot, of course.

You always had to mind your scalp in Comanche country.

Or breaking broncs for Johnny Sturges, until that one particularly nasty blue roan had bucked him off onto the point of his left hip, then rolled on him and gave him a stomp to punctuate the "ride" and to settle finally the argument over who was boss.

That had ended Bushwhack's punching and breaking days.

Fortunately, Abel Wilkes had needed a deputy and hadn't minded overmuch that Bushwhack had lost the giddy-up in his step. Bushwhack was still sturdy, albeit with a bit of a paunch these days, and he was right handy with a hide-wrapped bung starter, a sawed-off twelve gauge, and his old Remington. Now he grabbed the battered Stetson off the peg to the right of the one his gun had been hanging from, set it on his head, slid the Remington from its holster, holding the long-barreled popper straight down against his right leg, opened the door, and poked his head out, taking a cautious look around.

As he did, he felt his heart quicken. He wasn't sure why, but he was nervous. He worried the old Remy's hammer with his right thumb, ready to draw it back to full cock if needed.

Not seeing anything amiss out front of the marshal's office and the jailhouse, he glanced over his shoulder at Skinny Thorson once more. The outlaw was still sawing logs beneath his hat. Bushwhack swung his scowling gaze back to the street, then stepped out onto the jailhouse's rickety front stoop to take a better look around.

The night was dark, the sky sprinkled with clear, pointed stars. Around Bushwhack, Wolfwater slouched, quiet and dark in these early-morning hours—one thirty, if the marshal's banjo clock on the wall over the large, framed map of western Texas could be trusted. The clock seemed to lose about three minutes every week, so Bushwhack or Wilkes or Maggie Cruz, who cleaned the place once a week, had to consult their pocket watches and turn it ahead.

Bushwhack trailed his gaze around the broad, pale street to his left; it was abutted on both sides by mud brick, Spanish-style adobe, or wood frame, false-fronted business buildings, all slouching with age and the relentless Texas heat and hot, dry wind. He continued shuttling his scrutinizing gaze along the broad street to his right, another block of which remained before the sotol-stippled, bone-dry, cactus-carpeted desert continued unabated dang near all the way to the Rawhide Buttes and Wichita Falls beyond.

The relatively recently laid railroad tracks of the Brazos, San Antonio & Rio Grande Line ran right through the middle of the main drag, gleaming faintly now in the starlight. Most businessmen and cattlemen in the area had welcomed the railroad for connecting San Antonio, in the southeast, with El Paso, in the northwest, and parts beyond.

Celebrated by some, maligned by others, including Marshal Abel Wilkes.

The San Antonio & Rio Grande Line might have brought so-called progress and a means for local cattlemen to ship their beef-on-the-hoof out from Wolfwater, but it had also brought trouble in the forms of men and even some women—oh, its share of troublesome women, as well, don't kid yourself!—in all shapes, sizes, colors, and creeds. However, it being a weeknight, the town was dark and quiet. On weekends, several saloons, hurdy-gurdies, and gambling parlors remained open, as long as they had customers, or until Marshal Wilkes, backed by Bushwhack himself, tired of breaking up fights and even some shootouts right out on the main drag, Wolfwater Street. Marshal and deputy would shut them down and would send the cowboys, vaqueros, sodbusters, and prospectors back to their ranches, haciendas, soddies, and diggings, respectively.

The road ranches stippling the desert outside of Abel Wilkes's jurisdiction stayed open all night, however. There was nothing Wilkes and Bushwhack could do about them. What perditions they were, too! When he'd heard about all the trouble that took place out there, Bushwhack was secretly glad his and the marshal's jurisdiction stopped just outside of Wolfwater. Too many lawmen—deputy U.S. marshals, deputy sheriffs from the county seat over in Heraklion, and even some Texas Rangers and Pinkertons—had ridden into such places, between town and the Rawhide Buttes, to the west, or between town and the Stalwart Mountains, to the south, never to be seen or heard from again.

In fact, only last year, Sheriff Ed Wilcox from Heraklion had sent two deputies out to the road ranch on Jawbone Creek. Only part of them had returned home—their heads in gunnysacks tied to their saddle horns!

As far as Bushwhack knew, no one had ever learned what had become of the rest of their bodies. He didn't care to know, and he had a suspicion that Sheriff Ed Wilcox didn't, either. The road ranch on Jawbone Creek continued to this day, unmolested—at least by the law, ha-ha. (That was the joke going around.)

Bushwhack shoved his hat down on his forehead to scratch the back of his head with his left index finger. All was quiet, save the snores sounding from Skinny Thorson's cell in the office behind him. No sign of anyone out and about. Not even a cat. Not even a coyote, in from the desert, hunting cats.

So, who or what had made the sounds Bushwhack had heard just a minute ago?

He yawned. He was tired. Trouble in town had kept him from getting his nap earlier. His beauty sleep, the marshal liked to joke. Maybe he'd nodded off without realizing it and had only dreamt of the hoof thud and the bridle chain rattle.

Bushwhack yawned again, turned, stepped back inside the office, and closed the door. Just then, he realized that the snores had stopped. He swung his head around to see Skinny Thorson lying as before, only he'd poked his hat brim up on his forehead and was gazing at Bushwhack, grinning, blue eyes twinkling.

"What's the matter, Bushwhack?" the kid said. "A mite nervous, are we?"

Bushwhack sauntered across the office and stood at the door of Skinny's cell, scowling beneath the brim of his own Stetson. He poked the Remington's barrel through the bars and said, "Shut up, you little rat-faced tinhorn, or I'll pulverize your head."

Skinny turned his head to one side and a jeering warning light came to his eyes. "My big brother, Frank, wouldn't like that—now, would he?"

"No, the hangman wouldn't like it, neither. He gets twenty dollars for every neck he stretches. He's probably halfway between Heraklion an' here, and he wouldn't like it if he got here an' didn't have a job to do, money to make." Bushwhack grinned. "Of course, he'd likely get one of Miss Claire's girls to soothe his disappointment. And every man around knows how good Miss Claire's girls are at soothing disappointments."

It was true. Miss Julia Claire's sporting parlor was one of the best around—some said the best hurdy-gurdy house between El Paso and San Antonio, along the San Antonio, & Rio Grande Line. And Miss Julia Claire herself was quite the lady. A fella could listen to her speak English in that beguiling British accent of hers all day long.

All *night* long, for that matter.

Only, Miss Claire herself didn't work the line. That fact— her chasteness and accent and the obscurity of her past, which she'd remained tight-lipped about for all of the five years she'd lived and worked here in Wolfwater—gave her an alluring air of mystery.

Skinny Thorson now pressed his face up close to the bars, squeezing a bar to either side of his face in his hands, until his knuckles turned white, and said, "'The Reaper' ain't gonna have no job to do once he gets here, because by the time he gets here, I won't be here anymore. You got it, Bushwhack?"

The Reaper was what everyone around called the executioner from the county seat, Lorenzo Snow.

The prisoner widened his eyes and slackened his lower jaws and made a hideous face of mockery, sticking his long tongue out at Bushwhack.

Bushwhack was about to grab that tongue with his fingers and pull it through the bars, pull it all the way out of the kid's mouth—by God!—but stopped when he heard something out in the street again.

"What was that?" asked Skinny with mock trepidation, cocking an ear to listen. "Think that was Frank, Bushwhack?" He grinned sidelong through the bars once more. "You know what? I think it was!"

Outside, a horse whinnied shrilly.

Outside, men spoke, but it was too soft for Bushwhack to make out what they were saying.

The hooves of several horses thudded and then the thuds dwindled away to silence.

Bushwhack turned to face the door, scowling angrily. "What in holy blazes is going on out there?"

"It's Frank, Bushwhack. My big brother, Frank, is here, just like I knew he would be! He got the word I sent him!" Skinny tipped his head back and whooped loudly. Squeezing the cell bars, he yelled, "I'm here, Frank. Come an' fetch me out of here, big brother!"

Bushwhack had holstered the Remington, but he had

not snapped the keeper thong home over the hammer. He grabbed his sawed-off twelve gauge off a peg in the wall to his left and looped the lanyard over his head and right shoulder. He broke open the gun to make sure it was loaded, then snapped it closed and whipped around to Skinny and said tightly, "One more peep out of you, you little scoundrel, an' I'll blast you all over that wall behind you. If Frank came to fetch you, he'd best've brought a bucket an' a mop!"

Skinny narrowed his eyes in warning and returned in his own tight voice, "Frank won't like it, Bushwhack. You know Frank. Everybody around the whole county knows Frank. You an' they know how Frank can be when he's riled!"

Bushwhack strode quickly up to the cell, clicking the twelve gauge's hammers back to full cock. "You don't hear too good, Skinny. Liable to get you killed. Best dig the dirt out'n your ears."

Skinny looked down at the heavy, cocked hammers of the savage-looking gut shredder. He took two halting steps back away from the cell door, raising his hands, palms out, in supplication. "All . . . all right, now, Bushwhack," he trilled. "Calm down. Just funnin' you's all." He smiled suddenly with mock equanimity. "Prob'ly not Frank out there at all. Nah. Prob'ly just some thirty-a-month-and-found cow nurses lookin' fer some coffin varnish to cut the day's dust with. Yeah, that's prob'ly who it is."

His smile turned wolfish.

Grimacing, anger burning through him, Bushwhack swung around to the door. Holding the twelve gauge straight out from his right side, right index finger curled over both eyelash triggers, he pulled the door open wide.

His big frame filled the doorway as he stared out into the night.

Again, the dark street was empty.

"All right—who's there?" he said, trying to ignore the insistent beating of his heart against his breastbone.

Silence, save for crickets and the distant cry of a wildcat on the hunt out in the desert in the direction of the Stalwarts.

He called again, louder: "Who's there?" A pause. "That you, Frank?"

Bushwhack and Marshal Wilkes had known there was the possibility that Skinny's older brother, Frank, might journey to Wolfwater to bust his brother out. But they'd heard Frank had been last seen up in the Indian Nations, and they didn't think that even if Frank got word that Wilkes and Bushwhack had jailed his younger brother for killing a half-breed whore in one of the lesser parlor houses in Wolfwater, he'd make it here before the hangman would. There were a total of six houses of ill repute in Wolfwater—not bad for a population of sixty-five hundred, though that didn't include all of the cowboys, vaqueros, miners, and sodbusters who frequented the town nearly every night and on weekends, and the mostly unseemly visitors, including gamblers, confidence men and women, which the railroad brought to town. It was in one of these lesser houses, only identified as GIRLS by the big gaudy sign over its front door, that Skinny had gone loco on busthead and thrown the girl out a second-story window.

The girl, a half-Comanche known as "Raven," had lived a few days before succumbing to her injuries caused when she'd landed on a hitchrack, which had busted all her ribs and cracked her spine. Infection had been the final cause of death, as reported by the lone local medico, Doc Overholser.

Anger at being toyed with was growing in Bushwhack. Fear, too, he had to admit. He stepped out onto the stoop, swinging his gaze from right to left, and back again, and yelled, "Who's out there? If it's you, Frank—show yourself, now!"

Bushwhack heard the sudden thud of hooves to his right and his left.

Riders were moving up around him now, booting their horses ahead at slow, casual walks, coming out from around the two front corners of the jailhouse, flanking him on his right and left. They were ominous silhouettes in the starlight. As Bushwhack turned to his left, where three riders were just then swinging their horses around the right front corner of the jailhouse stoop and into the street in front of it, a gun flashed.

At the same time the gun's loud bark slammed against Bushwhack's ears, the bullet plundered his left leg, just above the knee. The bullet burned like a branding iron laid against his flesh.

Bushwhack yelped and shuffled to his right, clutching the bloody wound in misery. He released the twelve gauge to hang free against his belly and struck the porch floor in a grunting, agonized heap. He cursed through gritted teeth, feeling warm blood ooze out of his leg from beneath his fingers. As he did, slow hoof clomps sounded ahead of him. He peered up to see a tall, rangy man in a black vest, black hat, and black denim trousers ride out of the street's darkness on a tall gray horse and into the light from the window and the open door behind Bushwhack.

The guttering lamplight shone in cold gray eyes above a long, slender nose and thick blond mustache. The lips beneath the mustache quirked a wry grin as Frank Thorson said, "Hello, there, Bushwhack. Been a while. You miss me?"

The smile grew. But the gray eyes remained flat and hard and filled with malicious portent.

CHAPTER 2

Marshal Abel Wilkes snapped his eyes open, instantly awake. "Oh, fer Pete's sake!"

Almost as quickly, though not as quickly as it used to be, the Colt hanging from the bedpost to his right was in his hand. Aiming the barrel up at the ceiling, Abel clicked the hammer back and lay his head back against his pillow, listening.

What he'd heard before, he heard again. A man outside breathing hard. Running in a shambling fashion. The sounds were growing louder as Wilkes—fifty-six years old, bald, but with a strap of steel-gray hair running in a band around his large head, above his ears, and with a poorly trimmed, soup-strainer gray mustache—lay there listening.

What in blazes . . . ?

Abel tossed his covers back and dropped his pajama-clad legs over the side of the bed. He'd grabbed his ratty, old plaid robe off a wall peg and shrugged into it and was sliding his feet into his wool-lined slippers, as ratty as the robe, when his daughter's voice rose from the lower story. "Dad? Dad? You'd better come down he—"

She stopped abruptly when Abel heard muffled thuds on the floor of the porch beneath his room, here in the second story of the house he owned and in which he lived with his daughter, Bethany. The muffled thuds were followed by a loud hammering on the house's front door.

"Marshal Wilkes!" a man yelled.

More thundering knocks, then Bushwhack Aimes's plaintive wail: *"Marshal Wilkes!"*

What in tarnation is going on now? Wilkes wondered.

Probably had to do with the railroad. That damned railroad . . . bringin' vermin of every stripe into—

"Dad, do you hear that?" Beth's voice came again from the first story.

"Coming, honey!" Abel said as he opened his bedroom door and strode quickly into the hall, a little breathless and dizzy from rising so fast. He wasn't as young as he used to be, and he had to admit his gut wasn't as flat as it used to be, either. Too many roast beef platters at Grace Hasting's café for noon lunch, followed up by steak and potatoes cooked by Beth for supper.

Holding the Colt down low against his right leg, Abel hurried as quickly as he could, without stumbling down the stairs, just as Beth opened the front door at the bottom of the stairs and slightly right, in the parlor part of the house. The willowy brunette was as pretty as her mother had been, but she was on the borderline of being considered an old maid, since she was not yet married at twenty-four. The young woman gasped and stepped back quickly as a big man tumbled inside the Wilkes parlor, striking the floor with a loud *bang*.

Not normally a screaming girl, Beth stepped back quickly, shrieked, and closed her hands over her mouth as she stared down in horror at her father's deputy, who lay just inside the front door, gasping like a landed fish.

Abel knew it was Bushwhack Aimes because he'd recognized his deputy's voice. The face of the man, however, only vaguely resembled Bushwhack. He'd been beaten bad, mouth smashed, both eyes swelling, various sundry scrapes and bruises further disfiguring the big man's face. He wore only long-handles, and the top hung from his nearly bare shoulders in tattered rags.

"Oh, my God!" Beth exclaimed, turning to her father as Abel brushed past her.

Like Abel, she was clad in a robe and slippers. Lamps burned in the parlor, as well as in the kitchen, indicating she'd been up late grading papers again or preparing lessons for tomorrow.

"Good God," Abel said, dropping to a knee beside his bloody deputy, who lay clutching his left leg with both hands and groaning loudly against the pain that must be hammering all through him. "What the hell happened, Bushwhack? Who did this to you?"

He couldn't imagine the tenacity it had taken for Bushwhack in his condition to have made it here from the jailhouse—a good four-block trek, blood pouring out of him. The man already had a bum hip, to boot!

"Marshal!" Aimes grated out, spitting blood from his lips.

Abel turned to his daughter, who stood crouched forward over Aimes, looking horrified. "Beth, heat some water and fetch some cloths, will you?"

As Beth wheeled and hurried across the parlor and into the kitchen, Abel placed a placating hand on his deputy's right shoulder. "Easy, Bushwhack. Easy. I'll fetch the sawbones in a minute. What happened? Who did this to you?"

Aimes shifted his gaze from his bloody leg to the marshal. "Thor . . . Thorson. Frank Thorson . . . an' his men! Shot me. Beat me. Stripped me. Left me in the street . . . laughin' at me!" The deputy sucked a sharp breath through gritted teeth and added, "They busted Skinny out of jail!"

"Are they still in town?"

"They broke into one of the saloons—the Wolfwater Inn! Still . . . still there, far as I know . . . Oh . . . oh, *Lordy!*" Bushwhack reached up and wrapped both of his own bloody hands around one of Abel's. "They're killers, Marshal! Don't go after 'em alone." He wagged his head and showed his teeth between stretched-back lips. "Or . . . you'll . . . " He was weakening fast, eyelids growing heavy, barely able to get the words out. ". . . . you'll end up like me—*dead!*"

With that, Bushwhack's hands fell away from Abel's. His head fell back against the floor with a loud *thump*. He rolled onto his back and his head sort of wobbled back and forth, until it and the rest of the man's big body fell still. The eyes slightly crossed and halfway closed as they stared up at Abel Wilkes, glassy with death.

Footsteps sounded behind Abel, and he turned to see Beth striding through the parlor behind him. "I have water heating, Pa! Want I should fetch the doc . . . ?" She stopped suddenly as she gazed down at Bushwhack. Again, she raised her hands to her mouth, her brown eyes widening in shock.

"No need for the doc, honey," Abel said, slowly straightening, gazing down at his deputy. Anger burned in him. "I reckon he's done for, Bushwhack is." Beth moved slowly forward, dropped to her knees, and gently set her hand on the deputy's head, smoothing his thick, curly, salt-and-pepper hair back from his forehead. "I'm so sorry, Bushwhack," she said in a voice hushed with sorrow.

"Stay with him, take care of him as best you can, honey," Abel said, reaching down to squeeze his daughter's shoulder comfortingly. "On my way into town, I'll send for the undertaker."

Beth looked up at her father, tears of sorrow and anger in her eyes. "Who did this to Bushwhack, Pa?"

"Frank Thorson."

Beth sort of winced and grimaced at the same time. Most people did that when they heard the name. "Oh, God," she said.

"Don't you worry, honey," Abel said, squeezing her

shoulder once more. "Thorson will pay for what he did here tonight."

Abel gave a reassuring dip of his chin, then turned to start back up the stairs to get dressed.

"Pa!" Beth cried.

Abel stopped and turned back to his daughter, on her knees now and leaning back against the slipper-clad heels of her feet. Beth gazed up at him with deep concern. "You're not thinking about confronting Frank Thorson alone—are you?"

Abel didn't like the lack of confidence he saw in his daughter's eyes. "I don't have any choice, honey." Aimes was his only deputy, and there was little time to deputize more men. He needed to throw a loop around Frank Thorson and the men riding with him before they could leave town. This was his town, Abel Wilkes's town, and he'd be dogged if anyone, including Frank Thorson, would just ride in, shoot and beat his deputy to death, spring a prisoner, then belly up to a bar for drinks in celebration.

Oh, no. Wilkes might not be the lawman he once was, but Wolfwater was still his town, gallblastit. He would not, could not, let the notorious firebrand Frank Thorson, whom he'd had run-ins with before, turn him into a laughingstock.

Trying to ignore his deputy's final warning, which echoed inside his head, Wilkes returned to his room and quickly dressed in his usual work garb—blue wool shirt under a brown vest, black twill pants, and his Colt's six-gun strapped around his bulging waist. He grabbed his flat-brimmed black hat off a wall peg and, holding the hat in one hand, crouched to peer into the mirror over his dresser.

He winced at what he saw there. An old man . . .

His dear wife's death two years ago had aged him considerably. Abel Wilkes, former soldier in the War Against Northern Aggression, former stockman, former stage driver, former stagecoach messenger, and, more recently, former

Pinkerton agent, was not the man he'd been before Ethel Wilkes had contracted bone cancer, which they'd had diagnosed by special doctors up in Abilene. Abel's face was paler than it used to be; heavy blue pouches sagged beneath his eyes, and deep lines spoked out from their corners.

There was something else about that face staring back from the mirror that gave Wilkes an unsettled feeling. He tried not to think about it, but now as he set the low-crowned hat on his head, shucked his Colt from its holster, opened the loading gate, and drew the hammer back to half cock, he realized the cause of his unsettlement. The eyes that had stared back at him a moment ago were no longer as bold and as certain as they once had been.

They'd turned a paler blue in recent months, and there was no longer in them the glint of bravado, the easy confidence that had once curled one corner of his mustached upper lip as he'd made his rounds up and down Wolfwater's dusty main drag. Now, as he stared down at the wheel of his six-gun as he poked a live cartridge into the chamber he usually left empty beneath the hammer, his eyes looked downright uncertain. Maybe even a little afraid.

Maybe more than *a little* afraid.

"Don't do it, Pa. Don't confront those men alone," Beth urged from where she continued to kneel beside Bushwhack as Abel descended the stairs, feeling heavy and fearful and generally out of sorts.

Beth wasn't helping any. Anger rose in him and he shifted his gaze to her now, deep lines corrugating his broad, sun-leathered forehead beneath the brim of his hat. "You sit tight and don't worry," he said, stepping around her and Bushwhack, his Winchester in his right hand now. "I'll send the undertak—"

She grabbed his left hand with both of her own and squeezed. "Pa, don't! Not alone!"

Not turning to her, but keeping his eyes on the night ahead

of him, the suddenly awful night, Abel pulled his hand out from between Beth's and headed through the door and onto the porch. "I'll be back soon."

Feeling his daughter's terrified gaze on his back, Abel crossed the porch, and descended the three steps to the cinder-paved path that led out through the gate in the white picket fence. He strode through the gate and did not bother closing it behind him. His nerves were too jangled to trifle with such matters as closing gates in picket fences.

As he strode down the willow-lined lane toward the heart of town, which lay ominously dark and silent straight ahead, Abel shook his head as though to rid it of the fear he'd seen in his daughter's eyes . . . in his own eyes. Beth's fear had somehow validated his own.

"Darn that girl, anyway," he muttered as he walked, holding the Winchester down low in his right hand. *She knows me better than I do. She knows my nerves have gone to hell.*

Fear.

Call it what it is, Abel, he remonstrated himself.

You've grown fearful in your later years.

There'd been something unnerving about watching Ethel die so slowly, gradually. That had been the start of his deterioration. And then, after Ethel had passed and they'd buried her in the cemetery at the east end of town, that darn whore had had to go and save his hide in the Do Drop Inn. The gambler had had Wilkes dead to rights. The marshal had called the man out on his cheating after hearing a string of complaints from other men the gambler had been playing cards with between mattress dances upstairs in the inn.

So Abel had gone over to the inn, intending to throw the man out of town. The gambler had dropped his cards, kicked his chair back, rose, and raised his hands above the butts of his twin six-shooters.

Open challenge.

Let the faster man live.

Abel remembered the fear he'd felt. He had a reputation as a fast gun—one of the fastest in West Texas at one time. "Capable Abel" Wilkes, they'd called him. His dirty little secret, however, was that when he'd started creeping into his later forties, he'd lost some of that speed. His reputation for being fast had preceded him, though. So he hadn't had to entertain many challengers. Just drunks who hadn't known any better or, because of the who-hit-John coursing through their veins, had thrown caution to the wind.

And had paid the price.

The gambler had been different. He'd been one cool customer, as most good gamblers were. As Abel himself once had been. Cool and confident in his speed. That night, however, the gambler had sized Wilkes up, sensed that the aging lawman was no longer as fast as he once had been. Abel hadn't been sure how the man had known that.

Maybe he'd seen the doubt in Abel's own eyes.

The fear. That fear.

Abel had let the gambler make the first move, of course. Over the years, the lawman had been so fast that he'd been able to make up for his opponents' lightning-fast starts. That night, however, Abel would have been wolf bait if the drunk doxie hadn't stumbled against him in her haste to leave the table and not risk taking a ricochet.

She had nudged his shooting arm just as the man had swept his pearl-handled Colt from its black leather holster thonged low on his right thigh. Abel's own Colt Lightning had cleared leather after the gambler's gun had drilled a round into the table before him, between him and his opponent. Abel's bullet had plunked through the man's brisket and instantly trimmed his wick.

Abel had left the saloon after the undertaker had hauled

the gambler out feetfirst. He'd tried to maintain an air of grim confidence, of a job well done, but the other gamblers and the saloon's other customers all knew it to be as phony as he did. If that drunk, little doxie hadn't nudged the gambler's arm at just the right time, the undertaker would have planted Abel in the Wolfwater bone orchard, beside his dearly departed Ethel.

Leaving their old-maid daughter alone in the cold, cruel, West Texas world.

Now he swung onto Wolfwater's broad main drag, dark except for up at the Wolfwater Inn, half a block ahead and on the street's right side.

Abel felt his boots turn to lead. He wanted to do anything this night, except confront Frank Thorson and Thorson's men. Abel didn't know whom Frank was running with now, but for them to do what they had done to Bushwhack, they all had to be every bit as bad as Frank.

No, Wilkes wanted nothing to do with them. But he couldn't very well ignore them. He wanted to turn tail and run home and hide. Wait for the Thorson storm to pass. That's why he did what he did now. He quickened his pace.

There was only one thing worse than being dead.

That thing was being a laughingstock in front of your whole dang town.

Visit our website at
KensingtonBooks.com
to sign up for our newsletters, read
more from your favorite authors, see
books by series, view reading group
guides, and more!

Become a Part of Our
Between the Chapters Book Club
Community and Join the Conversation

Betweenthechapters.net